CITY ON THE LEDGE

PHILIP
KRASKE

CITY ON THE LEDGE

encompass
EDITIONS

Published by Encompass Editions, Kingston, Ontario, Canada. No part
of this book may be reproduced, copied or used in any form or manner
whatsoever without written permission, except for the purposes of brief
quotations in reviews and critical articles. For reader comments, orders,
press and media inquiries:

www.encompasseditions.com
or
www.philipkraske.com

FIRST EDITION 2012

ISBN 978-0-9880428-1-0

Cataloguing in Publication
Program (CIP) information available from Library and Archives Canada
at www.collectionscanada.gc.ca

cover design by Ismael Medina

encompass
EDITIONS

For Estherina

They say that these are not the best of times,
But they're the only times I've ever known.

—Billy Joel
Summer, Highland Falls

PROLOGUE

Quito, Ecuador, South America.

Alvaro the shoeshine boy is running towards death.

It is eight P.M. of an honest Thursday, and already colonial Quito has hunkered down for the night. The Indian traffic cops are hiking off home to see how their wives have eked the four hundred monthly dollars that the Force of Public Order pays its custodians. The beggars have tumbled into their doorways to nibble bread cached beneath the folds of their ponchos still stinking from the rain, and El Trole—the trolley—begins its night service that grants travelers one run an hour. The streets go still as a painting, as an unvisited museum.

Fog sits on the city. It coats in droplets every stop sign, every gate, bench, balcony and door; it turns the distant streetlamps into starbursts. All are silent, nothing drips. Tangled cables tacked along the cement facades calmly bear their burdens of power and data, and the national flag— red, blue and yellow stripes flown everywhere with the hope of a crucifix —hangs heavy like dripping candle wax.

In all Latin America, only Quito can achieve a mood of Gothic. You hear it in the clump of its Indians' hammy feet along the brick sidewalks, feel it in the anger of the storms that rake its streets. You see it in the hulking gray of its churches, the grim consummation of its wrought-iron gates, and the humorless stare of infants slung on their mothers' bent backs. Even the cobblestone streets, laid out by the Conquistadores centuries ago, lie in a gloomy grid, with no exceptions for the insufferable grades that mark the first upward jolt of the Pichinchas, the three green peaks that rise a mile over the city, witnesses to the itch-itch-itching of humanity bent on breaking its final limits.

Only Alvaro troubles this portrait.

The shoeshine boy slaps through these streets tonight, slaps because his shoes are teenaged-sized and his feet are not; slaps because the wet sprawls everywhere, on stone and metal, clings to his ankles and probes his jacket, seeks to root in his innocent heat. And Alvaro has heat to spare. The driving beat of his shoes—*la plata, la plata, la plata*—on the cobbles describes the importance, the sheer great sweet commercial bliss, of his mission: twenty *dólares* to bring the envelope to El Ejido Park! The man will wait for him at the start of *Friends,* and Alvaro knows that this is any minute now, even though he cannot read a watch.

He and his older brother Leopoldo, who is twelve, never miss *Amigos* reruns on the television at Televisiones Chimborazo, just off the Plaza

Grande and a stone's throw from President Atahualpa Tingo's office, where they spend the mornings cadging for shoeshine clients. La Rachel, the blond *Amiga*, is the most beautiful woman ever born. Alvaro and his brother each have a sticker of La Rachel on the inside of their shoeboxes, and they have cut their fingers and sworn on their blood that if La Rachel ever comes to Quito, they will shine her shoes for free, each one taking a shoe. And at the end, they will stand up and bow deeply and pronounce the phrase honed through many idle sidewalk hours: "It has been an honor—a great honor to the Ecuadoran nation—to clean your shoes, Señorita Rachel."

La plata, la plata, la plata—the silver, Latin America's ancient denominator of wealth. *La plata, la plata, la plata.* Alvaro's shoes sing, and the echo follows like a posse amidst the flat-faced buildings, for every street in the colonial district is a canyon four floors deep.

La plata, la plata, la plata. Alvaro's pace does not vary, though Quito lies at 2,800 meters, more than a mile and a half, above sea level. He passes a dozen Indian women, each with an infant tied to her back, standing like statues in a line before a closed door with a light on in the transom. He pounds through another silent four-way intersection, ears looking both ways for him around the corners. He doesn't notice—why should he?—a car two blocks up the steep hill to his left, its passenger window rolled down, and a man leaning well over from the driver's seat to watch him through the fog; and then speed ahead.

La plata, la plata, la plata. Alvaro zigs left at the intersection, zags right at the next. He weaves through the cement balls along the sidewalk that keep cars from parking there, and he keeps his head carefully down as he passes the gargantuan Iglesia de la Merced with its stark stone doorway in the massive white wall. A zig, a zag. He turns another corner, and the grade is downhill now, the going easier. He shifts his filthy wooden shoeshine box, no longer than his forearm and which he grips by its footrest, to his other hand.

Up ahead, he sees two people spying round the corner of the building into the next street. One, a woman, turns at the sound of Alvaro's feet, and Alvaro instinctively swerves wide—and nearly cries out in surprise, for the other person, a man, has now turned too, his face lit by the tiny, bluish screen of a video camera. Alvaro has seen tourists using them, and even once saw his own image when a tourist took his picture with him. The two persons watch him pass—*"Cállate, carajo!"* the man hisses angrily—and Alvaro pushes yet more speed into his legs. *La plata, la plata, la plata.*

In the next street, he sees what the two are filming: a man, half-way down the next block, with hair as golden as La Rachel's. It is short and forms a halo around his head. He is down on his haunches handing something to a man sitting in a doorway. Hearing Alvaro approach, he rises, and Alvaro hears the crackle of his knees; he recognizes this sound because he often hears it during his workday.

But this man is enormous, a giant! He carries a plastic bag and takes something out. And now he is moving into the street. Alvaro, now at full sprint—*la plata, la plata, la plata, la plata!*—barely gets past him. The man calls after him, but the words are truly those of a monster and echo over the wet walls like ghosts sent to pursue him. But they do not; they cannot. They fall behind. Alvaro is invincible!

He turns the corner. At the end of this street is Avenida de Guayaquil, a busy street because it soon merges with Avenida 10 de Agosto, which leads to the modern, northern section of Quito. After the daily afternoon rainstorm, he and Leopoldo always work this area, where there are men in business suits who want shines and tip well.

But now a broad figure—dark pants and windbreaker, white polo shirt—steps out of a double-parked car and hails him. Alvaro again swings wide, now as far as the opposite sidewalk. The man hurries across to intercept him. Alvaro puts on speed. The man is calling: *Espera, espera. Te doy dinero.* Wait, wait. I'll give you money. But Alvaro has been warned about *maricones*—homosexuals. One touch of their dicks with your bare hand, Leopoldo says, and you'll turn into one.

La plata, la plata, la plata.

La plata, la plata, la…

Jamming along the wall of a grocery store, Alvaro tries to slide past. But the man lunges and pins him with one huge foot, thumping his back against the bricks. His hand falls on Alvaro's arm like a shackle; the other snatches his shoeshine box, and Alvaro cannot leave it behind.

"Don't worry, kid," he says in a murky Spanish that slurs the Rs. He is kneeling and opening the flaps of the shoebox. "I only want to look at your letter; I'll give it back."

"*Por favor, señor,*" Alvaro squeaks, the breath knocked out of him.

Letting go of his arm, the man kneels and, careful not to upset Alvaro's three bottles of polish—red, black, and *color café*—takes out the half-sheet buff envelope that the other man, the one who spoke good Spanish, put in twenty minutes earlier. This man puts a small flashlight in his mouth, slides out the contents, and quickly flips through four photographs. The reflections from their glossy surfaces dapple the man's muscular face.

And now it goes stiff; whatever is in the photos displeases him. He has thick, fleshy lips, and these curl back from the flashlight like a dog's mouth, and a sound like a distant thunder simmers under his throat.

But Alvaro is not going to miss his money because of this *maricón.* Now catching his breath, he steals a hand under his woolen sweater and finds the knife in his belt. Very slowly he begins to draw it out. His thumb finds the button for the blade.

Still kneeling, the man taps the photos back into the envelope.

"Take that, *maricón!*" Alvaro cries. In one oiled movement, he jerks out the knife and swings at the man's face, the blade spitting out like a snake's tongue. The man jerks back just in time: only the very tip of the blade reaches him, tracing a finger-long gash under his ear. The man squawks and his light falls to the ground and goes out.

Alvaro grabs the footrest of his box. The man, who has fallen sideways, is leaning on one hand. He kicks at Alvaro, kicks hard because the boy has humiliated him, and his toe drives straight into Alvaro's right kidney. The boy staggers back against the wall, paralyzed with pain. He drops his knife and box, but can't bend down to pick them up.

Panting now, face tight, the man stands and presses a handkerchief against the wound and cocks his head against it to hold it in place. Alvaro in his breathless agony sees blood running over the white collar of his shirt and is glad.

"Who will you give the message to?" the man snarls in his pasty accent.

"A man is waiting for me at the Arch of Triumph in El Ejido Park," Alvaro manages to say. Even to breathe sends waves of pain through his back.

"*Who?* What man?"

"El Profesor." His back is aflame. "Don't hurt me any more, señor. Please."

"Okay, but don't tell him that I looked at the letter." He bends closer. "If you do, I will dump gasoline on you and burn you alive!"

"No, no, I won't tell anyone."

"I will find you if you do!"

"I won't tell anyone, not even my brother!" Alvaro pleads.

The man takes the envelope and tucks it into the shoeshine box. Then he bends down and picks up Alvaro's knife. For a terrifying moment, Alvaro waits for the stab, knowing that he is in too much pain to dodge. But the man looks down at him and nods.

"Good move. You almost got me."

He wipes off the blade on his handkerchief, pushes the button a few times and admires how smoothly the blade darts in and out, and drops the knife into the shoeshine box.

"Now go."

The weight of his whole body seems to crush directly on his wounded kidney, and Alvaro needs a great effort to walk. The effort will become ever greater over the following days, as the wound refuses to heal properly and gets infected. After several days he will die in Leopoldo's arms.

"Fast!" the man growls.

Alvaro makes a little jumping movement with his feet and shuffles them faster. After several steps, like an albatross trying to take flight, he finally works into a running stride, though it seems to split his torso down the middle. Turning onto Avenida de Guayaquil, he looks back. The man watches him flatly, pressing the handkerchief against his neck. Alvaro hopes it hurts like a sword run through his flesh, because that's how badly his side hurts.

1 Four days later, at six-thirty A.M., two men were playing basketball in La Carolina Park, in northern, upscale Quito. The night air still hung wet as washed bedsheets, but bright and abundant, for the gargantuan rising sun bowled waves of light across the deep eastern valleys and into the city, which lies, painted in white, ten miles long and half-a-mile thin on the ledge of the Pichinchas.

Rafael Ramirez took the ball at the top of the three-point line and concentrated, tugging down his jersey. His thick middle made a maternity gown of his Los Angeles Lakers jersey—number 32 for Magic Johnson—which got hung up on his belly every time he raised his shoulders. So he was always tugging it down; otherwise the shoulder straps fell off sideways.

"Okay, gonna moth'fuck you, man. A hard rain's a-gonna fall." His English, the fruit of two partying semesters in Miami, was a wreckage of undercooked grammar and the lyrics of classic pop tunes.

Paul Klippen set himself in a defensive stance and rubbed his hands on his shorts, waiting patiently. At thirty-nine, he was actually ten years older than Rafael but looked about the same age, being lithe and slender. His pretty hair was thick, brown and shiny, though his hairline had receded on the sides. He wore his only pair of glasses, with round delicate black frames, because he had none for sports.

Finally, Rafa performed on a stutter-step fake to his left. It would not have fooled a child, but the American, being a diplomat, shuffled his feet diplomatically in that direction. This the Ecuadoran took as his chance to bull his way up the right side of the foul lane, slapping the ball down, shouldering the American along. Nearing the hoop, he stopped and set his feet. With a tremendous grunt, he leapt and launched a hook shot. The American didn't really jump, but hopped up a few inches and raised his arms—the type of defense one plays against a young son. The ball bounced twice on the rim, rolled around it once, hung for a moment on the support, and grudgingly, poutingly, like a lady seated in the last empty place by a stern flight attendant, settled into the chain net.

"What skyhook, eh, man? Take your breath away."

"You're unstoppable today, Rafa," Paul Klippen admitted, glancing across the twenty yards of grass to where the Rafa's chauffer and bodyguard, copper-faced Indians, leaned back against the Mercedes, listening to talk radio through the open window. The one smiled at the other, and Paul wondered for the hundredth time what Rafa would say if they told him what a lax defense he offered their boss. Not that he feared their saying something: the lower caste of Ecuadoran society rarely speaks with the upper, which considers their opinions foolish and ignorant anyway.

"It makes 26 to 28, okay?" said Rafa. "One more basket and…We are the cham-pions, my friends!" he sang, throwing up his arms, which made his jersey ride up and the left strap fell off sideways.

"Something incredible just might happen."

Rafa jerked down his jersey. "Incredible? Go to the hell, man. Also I won you last week."

"That's true, isn't it?" Paul said, dribbling the ball back up to the three-point line.

"See? It has nothing of incredibilation." His jaw twisted sideways in doubt. "I can say this in English?"

"In Missouri, that would be 'incredibleness,' Rafa."

"'Incredibleness,'" Rafa repeated, looking up to his brain as if ordering it to remember the word. Then he assumed a defensive position, arms low and legs spread, as if he were trying to catch a runaway chicken. "Okay, Paulo, twist and shout, man!" he cried.

Paul set himself well to the left of the basket, crouched over the ball. He faked right, easily losing Rafa, came back to his left, gathered his legs beneath him, pushed off, and with a well-coached flip of the wrist, let fly. The ball kissed off the backboard and went in.

"Carajo!" Rafa grumbled. "Ain't no sunshine when she's gone, man."

"Sorry, Rafa, but I can't let down Uncle Sam." he said, though he knew that Uncle Sam would take his defeat with philosophy: Rafa negotiated more equably after winning a match, and today, with luck, the final agreement on their deal would come.

For what was really at stake this morning, as the rising equatorial sun coated the Pichinchas in emerald green, was Ecuador's future and America's most important interests in the country. These morning basketball matches were actually the center of American-Ecuadoran relations.

Which were officially at daggers drawn.

Three years earlier, in his inaugural address to the nation, President Atahualpa Tingo had called the United States "the bloodsucker *(sangijuela)* of the American continent." And this was indeed a great evil, for like most South Americans, Ecuadorans are taught that North and South America are one continent. The U.S. ambassador at the time had refrained from walking out, though the first thing the new ambassador had said when taking charge was that he intended to "set Tingo straight on just who sucks blood from who, and how much Congress pays for it." Which was why in two years Tingo had received the ambassador just four times, two of those with several other ambassadors present. Ambassador Frunk, a golf-course mogul who had contributed heavily to the U.S. president's campaign, stuck out his dresser-drawer of a jaw every time Tingo's name was mentioned.

So did many Ecuadorans. Nearing the end of his four-year term, President Tingo had turned nearly everyone against him. Two years earlier, his own vice-president had tried to depose him, the dirty work falling to the vice-president's cousin, who was chief of the central-region Army brigade. On the eve of the revolt, however, General Ronaldo Santamaria's feet went cold, and he called Paul, the U.S. Embassy's top political officer. Paul suggested a late-night snack, and in a Quito Burger King, over double-decker Whoppers, he listened to the general's diatribe against Tingo, commiserated copiously, and gently pointed out that revolt against a democratically-elected government, however badly run, was rarely a smart career move anymore. Times had changed, Ronaldo, alas! Besides, in Paul's opinion, though Santamaria was clearly the most capable general in Ecuador, the head of the armed forces was unlikely to admit it and step aside for him. Then Paul turned the conversation to domestic matters and promised to get Ronaldo's teenage daughter an appointment with a dermatological specialist at a top clinic in Miami, to see about her acne problem. The next morning, the vice-president announced that he was leaving the government to form a new political party.

In the last year of his administration, however, Atahualpa Tingo had learned of a miraculous alignment of interests with the Americans, though he mentioned this to no one. Paul himself had aligned them, on orders from Ambassador Frunk:

"Paul, you're the go-to guy in this dump, far as I'm concerned," he had told Paul one afternoon in his residence, double-whiskey clenched in his fist. He was wearing an orange golf shirt and violent purple slacks, these joined horizontally at his jutting middle; he resembled a child's plastic candy egg. He moved constantly, as if still on the green: a few steps to one side, a few to the other, a man lining up a putt. Paul felt uneasy, and not only because he was sipping a martini he hadn't asked for and didn't like.

"I just do my job, Bob," Paul said. The ambassador had everyone call him "Bob."

"You *more* than do it," the ambassador barked. "Everywhere I turn in this goddamn rabbit den, *your* name pops up." In a nasal whine, he imitated the diplomats, whom he loathed as 'entitlement fleas': "'The guy to ask about that is Paul Klippen.' 'Oh, that's Paul's side of the field, all that.' 'I never met the Interior minister, but Paul Klippen just had lunch with him the other day.'"

"Oh, that was nothing. Poor Alfredo needed to talk through some underwater mortgages he has in the Florida Keys. I looked up a few property brokers for him and worked out a—"

"Whatever. Cutting to the chase. I want two things done over the next year, and I'm tasking *you* with the job. Up to it?"

"I do my best to give the taxpayers their money's worth, Bob."

"Yeah: you and you alone," the ambassador despaired. He poked the air with his forefinger. "One: the intelligence boys are telling me that there's big-time labor unrest down in the lowlands—banana workers, mainly. Some pineapple."

"I've heard a lot of rumors too, but they seem to me—"

"They tell me there's eventually going to be a strike. Like shit. I want it headed off at the pass. I want it cut off at the knees. If they do get anything, I want the new wages—conditions, perks, whatever they want—I want it maybe one penny better than they have now. One thing I've learned in business is this: Never, never let the workers catch an updraft. Do that, you're all finished. Last thing I need is to get my bell rung by House Ag because the price of bananas has gone up on my watch."

Paul nodded silently, and risked a new swallow of his awful martini.

They were standing at the living room window that looked over the city. The sun was sinking behind the bulky mountains that stood like a vast theater curtain. The shadows on the lawn were visibly fading. Now they were gone. Quito went from full daylight to complete darkness in forty minutes.

After some searching, Paul found a reply. "It'll be tough getting President Tingo to stand for that, don't you think? He's very pro-worker. If it weren't for—"

"*Radically* pro-worker, the cocksucker."

"If it weren't for the conservatives opposing all his labor reforms in Congress, the—"

"Hell. Tingo's history by this time next year."

Paul took another sip to fortify his patience. "That's not quite the point I'm making here, Bob. I *mean* that, one way or another, he would have to endorse any big agreement between workers and plantation owners. And for just an extra penny of salary, he wouldn't. That's why the unions are going to strike *this* year. It's their last chance. He'll sign on if they manage a big increase."

The ambassador reset his feet. "All right, all right. You're the expert, I'm not. Do the workers down however you want, but do it. Oh, and don't bring in Harry Kruger unless you absolutely need to. You know those macho CIA types: walk in with a howitzer, blow the whole place away and call it a solution. Garf would give me hell big-time."

"Garf," short for "Garfield," was how he referred to the secretary of state, his golf partner since college.

Paul took the tiniest sip of his martini, which was so strong it nearly made his hair stand on end. "Consider it done, Bob. And what's number two?"

"Two—hah!" Frunk shouted, making Paul flinch. A new slurp of his whiskey. "The worker-strike shit is a kiddie cakewalk compared to number two." He reset his putting stance. "The latest goddamn constitution of this country forbids the presence of foreign bases. Don't know why. Ecuadorans sure made enough money off 'em."

"You mean our former coastal airbase down in Manta?"

"That's the one. Ask the local shopkeepers if they're happy about it getting shut down."

"Be that as it may, it seems that our airmen didn't make careful distinctions between Ecuadoran fishing boats and boats running cocaine. Mistakes were made, people died, and the locals took that, ah, poorly, to say the least. And then the base commander, far from offering sympathy, said there was nothing to the accusations that honest boats were blown out of the water. That rankled more than a bit,

I'm afraid." *And thank God all that was before my posting here,* Paul added silently, remembering the frazzled outgoing diplomat who had had to deal with the crisis.

The ambassador waved his free hand at the now-dark mountains as if they were blocking his view of the fairway. "Whatever. I want our people back."

Paul drank again and felt the angry burn on the back of his throat. "Back...on the base, that would be?"

"That's right. I'm gonna make that little bastard Tingo eat shit—*our* shit—just once before I blow this pop stand. Besides, the Pentagon wants it, Garf wants it, and the American people want it. 'America sees farther because it stands taller.' Remember that."

"Secretary of State Allbright's famous quote—yes." Paul chewed his lips pensively. "Still, changing the Ecuadoran Constitution is a rather tall order."

The ambassador waved a meaty hand in the air again. "No, no. I got you there. You don't have to change the Constitution. Hell, I *respect* their Constitution—at least till they tear it up for a new one. All you gotta do is get our people back *on the base*. Get it? Advisors, techies, trainers, a few pilots."

"Still: bit of an end run around the spirit and the letter, you know, Bob."

"Oh no, it isn't," said the ambassador triumphantly. "I had Elena look it up in the Constitution and translate it for me." He dug into the depths of his purple pants and took a dingy, folded three-by-five card out of his pocket. Not wearing his glasses, he had to hold it at arm's length to read it. "'Neither the establishment of foreign military bases nor foreign military facilities will be permitted. It is illegal to cede national military bases to foreign armed forces or security forces.' See? No problem. *Their* base—lock, stock and barrel. Just *our* personnel there alongside their own. They don't have to *cede* anything."

"Yes, that would be the famous Article Five. Article Four is about the same, just a little more prickly." Paul nodded slowly, looking out the window at the tortured rock of the Pichinchas outlined against a power sky fading to mauve. "Tricky. Tricky one, Bob." A careful smile. "But don't give it another thought. If America wants it, who am I to say it can't be done?"

Seven months and, by Paul's meticulously kept log, one hundred ninety-three meetings later with Defense, Agriculture, State, Commerce, CIA, FBI, DIA, the Navy, Panamanian banks and Filipino maritime officials, and eight different congressional subcommittees of every orientation, faith, and purpose—his record was nine meetings in a seventeen-hour sprint across Washington—the deal was about to be closed on a public basketball court. And just in time, for Tingo's term had just months to run and, out of the blue, the workers on the biggest plantation in Ecuador, Plantaciones Costa, had walked off the job. Within days, the strike had spread across the lowlands, and most ominously, the plantations were unable to resort to the usual tactic of hiring replacement workers. For once, workers had locked arms.

Rafa Ramirez's hook shot from the three-point line crashed through the chain net. "I win! Baby, we were born to ru-u-u-u-n," he sang, throwing his broad, teddy-bear arms in the air.

"The embassy flag goes at half-mast today, Rafa," Paul said, though he had had to miss his last five shots in order to lose. "No question about it."

"Half-mass?"

A media asta.

"Oh." It took Rafa a moment to get the joke. "Oh! Right! Yeah, have-mass. Ain't no sunshine, eh, man?"

Now they turned to the usual post-game free throws, ten each, one rebounding the ball for the other. A Delta Airlines 767 came in roaring—screaming—overhead, so close that Paul could see the rivets in the wings. The night flights from Miami and Europe were starting to arrive, and the present airport was only a mile away, right in the middle of the city. The new airport, already built across the valley, would open any day, had been the official answer over the past year or two.

Rafa tossed up a few of his hook-shot free throws, made some, missed others, and put on his professional scowl. Paul knew the gesture well.

"Okay, Paulo, now it is the time for that we are serious, okay? Takin' care of business…"

"And workin' overtime," Paul sighed, tossing back the ball. It was their usual routine to begin negotiations, and he had to suppress a groan every time he said it.

As usual, Rafa opened the proceedings with a spurt of Ecuadoran oratory:

"I mean, today over all, we are treating matters of the maximum importance for the life of the Ecuadoran state, and we need that you give it all you got, and do the maximum effort, and to practice a true, ah, seriosity—is this possible?"

"'Seriousness' would be my choice there, actually," Paul said as he rebounded a missed shot, once again longing for Rafa to converse in Spanish with him. But Rafa wouldn't hear of it. Doing business in Spanish wasn't "correct," he always said.

Rafa pounded the ball on the court, set his feet sideways to the basket, and tossed up another hook. "Seriousness. Okay, today we must to be maximum-security seriousness. In this moment in time it would be necessary to open, ah, open your heart and give it all you got for that we make an accord that is feelin' groovy for the two of us and for our nations. We are the world, we are the children, okay? I believe, Paulo, that we can terminate our negotiations today."

"Oh?" Paul had a bad moment, till he realized that Rafa had meant "*finish* our negotiations."

"Yes, we are young men, Paulo, oh so young and free, and we see what changes need to be effectuated in the world for that everything continue singin' in the rain. Our generation must to play the paper that history give for it." He shot.

"That's 'play the *role*,' Rafa," Paul put in, for some of Rafa's mistakes bit too deeply. He caught the ball and bounced it back.

"The *role*, yeah, thanks. Okay, Paulo, my Uncle Tata, the president of the Ecuadoran Republic, he is agree with all the things importants that we have talked, except one detail or two. Really, no problem. Don't worry be happy."

"Well, that's good news," said Paul cautiously. "So, first: we have agreement on the banana negotiations: whatever the price that the owners reach with the unions, even if it's one penny, Tingo will sign off on it, right?"

Rafa lined up another hook shot. "Right. The unions—I hate to those guys, man. Baddest man in the whole damn town. I don't know why Uncle Tata loves them."

"Their blind support and votes must have something to do with it."

Rafa shrugged and tossed up a shot: out. "Yeah, is truth: when a man loves a woman, can't keep his mind on nothin' else."

Paul chased the ball down the baseline and snapped Rafa a pass. "All right, and when he accepts the wage, twenty million dollars will appear in a Panamanian bank, which he can draw whenever he wants."

"With two millions for me." Another piratical grin as Rafa whipped another hook shot towards the basket: in. "And real quiet, right, man? Like, 'Hello darkness my old friend,' huh?"

"Oh, the darker, the better, Rafa, believe me. And once the money is where it needs to be, your kind Uncle Tata will sign an agreement renting for just one dollar the fine services of the United States Air Force—trainers, mechanics, pilots, no more than a hundred at any one time. And if someone leaves a drone aircraft or two tossed in the corner under a tarp, nobody is going to make a fuss, right?"

"Yeah, right, Paulo, except, ah…" The grin faded. "Hey, that's ten. It's your turn to shoot."

"Now, did I hear 'except,' Rafa?" Paul walked to the foul line, dribbling the ball as casually as he could.

"Yeah, one thing that we must to talk, Paulo: the new salary for the workers, the advisors in the airbase of Manta—fine, no problem, don't worry be happy."

"Yet I find myself worried and unhappy, Rafa. What's the problem?"

Rafa grimaced hard, like a man who has farted in the elevator. "Well, the president is nervous about the money. Where is gonna come from those twenty millions of dollars? Yeah, okay, I asked to you before, and you said is your problem, not the mine. Okay. But also he is reading every day that there are many bad-bad Leroy Browns cutting your budget."

Bouncing the ball a few times, Paul chuckled and shook his head. "I'll give you that one, Rafa: Leroy Brown is a pale choirboy beside those congressmen."

"And the president, Uncle Tata, he wanna make plans, he wanna know everything is gonna be all right uh-huh uh-huh."

Paul drew a breath, took aim with what concentration he could spare, and shot: out. *Well, this is no time for people to get nervous,* he told himself.

"This is between me and you and your uncle—okay, Rafa?"

"Yeah, sure, Paulo: sunshine on my shoulders."

"We—the American Embassy—we know what the new salary for the workers is going to be already." He raised a hand in caution. "More or less. Within a dollar or two."

Rafa's brown eyes grew wide in his round face. "Really? *Really?*" He lowered his voice. "Hey, Paulo, you doing like, like, like 'do a little dance, make a little love'?"

Paul shot: in. "Let's just say that we've got a handle on it. And we've made a deal with the top banana-plantation owners: if we at the embassy keep salaries low, they will put up the money for your uncle."

"But they *hate* to Uncle Tata. They prefer killing to him!"

Paul spoke quietly. "They don't know it's for your uncle. All they know is that if we keep the new salary below a certain amount, they will thank us by putting twenty million in a Panamanian account that we specify. And believe me, they're so worried about the strike that they're happy to do it. Twenty million is nothing compared to what they might lose if the workers get a decent wage out of the strike."

Rafa caught the ball but didn't throw it back. His mouth hung open in an O. "And you can make that to happen, Paulo? Make all our dreams come true—even with the negotiations with the workers? That's great balls o' fire!"

A mysterious smile. "For the U.S. State Department, Rafa, it's all in a day's work. Now, do we have a deal?"

2 As Paul Klippen was preparing his scheme, Mary Swanson was dragging herself up to Quito from the Equatorial Line Monument, to which she had coasted on her bicycle from the city.

She was twenty-eight, from Lancaster, Pennsylvania, and still young enough in the Foreign Service to not speak Statese. She could still see the difference between "important" and "vitally important," could still be active without being pro-active, and could still write a sentence of less than six words. She could still shake a hand with real warmth, ask questions with sincere curiosity, and smile her own smile, which as yet held no whiff of protocol, corporations, or skulking intelligence agencies.

Her legs and lungs were also her own and not an Olympic champion's, and at the moment this was a drawback. The Equatorial Line Monument, known locally as "Mitad del Mundo" ("Middle of the World"), stood at 2,483 meters, which is four hundred meters lower than Quito, some ten miles south. But just why those four hundred meters—the height, she remembered reading somewhere, of a hundred-story building—had to be climbed in one gargantuan leap, rather than in gentle stages, was still a mystery to her. Maybe the highway engineer's mother-in-law had been a cyclist.

Up she rode, sweat pouring into her eyes, streaking her cycling glasses, gushing through her hair and down her neck as she ground yard after yard in first gear. She was on the worst part of the return trip, which she called The MaryMaker, the third and worst grade coming back from the monument. It featured a sudden upwards bump—as if a giant egg were forcing its way through the surface, for its last 150 yards, and Mary was certain that it was the result of some miscalculation of the surveyors or the builders.

No, she had to stop. The MaryMaker had done it to her again. She wiggled her shoes out of the pedal traps and put them down with a clack on the pocked tarmac of the highway and jerked off her cycling glasses before they steamed up. Then she hung herself by the waist over the handlebars. For half a minute, she gulped air, too weak even to grab her water bottle. The humidity and cool air and burning sun made steam rise off her forearms and back.

"Well, I could have just stayed in bed"—she gasped again—"and decided to stand up to *Cosmo* culture—dammit."

She finally pulled herself erect and took her water bottle out and with her teeth jerked up the nozzle, but could not drink—was still panting too hard. "Nothing really wrong with being big, is there? Course not. Long as you take care of yourself. Besides, I am—god*dammit!*—I am what they call a *large-boned* woman, right? And my guy thinks I'm terrific, and that's what counts, right?"

Finally, she drank.

All her life, Mary Swanson had been chubby. Till two years before, she had always been good ol' Mar', great for a laugh at the pizza joint but nobody you'd like to find waiting for you between the sheets. Of course she had dieted, of course she had exercised, of course she could hardly lose five pounds without turning into a nervous wreck.

The unchanging opinion of her ever-skeptical mother, editor of a successful fashion magazine, was that Mary never had any discipline.

Then Mary finished her Master's in International Relations and against every expectation, passed the Foreign Service Entry Exam on the first try, an amazing achievement for a person under thirty. And now something happened. Without any effort, she began losing weight. It was only after her pants became noticeably limp that she realized that she was eating less and eating less often. When it continued, she went to a doctor and got checked for everything except the Ebola virus: nothing. Still her weight fell.

She went through nearly a year of diplomatic and language training, spent a year at Consulate Barcelona on a State Department research project, and now with conscientious exercise and a dietician's advice, her weight continued to decline. The lifelong python wrapped around her midriff crept away and allowed deep curves to show. Wedge-like islands of cheekbone jutted out of the receding mass of her cheeks and gave dimension to her wide, pleasant face. If it missed high beauty, this was only due to her tiny, even rows of teeth and smallish eyes. She let her curly hair grow and found a hairdresser who dissolved its bushiness and gave it form.

For the first time in her life, men began to look at her twice. She let herself be picked up by a laughing Swede at a cocktail party, and enjoyed herself so much that she did it regularly. Just to be desired, and by good-looking men, was a thrill.

By the time she reached her first real posting, at Embassy Quito, she was fifty pounds lighter than in high school. She arrived each morning looking not good, but impeccable. Her blouses were spotless and perfectly ironed, her shoes gleamed, her nails glowed. If she wasn't a goddess, she knew how one felt.

Except during the MaryMaker.

She gulped water and looked around. "At least they could give you a decent view for your trouble," she muttered.

For the area around the equatorial Line Monument, north of Quito, is oddly barren. Dull factories and warehouses—a soft-drink bottler, pharmaceutical distributor, a cement manufacturer, a slaughterhouse—lined the highway on both sides. Behind them, nothing: yellow sand showing through scrub right up to the tops of the mountains. A bus carrying employees from Quito pulled up to the gates of a lingerie maker, and two gray-uniformed guards holding assault rifles opened the gates. Mary checked her watch: seven o'clock, which was the starting time for some companies and all schools.

She heard a gentle pounding to her right and turned. A man came trotting along the three-foot alley between the barbed-wired-topped walls of the bottling plant and a warehouse for cut flowers, a major Ecuadoran export. On his back, he carried a tall sack the size of a garbage can, supported by a thick rope sling that ran from its base to the man's forehead.

"Buenos días," he muttered, stopping and swinging his load down to the ground—potatoes—and looking down the highway for the local bus to Quito. He was short and squarely built, as if with an erector set. The muscles in his vast neck, inflated like a bullfrog's until now, relaxed and disappeared. Then he stared at her. *"Dios!* A woman!"

Mary grinned. "And you are a man, right?" she said in Spanish.

"Yes, of course," said the farmer with a puzzled laugh. A sense of irony, Mary had found, was missing from the Ecuadoran character. *"Chooo-ta!"* he exclaimed again. "But you are…" He looked closer, walking right up to her, staring. "Are you la Mary? The one from *Hablemos?"*

"Yes, it's me."

"Chooo-ta! By god, what a coincidence then! Everybody in my village watches your show. Except last week, or the week before—I don't remember then. We didn't see it. What happened then?" Like many country Ecuadorans he had the habit of putting *pues*—then— at the end of most sentences.

"Well, it was only six programs. It's over now," she panted.

Hablemos, which means "Let's Talk" in Spanish, had been a miniseries, a half-hour every Tuesday at prime time, sponsored by the American Embassy and a local department store. It consisted of a ten-minute documentary prepared about some aspect of American life, and then a studio-audience Q-and-A with Mary about America, particularly for people interested in immigrating or doing business there. But the questions had quickly veered off into other areas, such as what Mary thought of Ecuadoran men, what she thought was a proper division of household work, or what was the fastest way to learn English. On the last program, a woman gravely asked her which of the lovers, the man or woman, should put the condom on.

And Mary had risen to the occasion. She was a natural ham. Her dreary youth of always being the fat girl had whetted her sense of humor to a fine edge. She joked about the effects of altitude in the Andes, the rain in Quito that came so punctually every afternoon "that God set His watch by it," even Ecuadoran machismo: "When a guy tells me he's a great lover, I always agree. I answer that his wife or girlfriend told me he's the best lover on the block." Her Spanish was still far from perfect, and when she was stuck for a word, she did a pantomime till someone in the audience shouted the answer.

After the three originally-scheduled programs, *Hablemos* turned into the most popular show on Ecuadoran television, and was extended to three more segments. The embassy, glad to combat America's reputation as hemispheric bloodsucker, was delighted. At the last program, the audience shouted, *"La Mary, presidente! La Mary, presidente!"*

"All over," said the farmer pensively now. "All over. That's too bad then. Well, my son said that I can see them again on the Internet."

"Oh, you have an Internet connection in your village?"

"Well, I don't use it," the man said with a giggle. "I don't need it. But the young people love it. They like to play computer games."

It was unlikely that the man could read, Mary figured, much less use a computer. "Where are you going with that big load?" she asked, finally getting her breathing under control. She wiped her face with the sweat-crusted handkerchief that she carried in the rear pocket of her cycling jacket.

"I'm going to the market in Quito then. I have a cousin who works there, and he will pay me for the potatoes."

"Did you grow them?"

"Yes, ma'am. I have a little orchard in the valley near Casitagua then," the man said with pride, waving a hand up behind the factories. Casitagua being the other side of the mountain ridge, Mary figured that he had walked at least three miles.

"Why don't you buy a car? That way you could pull me up this hill."

"Chooo-ta!" the man sighed again. "I get only 27 dollars for the whole sack then! And I have to buy new shoes for my little daughters, the twins. That is fifteen dollars then!"

"Do you go to market every day?"

"Chooo-ta! I would be a rich man that way. No, Miss Mary, no. I go

when I have a full bag then: two or three times a week."

Mary sipped more water and put away the bottle. Her breathing was finally coming back to normal. "Well, I have to go," she said, wiggling a shoe into the pedal trap till it clicked and locked. "The president is going to call me at nine o'clock in the embassy."

This made no impression on the man, who looked doubtfully at her. "You are going by bicycle? Why don't you wait here with me and take the bus then? It is much easier and faster. They can put your bicycle on the roof and tie it with rope then. Look—you can use my rope." He offered her the sling-rope.

"Oh no, that's very kind. I like the exercise."

"Yes, the TV says that exercise is very important then," the man said thoughtfully. "There is also an exercise program in the morning. I never exercise."

"I think you get a lot of exercise carrying that bag to the market."

The man regarded it doubtfully. "Yes, but it's not the interesting kind that you see on TV then. You know," he added, making a general motion of swinging his arms wide. He frowned. "Miss Mary, I am trying to remember a word then. What was the funny word that you said on your program?"

"Did I make a mistake? Sometimes I make mistakes in Spanish."

"No, it was an English word. Do you remember? You said some English words that sound strange. I was watching on the television in my brother's house then. I don't have a television—I'm saving my money for one then," he added sheepishly.

"Um—*splurge?* That means to spend a lot of money."

"Yes, but there was another word then. It sounded like a bird's call."

"A bird's call?"

"Yes, but funny. Everybody laughed—a lot, a lot, a lot."

The question from the audience had been, What were the strangest-sounding words in English? Her answers had the audience splitting its sides. "I said several words. I don't remember—"

"Ah! *Petróleo.* Maybe *petróleo?*"

"Oil?"

"Yes! That's it!" And the man repeated this in the same interrogative tone: "Oil? Oil? Oil? It is a funny word for *'petróleo'* then."

Mary pointed down the grade, where a small bus came moaning up the highway in first gear. "There's your bus."

The man jumped up and began digging in his pocket. "It costs forty-five cents now! And it will go up soon to fifty! Robbery then!"

"Yes, things are so expensive nowadays." Mary pushed off and quickly stuck her other shoe in the trap. "Adios! It was nice to talk to you."

"Adios, Miss Mary! Oil? Oil? Oil?"

Mary began grinding her way up the MaryMaker—after fifty yards, she was past it, and the grade slowly leveled off. A minute later, the bus chugged past, full of country Indians, and every single person aboard was jammed against her side of the bus, waving at her out of the little half-windows, for apparently the farmer had bragged to everyone aboard.

"Hola, Señorita Mary!"

"Buenos días, Mary!"

"Oil? Oil? Oil?"

A young mother who could not have been sixteen yet, was waving madly with one arm out the window and holding her nursing baby with the other, blouse pulled up, breast big as a loaf of bread flopped out over the bra.

"Mary, te quiero!" ("I love you!") she squealed.

Mary smiled, panting too hard to talk.

After a moment, the bus passed. Mary waved to the people in the back window.

"My god, I'm a star. What would they say back in Lancaster?" she murmured.

3 *"Chencho! Trae el maletín! Ya!"* ("Chencho! Bring the briefcase! Now!") Rafael Ramirez snapped to his chauffeur, and Paul heard the echo of five centuries of Jesuit monks, Spanish viceroys, and Andalusian army generals decked out in black silken capes: mamas' boys turned into little Cesars.

How little has changed here over time—it's astonishing, he reflected. *Five hundred years and a veritable revolution in humanity, but here the upper class still considers the lower cannon fodder—and the lower has always believed them. No wonder the Internet has been such a revelation.*

His driver jumped, grabbed a briefcase out of the back seat, and came trotting across the grass, the dew on it making a mess of his black-leather shoes. He handed it to Rafa, who laid the briefcase flat on the man's outstretched forearms; it seemed to be a common practice between the two of them. He opened the top, took out two documents and a pen, closed the case and laid them on top.

"Stand this way," Rafa snapped, turning him around. The huge, oily Ecuadoran sun was up, and he made the chauffeur look into it rather than himself.

The documents were in Spanish and English, one a copy of the other. At the bottom of the second page of each, the president had signed them and put his seal.

"See? All is signatured and feelin' groovy," said Rafa.

"Fine, looks good, Rafa," Paul murmured. He signed each document on the dotted lines. Another airliner screamed down its glide path to the airport.

"When the president receive the twenty millions, he gonna give the order to the chief of the Forces of Air, and you can to bring your people to the base when you want, no problem."

"Fine," said Paul, taking the English copy.

Rafa put his copy in the briefcase, closed it, and with an upward nod sent the chauffeur back to the car. "My uncle, he said he don't like doin' this—oh no, it just don't fe-e-e-el right. But he need to make money before to leave the Carondelet." This was the Ecuadoran White House.

"He *needs* to?" Paul walked over to the base of the basket support and picked up his basketball bag. He slid the contract into a file inside and zipped the bag shut tight. "That surprises me. I thought he was doing very well financially," he lied, pulling on a U of Missouri sweater over his damp tee shirt. They began walking to their cars parked along the street.

"Happened to him a real bad thing, Paulo."

Paul painted alarm on his face. "Is that so? What bad thing?"

"A few months ago. He had a ship; it was a oil ship confisked by the Ecuadoran government two years ago because for the bad papers."

"Confiscated."

"Yeah. Well, the only one bad, corruption thing that Uncle Tata he did in his time of president, he stole that ship. He had a company who bought her for nothing from the Ecuadoran government. He register her in Bahamas. And the ship, she make a lot of money, carrying the oil, you know? And containers on the top? But you know what passed? The ship, she disappeared."

Paul stared. "Disappeared? You mean sank?"

"No, no—not get on the bottom. Disappeared. The ship it was in the Filipinas and going to the Indonesia for getting more oil and—*bloop!*—one night some pirates go to the ship, they put everyone in the little save-life boats. Bye-bye, dancin' the night away. The captain he say, 'How you gonna drive the ship without that you got the people?' The pirates they say, 'Ah, no problem, don't worry be happy.' The ship, she not went to Indonesia, she not went to anywhere. Disappeared."

"Just disappeared—incredible."

"Yeah, the answer, my friend, is blowin' in the wind." He swept the sweat from his forehead into his spiky hair.

Paul frowned. "You would think they would have time to get off a radio signal."

"Yeah, the captain of ship, he taked four days for that he was rescued, later talk with the police, officials maritimes, everybody. They look, but not ship. Okay, maybe she sinked."

"Well, if the new crew didn't know the ship, that'd be my guess."

Rafa shrugged sadly. "Well, bye-bye love, bye-bye happiness. So it result that Uncle Tata, he need the money of the banana growers for that he sit on the dock of the bay wastin' time when he retire. Twenty millions, wow!—that's the way we like it, uh-huh uh-huh."

They reached the cars.

"Well, I'm glad that we could help out, Rafa. Wait. I have something for you."

Paul opened the trunk of his car, dropped his bag inside, and took a new, leather basketball out of a plastic bag. He tossed it to Rafa. "Here—to celebrate our deal."

The huge, round face lit up. "B.W. to Rafa from your friend *Lebron James*," he read. He stared at Paul. *"Paulo!* Oh, Paulo, you are my brother! Like, you ain't heavy, you're my brother!" He grabbed Paul's hand and pumped it wildly.

"My pleasure, Rafa. That's with my thanks."

Rafa turned the ball over and over. "Hey, Paulo, how'd you get this?"

The ball had actually ridden in Paul's trunk for the last month. Paul thought that a last-ditch bargaining chip might come in handy and by phone had plowed his way through James's personal staff to wring the autograph out of him.

"The U.S. State Department, Rafa," he said airily. "For miracles, press one; the impossible, press two."

"It's incredible, it's—"

"Hey, guys! Who won today?" Mary Swanson pulled up on her bicycle.

Rafa ran over and showed her his ball. "Paulo, he gave me it. Look—Lebron signature it!"

Mary stared, wide-eyed, then looked at Paul. "Wow, that's pretty good. All I ever got was this lousy tee shirt."

"Well, I have to fly up to Washington later today," Paul said. "I'll stop by Cartier's for you."

"Guys—you all talk the same line."

"Hey! I winned!" said Rafa proudly. "Suddenly death overtime."

"Rafa won by two baskets," Paul explained, "and I died suddenly."

"You deserved it—a disgrace to the Republic, Paul," Mary deadpanned. "Well, I've got to get going before I get cold. See you in an hour, Paul. Don't be late. And no wet hair."

"Wet hair is for frogmen, not diplomats."

"Nice to see you, Rafa," said Mary, pushing off.

Rafa watched her as she rode off, picking up speed as she stood on the pedals. "She got some good legs, huh? Hey, Paulo, have she a boyfriend?"

"Mary?" Paul thought. "Yes. Yes, that would fit. I would say she does."

Rafa scowled. "Raindrops keep fallin' on my head, man. Okay! See you next week! Hey, thank you again, man." He looked at the ball. "This is, this is—I just want to celebrate another day o' livin'!"

"I'm glad, Rafa. Enjoy."

A moment later, he was driven away in his car, which swerved importantly across three lanes of the street, siren blaring, Rafa waving through the back window. Paul waved back.

"Actually, Rafa, that was a Navy Seals unit that took your uncle's ship—though that's not really my end of it. Sailed it to a dirty little breakers' yard in Goa, India, I guess. Repainted, refitted, re-registered—happens to a few ships every year: just disappear into thin air. But it wasn't Tingo's boat to start with—not by rights, it wasn't—and we needed him to need us, didn't we?"

He closed the trunk and, before getting in the car, stood with his arms on its roof, the grand equatorial sun warming his back. A white feather boa of vapor crawled along the green skin of the Pichinchas, god-like in their immenseness. *What a tourist I am,* he thought. *I must look at them twenty times a day, they have so many moods.*

But that was just as well, he reflected, as the bear-hug of fear closed around him. For the die was now cast, and by this time next week, he might be far away with no vista longer than the walls of a prison cell, because State wasn't going to be happy if his plan—not the one-hundred-ninety-three-meetings plan, but his own personal plan— went wrong. Or if it went right and State found out. He shivered despite the warming hand of the sun on his back. He wondered if he would end up in Guantánamo, under the tender care of the water-board specialists.

"Or maybe they'll just dispense with the niceties and dump me out at sea, like Bin Laden."

He finished saying this, waited a beat, and then opened the car's door. Because he really was taking a dangerous gamble, CIA station chief Harry Kruger really did have a dirty mind, and bugging diplomats' cars really was his idea of fun.

4 Directly on the other side of La Carolina Park from the basketball courts, Rodolfo Ilahú sat fretting in his office at TeleMax8, on Avenida de las Amazonas, Quito's main business street. TeleMax8 was the flagship operation of Grupo Ecua-Max Media, which had a two television stations, four radio stations, and three magazines of journalistic standards that flexed to every market.

Rodolfo was fretting because he needed Something. Monday was always a slow news day to start with, and the news had been tepid the past weekend, or to put it another way, image-less. Slouched at his oaken desk, he reviewed its indecorous monotony:

Universally despised President Atahualpa Tingo, his approval polls now in the teens (except in his native Amazon Province, where they were at nearly eighty percent) was having yet another spat with the leader of the opposition party. This idiot, an uncle of his sister-in-law, had again claimed on a Sunday TV talk show to have "more pants"—i.e., to be more of a man—than the president. Tingo had retaliated that evening in a press conference, saying that he found his dignity "irrevocably wounded" and challenging the other man to a fight "with our shirts off." That was for the moment the leadoff story, and even Rodolfo had to admit it was thin: all words, no blood.

The Petróleos Andinos story was no better. On Friday Petróleos had finished re-negotiating its debt with DynoBank, the New York investment firm, though "negotiating" was probably a generous term. The more details leaked out, the more it seemed that Petróleos had got its way, at best, on the letter font of the contract. It was outrageous, it was little less than a formalized robbery—but only if someone talked the viewer through the details and explained why. And Rodolfo held no truck with talking anyone through anything, whether in newcasts or in life. He had, in fact, a profound distrust of thought and words in general, and protected his viewers from them as a mother protects her children from cars and colds.

Besides, the bright spot in the story was not the deal at all but DynoBank's spokesman, who had made great footage: thirty-year-old Jay Streets, with his blond hair, chiseled jaw, and eyes blue as Arctic ice. He was a recently retired pro-football player, and had kindly brought along some NFL footage for the local stations. But he was now back in New York with the negotiating team. No, that story was dead.

Then there was the banana-workers strike in the Pacific-side lowlands, now two weeks old. It was *the* big ongoing story, as Ecuador is the world's leading exporter of bananas, which are themselves Ecuador's second-biggest export-earner after oil.

But images? Zero. How do you take pictures of people *not* working? The strikers from Plantaciones Costa, the biggest plantation in the country, had come up from the lowlands by the busload and were now camped, annoyingly peaceful, in Quito's El Ejido Park, not a mile up the street from his office. For the last ten days, his reporters had done stand-ups in front of women calmly stirring pots of soup over camping-gas fires, or washing infants in the street fountain under the glum gaze of riot police sitting on their water cannon. A week ago, four strikers had got drunk and brawled with police;

but this had happened at three A.M., and by the time a camera crew could get there, the bloodied men had been driven off in a police wagon.

In short, it was a news day as flat as his wife's behind.

Yes, Rodolfo Ilahú, paunchy, forty-five, with a thinning head of dyed, jet-black hair, nurtured and puffed up so that every strand did the work of three, crouched at his desk, jerking his computer mouse down the list of items from the news services, considering one and another, determined to pull a rabbit out of his hat. Whatever—an explosion, a scandal, a Guatemalan drug-bust gone bloody. The first item of the day was what hooked viewers and kept TeleMax8 News number two in the ratings. And ratings protected Rodolfo's cushy lifestyle: teenage kids in school in Arizona, house full of servants for his lazy wife, lover-secretary who took home an extra paycheck, and a constant stream of money-filled envelopes from military officials, bankers, politicians, businessmen and everyone else who needed to ensure an understanding slant when scandal broke.

On and on he dashed through the wire-service headlines. Rodolfo knew better than to leave the lead story to his staff. It consisted of the usual upper-class Ecuadorans holding college degrees earned through creative mixes of study, cheating, bribery and purchase. All had gotten their jobs through *palancas*—"levers"—which is what Ecuadorans call "connections." The staffers were fine for filling out the news with car accidents and restaurant poisonings; the lead was what got ratings.

He tried the international news beyond Latin America. A fifty-mile traffic jam in France, a collapsed bowling-alley roof in Texas—blah.

"Where's a good volcano when you need one?" he whined quietly. Volcanoes had real grab in Ecuador: in 1999 the one behind the Pichinchas, Guagua, had burped for a few days and dumped so much ash on the city that everyone wore surgical masks for a week. In 2006 lava flowing from the Tungurahua had missed the city of Baños by a stone's throw. "Please, San Antonio," he murmured, fingering the cross under his shirt and tie, "help me out here."

San Antonio's answer came in the form of a buzz from his pliant secretary, Monica: "Don Rodolfo, there's a young man with an amateur "investigative" video here. He says it's electrifying. Would you like to see him, or should I send him to—"

Rodolfo would see him. Waiting, he raised his eyes to the ceiling. *Please, San Antonio. Please.*

Jorge Santillamén quickly stoked Rodolfo's hopes. He was a university student of about 19, with a small helping of Indian in his otherwise European blood. He was deferent, referred to him by the honorific *Don* Rodolfo, and politely thanked Monica for getting him in so quickly.

I can get out of this for three hundred dollars tops, Rodolfo thought with relief.

He lowered this price much more when he saw that Jorge carried only his digital camera. This meant that the video on offer was the original and that most likely no copies had yet been made.

He told the kid to sit and gave him the usual speech about how he was always on the lookout for good footage that would "inform and enlighten and/or delight the Ecuadoran public. It is my sacred duty to my people, and I spare no effort nor drop of sweat in this calling," he finished, enjoying the awe in the kid's eyes.

As trained, Monica had waited till he finished his oratory and now brought in coffee. "So tell me about your film," Rodolfo said as he stirred the fourth heaping spoonful of sugar into his cup of *tinto*. "Where did you take it, when, why…"

"Okay." Sitting in the chair in front of Rodolfo's desk, Jorge leaned forward and slashed a long hank of hair out of his face. "Thursday night I was—"

"You took this film Thursday?"

Jorge nodded.

Old news. Rodolfo nearly fainted. "Why, ah, why didn't you bring in the tape the next morning? Or Saturday or Sunday?" Rodolfo asked.

"Well, I didn't look at it on Friday—I had exams. And then on the weekend, I just figured you'd be closed."

"I'm afraid that television stations don't close for anything," Rodolfo chuckled sadly, though he bitterly wished this wasn't so. He nearly threw the kid out right then, but the prospect of more searching through the wire services depressed him. "All right. Friday night, then, what happened?"

"I was in the center of town—over by the La Merced Church? I was in a taxi with my girlfriend. We were going to a party down in the southern sector of town. And we passed this big guy with blond hair. My girlfriend recognized him: it was that guy who was meeting with the press because his company is negotiating with Petróleos Andinos. Remember him? Jay Streets?"

"Yes, more or less," Rodolfo said.

"*More or less?* With every girl in Ecuador panting for this guy?"

"Well, this is a serious TV station," Rodolfo retorted. "We don't make stars of spokesmen." But he raised the price for the video by fifty dollars.

"Well, I didn't mean *that*," said Jorge coloring.

"Anyways—he was doing something, maybe…naughty?" Rodolfo said hopefully.

"Not exactly naughty—worse. He was carrying this plastic bag, like for groceries. At first I thought he was a tourist—well, he kind of was, really. And he was doing something incredible. When we passed, he took some money out of a bag—a thick bunch of dollar bills. And I thought, 'What's he going to do with that?' I turned around to look through the back window and I saw him kneel down and give the money to a beggar. *To a beggar!*"

"Ah, I see." With alarm, Rodolfo realized this was the crux of the story.

"And then he went a couple steps down the street and gave more money to another. That's when I told the taxi to stop and ran back there with my girlfriend. He was giving away wads of twenty-dollar bills. The guy—the beggar—was just staring at the wad in his hand. He couldn't believe it!"

"Pretty…pretty strange, all right." Rodolfo had a vision from the evening before, Mónica splayed over his desk, nylons a mess around her ankles and her skirt crushed up around her waist.

"Yeah—strange and *insulting*. This guy must be a millionaire! Anyway, we ran after him and started filming." Jorge had got up and connected his digital camera to the television.

Rodolfo performed his best Sigh of Gravity. "Now, I must advise you, Jorge: the video will have to be of the very top quality to make our program." Out of respect for the kid's feelings, he didn't tell Mónica to start the downlink from Mexico—the Mexicans always had something, even if it was just a drive-by in Ciudad Juarez.

At first the video was dark. Only when the American was direct-ly under streetlamps were his features visible. He knelt into a door-way, fumbled with something in the plastic bag he was carrying, and handed something to a shaky hand. Then the American stood up, walked away from the camera several steps, stopped and did the same thing in another doorway.

"See what I mean? This guy is giving away stacks of money!"

Rodolfo nodded wisely, wishing it was himself in the doorway.

"Oh, this was a shoeshine kid," Jorge said.

The camera jiggled and swung around, following a kid run-ning along with a shoeshine box. He rounded the corner, and the American tried to stop him, holding up a sheaf of money. But the boy slipped past and ran on. At the next intersection he turned right and disappeared round the corner.

A three-second gap of black. "Just a second. It comes back now," Jorge narrated.

Now Streets, walking fast, passed under a streetlamp—the glim-mer on his leather jacket outlined his torso. Yes, it was definitely the American spokesman from the bank: the strong, white face and shimmer of blond hair were unmistakable. A white plastic super-market bag hung from the fingers of his right hand.

Another gap. Now Streets stopped at a bench that a man was sleeping beneath. He pulled out another stack of money and laid it on his chest.

"Isn't that the most pathetic thing you ever saw?" Jorge exclaimed.

Rodolfo nodded. It was. It was a pathetic waste of valuable money and his own valuable time. "Well, Jorge, I'm sorry to disappoint you, but the standards of TeleMax8 are such that—"

"Wait. We're getting to the best part!"

Now the man stopped. The shaky glow on his face indicated a fire. He put his hand in the bag and pulled out what was apparently the rest of the money—a stack as thick as a brick—and wadded up the bag, looked around for a wastepaper basket, and then like a good American stuffed the bag into his jacket pocket rather than litter the street. With a huff he settled his shoulders and walked slowly for-ward, picking his way with care, towards the fire. It seemed to come from a gap in the exterior wall of a building.

The camera jiggled; running footsteps sounded.

"Okay, so here we ran up behind him as fast as we could," said Jorge.

Rodolfo ground his teeth.

The scene, far better lit than the others, was the ruins of an old building that had collapsed a few months earlier; Quito's daily rain often weakened the ancient cement. Rodolfo remembered the place because five people had died in the collapse and his program had got two or three decent reports out of it. Much of the debris had now been cleared away, but massive log beams still stood at angles, and stone building blocks littered the ground. To the right and the back, vestiges of roof remained, and tucked under them and against the adjoining walls of buildings were two campfires that burned bits of board and kindling. Children waddled aimlessly, one with a spoon clutched in both hands like a cudgel. At one fire, three men sat on some stone blocks, sharing a bottle between them: *aguardiente,* to judge by its transparency. At the other, two chunky Indian women cooked on little tin pots held over the flames. A third woman, kneeling, was holding up a tiny wool sweater to dry it. The only audio was of squeaking children.

Then everyone froze. The American was walking over to the women at the fire. Two jumped back against the wall of the building, but the one drying the sweater only watched him. The men looked on; one tried to get up, but fell drunkenly back on his behind. The American said something unintelligible; Rodolfo remembered that he spoke little Spanish, hardly more than greetings. The American looked down into his hands—he was in profile—manipulating the thick sheaf of bills. He pulled out part and offered it to the woman.

The woman looked at it, immobile. "Por favor," said Streets with impatience. Nothing. He shrugged. Then, looking around, he bent down and put the money on the ground. He took some object—it was in the shadow of his leg, but most likely a rock—and put it on top. Then he walked to the other two women. They squawked in fright. Streets divided the remaining money in two parts and laid them on the ground, placed a stone on each. He rose and huffed sharply, and his steamy breath came out in a cloud: a dirty job done. "Adiós," he said, and walking away added something in English.

"I took the film to my neighbor. He's from Norway," said Jorge. "He said, 'Lighten up, girls, would you?' Isn't that just incredible?"

Rodolfo sighed. He had been sitting on the edge of his desk, but now walked towards the television and began his spiel: "Well, Jorge, I can understand why—"

"Wait—the last part!" cried Jorge, grabbing his arm.

Now a man charged—staggering—at the American, an empty bottle held high. In Spanish: "What are you doing with my wife? Nobody touches my wife except—"

Which is as far as he got before the American bent and came in low and fast, and plucked him off the ground by the knees. The Ecuadoran squawked, the bottle flew away. The American swung him around like a baby and laid him gently down.

The American glanced at the others—no more takers—and with a shake of his head turned away towards the sidewalk. The camera went black.

"That's it!" said Jorge. "Fantastic, huh? We figure he gave away ten thousand dollars in fifteen minutes."

Rodolfo dropped into his seat behind his desk and propped his tubby face on his fists. He tipped his head to each side in a rendering of Careful Consideration. He felt more solid rejecting a piece this way. "Well, I guess that as a human-interest piece, it has—"

"When I got home and some friends looked at it, we were just about ready to march over to the American Embassy and throw rocks. I mean, by day the bank people extort *even more* millions from us, and by night they throw a few bucks into our beggar's hat? That's what it is: gringo guilt money!"

Rodolfo nodded, though in reality the idea rocked him like a swat from a baseball bat. Gringo guilt money—yes. Gringo guilt money was a story with good, long legs and miles to run.

"I mean, it's not enough they take our oil for nothing," Jorge cried, swatting away his forelock again. "But on top of it, they give back a few pennies to street people and go back to the hotel thinking that they're good Christians? That's filthy! That's just the kind of thing that…"

Jorge rambled on, and Rodolfo leaned forward and reached for his elegant teak cigar box. It had a broken corner, this a pleasant souvenir of his last secretary, Juliana, who had shoved it off the table the year before in a moment of ecstatic carelessness. Now he took out a cigar and smoothed it with his fingers and cut off one end, thinking.

Guilt money—and images to boot. Yes, that would do for both

the midday edition and the six-o'clock—if properly presented, inter-cut with anodyne statements by Streets on behalf of the bank, with a little of his football footage, and with a quote or two about the new agreement from outraged Petróleos execs. And there was another benefit. Rodolfo had been taking heat from the Ecuadoran left—damned Communists, the lot of them—for ignoring the working man. Now he could shut them up for a while.

"And besides, I looked this guy up on Wikipedia, and this guy played five seasons in the American rugby league"—which is what Latin Americans call American football. "He must be a multi-multi-millionaire," Jorge was exclaiming. "Even if it *is* his own money, what's a few thousand dollars to him? Nothing. Less money than he blows on one dinner in a New York restaurant. See? It's just guilt money."

Rodolfo made his plans. He would get Luis Alfredo Valverde to do the report. Valverde was a frothing Commie who always wanted to put on stories about poor farmers. His father owned Ecuador's big-gest supermarket chain and had threatened to take his advertising elsewhere unless TeleMax8 gave Luis Alfredo a job and got him out of the house. Rodolfo drew a breath.

"Jorge, journalism is the backbone of our democratic society and the tireless, holy defender of our rights and liberties. It is to the re-porter who joins his weapons to our struggle that the greatest thanks, appreciation and praise must flow, and his accomplishment and con-tribution must be taken with an esteem reserved only for saints and our greatest national heroes. In thinking about an adequate com-pensation for this work, which you have done with admirable clarity, coherence, and risk to life and limb, I am impressed by your dedica-tion to the Ecuadoran democratic spirit, our sense of justice, truth, dignity, and humanity, and the rigorous investigation of those who may not have at heart the best interests of our beloved and beauti-ful fatherland.

"My funds are extremely tight in these times of economic uncer-tainty, as I'm sure you, in your magnanimity and great sense of cul-ture, can understand. I am, however, in light of the impressive and important work that you have exhibited to me, disposed to make an important financial and monetary effort to express, if only in token form, the gratitude, delight, and admiration of our company and the Ecuadoran people. I say, as I should say, that I hope and expect that two hundred dollars would constitute neither a stain on your honor nor an inadequate reward for your Herculean efforts."

All of which purled from Rodolfo's mouth as smoothly as smoke from a chimney, since Ecuadorans set great store by oratory, and Rodolfo had long ago discovered that plenty of calligraphy around the final price made the seller more amenable to being cheated.

Jorge swallowed hard. "Two hundred dollars? Oh. Well, okay."

Rodolfo stuck his hand out quickly to seal the deal. Then he walked around his desk and buzzed Mónica to bring in his checkbook. "Can I also throw in a cigar for your good father?" he asked, taking a new one out of the box.

5 Paul Klippen needed an effort not to grimace every time he entered the office of George Kaufman, the deputy chief of mission, the number two man in the embassy.

His office décor, carried across three decades and a dozen diplomatic postings, was a running battle between Oval Office and OK Corral. Every thrust of elegance had a parry of tackiness to thwart it. On his desk stood a plaster bust of Lincoln—wearing a beaten, stained five-gallon hat. Beside a framed citation from the secretary of state hung a framed U.S. Cavalry stirrup. A shapely wine decanter shrank from the dented WWII canteen—Kaufman's father's—beside it on a tea trolley. His desk was neoclassic maple, the chair behind it a chipped, dented, pocked pine thing that Kaufman had bought at a U.S. airbase antique auction: it had reputedly been General Eisenhower's in England before D-Day, and Kaufman showed everybody the carved *HOW LONG?* on the right armrest, which he swore Ike did while waiting for the Channel weather and tides to turn. But the letters, Paul had noticed, were slanted almost perpendicular to the armrest, and Kaufman left-handed. Just to settle the matter, Paul had looked up Eisenhower and found that the good general had been right-handed.

Happy to turn his gaze elsewhere, Paul watched Mary enter Kaufman's office and greet everyone, place in the center of the table a pot of coffee—she made it herself for every meeting—and take her place for the bi-weekly "country team" meeting.

"Walt!" she cried. "What did Louise tell you? You keep eating those things and you're going to turn into a beach ball!"

Walt Boam, the Foreign Commercial Officer, nodded and giggled and took another bite of a powdered donut, listening to his cell phone.

Mary leaned over and said into it, "Walt's turning into a beach ball. We're all disgusted with him." Walt stared at her, scandalized.

Paul laughed and clapped his hands.

Walt giggled and said, "Marty, I'm gonna have to call you back… No, nobody's disgusted with me, I think." Another giggle.

"Bravo, Mary!" said Paul. "In the history of the State Department, nobody's ever gotten Walt off his cell phone so quickly."

"Ta-da! It's magic," she laughed.

Yes, that was it: she was in love, Paul realized. She was right in the curl of the wave of it. Hardly an hour after one of her daily "down and backs" to the equatorial Line Monument, and she sat feminine and strong and radiant—though she wore but a light-blue suit and white blouse, simple gold chain at her throat, and a delicate watch. His friendship with Mary was natural and strong, and had quickly become an alliance. Without her knowing, he had lobbied the ambassador hard to get her on *Hablemos*, which he knew would quickly boost her career.

Still, he wondered now why she had not told him about the man in her life. They often lunched together and she had come several times to his house for Sunday lunch.

"All right, let's jump-start this puppy," Kaufman declared in a nasal Wyoming drone. George never started anything without jumping it too, Paul despaired.

Kaufman walked to the meeting table, stepped over his chair's back and dropped his bony rump on the seat. He smoothed his red-white-and-blue suspenders and rolled up his sleeves, rolled them and rolled them till they were two tourniquets over his thin biceps.

Are you going to chair an embassy meeting or play poker, George? Paul wondered silently.

His ablutions finished, Kaufman passed around the morning agenda as if dealing the first hand. "Well, Mary Swanson is here, and that's really all we need."

"The madding crowd," said Mary with a dismissive wave of the rest of the room.

"Absolutely true, Mary. These guys"—a hopeless shrug their way—"I think they just come to get away from their desks for an hour."

With Mary looking the other way, Walt Boam stole another powdered donut from the plate that Kaufman always put out. But he saw
Paul watching him and giggled. Paul winked.

Paul did not care for Walt, either. He was an Economic Officer, a
back-slapping, put-it-there type, an African-American mover and
shaker who knew by name every top executive in Ecuador. He had
been in the country six years—two whole tours in the same place,
which is rare at State. On weekends, he loved crashing through the
jungle with his children in his fortress-like SUV. He had a framed
photo in his office of himself crouched before *Epipedobates Anthony,*
a red frog with lime-green stripes—the most dangerous reptile in the
world: with a single touch, convulsions were the result. Visiting biol-
ogists often consulted Walt on the best places to find one Ecuadoran
critter or another.

His respect for Ecuadoran humans, however, was as low as a frog's
belly and reserved strictly for the rich. As far as Walt was concerned,
Ecuadorans either drove good cars and wore suits to work, or could
safely be regarded as ants. He had seen Walt pay a street shoeshine
boy five dollars and wait for the kid to dig out four dollars change
from two different pockets and his sock.

"I'm sure glad you got the rotating spot for junior dips, Mary," said
Walt with a giggle. Already there was powdered sugar on his dark
cheeks. "I mean, really, having a woman here—really throws a whole
new light on things, doesn't it?"

"Well, thanks, Walt." To the others, fluffing her curly hair: "See,
guys? Walt knows how a girl likes to be treated." It was cover fire for
Walt's clumsiness; Paul alone appreciated it.

"Darn right," Walt said—and giggled again. It would surely be,
Paul thought, his last sound on earth if someday he and his SUV
sank into jungle quicksand.

Paul looked over the agenda. "George, point three here would really
be better dealt with at a later time, don't you think? The ramping-up
of chamber-of-commerce interest in a bilateral textile-manufacturing
accord with Mexico is just reaching maturity now. Next week we'll
have something substantial to talk about—one man's opinion here."

"Point three, huh?" said Kaufman, hooking half-moon reading
glasses behind his ears. "Yew betcha. All right, people, let's strike that
for the time being." And he launched into one of his many, many,

many set pieces: "You know, an agenda isn't written in gold, people. Till the moment the meeting starts, it's perfectly legit to add or subtract items. I mean, the agenda is here to serve *us*, not *us* to serve *it*. This is a point that really has to be impressed upon…"

There was little to do once he'd got up a head of steam, so as George blabbered on, Mary reached for the coffee and filled two cups, one for her and one for Paul.

"Hail Mary, Queen of Coffee," Paul murmured after a careful sip. "Perfection—*merci bien*."

"That said," Kaufman finished at last, "let's get down to beeswax. Point one: DynoBank's rescheduled debt with Petróleos. Local papers are raising the dickens out of it. The overnight note from the Ecuador Desk this morning is recommending a general press release for Latin Am, touching on reservations about some clauses of the new ag'ment, a plea for understanding, times hard for one and all, Dyno's statement does not in any way, shape, or form constitute the policy of U.S.G. But they give us leeway on issuing as we see fit."

"Refraining at all times from using the term 'draconian,'" Paul said dryly.

"Oh, c'mon, Paul. It's not that bad," Walt Boam said.

"Did you *read* that new agreement?" Paul answered. Walt's silence said no. "For the new loan extension, Dyno gets ten percent *above* what they're already owed, paid every six months on the dime, and if they don't get it, they automatically—automatically, as in no questions asked—the next day take over another 27 percent of the company stock—bringing their total to 49 percent—*and* they seat two people on the company board. That's the collateral: 27 percent of stock and two seats. Have you ever heard of anything like that?"

"Hey, man, there's a lot of risk there. Petróleos is a three-ring circus—well, it *can* be. Heck, I give Dyno all the credit in the world."

"With all respect, Walt, I would give them somewhat less," said Paul.

"*Moving on*," Kaufman said, with a light snap of his suspenders; he loved policy and hated debate of it. "I say our comment is: Dyno's statement does not in any way, shape or form, reflect on blah-blah-blah. And I'd attach on a reiteration of our vital hopes for a steady expansion of Ecuadoran industry and economy, blah-blah-blah, as being good for both our great nations, blah-blah-blah. Thumbs up or down, people?"

"Yeah, sure, I'd go with that," Walt said, reaching for another donut.

"Actually, George, I wouldn't mention the matter at all: benign neglect," said Paul. "No release, no statement, nothing. Anything the Great Satan might say at this point would only be twisted around by the left and thrown back at us."

"Yeah, well, just seems to me that, hell, just for general PR, we oughta say *something*," Kaufman said uneasily. "Mary, you're the most popular woman in Ecuador. What say?"

"I guess I'd side with Paul," she said. "Why associate ourselves with DynoBank? May as well hang a sign out front saying, 'Baby-eating Scrooge capitalists get free embassy parking.'"

The men laughed.

"Yeah, well, all right, a-a-a-a-h, for *now* we'll just kind of decide not to decide...." Which was how Kaufman decided anything.

"Who's deciding things without my permission?" Harry Kruger asked as he strode in, a scowl on his massive lips. He was wearing a black corduroy shirt and tan chinos under a gray shapeless windbreaker with Massachusetts Institute of Technology stamped on its left side. His shoes were black and made for running, like a basketball referee's. "Not to mention starting meetings without me?"

"Afraid we thought you weren't coming, Harry," said George Kaufman, which was as close as he ever dared criticize Harry.

Harry tossed his windbreaker onto the coat rack. "Yeah, sorry if I'm late, but I'm CIA head of station, and I really don't give a fuck," he added, his fat lips re-forming into a rubbery grin. Those lips, Paul thought. They were the cardiogram of his soul.

"Two honest statements in a row," said Mary. "You're slipping, Harry."

"Keep that up, and they'll send you to a CIA shrink," Paul added.

"We were on Point Two, Harry," George Kaufman said with a tiny cough, handing him an agenda. "So moving on, Paul, can you—"

"Look: I'm an invalid." Harry swiveled his rude wrestler's bulk like a model and pulled down the collar of his shirt. "No kidding: can't hardly turn my head. Ten stitches I got. Guy tried to take me down with a switchblade—a six-incher." A broad surgical bandage was stuck on the side of his neck, just below the ear, though the upper end reached into his salt-and-pepper scalp.

Walt Boam, who had a fascination with espionage, bolted forward in his seat, eyes bulging. "Whoa! That's a real rip, Harry."

As Harry preened, Paul wondered if that was even close to the real story. He had observed spooks for years, and it startled him how many were the emptiest of empty vessels, men just begging to be filled with a message, a mission, a life. Truth for them was the merest calculation of interests: how much a story benefited or hindered career or agency or nation. And how they hated people for whom the truth had an intrinsic value. Hence Harry's impatience with diplomats and politicians and anyone else who dealt in facts and the conflicts that resulted from them, and his unalloyed belief in his agency as the last bastion of Western civilization. Of all government workers, spooks were the only ones Paul loathed.

"Hurts like hell too—and it's been three days," Harry was saying. "No, four. It was Thursday night. Ruined a good shirt too."

"So, Harry: your Purple Heart in the war on terror," Paul said. "Congratulations."

"Oughta be—*was* line of duty." Kruger finally lowered his thick, shapeless frame uneasily into the open chair as if it might collapse; then slouched back, knees open, lips sagging, and snatched up the agenda as an eighth-grader does a math lesson, defying it to interest him. "I want workman's comp and a nice blowjob from Miss America too—settle for you, though, Mar'." He dropped a hand on her knee beside him.

"You CIA guys are so suave and sophisticated," Mary said, snatching his hand and dropping it heavily on his own. "They must teach you that stuff at spy school."

Harry grinned, still looking at the agenda. "Just like James Bond, hon.'"

At about the time she had started with *Hablemos*, Mary had gone to bed with him, once, both out of loneliness and her intoxication with her new attractiveness to men. And how she had regretted it: he had pestered her ever since. He simply could not believe that she wanted nothing more with him.

Kaufman harrumphed and launched another set piece—"The Very Fine Line Between Good-Natured Ribbing and Sexual Innuendo"— but Mary, who was learning how little respect one needed to lavish on Embassy Quito's number-two man, cut him off:

"Of course, there is an upside there, Harry, now that I think of it. I mean, *I'd* get a Purple Heart, too."

Both Harry and Paul laughed; Walt and George hocked up a few careful chuckles in order to go with the flow. Walt reached for another powdered donut while nobody noticed; Paul counted it his third.

Kaufman: "Okay, Point Two: Paul Klippen, up-to-date us on the banana negotiations."

"Interesting, that one," Paul began. "My source says that Plantaciones Costa has now agreed to actually negotiate a global agreement for all plantations, which is actually against the labor laws because all negotiations have to be on a plantation-by-plantation basis, not—"

Harry slapped the agenda on the table. "Agreed *how?* Formally? Informally?" He sat, lips round, slowly puffing out his cheeks like a bottom-feeding fish in a tank.

"Formally, like everything else in this country: it doesn't exist till it's put in writing," Paul said.

"Oh, that was smart," said Walt Boam sourly.

"The *fools*," Kruger muttered, looking up at the ceiling.

"It's a big chink in the armor, all right. And it's going to be a single per-diem wage for everybody: pickers, washers, transporters—the lot. But fear not. Beyond that, nobody's giving an inch: Costa won't go a dime over fifteen dollars, and the workers want upwards of thirty dollars per diem."

"Bastards—those absolute bastards!" Walt said through gritted teeth.

"My source says the owners are desperate. Bananas ripen so quickly they can't go another week this way before the heavy losses start. And the strike's spreading. Easily eighty percent of workers have stayed away from work, no scabs are coming in to replace them, and it's expected to be near a hundred percent by the end of the week."

"A hundred percent!" Walt moaned.

"It's a challenge all right," said George Kaufman, adjusting his suspenders.

Paul noticed the secret, tight smile that had bloomed on Mary Swanson's face. He noticed it whenever the matter of the banana negotiations came up. Now she covered it with her coffee cup.

"The windup being," Paul ended, "that they've made no headway since that one agreement, and the thinking now is that the two sides will go to an arbitrator—"

"An arbitrator?" Walt gasped. "God—Costa's against the wall *already?"*

"That's how I hear it: they're ready to do anything," Paul said evenly, though he nearly chuckled with delight to see Walt jerked out of his complacence. "A few names have been suggested, though half-heartedly."

"Jesus, Harry, can't you *do* anything?" Walt whined. "I heard that a few reefers were hanging offshore waiting for cargo, but I had no *idea* it was this bad."

"Reefers, Walt?" Mary asked.

"Refrigerator ships. You gotta have 'em for bananas. You don't even *harvest* till you have your ship scheduled."

"Klippers, who's your source in the negotiating room?" Harry asked Paul. Paul smiled philosophically. "Well, now, Harry, *sources.* That cuts a little close to the bone, don't you think?"

"For Christ's sake, Klippers! This is—"

But Paul was waving him down. "It's someone on the plantation-owners' committee, but you surely know that. What difference can it make exactly who?"

"Heck, Harry," said Walt, "a lot of growers cry on *my* shoulder. I can get the skinny if you're—"

But Kruger had no ear for him. "All right—forget it. Point is: from now on, Klippers, no more contact with him till this is all over, understood?"

Which cut even closer to the bone, and made Paul, who in a debate measured every gesture, clear his throat. "Agent Kruger, the U.S. State Department has a very active and *legitimate* interest in—"

Kruger massive CIA index finger stabbed the table, which is what he did to lay down the law: *"No. More. Contact.* Read my lips, Klippers. There's *too much* on the line. We can't take *any* chance that the embassy is seen working this game."

Kaufman looked on, wide-eyed, as he always did when Harry took over a meeting.

"Now do I have your word on that?"

Paul spoke softly. "My goodness, Harry, is that your waterboarding voice? I would think that—"

"Goddammit! I said, *Do I have your word?*"

Paul considered this question, then picked up his coffee mug, swirled its last contents, and drank them. "Mary, I'm going to pour myself just another half here. What say ye?"

6 Rodolfo Ilahú waddled with an ant's flurry along the stale corridors of TeleMax8.

He didn't find Luis Alfredo Valverde at his place in the newsroom, if that was the word for the maelstrom of desks that his staff shared with quarrelling soap-opera writers and the accounting department. He finally ran him to earth in the staff meeting room, in English class, with the vile Chris Carf, the orange-haired, brown-mustachioed English-as-a-second-language teacher. The company paid for classes for a half-dozen staffers because they had more and more relations with Asian and European news outlets.

Chris, twenty-four dogmatic years old, a recent graduate in Spanish from the University of Washington, was standing beside a frazzled oilcloth flipchart, tall and rail-thin like his Oregon Trail descendents. He had one foot on a chair and was beating time on his knee as he chanted with his six students around the table: "Mr. JONES has BOOKED Flight TWELVE-oh-THREE to New YORK. Mr. JONES has BOOKED Flight TWELVE-oh-THREE to New YORK." It was a modern method developed by "Bulgarian linguistic scientists" that allowed adults to learn English by ear, like children, this according to the assurances of EnglishItUp Language School. The method was guaranteed, and best of all, required no homework. Rodolfo was skeptical. His cousin Jacobo, director of personnel, had contracted EnglishItUp, and had surely taken a quiet kickback as well.

As Rodolfo entered, Chris raised a policeman's hand before his face, not taking his eyes off the class, and shook his head. His hand did not miss a beat.

"Mr. JONES has BOOKED Flight TWELVE-oh-THREE to New YORK," chanted the students.

"And...*will!*" cried Chris, in time with his beating, like an aerobics instructor.

"Mr. JONES will BOOK Flight TWELVE-oh-THREE to New

YORK." Two secretaries, two reporters, and two staff from the weekend-programming department—all sat slouched as if melted around the meeting table: "Mr. JONES will BOOK Flight TWELVE-oh-THREE to New YORK."

"And...*should!*"

"Mr. JONES should BOOK Flight TWELVE-oh-THREE to New YORK."

"And...*can!*"

"Mr. JONES can BOOK Flight TWELVE-oh-THREE to New YORK."

Finally, Chris turned to him. "Good morning, Rodolfo. Do you mind? We still have a few statements left." "Statements" were the repeated sentences, all organized by the Bulgarian linguists.

"Ah, I need to the Mr. Valverde. It is an urgent—"

"'I *need* Mr. Valverde,'" Chris corrected, and ran his tongue thickly over his teeth. "Just two statements left." To the students, beating on his hip: "Mr. JONES hubs in FRANKFURT for his connecting FLIGHT to Dubai."

"Mr. JONES hubs in FRANKFURT for his connecting FLIGHT to Dubai."

"And...*could!*"

Five minutes later, the students tumbled out of the room like gassed rats, and Rodolfo went in and put Jorge's video into the room's machine. "Take a look at this," he told Luis Alfredo in Spanish. He repeated Jorge's story in a few sentences. "What kind of report would you make of this?"

Luis Alfredo had sleepy black eyes, a coke-fiend's sniff, and a narrow, disappointed face. He watched the tape with his thin arms folded over his chest. "That's the DynoBank guy, isn't it?"

"Uh-oh," sang Chris. He was rolling up and tying his flipchart. "English. We're still in the room. Do we remember the rules?"

The Ecuadorans ignored the rules.

"And he's giving money to those people? Seriously?" Luis Alfredo asked.

"The camera followed him for ten minutes," said Rodolfo. "He gave out thousands of dollars—in twenties."

"*Thousands?*" said Luis Alfredo. "*Chooo-ta!* What for?"

Chris laughed disgustedly. "What's it matter to him?" he said in

Spanish. "He must be stinking rich. God, that is *pathetic*. He could give away ten times that amount and still have enough for his Ferrari." He ran his tongue over his upper teeth again.

Rodolfo noted that his instinct had been right: properly presented, this story had heat.

Then came the sequence in the ruins, by the fire. Streets put some money under rocks, and the terrified women pressed back against the wall as if before a firing squad.

"That's it, you bastard," Chris sneered. "Just leave it on the ground and let them bend down and pick it up. And if it's all wet, well, that's just too fucking bad for them. You won't worry, will you? Just go back to your nice apartment and your silicone babes. You've done your duty, and it didn't even hurt, did it?"

The man attacked Streets with a bottle, and the sequence ended. Luis Alfredo shook his head. "Absolute dynamite, man—rich bastard like that giving out bar tips? We ought to send a copy to the gringos at the embassy."

Rodolfo felt that things were on track, and that was enough work for one day. He took out the video cassette and slapped it into Luis Alfredo's hand. "That's going to lead the midday news, so play it big. Report it as if *our* people shot the footage. Call DynoBank's central office in New York and get a statement from Streets. Chris, help Luis Alfredo with the English." He took out a roll of cash and gave Chris two twenties. "That's for your help. Now get going."

7 Paul had served Mary and poured a precise half-cup of coffee for himself by the time Harry Kruger finished ranting about how the banana negotiations were too important and that Langley was giving the case top priority, and that senators and congressmen were banging on Langley's door to keep the price down.

"They hear 'rising fruit prices' and they get hives, and then they go to Langley, which is where all the world's problems come calling for a solution."

Twice George Kaufman had tried to start a sermon, the first beginning, "The State Department and the intelligence services have enjoyed a long and close relationship"; the second, "In any conflictive differing of opinions, my philosophy is to try to find common ground first because nine times out of ten…" Kruger had smashed both like a car through hedges.

"Now: are you on the wavelength, Klippers?" Harry's lips had come to rest in a menacing rictal oval, framing his thick teeth. "No more contact."

"Harry, I know of no injunction from our secretary of state directing foreign-service officers to kiss the Company's nether parts."

"I'm not saying *that*, Klippers," Kruger moaned. "Diplomacy is just fine for keeping the ball rolling, day-to-day issues. But results-when-the-crunch-is-on is *my* department. I don't want *any* possibility that it looks like we're influencing the negotiations."

"When we really are."

"No, no. We're letting this thing run its course."

"Exactly! Which is as it should be," said Mary. "Thank you, Harry."

Paul chuckled skeptically. "Harry, *please.* You sound like a stoned kid telling his parents he never touches drugs."

Walt had sat up, donut frozen in mid-upswing to his mouth. *"Run its course?* Hey, now just wait a minute here, Harry. I have friends— real power boys in the fruit industry—and you can get religion just listening to them. I told them we had a handle on it. Now we do, don't we?"

"Really, y'know, when you look at it," Kaufman began, smoothing his suspenders again, "what we have here is the oldest of embassy dilemmas: a structural overlapping of functional competencies."

Paul: "Harry, a question: Given that this issue is so important, *why* didn't you fine professionals in the results-when-the-crunch-is-on department cut it off at source? The groundwork for a strike of this magnitude, that paralyzes the biggest plantation in the country and spreads to others, was surely laid *months* ago."

Again, from the corner of his eye, he saw Mary smile into her coffee.

"Two *years* ago," Harry grumbled, snatching a donut, "but who's counting? Ancient history."

Paul: "A question of two years is hardly ancient. If I'm supposed to stay away from the negotiations, I'd like an answer, please. How did workers of the biggest company in the banana industry go on strike and drag management to the negotiating table? Or did you fine *results* people, to put it charitably, get caught napping?"

"Well, it's not *our* country, Paul," said Mary. "If these people want to strike, that's their right."

Paul watched Harry and waited.

With a growl, Harry lurched forward to the table and pointed an accusing finger at Paul, though he had no accusation to put with it. "It's because their leader played it smart, okay? He—"

"Sixto Carrasco, you mean?"

"No, no—he's just the movement's mouthpiece. He's a lawyer who made a splash defending a few workers and talking trash about America. He's damn good at it, and now it looks like he's going to run for president."

"Yeah, he's number two in the polls and rising fast," Walt griped. "Can't you *do* something about him, Harry?"

"Later," said Kruger, waving this aside. He fell back in his chair and raised one cast-iron knee on the other. "Look, story's this. The strike seriously started its takeoff roll"—he thought—"call it a month ago. Carrasco simply hopped on the bandwagon before it left without him. There's another guy—little hood-slash-conman called Segundo Verdes. He and his crew did the heavy lifting. They worked the base communities, especially Costa's five big plantations and the little feeder farms that fill out its export quotas when they're a little light on the harvest. He—Verdes—he's the one that really wrapped it to-gether, starting from around two years out. We got wind of him, sure. We tried to find him and pull him in for a full and frank exchange."

Paul smiled over his coffee cup. "Ah, my favorite euphemism."

"Turned out he'd done his homework. Doesn't live anywhere, no family. His team changes, depending on when and where he needs them. He appears and disappears, lives off the land; people give him sandwiches. They call him 'El Profesor.' Everybody in the Pacific-side lowlands knows *who* he is, nobody knows *where* he is. Our file on him hasn't run its first megabyte yet."

"Wow! He sounds like a pretty remarkable guy!" said Mary.

Harry only grunted.

Paul: "Why 'El Profesor'? He was a teacher?"

"'Cause of his style, I guess. No rhetoric, no bullshit. Speeches hardly last five minutes. Pops up in a village, hands round some yuca, talks up the movement, says everybody's got to be ready when the balloon goes up for the strike. And that means everybody *in the village,* not just the plantation: won't do any good to walk off the job if the grower can simply hire replacements the next day. Before the local cops can be rousted out of their hammocks, he's slipped off through the swamp. Three months ago, Costa sent out dogs and a helicopter after him. Couple of us here helped out too. No good."

Paul: "Computer? Cell phone trace?"

"Nothing. Not a thing. Not even a voice print."

Paul whistled. "Well, well. So he's been trained by someone, hasn't he?"

Harry shrugged unhappily. "We don't know. He has *some* link with Spain, though how far, what for, how much money…we never got confirmation."

"Spain? Harry! This is getting serious!" Walt cried in alarm, swatting the powdered sugar off his cheeks. "Who the hell is this guy? Commie? Al Qaeda?"

"I wish he was—then I could tear some budget and muscle out of Langley. He didn't pop up on the grid till about two years ago, taking an Iberia flight from Mexico City to Madrid. There's some murky stuff about him living in L.A. for a few years, and contacts with Spanish spooks, but nothing concrete. We can't even locate him re-entering Ecuador." Kruger opened his hands and let them drop. "That's it—whole file."

"So if he's here, he must've swam from Spain," joked Kaufman.

Paul: "That's 'swum,' George: swim, swam, swum. Harry, the Spaniards' incentive, now what would that be? Thinking of their own fruit industries, right?"

"What else? The Spanish are in the banana business themselves—big Canary Island operations. Ecuador is the bargain-basement floor of the world banana market: two hundred seventy dollars a month minimum wage. If labor costs rise and the per-ton goes up *here,* it goes up in all Latin Am. And that makes Spanish bananas and plantains more competitive on the world market. Spaniards have to blow fifteen hundred per worker per month."

"Okay okay okay, 'History is bunk,' to quote the Bard," Walt said impatiently. "You gonna take this guy out or not, Harry? My friends are getting ulcers over this thing."

"Walt!" Mary gasped. "Come on! That stuff went out with the Cold War. We don't do that now!"

"Not as often, anyway," said Paul quietly. "But business is business, dear."

To everyone's amazement, Harry Kruger had started laughing—laughing and shaking his head in pity. "Take him out? Jesus Christ!"

"You guys, *come on!*" said Mary. "Ecuador isn't some satellite state of the Soviet Union."

Kruger frankly patted her knee. "Mary, do yourself a favor and get out of the diplomatic game while you can, huh? See how stupid it makes you?"

"Hey, that's pretty judgmental, Harry," sniffed Walt.

Kaufman: "You know, interdepartmental relations are really not the smoothest area of embassy—"

"What the fuck does it matter *now* if we 'take him out'?" Kruger roared, silencing everyone. "You dipshit dips! Look out the window for a change. The strike's a *reality*. It's now! It's happening! The plantations owners have been dragged kicking and screaming to the negotiating table. And now, to top it off, *now* the shitheads have gone and agreed to negotiate a single per-diem for the whole industry! Fuck's it matter *now* if we kill Verdes—kill him and wave his head on a great big fucking flagpole? We kill him, and his number-two man steps into his place at the negotiating table. Big fucking deal! The hard part, the *impossible* part, getting a hundred thousand dumbshit peasants to lay down their tools all at once, on cue, and stay that way, *and* nobody steps in as scabs—*that's* done."

Paul: "Indeed. You certainly have to hand it to him."

"Damn right you do. Like I cabled Langley last week: strategically, the guy's a genius. And it's only because I've been on this thing from the start that we've still got a card to play in it at all. *Which means,* Klippers, that you're not going to touch this thing with a ten-foot pole. And it means that *you,* Mary—you're going to have to pitch in, and if you need to use your pretty ass, you do it."

Kaufman: "Now Harry, that really goes beyond the—"

Kruger jabbed Mary's knee hard with his forefinger, and his big lips were a hard, straight line. "Mary, tonight you're in El Ejido Park where they're all camped out, and you're going to find Verdes, get it? He must be in there somewhere—he gives the workers a pep talk most nights. Get in close to him and get him to tell you his plans. Background, program, anything you can get. Especially if you can find out what kind of per diem he'll finally settle for, or who he's thinking for an arbitrator, I'll give you a free night in my bed." Kruger stood up, pulled his pants up to his bullish torso, and pressed his neck bandage in place. "That's enough playing office. I've got work to do."

"Why would he talk to me?" asked Mary.

"Because you're a *brand,* babycakes! You're the only face-slash-personality we've got around here, and that tells him you can't be Company."

"Why not?"

Kruger rolled his eyes, a man talking to idiots. "'Cause we don't exactly make a habit of putting our agents on national TV, do we? Plus you're sweet and sexy, *and* you've got a D cup to show him. If he isn't a complete fag, he'll talk to *you* where he won't talk to *me.* Now *do it!*"

"I'll, I'll see what I can do," Mary murmured.

"Good. At least there's one dip around here making a contribution to the cause." He snatched his windbreaker in a fist and headed for the door. "Christ. Sometimes I think we ought to post all you State Department types to Uzbekistan and run foreign policy straight out of Langley—save us all a lot of trouble."

8 Bent over the table right there in the meeting room, Luis Alfredo worked up a script for the report: the when, where and who, the probable why. He thought up questions to ask Jay Streets, and Chris translated them into English, though with the care and precision of an accountant, which nearly drove Luis Alfredo insane:

Do you also feel sorry for the Ecuadoran people after fleecing their national oil company?

How do you expect Ecuadorans to survive on the little money that you give and all that you take?

Isn't the pittance that you gave these people a reflection of what DynoBank did to Petróleos?

Then they went into the newsroom to call Jay Streets. Since Luis Alfredo's English was still dodgy, he asked Chris to do the interview.

"Okay, I *think* I'm ready," Chris said, looking over the questions and running his tongue over his teeth behind his lips. It made Luis Alfredo shudder; it looked like a rat running around and around inside his mouth. "Now, what kind of tone should I adopt in this interview, Luis Alfredo? Should I make it a tough, aggressive tone? A more scholarly—"

"Chris! Please!" he said in English. "Only call and make the questions to the Mr. Streets. We have to finish the report *now!*"

"'*Ask* Mr. Streets *the* questions.'"

"Yes, but we call now-now, okay? I need finish this section of the report to carry to the montage people! The news it begin in only forty minutes and they need to do the montage and record my report and—"

But Chris was grinning and shaking his head. "Yes, yes, yes, Luis Alfredo. I understand that. But the interview is the key to the report. And the *opening tone* of an interview is all-important," Chris said as if he did interviews every day.

Luis Alfredo jumped up and jerked his desk phone near. "Please, call to him. Obtain him on the phone and read the questions. *This* will decide the tone," he said.

"O-kay," sang Chris. "You wanna blow this, it's *your* problem."

Luis Alfredo dialed the New York telephone number of DynoBank and handed the phone to Chris.

Chris smoothed down his mustache and crossed his thin legs, letting the free one swing in a lazy circle. In his right hand he held a pen over Luis Alfredo's pad. *Dumbass. You can't deal with New Yorkers like you're some momma's boy,* he thought. *Besides, a good translator has to take into account the culture of the people he's translating for.*

"Doynobyank," answered a woman in nasal Brooklynese.

"Good afternoon," Chris chirped. "I'd like to speak to a top executive in your organization, please: Jay Streets. You can tell him that—"

"Transferring."

New Yorkers don't give a shit about anybody, Chris reminded himself.

"Public Relations Depwotment." A woman's voice.

"Mr. Jay Stree–"

"Yes, the operator told me. Mr. Streets is out at this point in time. Can I take a message?"

"He's out," Chris repeated to Luis Alfredo in Spanish.

"*Mierda!* Okay, get the president of the bank—or someone in PR. Anybody who can give an official statement or some kind of—"

"I'll take care of it," Chris said with a motherly nod. "Listen, I'm calling for a TV station, and I've got some extremely important questions to ask your company about the behavior of its employee ethics, so you'd better to put me on with whoever tells P.R. what to say and how to—"

"P.R. spokespoison—yeah. Just a moment."

The hold music started. Chris swallowed his anger and gave Luis Alfredo a consoling thumbs-up.

"Yeah, this is Rochelle Smith," said another woman. "You had a question for us about our employees?"

"Hello, my name is Chris Carf and I'm calling from Quito for TeleMax8. Uh, that's a television station here. We have come across *startling revelations* regarding, you know, the behavior of the people you sent here to negotiate an Ecuadoran company's debt? The report is going to go on at noon, and we'd like a statement from you."

Silence. "Where'd you say you were callin' from, sir?"

"Quito."

"Quito. Zat like Key West?"

"Quito, *Ecuador.*" Chris scowled at Luis Alfredo. *These Americans—what the hell do they know about the rest of the world?*

"Oh, right. That—yes. That's down by Venezuela, right?"

"Colombia."

"Okay, Colombia," the woman said with patience that cut Chris to the quick. "And you have startlin' revelations about *what?*"

You take shit from New Yorkers, and they'll walk all over you, thought Chris. "Listen, honey. This station has *in its possession* original video footage of one of *your company's* top executives strolling around the city in the dead of night giving out thousands of dollars to the poor."

"And just what's the revelation? *Honey.*"

"The revelation is that he's an executive with your bank, and he was here re-negotiating the debt of Petróleos Ecuador, and people here aren't too happy about the conditions that the bank set. But it seems he has plenty of money to dribble out among beggars in the street."

An impatient sigh. "So what?"

"So just what do you think people here are going to think about DynoBank if its execs are robbing the country *by day* and giving a few bucks to street people *by night?*"

"I don't know: that we do business well but we also have a heart?"

"Oh. Oh, great. Is that your statement for the press? You can just take millions from this country and give back a few pennies in return?"

A pause. "Tell me something. You said this guy in the video— Wait. Who was it?"

"Nothing less than Jay Streets. He was down here—"

"Yeah, he was out of the office all last week." The woman needed a moment to digest this. "All right, you said he was doin' this at night. Was he doin' this, handin' out money, in some official capacity? Or was he on his own?"

"Uh, it's kind of hard to tell in the video." Chris ran his tongue over his teeth. "Probably on his own." Luis Alfredo snatched up the list of questions and shook in front of his face; Chris slapped it away.

"Sounds like it. Well, whaddaya want me to say? In the first place, he's no exec, any more 'n I am. And if somebody from our company wants to help out the poor, and it's his own money and he's on his own time? Hell, more power to him." A giggle. "Course, if he wants to give out cold, hard cash to the needy, I wish he'd look a little closer to his desk."

"Yeah, except for one little thing," Chris retorted. "It's going to look to a lot of people here like you treat this country like it's your own personal preserve. Like we'll rob your country blind by day, but we'll give you back—"

"A few bucks by night. Yeah, you told me."

Silence. Luis Alfredo was waving his arms, trying to get Chris's attention. He swiveled away.

"This goes on the air, honey, and you've got a bombshell exploding in your face."

"In Ecuador, right, *honey?* Which is near—was it Colombia or Venezuela?"

Chris fell into that one. "Colom…"

The woman started to laugh.

He snapped, "Listen, honey, within twenty-four hours, the whole world media is going to be clamoring about this footage!"

"The world media too, huh? Lord help us!"

"They're totally grotesque—this millionaire exec handing out a few bucks here and there to people who live in utter, desolate poverty!"

The woman barely managed to stop laughing. "Okay, okay. You want a statement, here's our statement. Ready?"

Chris swung round to the desk, clicked out his pen and nodded broadly at Luis Alfredo. "Shoot."

The woman spoke slowly: "Dynobank's position on this matter is, 'Kiss my ass.' Bye. *Honey.*"

The phone went dead, and Chris sat immobile, hunched over the paper, pen poised: *Rochelle Smith: "Dynobank's position on this matter is*

He ran his tongue over his teeth. Again. It made Luis Alfredo sick.

Then Chris continued: *that it is not responsible for rogue employees nor for the foreign government it gives credit to. DynoBank is profoundly sorry about the crisis of poverty in Ecuador, but it recognizes that every society is composed of winners and losers, and that it must work with the winners in order to make a profit/profits. However, this does not mean that DynoBank does not yearn for the day when upper-class Ecuadorans choose to end their totally grotesque treatment of the poor and take them in as stakeholders. Meanwhile, we suggest that poor Ecuadorans try to educate themselves, drink fewer alcoholic beverages, and prepare to take their place in society as top-flight citizens. Ecuador's problems are Ecuador's. DynoBank has nothing to do with them.*

"Okay, thank you so much!" said Chris into the phone. He hung up and added, *We wish the Ecuadoran people the very best of luck.*

Luis Alfredo was twisting his neck to read the pad; Chris was pleased with how wide his dark brown eyes grew. "What is 'stakeholders'?" he asked.

Chris nodded, re-reading the note. "Okay, Luis Alfredo, let's translate this text very carefully."

"But only I want to know 'stakeholders'!"

"Patience. Start at the beginning."

Luis Alfredo snatched the paper and ran off to find a cameraman to film his report. Rosco, the control-booth guy, had lived in Canada for two years. He could translate 'stakeholders.'

Chris watched him dash away. He ran his tongue over his teeth three times in succession, which was what he did when he made important decisions.

Time to change countries again, he thought. *Yup—time to change; these kinds of things, you can just feel 'em in the air. At least it's only the beginning of the month; I'll only miss three days' billing. But what the hell—I just made forty bucks! I've never given a damn about money, anyway—not like some people. Yup, time to take another jump south, down to Lima. Hey, I haven't paid my rent this month yet. That'll make up for the three days.*

Chris put on his jacket, wondering how he could get out of his rented room with all his stuff, and without Señora Carmencita, the owner, seeing him. His belongings fitted easily in his backpack; that was no problem. Wait. Today was Monday. She always went to the supermarket on Monday morning. With any luck, he could be at the bus station in an hour.

9 Paul Klippen checked one last time to be sure he had the signed document from President Tingo authorizing an American presence on the base in Manta. Then he looked into his blackmailing materials. He would have fifteen minutes in the back of a taxi to do the deed, and he had read that the trick to blackmail was to push the victim right up the scale till the pain was shrieking, and not let up till the fix was officially in.

First he counted the pages in the file, documents relating to Doctor Melero. The bitterest, signed by a dozen researchers that Paul had lined up, complained that ten years earlier, the doctor had given them no credit at all for their enormous contribution to his research projects—far more enormous than the doctor's own. And one of the projects had led to a lucrative medical patent. This document would lend credibility to the centerpiece of his blackmail presentation: the video-recorded testimony of a Princeton medical researcher who had his own axe to grind with Melero. Eighteen years earlier, the researcher, who had done research for his Ph.D. in the same laboratory as Melero, had taken ill with testicular cancer. Recovering nearly two years later, he discovered that Melero had swiped all his research and turned it into his own doctoral thesis, finished his degree, and gone on to greater things. Surely Melero, whose name was now short-listed for the Nobel Prize, would like to keep these documents secret, and would do Paul a little favor in exchange.

Yes, all twelve pages were there. Then he slipped a pen drive into his smartphone and watched a segment of the testimony of the Princeton researcher: "Hay-ell yes, my thesis was all set to present," the man griped in a Louisiana accent. "All that Antonio guy did was change a few dates, change mah name for his—and that was it." The sound and picture were excellent. It would do.

He checked to be sure the battery was topped up, then turned off the phone. Where blackmail is concerned, Paul reflected, image is everything. Even a bank robber must polish his gun before walking up to the teller.

"Hi, Paul. Saw your SMS. What did you want?" Mary Swanson was standing in the doorway, empty coffee cup still in hand.

"Ah, my favorite pair of cheekbones." Paul put the smartphone in his carry-on and snapped it shut. "I have to run up to the States—check in with the mother ship, couple of meetings. Need me to bring you anything?"

As Mary answered—a couple of books, a hairspray—Paul stepped past her and closed the door. Then, from the pocket of his suit jacket, he took out a device the size of a deck of cards and turned it on.

"Actually, Mary, it's something else. Please." He motioned to the small round meeting table and placed the device on it. "Have you seen this photo of Cindy?" he said, pointing to a framed photograph on the wall beside the table. Paul's British wife, blond hair flying from under her helmet, was rappelling down the side of a sheer cliff. Far away, hundreds of feet below, was the sea.

"God, that looks high," Mary said with a shiver. "Where was that?"

"In Norway a few years ago, before her accident."

Two years earlier, Cindy had slipped on ice getting out of her car, banging the small of her back on the car's doorframe, and hurt her spinal column. The spinal cord was bruised, though not broken, the doctors had said. Cindy had been in a wheelchair since.

"By the way, there's some good news there. Remember those expensive growth-hormone treatments I told you about some time ago?"

"Yeah—a thousand dollars a box. Ouch."

"Well, they turn out to have been worth it. Cindy doesn't want me to tell anyone, but…just a second here." Paul quickly wiped his eyes, though without any embarrassment. Mary was one of the few people in the embassy with whom he put aside the diplomatic mask; with the rest, he treated State Department life as a grand chess game, and if at times he needed to be false and calculating, he at least had the consolation that he was steadily winning the game. "She's moving her right leg now. And some feeling is coming back in the left."

"Really? That's fantastic!"

"I've never seen her so happy since A-day. That's what we call the accident. She's going like hell at her therapy. The doctors have to tell her to take it easy. It's a good thing she has her ceramics to keep her busy. She's received several orders for busts recently."

"That webpage is really working for her, huh? Uh, Paul, what's this?" Mary pointed to the black box.

"This little beauty distorts noise and foils any listening bug Harry and his buddies might have left behind." He picked it up and walked around the little office, swinging it around as if spraying the room with freshener. Then he looked at the little meter on it. "It also detects the little things. Okay, it would have picked up anything by now."

"Do you think Harry would…"

"I *know* Harry would. I sweep my office all the time. Last year—before you arrived on post—I found one."

"No! You're kidding!" Mary gasped.

"Not a bit. I took it to Harry and told him I'd stumbled across it on the back of my computer screen."

"What'd *he* say?"

"Nothing. Just laughed and said someone on his staff was doing—wait for it—'a training run.'"

"Oh my god."

"I told him I'd take it as a joke this time; next time I'll go straight to the undersecretary of state with it."

"I'll go with you."

Paul looked at his watch. "Mary, I've got to run for my flight. This is none of my business, really. I got you in here because I just want to make sure I have something straight." He hesitated, pushed his round glasses back a bit. "That message from Segundo Verdes you gave me last month? By the way, I sent a classified cable to Washington on it, not mentioning you by name."

"That's about all he wanted—fine. So?"

"Ah, look, Mary, unless I'm quite wrong, I get the feeling you've seen Verdes since then. Romantically. Correct?"

"Oh, Paul!" Mary sighed hotly, her hands disappearing up into her curly hair as she gripped her head. "I'm sorry. I knew I should have come to you, or put it on the record or—"

"Oh no—no no no, Mary. That would be a very, very thoroughly bad idea." He checked the gizmo's meter again. "Considering what Verdes is mixed up in, you're far better keeping it off the record. Look, if push comes to shove, blame it on me: say you came to me with it, and I advised you to keep it under your hat till after the banana crisis is over. I can take the heat on that."

"Oh, thanks, Paul. That's really a load off my—"

Paul waved this away. "No, I just wanted to satisfy my curiosity and know how things stand, just in case…"

"In case of what?"

Paul changed his mind about something. "Nothing. Harry's bit on him today was, well, astonishing."

"He's an astonishing man," Mary said softly, eyes down. "Decent, romantic, funny. I swear to God, Paul, I can't live without him."

"Mary, save that for your sister, would you?" Paul chuckled, embarrassed.

"Sorry—girl talk. Harry doesn't know the half of him. Hondo—that's what people call him—told me I'm not to be his spy in the embassy or anything like that."

"Good of him."

Mary fingered the gold chain at her throat. "How did you figure it out—Hondo and me?"

"Well, that 'He sounds like a remarkable guy!' in the meeting. That did kind of, shall we say, speak for itself."

"Oh my god. Do you think anybody else—"

"Among our company at the table? Please—you give them far too much credit."

"Oh, that's good! Hondo is really careful about seeing me, but you never know. And since the strike started, he hasn't, you know, come by." A smile. "Well, just once."

"That's smart. Best thing you can do. And now Harry has kindly offered you a chance to meet him officially. That will ease the—"

"I'm hoping he'll ask me to marry him."

Paul froze. "Married. It's gone that far?"

"Yeah. Oh God, Paul, I'm going crazy trying to figure out how I'm going to explain all this!"

Paul grinned, getting to his feet. "I've got to get moving for the airport. We'll talk about this when I get back. But Mary, if you've found the right guy, explanations are the least of your worries, believe me."

"I hope you're right," Mary said warily.

Paul pulled her close and pecked her on the cheek. "Congratulations. And don't worry about all this," he added, grinning broadly and waving a hand around. "After all, this is the U.S. State Department. We never met a truth we couldn't finesse."

10 The romance of Mary Swanson, junior U.S. Embassy Public Affairs Officer, and Segundo Verdes, union organizer, had begun six weeks earlier.

With only two days to go till the event, the organizer of the Miss Tumbacado Beauty Pageant called Mary and asked her to be a judge. One of the four judges had cancelled—or been cancelled, having been arrested for running three companies without business licenses, normally not a grave offense in Ecuador, but one was a cocaine factory and the other two whorehouses, and the local police had neither been informed nor paid off.

Mary was a natural choice for the pageant. By then she had already done three segments of *Hablemos* and was the most important face on Ecuadoran television. The pageant organizers even sent a car for her, as the trip to Tumbacado, a city of 130,000 people, meant a long drive down through the Andes to the Pacific-side lowlands, this on a busy, snaking highway that every few miles surprised the driver with basketball-sized rocks newly-fallen from the vertical cliffs above the road. Cayetano, her driver, was a careful, serious man of forty-two who had three grandchildren and reflexes like a cobra's, which now and then were all that saved them from a rock or a bus or an oncoming car passing another on a blind curve.

"Some people have a sixth sense that tells them when they can pass on curves," Cayetano explained, jerking a thumb back at the ten-seater bus that had nearly ended their lives. Mary's hands were still locked on her skull. "My brother, for example: he has it, so he drives a bus between Guayaquil and Cuenca—makes almost five hundred bucks a month if he works weekends, the lucky guy. Me, I don't. I can only drive cars as a chauffeur," he added sadly. Mary agreed this was a disadvantage in his trade.

The beauty contest was held in a high, gaunt cement gym that also served as cinema, sports arena, beer hall, dance hall, flea market, and cattle corral during floods. The basketball-hoop stands had been rolled to one side of the makeshift stage, where they held back a dozen orange-painted wooden benches piled up against the wall like a train wreck. A sheep-rug buyer had occupied the place that morning, and a Swiss NGO teaching baby hygiene that afternoon. Both sheep and babies had left their smells scrawled as gaudily as graffiti across the close air. By the end of the beauty contest's swimsuit pass, however, they had been drowned in the sour cloy of sweat emanating from the jam-packed cement risers.

Things were not going well.

Sandwiched with the other three judges between the stage in front of her and the throbbing crowd behind, Mary knew with rising dread that she should have stayed home. She had dressed for the heat, but already her blouse was plastered wet to her back, and sweat streamed in busy creeks through her hair. The roaring batteries of giant fans—four of them, each six feet high, to either side of the stage—might have been blowing into the ocean for all the effect they had, and she fanned herself with a program till her wrists ached.

The crowd had focused its love on two favorites of the eleven girls competing, and its hatred, utterly inexplicable, on one modestly handsome girl whose round face balanced on a thin neck like a daisy atop its stem. The pageant consisted of an evening-wear pass, a swimsuit pass, and a dance to the chug-a-chug *cumbya* of the five-piece band in the back left corner of the stage, the girls now dressed for the discoteque. Every time the daisy-headed girl had her turn at the front of the stage, two things happened: a well-defined point of cheering burst from the crowd, somewhere high up and directly behind Mary; and boos and catcalls erupted from everywhere else. The girl played directly to her little fan club, grinning and waving secretly. Mary had to give her credit: for a girl of nineteen or twenty, she ignored the boos with admirable calm.

"What's going on with that girl?" Mary asked the judge to her left, who was the ex-mayor of Guayaquil.

"Is normal," he murmured in his cut-and-paste English. "Is the daughter of Sepúlveda, president of the cement factory of Tumbacado. Is the second year that she is present in the concourse"—his word for *contest*.

Mary was glad when the judges retired behind the stage to a dingy dressing room for basketball referees, to cut the contestants from eleven to five. Sepúlveda's daughter didn't stand a chance—and just as well. With her out, she thought, maybe some civility might return to the proceedings.

To her amazement, the other judges didn't see it that way. The Sepúlveda girl had the best clothes by far, they said, and that had to be taken into consideration.

"That's true," said Mary. "But her family is rich. Her father probably paid three or four times what the other girls did for clothes. We can't let *that* determine our choice."

But apparently they could. Each judge had five votes to cast on a whiteboard list of all the candidates, and the Sepúlveda girl was solidly in. She was in, only one of the two audience favorites was in, plus three others—all prettier than Sépulveda but less than the favorite.

Well, maybe they're just playing to the crowd. At least the final decision will be a snap. Mary thought as they trooped back past the pile of orange benches and around the front of the stage, where the ex-mayor handed the results to the emcee.

He was a schmaltzy old bastard who waltzed around stage wearing an impeccable *guayabera*, an embroidered, billowing white-linen shirt worn outside the pants. He waved the results envelope around and bleated that this was "the most difficult pageant he had ever seen, with eleven flowers of God so perfect, so beautiful, so sublime in every respect that any one of them could be the Virgin Mary."

And he introduced the judging panel, calling it, "the most excellent panel of judges ever created in this country and all Latin America, on whom there hangs the destiny of these gorgeous, talented creatures, the very cream and excellence of Tumbacado. We express to them our most sincere gratitude and our most profound sympathy for the momentous judgment that they must render—no less dire than that of King Solomon, a judgment sure to be written into the history of our city and into that of the Ecuadoran nation."

Mary kept a straight face, but it wasn't easy. The audience roared its approval of the oratory.

Can't we get on with this? Mary wondered, waving to the audience, arm low so that the sweat stains of her armpit weren't too visible. In addition to her and the ex-mayor of Guayaquil, the other judges were a highway commissioner and a fluffy-haired skeleton who was a top fashion designer in Quito.

The judges sat down again, the emcee announced the five finalists, and each girl presented herself, still dressed in dance clothes, for a brief interview with the emcee.

Each girl answered the same three questions—*What would you do on the morning after being chosen Miss Ecuador? How would you spend a million dollars? Where would you most like to travel?*

The answers were all painfully sappy, the Sepúlveda girl's no worse than the others', but the rumbling boos aimed at her made the judging table vibrate. They scarcely fazed the girl, though, who heard only the cheers from her fan club. The lion-haired emcee merely waited for each storm to subside, nodding wisely. Out of the corner of her eye, Mary saw three jack-booted policemen storm up the risers, but when she turned around to look—some of the partisans had apparently started using their fists—the ex-mayor beside her quickly turned her back.

"You not like see, Miss Mary. Is very disagreeable. There is much silly people in here, you know."

So Mary kept her eyes nervously forward, hoping that she would get out before a riot or a human avalanche engulfed her.

At last the interviews ended, the band began to play, and the judges, Mary leading because she was the only woman, again walked behind the stage, past the gargantuan fans and orange benches, and into the dressing room. As she waited at the door for the men to open it for her, she glanced at the back of the stage. Each girl had a changing booth there, all open in order to benefit from the fans' draught. Each of the remaining five huddled with—apparently—her mother, listening to the crowd and talking excitedly. The Sepúlveda girl and her mother, unlike the others, had taken out rosaries and were fervently turning them over with their thumbs, eyes shut, whispering Hail Marys.

Well, God had better help you, sweetie, because I'm not going to, thought Mary. Yet God, it turned out, was indeed pulling for her. In the oven-like room, the judges worked quickly. Each now had only two votes, one for queen, one for princess.

The Sepúlveda girl won, and on the first round of voting: three to one. The audience favorite, Conchita Hernandez, was awarded princess.

"So! We have our queen and our princess," exclaimed the ex-mayor. "Excellent!"

"Let's go!" said the fashion designer, heading for the door. Mary grabbed his arm.

"Now just wait a minute. We can't go out there! That girl is as plain as can be!" she snapped in Spanish. "Conchita is ten times prettier."

The men smiled at her indulgently, as if at a senile grandmother bragging about her tickets to a Frank Sinatra concert. The roads commissioner turned a faucet on the filthy sink, but it spun uselessly under his thick fingers.

"Besides, the audience likes her best," Mary went on, "and we have to take *their* opinion into account too, you know."

"Ah, Mary, that would be a great error," pontificated the fashion designer softly. He had big, sensual eyes and hair so puffed and lacquered that it could have protected him from a falling meteor. His neck was as thin as a chicken's and more wrinkled. "To listen to the riffraff can only lead to disaster."

"And you think Berta Maria Sepúlveda is actually more beautiful?"

The designer thought. "She has an air."

"An *air?*"

"She wears her clothes with extraordinary grace, don't you think, Iñigo?" added the ex-mayor, who was sweeping a damp handkerchief over his bald head.

"Extraordinary grace—that is the word exactly, Santos," said the roads commissioner.

Mary wanted to argue, but couldn't. It was like a nightmare: the windowless room, the boiling heat, her soaked blouse clinging to her, the men's quick glances at her bosom—she might as well be topless. The designer was rippling his *guayabera* to make a little breeze by his skin.

"All right," Mary said hopelessly. "All right, let's go. But you guys had better protect me if the crowd gets violent!"

"With our lives," said the fashion designer gallantly, though he was so thin that a beefy ten-year-old could have wiped the floor with him.

"Is no pro'lem, is no pro'lem," said the ex-mayor kindly in English. "Happens the same every year. Is no pro'lem."

"No pro'lem," parotted the roads commissioner.

They returned—the audience sizzled with anticipation—climbed eight rickety steps up to the stage, and stood some steps behind the emcee. Uneasy, Mary eyed the twenty jack-booted policemen, all full-blooded Indians, who had lined up at the foot of the risers, sour and flat-faced like the Easter Island Statues. The judges' table had disappeared. The audience, roaring now, swung and bucked like an angry bull in a too-small pen. The emcee smiled and signaled for quiet.

"Oh my god, this is going to end *so* badly," Mary murmured to herself.

The three runners-up were named; each shuffled over to receive a kiss and a trophy from the last year's Miss Tumbacado, whose batter-thick makeup could not hide the bags under her eyes; her reign had been a trying one.

As the last of these was called Mary realized what was going on. For her eyes had wandered up to the central section, about ten rows up, to Berta Maria's fan club. There stood Señor Sepúlveda, as thin as his daughter and with a face just as round, dressed all in white except for a crimson tie and crimson kerchief in his pocket. He stood with his arms folded over his chest, stood like a farmer inspecting his lands, and much satisfied with his hard-won crop.

No wonder the other judges are so damn convinced! Because you convinced them, didn't you? This whole thing is rigged!

The emcee named the princess. Conchita, stunned, shuffled numbly over to receive her trophy. And Berta Maria shrieked with joy as the band exploded with song. The Miss Tumbacado kissed her, slipped the Miss banner over her shoulder and planted the tiara on her head, and with a wave to the crowd floated away off stage and disappeared. She had evidently learned a good deal about Tumbacado crowds. Ten rows up, Sepúlveda went red and pulled out the crimson kerchief and dabbed his eyes. Around him, everyone was hugging each other; his buddies pounded his shoulders and pumped his hand.

"Is wonderful, no?" the ex-mayor remarked, beating his hands together wildly.

"Oh, wonderful. Absolutely," said Mary.

The crowd knew perfectly well what had happened. People swarmed down the risers, chanting "Con-chi-ta, Con-chi-ta, Con-chi-ta!" Two or three of the policemen swung their nightsticks; most used them mainly to shove the crowd back from the stage, but soon they were backed against it, and the stage itself began to tremble. The band played more frantically, but the roar of the crowd—men and women, young and old—overwhelmed it: *"Con-chi-ta, Con-chi-ta, Con-chi-ta!"*

Conchita was delighted. She stepped up center-stage, right in front of Berta Maria, and did a nice curtsey. The crowd roared its approval: *Conchita Reina, Conchita Reina, Conchita Reina!* Conchita Queen.

Conchita stepped down between the policemen and was hoisted onto two shoulders, and the crowd, like slowly flowing lava, started to move towards the exit—which was a good thing because the policemen were losing the battle. And just before Conchita ducked her head under the door, she swiveled around to the stage stuck out her tongue at Berta Maria, who burst out crying.

Behind her, Mary heard a deep, clear voice in English: "Miss Swanson, may I suggest that you come with me?" Mary turned and looked down. A man—Ecuadoran—stood by the stage. He was standing on a step-ladder, which he had set in one of the empty dressing booths for the contestants. "It is perhaps dangerous to be with that multitude, and the streets of Tumbacado are bad illuminated. And..." he hesitated. "I need to give you a message for your embassy. It's, well, rather urgent," he added apologetically.

Mary looked back at the stage. The band was still going at it, but the judges and everyone were heading for the stairs. The fashion designer was wrinkling his nose at the "riffraff" who would never buy his creations. The police were fighting with some dozen young men at the base of the stage. Sepúlveda the cement king and his wife and two sons had mounted the stage and run over to Berta María, the father wiping his crimson kerchief all over her face and making a black gravy of her mascara.

"Okay—just a second," Mary told him.

She walked over to Berta Maria and, pulling her away from everyone else, threw her arms around her.

"You were fantastic!" Mary shouted in Spanish. "Fantastic!"

"But, but…" burbled Berta Maria, glancing at the crowd oozing out through the exit.

"Oh, don't worry about them," Mary said, throwing a hand that way. "You, you, you have an *air*, Berta. The air of a queen. They don't."

Berta Maria's face lit up. "Really? *Really?*"

"Absolutely! Everyone said it in the voting. Good luck!" she added, dashing away to the man and his urgent message.

And now that she thought of it, he had beautiful green eyes.

11

The irony, when it was all said and done, was that Luis Alfredo Valverde gave his report straight, avoiding any sarcasm or bombast. He identified Streets as the DynoBank spokeman, added a clip of him speaking for the bank, then showed Jorge Santillamen's video footage, adding only a bit of commentary before the final sequence in the building ruins. He finished with Rochelle Smith's message in full, and signed off.

But the item had led the news, and the anchorman's summation— "That will certainly make every Ecuadoran think of the dignity of his country"—added a tang of bitterness. Dignity, in the form of indignation, exploded throughout the country. DynoBank's Quito branch received dozens of angry calls, the Guayaquil branch a bomb threat that allowed everyone to take the next day off, and between the two branches some eight or nine account cancellations. The opposition political party requested that the government "save the honor of the nation" and issue a sharp rebuke to DynoBank. The Ecuadoran Commerce Ministry burped out a murky statement that they would send the bank a protest.

This reaction found many fraternal echoes throughout Latin America, for Rodolfo Ilahú was not remiss in notifying his brother news directors north and south of the equator, and making a pretty penny selling copies of Jorge Santillamén's footage, along with a facsimile of Rochelle Smith's quote. And the farther away the story got from Quito, the more starkly and disgracefully it played. Bilingual dictionaries were opened and consulted all over the continent. The line that got most play was "*upper-class Ecuadorans choose to…take the poor in as stakeholders…*" Diligent reporters discovered that "take in" could mean "to cheat." So they translated the phrase this way: "upper class Ecuadorans choose to…cheat the poor."

"Stakeholders," however, stimulated the greatest creativity. Rosco, the control-booth guy who had lived in Canada, had been as puzzled as Luís Alfredo, who with laudable prudence clove to a literal "people who hold fenceposts." Venezuelans called them "fencepost people," Uruguayans "fencepostists," and the leftist Bolivian media "people dumb as fenceposts." There was something for every taste.

But the result was the same. By the end of the day, DynoBank branch offices were being egged from Tierra del Fuego to Tijuana. *Porteños,* the touchy inhabitants of Buenos Aires, lumped DynoBank in with the rest of their lubricious financial community, and a small crowd treated the terrified employees to a *cacerolada,* whacking on frying pans on the sidewalk in front of the little branch office, where only four people worked. The branch manager, a born-again Christian from Dubuque, trusting that people were reasonable if you just reasoned with them, tried to calm the mob with his Iowan Spanish. This ended in a thorough beating of the poor man, but a cabbie filmed it and, like Rodolfo Ilahú, made a small fortune selling the footage to news programs. For everyone south of the Rio Grande, DynoBank was the new cigar-champing Gradgrind of the earth.

Which was when Jaymond Arthur Streets stepped into the breach.

He had starred at quarterback in high school, starred at defensive back at Notre Dame, and starred at wide receiver during his five seasons in the pro ranks, all in New York. He played in two All Star games. His fourth season was marred by a shoulder injury, and after his fifth season the doctors told him that he was risking chronic, inoperable back pain if he continued his career.

"So I listened to the doctors and listened to my common sense, and I said, 'Enough is enough,'" he told *Football Fanatics FanGuide.* "Yeah, I could go on another season or two if I had to—and if the team really needed me, like if a championship hung in the balance. Then sure, maybe I'd make this effort. But when the clinch comes down, you just gotta listen to your common sense. Same as doing drugs, smoking, anything—just don't do it. I've pretty much achieved my objectives. I never got a ring, but I've done two All Stars, made some really clutch catches, and generally contributed a positive role. And I've had a lot of fun too. I wish I could go back and do the whole five seasons again, but you can't, and that's that. Time to clean out my locker and move on. I've got offers, I won't be bored."

One of those offers was the brainchild of Roger Asquotti, DynoBank's director of public relations, who had been bullied by the marketing brass to raise the bank's profile among the just-out-of-college segment for Dynobank's Pensions and Long-Term Investments unit. Soon he presented Jay to the weekly meeting of department directors. As one they approved, taking their photos with him and nearly assigning him a windowed office bigger than Asquotti's—had Asquotti not intervened.

For his part, Jay knew how to play his role. He emphasized his future with the bank rather than his past in football, played down his stardom, and said that he would be working on his unfinished degree in Journalism/Public Relations. After his first year in the bank, Asquotti attended the little champagne party that Streets had in his office when he'd finished the last exam.

Jay was no loafer. He went at his new job as he had done with every sports challenge in the past: full tilt. Over several months, he mastered the vocabulary and concepts of high finance, and could speak intelligently about the vicissitudes of the markets. He spent two weeks each in the pits with the currency, stock, and commodities traders, and slowly arrived at a basic understanding of their work. He could take a speech or a press release or talking points for a public appearance and break it down into language that sounded as if it actually came from him rather than the marketing and ad staffs. He even righted his grammar, since Asquotti took a vindictive red pen to his e-mails.

And he was a perfect spokesman, simply beautiful: curly-blonde, blue-eyed, square-jawed, long and slender with muscular shoulders. His nose was a straight, narrow blade and his teeth two straight lines of brilliance. Photographers fairly drooled through their sessions with him. In one ad Jay peered intently at rows of numbers on his computer screen; in another he stretched, jacketless, tie dangling, to pluck a sheet from the printer, muscles rising like a choir on his perfect shoulder. He could sit on the edge of his desk, look into the camera, and with an athlete's direct enthusiasm talk about the wisdom of starting a pension plan early. "'Cause someday, dog, you're gonna be old like me," he added with a grin. Pension sales soared.

When the Quito crisis broke, responsibility tumbled down DynoBank's organigram like a boulder; its first victim was Rochelle Smith. Cited by Latin American reporters with truly hair-raising pronunciations of her first name—*roCHEL, raKEL, roCHAYay*—she did not survive even the first twenty-four hours. The moment she admitted having spoken to a reporter from Ecuador, her fate was sealed. Of course, she flatly denied the statement attributed to her, and everybody believed her—and knew that she was history.

Even Roger Asquotti believed her, and nodded so sympathetically that Rochelle thought she had a chance. Little did she know: a head had been ordered to roll by the company brass, and Asquotti had itched long and deeply to roll Rochelle's. He loathed her. He loathed her streetwise directness in meetings, her too-short hair, her high necklines, and her stiffly asexual demeanor. Rochelle spoke her mind and took shit from no man—an unwise course in life, as Asquotti meticulously, succulently, painstakingly explained to her towards the end of his dismissal chat.

Then came Jay Streets's turn, and Roger Asquotti awaited him with, if anything, even greater pleasure: not only was he chucking Miss Take-No-Shit out on her well-shaped can, he would have a chance to dump the young Adonis out of his artificial-turf crib and make him face real questions for once. Fifty-five, pot-bellied, his face a moonscape of crevices and craters, husband of a puddle of couch flesh and father of a gambling junkie, Roger Asquotti wished every possible ill on mankind and looked forward to the day when the earth showed a little chutzpah and eliminated the whole damn lot— young and old, rich and poor, Christian, Muslim and everything in between—with a year of 150-degree temperatures.

Jay entered Asquotti's office with neither a suit jacket nor a hint of trouble on his open brow, straight as the prow of a ship. It was the face that now adorned DynoBank ProYouth credit cards. His blond hair sparkled with highlights, his woven-leather belt lay level as water across his stomach. He wore a cobalt-blue shirt and pants of the lightest spring green. His silk tie had a potpourri of exploding colors, also on a background of the lightest spring green.

"Rog', wussup? Pretty funky about this Quito thing, huh?" He dropped into the chair in front of Asquotti's desk and propped an ankle on a knee.

Aren't you the cool one, thought Asquotti. *I'm your boss. What do you think this is? A schmooze on the goddamn* Tonight Show?

"It most assuredly is," he said with dim sadness. "I hear that our manager in Buenos Aires got beaten up by a crowd of protesters."

"Guy should've put on security, huh?" Jay asked.

That's it—the inevitability of justice, thought Asquotti. *Everyone gets what he deserves, right? Even poor Morrison down in B.A. Not because a mob grabbed him but because he hadn't taken precautions first.*

"That's for sure," Asquotti chuckled sadly. "A few more of our branches have gotten egged too. Jay, we're going to have to make a statement."

"Yeah, that was my first thought: get out there in front of the curve on this thing, and fast." He shrugged, amazed. "And you know what the grabber of all this is, Rog'? It wasn't even my idea—I mean, giving away the money down there."

Asquotti had no trouble believing this; Jay loved money. "You don't say?"

"Heck, no. All right, get this." Jay sat forward and propped his elbows on his knees, his taut back arched, hands up for gestures.

Are you going to have an adult conversation, thought Asquotti, *or order a zone defense from the bench?*

"All right. Last month, my grandmother died, and I got an inheritance—that is, me and my sister, to be exact. Few grand—nothing to write home about. Well, the old doll always liked me in a suit, so I went over to Frank Yang's on Ninth Avenue and did the whole wad: jacket, three or four good silk ties, extra pants. Ever been there?" he asked suddenly, startling Asquotti.

"Afraid not. I'm only the office boy."

Streets laughed a note. "Yeah, right. You don't do too bad for rags yourself, dog. I seen some of the secretaries lookin' your way."

And with that little ghetto writhe too, Asquotti thought. *How easily you hand round the compliments. Because you really believe them, don't you? Or at least you believe in their power, just like Jesus telling*

Lazarus to get up and walk. Well, why not? You've seen it work with all those fans reaching out to touch the hem of your kneepads.

"Anyways, then my sister Beth—she's this sociology prof at Saint Olaf College? That's about an hour south of the Twin Towns. Kind of lefty-radical and all, but she's a good egg. She told me to give her part of the cash to street people in Quito. 'Cause I told the family I'd be going down there, right? And at first I'm like, 'Yo, I'm *sure* I'm going to go walking around some town in South America handing out money.' But she turns the screws on me—that's Beth being Beth, you know. She said that even twenty bucks in the hand of some beggar was like a million dropping on you or me, and you can be sure she's right 'cause she knows all that stuff from A to Z. She's an expert."

"I'm not, and I'm damn glad."

Jay's forefinger jabbed at him. "Yo, truth in spades there, Rog'. Morbid stuff, y'ask me. Anyhow, cutting to the chase, at first I like no-wayed the whole deal. I mean, I'm talking like for *a whole week*. But she kept bringing up this pretty big favor that she did for me a year or so ago, and she kind of twisted my arm with it."

"Must've been a big favor."

"Yeah, big as in 'killer big.' I like needed an excuse, like I was in Minnesota on a certain weekend, right?"

"Don't we all?" Asquotti said with a bishop's nod.

"I mean, actually, we were on a time-out, me and this girl, but you know, just to have everything right? I asked Beth to call me up when the girl was in my apartment and do this one role-play bit with me."

This surprised Asquotti. "That was a big favor? That's the least I'd do for *my* brother."

"Yeah—exactly." A roll of the eyes. "Well, you gotta know Beth. She's kinda, y'know, religious. Doesn't like to lie."

Asquotti said nothing and enjoyed seeing Streets squirm. *Isn't that the life of an athlete? Stand by the rules till the going gets rough. Then cheat.* "In short, you owed her."

"Big-time, off the charts—in *her* book, anyways," Jay added. "So on the last night of, y'know, being in Quito? Thursday, must've been. I finally got up my nerve and went out and just got rid of the money as fast as I could. Took me a couple of hours to find enough people on the street. There was like *nobody* out there. And it was dark as hell. I just started stuffing handfuls of twenties into people's hands like they were tickets to a game. I didn't know if they were poor or not—'course none of them were wearing Armani, that's for sure. I had a whole fat wad of bills to get rid of, and I wasn't too choosy."

"And you were filled with a sense of purpose and goodness, right?" Asquotti asked.

Another roll of the eyes, though this time denoting disgust. "More like, I was scared shitless most of the time. Okay, a deal's a deal, but it'll be a cold day in Bermuda when I ever ask *her* for a favor again."

The 'favor,' Asquotti noted, had a nascent New Yorkishness in it: *fay-vuh. How protean athletes are,* he reflected. *You simply adapt to whatever—the new team, the new city, the new woman. You have no center except the game and the money, do you?* "And the man who came at you with the bottle, by the fire?" he asked, referring to the video tape.

"Oh, he was just this drunk guy. There were a few of them kind of sitting off to one side there, wrapped up in ponchos. You don't see them too much on the clip. This one guy with a bottle in his hand tried to jump me, but he was pretty wobbly, so I just got in under his beltline real quick and got him off his feet. Once you get a guy off his feet, you can pretty much do whatever you want with him."

Ah, technique! Technique that knoweth neither good nor evil. How we'll love even a serial killer if his technique is refined. "Sure you didn't hurt him?"

Streets replied stiffly: "I think that's pretty clear on the film, Roger: I just laid him down real fast."

"Game over—no harm, no foul."

Streets laughed. "Right."

"And you didn't see the camera? Twenty minutes or so, following you around?"

A bothered shrug. "I think I did at one point, to be honest. I spotted it down the street. But I heard two people talking, and I figured that for whatever reason, one was filming the other. I mean, heck, what was *I* doing that was worth filming?"

Asquotti assumed a judge's demeanor—the one he used to fire people—and was disappointed that Streets did not shift uncomfortably. It was not his obvious wealth that made him fearless, he reflected; it was his simple, stainless-steel belief in his coolness. "Well, Jay, let's talk about what we're going to *do*."

"Right. Trouble is, you know…" Jay shrugged and threw his big hands wide. His long fingers were probably the only part of his body that suffered some defect, for through his long sports career he had broken most of them at least once, and at his first interview with Asquotti he had explained where each odd lump on his knuckles had originated: a high school state semi-finals basketball game, a practice before the Sugar Bowl against Texas Tech. "Trouble is, Rog': what do we do? I mean, I don't really see the window of op here. A press release saying that there was a complete misunderstanding— that's about it. If people make a conscious decision not to believe that, what can *we* do?"

As if every decision were conscious, thought Asquotti, delaying a moment to savor the thrust of the knife. "I was thinking….a press conference. Statement, Q and A, thanks for coming. You could get up in front of everyone and set the record straight."

To Asquotti's disappointment, Streets weighed this evenly. "Yeah, a conf. That'd be one way of dealing with it. I suppose it'd ram home the point that it was all on my own time, not the bank's." A grin. "I haven't held a conf in a long time."

Which spoiled all of Asquotti's fun. "Well, I've already made the arrangements, and it's on for two o'clock today."

"Two o'clock?" Now Asquotti saw some resentment, and relished it. "You put me up for a press conference today at two?"

"That's right—that'll catch the evening news both here and in Latin America." Asquotti wanted to laugh with glee.

"But Rog', look at me. Do I look like I'm *dressed* for a press conf? I'd need a light-blue shirt, or maybe white. I'll have to think over a tie and what kind of—"

"What—it's a question of clothes for you?" Asquotti asked incredulously.

"Hell yes, and besides…" Streets puzzled, head down, and Asquotti glimpsed the athlete before the game. "Thing is, something like this, you gotta walk in, like, really *up* for it." He got up, still thinking, look-ing over his clothes. "I'll have to do something about this—and fast," he murmured.

As he was leaving, Asquotti called him back. "Jay, just one thing— a suggestion. Why don't you tell the media it was *your* money and *your* idea, not your sister's?" He raised his hands in defense. "Not because she's leftist, mind—free country, me. But it could be tricky legally—bringing her name into this, I mean—and your story'll play better."

"Yeah, make it seamless—I get it," said Jay slowly. Then he pointed his trigger finger at Asquotti and pulled it. "You rock, Rog'. I would never have thought of that."

He left, nearly colliding with Katya, the gorgeous blond Russian twenty-nothing who turned Asquotti's bowels to water. She brought in his coffee and cookies each morning. Now she curved into Jay, grabbing his tie. "Hey, Zhay, you got cool tie. Maybe some day you gonna teach me how is it tied? My dad he always wish I make his tie American-style, but I don' know how." All this with a grin as wide as Siberia.

"Love to, Kats. Gotta run, though. Total clutch moment, company rep hangin' in the balance, time for just one more play."

"Rain-rain check, so?" she said, wiggling his tie.

Jay bent down ten inches and pecked her on the forehead, which shocked her enough for him to slide the tie away. "Kats-babe, rain-rain check is the word, and don't you forget it." He dodged away down the hall. "Hey, that English is pickin' up, girl. Keep at it," he called.

Briefly, Katya glowed like the star on a Christmas tree, then turned and composed her face for the Gulag, and entered the office of the director of public relations, whom she refused to call Roger.

12

He had seen her sweat-soaked blouse and somehow bought her a white tee shirt with "Tumbacado, Ecuador" written across it in big red, yellow, and blue letters. The size was perfect. Holding her blouse, he had turned around while she put it on in the alley behind the gym where the contest had been held. "I couldn't invite you to dinner like *that*," he had explained as he folded her sweat-soaked blouse and slipped it into the plastic bag that had carried the tee shirt.

Then they had walked ten minutes across town to a restaurant off the city's main street. On the way, he apologized for the inconvenience of the beauty pageant; he had arranged everything—even, to her amazement, the arrest of the fourth judge—to get her there, for he wished to get a discreet message to the American Embassy. "I'm sorry, but it *was* necessary. I hope that dinner will make up about it."

It was midnight now in Tumbacado, and the hot equatorial air, thick as gelatin, was finally relenting. The bar-restaurant he had brought her to served a surprisingly delicious chicken dinner—surprising because the restaurant was cracked and crumbling, a cement cavern the shape of an open shoebox lying on its side. Everyone ate at small square tables set up on the sidewalk. Mary wondered what they did on rainy days because there was certainly no room for dining in the restaurant, which was occupied almost completely by the bar running across its width. Its entire cement interior, lit by bare lightbulbs, had been spray-painted in day-glow-green. High, frail stools leaned against one another along the bar, furry ceiling fans blew waves of tepid air, and a skyline of liqueurs, local *aguardientes* and beers populated the back counter. A stern, nunnish woman stood in the far corner frying chicken and *cuy*—hampster, the other house specialty, which came served splayed on the plate, tail included. Her skinny husband in a spotless white shirt served the tables, ducking again and again under the bar through a hole in its middle.

"In short, Mary, would you please say to them that I'm not a monster?" he finished. "We're not communists, we're not interested in revolution or taking over the government. Our goals are modest—completely local. A decent daily wage, some services and safety procediments to keep workers safe. Nothing else."

His name was Segundo Verdes but he had told her from the first to call him Hondo. He was well-made: square, neat, mid-thirties: skin done in copper, sharp cheekbones in Inca, and his eyes bright, live emeralds. He wore a khaki safari shirt: cuffed short sleeves and big pockets stuffed with papers and pens. His forearms were round as salmon and capable, his wiry hair lay parted on one side, oiled down to stay put.

Everything about him, in fact, was efficient, harnessed to the goal. Hondo ate more quickly than she, though he did nearly all the talking as he explained his union movement. At first Mary mistook this for hunger. But little by little she noticed his tenseness—the thrust of his body over the little table, legs wide, feet planted flat as if he were ready to spring up. He often glanced over her shoulder down the street, and Mary realized that he was very subtly on the alert.

"Are you on the lookout for your wife?" she said at last. "'Cause if you are, I don't mind playing my role. You know, a scream, a slap in the face, and *'You bastard! You told me you're divorced!'*"

Which had made Hondo humph once and raise his thin, fine eyebrows—which was how he laughed, Mary was learning.

"Oh, you know, the, the parade," he had said vaguely.

A stone's-throw away, their street crossed Avenida 27 de Mayo, Tumbacado's main avenue, where Conchita, the runner-up, floated past at intervals. She was being driven up and down atop a Jeep Cherokee, legs crossed over its windshield, a forest of flowers in her arms that allowed her only the smallest waves to the crowds along the street. Berta María seemed to have been forgotten.

"Well, you don't sound like any monster," Mary said now. "And I can tell people at the embassy for you, but—"

"Especially say to Mr. Klippen, the first political officer," Hondo said, surprising Mary. "Is that possible?"

"Yeah, he was one of the first people I made friends with at the embassy."

"And please avoid to Mr. Kruger, your CIA chief. Everything I hear about him shows that he is a thug."

"You know he's the CIA station chief?"

The eyebrows jumped in surprise. "Of course. This position is declared to the local government, and our Spanish friends have excellent sources there. Do you know him?"

"Well, everybody *sort of* knows Harry," Mary said awkwardly. She had had her one-night stand with him just a few weeks earlier and was already tired of his pestering.

A chant crackled again from down the street as Conchita sailed past: "*Conchita reina, Conchita reina, Conchita reina.*"

"But why don't you talk with him yourself? I mean, why do you need *me* to give your message? And why me, anyways?"

"On *Hablemos,* you seemed to me a person very reasonable. You listen. Your mind is open, not like the usual diplomat. These are unique qualities. I'm sure that your Mr. Klippen is a good man, but how can I trust to him? He could be CIA agent himself. And as I'm sure you know, Mary, the CIA has been historically very hard with union movements in Latin America." His mobile eyebrows traced a jagged lightning line of anger. "Very hard."

"Then maybe if you sat down with him, he'd—"

"I cannot be captured, Mary. The CIA would torture me for information and then kill me immediately. It is clear."

"Hondo, *please!* Harry Kruger wasn't born yesterday, but he wouldn't kill you. We don't do things like that anymore. That was the bad old days."

"Well..." Hondo finished the last of his chicken, his eyebrows knit together. They expressed him almost as well as he spoke, wondering, scolding, inquiring, bestowing praise. They asked where his mouth did not, and approved or disapproved when he was too polite to.

A boy—a barefoot street urchin whose hair grew over his head like carrot leaves—ran up and tugged at his sleeve. Mary thought he was begging, but Hondo leaned over and let the boy whisper in his ear. "Bueno, bueno," he muttered in evident satisfaction, eyebrows bobbing. He pulled out a pen and notepad from the pocket of his khaki shirt, and on his thigh scribbled a message. From the other shirt pocket he took out a bill—twenty dollars—and gave it to the boy, who gasped.

"Chooo-ta! Veinte dólares!"

"Take this paper to the same man—now," he commanded in Spanish.

"Sí, señor!" With evident joy in this fortune, the boy dashed away.

"That is one of my *chasquis*," Hondo said. "I have networks in nearly every city of Ecuador. Have you ever heard of them—the *chasquis*?"

"No."

"The *chasquis* were the message runners for the Incans. They ran—*ran*—day and night, all the distance of the Andes delivering messages, passing them from one runner to the next one. In a question of days, an Incan message could travel more than a thousand miles."

Mary thought a moment, trying to anticipate what Paul Klippen might ask her. "Hondo, who, or what is your model here? I mean, they're going to ask me that. Are you like Chavez? Castro?"

Hondo smiled, and Mary thought she saw some pity in it. "My model? Always Claudia Schiffer. She's a bit past the prime now, but that's all right."

Mary grinned. "Loyalty in a man—how rare."

"It's one of my prides." He took out a clean handkerchief—Mary wondered who ironed it—and wiped the perspiration from his forehead. "*Caramba,* the *ají* sauce here is potent."

"I tried it once when I first got here, and I had to swallow a gallon of water. Anyway, what can I tell them?"

Hondo's eyebrows again fell into the basement of their wide range. "Oh, what use have someone for a political model?" he grumbled. "My model? Perhaps Madre Teresa of Calcutta. Or Harriet Tubman of the Underground Railroad—a remarkable woman. I have read four biographies of her. Clara Barton also."

It took Mary a moment. "The founder of the Red Cross."

"Magnificent. Or Lenny Bruce: 'Communism is like one big phone company.' Absolutely true. Have you read his *How to Talk Dirty and Influence People*?"

"I guess not." *But you have,* Mary thought. *You've read Lenny Bruce and Harriet Tubman.*

"It should be required reading in every high school. Or Bill Gates, the billionaire—why not him for a political model? A union movement is as any another: it needs a burst of imagination, then planning, then a careful development."

"He's a capitalist, though."

"Who cares? Read John le Carré, or Dickens before him. Good people make that the world is good—it doesn't matter the *ism*. Where we don't have the good people, we need the good agreements. This is why that we will hold the strike: because landowners are as all Ecuadorans: loving parents but cruel businessmen. The world outside of the Ecuadoran's home is the enemy territory. To defeat the enemy, any means are fine. So they have no, ah"—he thought—"no *qualms* about killing us or starving us. We are not family, we do not count. Please say me to shut up, Mary. I'm starting to sound like Trotsky, *caramba!*"

Down the street, Conchita passed by again, waving left and right. A middle-aged man in a light-blue *guayabera* had got up on the Jeep with her, flashing a leering grin and waving broadly.

Hondo looked over that way; his eyebrows bounced once and froze. "Oh, that is bad: Jesús Calderas, the mayor. I hope poor Conchita doesn't fall into the hands of *him*. That would really be a horror. He keeps a house of prostitution of high class in three floors of an apartment building in central Guayaquil. A girl was thrown from a ninth floor there last year because she refused performing some act that a client demanded. The police called this suicide." He looked down into his Coke, eyebrows high. "My god."

At another table, a cell phone beeped. The man got up and handed it to Hondo and stood beside him. The cuff of the man's pants had a bulge, and Mary realized that he had a gun holster strapped to his ankle.

Of course, that's why Hondo had to eat so fast—to be ready to hustle if anyone comes gunning for him. Jesus! What a life he must have!

Hondo said "Yes?" and listened to the phone, elbow out, eyebrows high. Then he grunted, handed back the phone and barked to the man in Spanish, "Dammit! All right, tell him I'll take care of it on Thursday. For the rest, let's see...."

The bodyguard, a thick-limbed black man who looked as if he wrestled crocodiles for a living, nodded and muttered "Thursday" into the phone.

"For the rest, this. One: tell Safiro to move the meeting point to Telmo's. Two: tell Juan de Dios that El Macaco is fired. El Macaco must return whatever money he hasn't spent, and if it's less than half of what he stole, Juan-de must break his ribs. That damn Quevedo group is a bunch of thieves, and when I get there, I'm going to clean house."

The bodyguard nodded and sauntered away, repeating all this to whomever was on other end of the line.

Hondo looked at Mary and made a small shrug as an apology. "Jorge is one of my assistants. The Spanish government sent some people to train them last year. They've been very kind."

"Including the part about not giving away your position on a cell phone by speaking?"

The eyebrows bounced again. *"Choosa!* And much more. My god, what a black world those high-tech companies are making for us. They give us instant communication but take away our freedom of speech. They no longer are neutral. I often wonder how much longer any type of rebellious activity can survive. I have thought of writing a theme on this subject when I have a quiet period. 'Theme' is the correct word, yes?"

"Maybe 'essay' would be better. Your English is excellent."

"I learned a good deal from Morman missionaries in Guayaquil, and then filled it out living in Watts, in L.A.," Hondo said.

"You lived in America?" Mary exclaimed.

"Almost ten years." But Hondo was looking down, and his eyebrows had knitted themselves together. "It is terrible to speak in that way—to my men, isn't it? It makes me to feel cold inside—prickly. Do you feel that? Sometimes during *Hablemos*, when I saw you, I noticed that you are sometimes, ah, stiff when you said the U.S. Government's policy."

Mary shrugged. "Sometimes you just have to do your job."

"Yes, 'just doing your job.' A terrible phrase; it smells of conformity. I learned that from le Carré. Have you read his *Russia House*? Excellent."

"I guess not."

"Put it in your list. It's a horrible thing, you know, when you must to speak in the voice of another. But that is the voice which I use when I order that a man's ribs are broken: the voice of the movement. It can make you—"

"You must be an awfully lonely man!" Mary blurted.

Hondo looked at her, his face still.

Mary blushed. "I'm sorry—that just kind of jumped out."

Hondo's eyes turned away as Conchita passed again, and he stayed that way for some moments. "There is something in what you say, yes," he said quietly. "Of course, constantly I'm in the company of my team. And my men are good and dedicated, yes. I'm afraid, though, that they've rarely been more beyond than the fruit plantations. The most have never been to Quito. One of them cannot read—a common problem in Latin America."

"You're not married?"

"With one of our simple country girls? With a Conchita?" He nodded down the street, and his cocked eyebrows told Mary how ridiculous that would be.

"I see your point."

"I'm—there was an excellent phrase…Ah! I'm 'the odd man out.' It has been a normal condition of existence for me." His eyebrows jumped and returned to normal. "But it's like a limp, or perhaps a scar. With time, I am accustomed to it."

"I know what you mean," Mary said, feeling tears peeking out from the inside of her eyes. "I used to weigh fifty-seven pounds more than I do now."

Hondo's eyebrows jerked, and he squinted so deeply that his eyes were tiny green specks. "Yes. Yes, very good. There it is."

"There what is?"

"I saw you on television and I thought, 'What an unusual person. A woman with sense of the humor and a true sensitivity to people.' I had the feeling it came from pain. And then tonight with that girl who won the contest of beauty. You consoled her. You raised her from a very bad feeling and made her understand herself a queen. Only a person who understands pain could know how to do this so easily."

Jorge lumbered over again. "Hondo, blue warning from Cándido."

Hondo jumped up and gave Jorge a ten-dollar bill and nodded towards the bar, where the waiter was toting up bills. "I'm afraid, Mary, that I have to keep moving—it wouldn't do to spend the night giving explanations, or worse, to the national police."

Mary looked around. "I think we're pretty safe here."

"They just received word that I am in the area. My men monitor police communications—another of the Spaniards' lessons."

Mary was standing now too, and took a step backward in surprise.

"Though I would be grateful for that you didn't mention this fact. They may know it already, but I don't want that the Spaniards get in trouble."

"No, that's, no, that's fine," she sputtered.

"Wait here for a minute. One of my men will come and accompany you to your hotel. He will tell you that his name is Donaldo."

Mary could hardly contain the sudden, failing sense in her stomach. "Gosh, and we were having such a good conversation."

"Hondo. *Ya!*" Jorge hissed, coming back, and heading off down the street towards the parade.

Hondo started after him, then turned. "Can I visit you in Quito?" he asked.

"Yes, I'd love it!"

Four days later, after work, she was unlocking the front sidewalk gate of her house—she rented the upstairs apartment over a beauty salon—and he appeared out of the darkness with a bunch of roses and a lasagna dinner, complete with two bottles of ice-cold white wine in a refrigerator box. And he'd brought her a book: *The Russia House.*

"I thought that you would like not to cook tonight," he said with that curiously apologetic tone.

"Do you have another message for the embassy?"

"Today my messages are for you."

As were the ones that would begin to come every three or four days, unsigned postcards from tiny towns in the Pacific lowlands: a drawing of flowers, a funny stick figure of a man riding on the roof of a bus reading a book, or at most a few words that would mean nothing to anyone else: *Read Lenny Bruce?*

And with each one Mary fell more deeply down the well of love.

13 *It's a personal challenge,* Jay told himself.

In his junior year of high school basketball, he had complained to a reporter about a referee who had called him for traveling in the last minute of the game. The ball had then gone to the other team, who scored and won the game. And though Jay could see on the game film that his gripe was justified—the call was wrong, he hadn't taken too many steps—he could also see that Coach Dempsey was right when he said that in life complaints are useless, or even worse than useless:

"Once it's in print, Jayster, you're cooked. You say you're right? Big deal. So does your mother. And complaints about refs are the worst: you look like the biggest loser who ever came down the pike. There's no percentage in it—none. With bad luck there's just one thing to do: open wide, swallow, and say 'thank you' when you're finished."

Jay cared about his image almost more than his health. In the following ten years of sports, neither complaint nor criticism ever came from Jay's mouth again.

It was with this in mind that he prepared for his afternoon press conference.

He drove home and carefully chose an outfit, then returned to his office and rehearsed answers to likely questions and looked over the questions Asquotti sent—considerably more pointed, if not insulting, than his own, but that was just as well. Jay knew the value of a thorough rehearsal. He had never done a sit-down interview in his life without going over all the bases beforehand. His opening statement—*I know it's just a small part of my total assets, but for once I wanted to give real money to real people instead of giving money to NGOs*—was designed to block as many uncomfortable questions as possible.

Chewing on a number-two pencil, he wrote out and rehearsed answers to Roger's questions:

How do you reconcile giving peanuts to street beggars and working for a bank and making a terrific salary? Not to mention being a millionaire?

Do you think the bank ought to change the conditions of its loan to PetroEcuador, which are the hardest conditions that a bank has ever imposed on it?

Does your solidarity with the poor of Ecuador make you uncomfortable with your rich lifestyle?

After ninety minutes, he could weave through these like a slalom skier. But just for good measure, he called a friendly sports reporter, Clyde Sakowicz at the *Times*, and outlined the situation.

"See where I'm coming out here, Sax? If you could show up and toss out a football question or two, it'd remind everyone that I'm still Jay Streets and not just some victim of a YouTube scam."

"You got it, man. Anything you want me to ask?"

"Whatever. Like, how is my back, any chance I'll come back to football, or, maybe, like, who am I looking to for a ring next season?"

"Done."

"Great. Beer's on me, buddy."

"Hold ya to it."

Jay hung up. "Good ol' Clyde—cool." he muttered.

The only step left was to call Beth, his older sister—and Beth was not cool at all.

He sat for a long minute, hand poised over the phone. Beth would most likely never know the difference. This press conference was at best page 15A of *The New York Times*, which meant that it wouldn't get within a mile of the Twin Cities media. And even if Beth did find out, she wasn't likely to raise a public stink. Beth was a good trooper; at most he would get a puzzled phone call from her.

But no—that was how every dumbshit in the world ever got caught—thinking nothing would happen. A reporter might call up to check out the story, might hear the puzzled *"What?"*, and might put two and two together.

Cover your ass, Jay decided.

He called her at home, since she made a point of walking the mile home from college after her morning classes at Saint Olaf's and feeding her twin daughters by herself. To Beth, it was part of bonding with them; Jay called it "her nun bit," which was of a piece with her pioneer-woman dresses and eternal knitting. Her husband, a barrel-bodied Lutheran pastor, kidded him mercilessly about his good clothes.

Jay told her the situation. "And don't get me wrong, Betho, it's not like I minded doing you the favor down there, and okay, it did a lot of good, spread around some cash to people who didn't have any. But you see what I mean? It's kind of landed me in the old crap pile over here." Profanity with Beth was out.

"You mean I got you in *trouble? Jaymond!* I am so *sorry!* It never occurred to me even once that this could occur! Honest! This is awful!" She was the only person on earth that called him by his full first name.

"Well, I'm not exactly in trouble, Beth. It's just that—"

"But your company got in trouble! And you got called on the carpet by your boss!" Suffering and guilt were Beth's specialty. She could moan over stepping on an ant; Jay had seen her do it.

"Oh, don't worry about that. The bank needs me. Since I started as spokesman, we've totally cleaned up on the 25-to-35 end of the pension market." *Which of course means nothing to you,* Jay added silently.

"Well…all right, if you say so," Beth said. "I still feel bad, though. I'll never ask you to do that again, Jaymond, I promise!"

Jay moved in for the kill. "The thing is—the reason I'm calling—is this. In about ten minutes, I have to give a press conference to just about every media outlet in Latin America. And okay, it's like my boss, see, he suggested that—"

"Just a sec', Jaymond." She walked away from the phone, and Jay heard, "Chrissy, now that's not like you. You have to happy-face Katie. Remember? 'Happy faces, happy days-es'? And if you don't, there's no sweetie after lunch. Get it? No sweetie for my sweetie."

Not like you. Jay rolled his eyes. Beth knew every euphemism in the book.

"Yeah, okay, I'm back. Chrissy's really jerking my chain today, Jaymond. They take turns, you know."

"Got it organized, huh? Just what I'd expect from a Streets."

"Hah-hah. You'll get your turn, buddy-boy. And we'll see if you walk two miles home and back to give them their lunch."

"Probably not," Jay chuckled, wondering how she had got this way. *It was Mom. Mom ruins everything she touches—even Dad.*

He took a breath and made his pitch. "Look, it's like this, Betho. For this press conference I have to give? Since I have to tell this whole story, my boss—you know, the one whose carpet I got called on today? Well, I told him the whole story, straight up: it was *your* half of the inheritance that I gave out, and all your idea. But he kind of suggested that I tell the media it was *my* money and *my* idea."

Silence: an ocean of it. Jay pressed the phone against his thigh and groaned. "Why the fuck did I call her? Why?" he whispered.

"Oh!"

"He said it would sound better this way, and you know, since the bank is looking pretty bad because of all this, he's probably right."

Silence. The children squawked in the background.

"This way," said Beth.

"I mean, he's an old hand at the PR game—rocks big-time; I've learned a helluva lot from him."

"Uh-huh. Uh-huh." A huff. "Well, I don't know, Jaymond. I mean, that's a *lie!* Why can't you just tell them the truth? The truth is the greatest power of all."

Which was surely a line from one of Richard's sermons. "Yeah, Beth, but it just…*sounds* bad."

"No, it sounds perfectly fine. 'My sister asked me to give away her money, so I went out one night and did.'"

"Yeah, and then they ask me why I didn't give away *my* half, too, and I look bad."

"No, you won't. You'll look—"

"Beth, I have *twelve million dollars* in the bank. You're a college prof, and you don't. Don't you see a kind of, of…" He fought for a word. "Of disconnect?"

"Well, it's the truth. If you're ashamed of it, why didn't you give away—"

"Because this is *television,* Beth. They don't *know* you. They know *me. I'm* the one viewers can cog into. *I'm* the reason this is news at all."

"Anybody can identify with doing a favor for his or her sister," Beth said simply.

"Yeah, but the first question they're going to ask me is still why didn't I give away *my* half, too? Especially since I have so much more to give away. And heck, Beth, it's not like I'm a Scrooge or anything. I do give money to charities—lots of 'em here in the Apple. Even tomorrow night—I'm scheduled at a benefit. But you know how people are: they want a nice, seamless story."

"Yeah, like in their stupid soap operas and romance novels. If they read. Did you know that 53 percent of Americans over the age of thirty-two haven't read a book in the last five years?" Beth read nothing but sociology books on how the country was disintegrating.

"Beth, please: you've got to give me a break here. I have enough headaches. I'm news, literally, all over Latin America. Our bank branches are being egged down there."

"Oh, *our* branches? Like you have one, too?"

"Our—*DynoBank's*—branches," Jay moaned. "Really, Beth, in New York, you wouldn't believe the pressure day after day. New Yorkers are like killer sharks. The woman that the phony press statement got tagged on? Not her fault or anything? She was history before morning coffee break. "

"Wouldn't be because she was a woman, would it?" Beth sneered.

No—because she was a smartass. "Well, she didn't handle the whole thing too—"

"CHRISSY! I SAID NO!"

Jay jerked the phone away from his ear and sighed.

"Sorry, Jaymond. What were you saying about your co-worker?" Beth asked with brittle urbanity.

"Nothing. Just that she didn't handle it too smart when this guy called up asking for a statement. Beth, look, I'm in a jam here. I know this compromises your principles. I do. I comprehend that totally, and I *know* I'm asking a lot."

A huff. "Jeepers, Jaymond. And I mean that—*jeepers.*"

But this was a weakening, he realized. He'd found the key: get her to martyr herself. "Of all the things I could ask you to do, I *know* it's the worst."

"But couldn't you just explain that you took the time away from your official duties to do this for a friend or something? I mean, we *are* friends." But she was pleading now; Jay knew that all he had to do was keep pressing.

"No, no, no. Then I've got to start pumping out explanations, and then I've got *more* problems. Reporters are merciless, Beth. All it takes is one of them to call you up and check out my story, and I'm toast. Please: can't you bend your principles *just once?*"

Silence. Jay sat, holding his breath.

"Well…Well, yeah, okay, Jaymond. Tell 'em, tell 'em whatever you need to tell 'em. I'll back you up if anyone calls. You know the truth and I know it, and that's enough in God's sight far as I'm concerned."

Why wasn't it good enough ten goddamn minutes ago? "Great, Betho, thanks. That takes a load off."

"Well, I guess it's for a good cause. Hey, when you gonna come home? I was up in Saint Paul last week and Mom and Dad are getting pretty lonely for you. It's been—what?—three months?"

"Yeah, I'll have to fly out one of these weekends, take the folks out to a decent restaurant or something." Already he dreaded his mother's jabs about his sex life: *Aren't you ever going to stop playing around and marry one of these girls?* "I'll look into flights."

"Yeah, well, look hard. You owe them a visit. And get that *New Yawk* accent out of your voice too, would you? You're starting to sound like The Godfather or something. Hold on: Chrissy and Katie want to say good-bye."

Jay heard a distant squeal, squawked a good-bye and hung up. He swung around in his chair towards the window thirty floors over Manhattan and dropped his face into his hands. "Never again," he whispered. *"Never* a-fucking-gain. I'm not getting down on my knees for that bitch ever again." He jumped to his feet, snatched his suit jacket and threw it on. "Not for Beth and not for a pack of screaming reporters, either. I want to give away money to poor people? Shove it, folks: it's my money, the poor need it more than I do—end of story. I'm gonna steamroll those bastards."

And he did. Jay spoke with such simple conviction that by the time he had finished, all the Latin media were calling him the new American Robin Hood.

14 In the morning, not all that fresh after the night flight, Paul Klippen shaved in the airport restroom and hit the ground running in Washington. In six hours he was in seven meetings, none lasting more than fifteen minutes, at Commerce, at Agriculture, on the Hill and in the third ring of the Pentagon. Here he thanked a senator, there he dropped off a report, here he requested a bit of extra budget, there he complied with a Navy admiral's request for an authentic Amazonian bow and arrow—kindly supplied by Walt Boam. It was grueling, but at least everything was going to plan.

His next-to-last meeting, at State, was the definitive one: the official green light for Operation Flexible Channel—the department's ghastly name for Paul's operation—from the assistant secretary for Latin American affairs. Paul was glad that the meeting started on time, for in an hour he would have the crucial meeting to start the operation with three other people, including Harry Kruger and Doctor Antonio Melero, whom they would ask to arbitrate the banana negotiations and set a final per-diem price for labor. Paul was then scheduled to escort Melero to the airport for his flight to New York, which was when he planned to present the doctor with the evidence of his various misdeeds and make sure he arbitrated correctly.

Paul knew the assistant secretary to be a wheezing, long-winded Ohioan who stammered a lot, so when he was told that the meeting had been assigned to an aide, he considered it a lucky break. And indeed, Janet Ruddle was a brisk woman with not a moment to spare. Tall and long-hipped, open suit jacket fluttering behind her, clipboard swinging, she whisked him up two floors, down three halls and into a colorless, windowless meeting room that she locked behind her with a complicated security key.

"Sorry for the long walk. Every other secure room was *slotted*," Mrs. Ruddle explained over her shoulder with an apologetic flash of long teeth between orange-painted lips.

"Just as well. Slotted rooms tend to be draughty," Paul deadpanned.

Mrs. Ruddle, however, was concentrating on the little column of tiny lights, like a traffic light, beside the door. The lights blinked: red, then yellow, then (with three tiny beeps) green.

"A-a-a-all right, we're secure," she said at last. "We may talk freely."

"I'm glad to hear it."

"Nevertheless, no note-taking will be tolerated," she added, placing her clipboard on the meeting table and shifting its top page, a broad square almost as big as a vinyl-record jacket, to the side. Then she turned her chair at an angle to the desk and sat down, smoothing her behind as if wearing a skirt—she wore slacks—and crossed her legs.

Paul wondered yet again why people in the Washington office always assumed the role of mother-superior of the convent.

"All right." Mrs. Ruddle cleared her throat loudly. "Now, the assistant secretary *has* decided to move forward with Operational Phase Two of Operation Flexible Channel, Paul, though with certain *reservations,*" she announced. "With caveats. With *ground* rules."

Paul said a silent prayer for the day that *rules* might someday be unshackled from the *ground*.

"That's certainly good news, Mrs. Ruddle. Time is truly of the essence. The banana negotiations are continuing as we speak. Our contacts on the plantation-owners committee have already steered the talks towards the naming of an arbitrator. They're stalling till I give them the name."

"An excellent point, Paul, which the assistant secretary *has* intaken." She placed emphases in her sentences in the strangest places.

"Good. Haste is important."

"Hence the ground rules," Mrs. Ruddle said with the nurturing smile of the mother she surely was. "The main one outstands: he doesn't know that he *knows*."

"In case the bad guys catch the good guys doing something illegal," Paul said with a smile, and Mrs. Ruddle nodded solemnly.

"For example, yes. Such is the assistant secretary's *thinking*: any and all *activities* touching on influence-oriented areas are to be strictly arm's-lengthed. The figure of the secretary of state should also be ring-fenced—strictly need-to-know, e.g., a contingency spikes up in which there is a *necessity* to loop him in." She raised a finger. "Deniability is everything."

Paul agreed, and silently wondered if deniability wasn't turning into a virtue, like courage or charity.

"And budgetarily speaking, the assistant secretary is pleased that your triangulation of funds will be obviating." Paul puzzled over this while Mrs. Ruddle examined the checklist on her clipboard. Her orange fingernail stopped at another point. "This notwithstands the fact, Paul, that the assistant secretary had a concern on the Foreign Corrupt Practices Act. He hopes that Operation Flexible Channel will not repercuss there."

"Not in the least, Mrs. Ruddle. The FCPA forbids American citizens and corporations from paying foreign officials to do their bidding. We can't possibly be accused of bribing President Tingo. For one thing, not a cent of U.S. taxpayer money is involved. Second, I have arranged matters so that we avoid any connection with the exchange of money."

"There's no connection at all?"

"None. I took a lesson from the money-launderers on that one. If we manage to get a low wage for the workers set—and we will—the banana barons in Ecuador will thank us by making a twenty-million-dollar deposit in a corporate account in a Panamanian bank. They don't know why or for whom. Only the bank manager that I've arranged things with has an inkling. In several months, when President Atahualpa Tingo has finished his term in office, he will go to that bank and ask for a loan. The bank, after taking out a nice commission, will then issue Tingo a loan for twenty million dollars. That is, *on the books* it's a loan, though quietly paid back the same day from the corporate account, no interest accrued. The account will then be closed, with nobody the wiser."

A flash of teeth. "Oh, very nice, Paul. *Very* nice!" Mrs. Ruddle scribbled a long note.

"The bankers in Panama made some excellent suggestions as to the transaction details and type of account. They'll have earned their commission."

Mrs. Ruddle's head bobbed up from her checklist. "He also *empathizes deeply* about your desire to copy in Langley only in an ongoing Operational Phase Two."

"Which begins in just an hour, when I attend the Committee on Agricultural Arrangements with our special guest, Doctor Antonio Melero."

Paul hoped that Mrs. Ruddle would take the hint, but she swung back to her clipboard and ran down her checklist again.She was about fifty, he noted, square jowls just beginning to hang from her cheekbones, and had obviously spent a good deal of time on her coiffure that morning, curling under her overworked, dry hair along the temples and above her forehead. Her earrings were ugly little orange droplets veined in black.

"*Now*," she said momentously, "I believe *you* have something for *me*."

"I certainly do," Paul said, snapping open his briefcase's latches. From long practice, he had set the combination locks to their proper positions just before the meeting, and kept the briefcase well under the table where nobody else could read them. He took out the proclamation from President Tingo allowing American personnel on the base in Manta. "Tingo has the Spanish copy."

Mrs. Ruddle glanced over it. "Yes, that's exactly *what* the assistant secretary was *targeting*, that will do splendidly." Another smile flashed. "And I would *imagine* that this required tedious negotiation?" she added with sudden sympathy.

"Nothing that made me lose my beauty sleep."

"Oh, that's good," Mrs. Ruddle said, swinging back to her clipboard, fingernail clicking against each point of her list. "Oh, and I am authorized to *convey* that the assistant secretary is extremely *interested* in the turnout of this operation. He emphasized that this will definitely feed back *into* your career, Paul."

"He's truly too kind."

Another look at the list, of which Mrs. Ruddle had reached the final item: QUESTIONS. A purse of the orange lips. "Are there any questions?"

"No, I think everything is pretty clear." For Paul knew that the less he asked, the better. "Or rather, just one." He pointed to the big square of paper that Mrs. Ruddle had laid to one side. It was printed in a hodgepodge of orange and brown blotches: autumn leaves. "May I ask what that is?"

"Oh that!" she said with a pleased smile, a natural one, which Paul realized was a much more frequent visitor to her face than the stern flatness he'd seen. Even her jowls disappeared. She picked up the paper and handed it to Paul. It was actually a thin cardboard, of the type used to make file folders. "This is a printout for a member of our group who works just down the hall—to kill two trips with one."

"Your group?"

"The State Department Scrapbooking Crop. I'm president."

"Scrapbooking *Crop*," Paul said blankly.

"State *used to* give us five hundred dollars a year—took it out of the curtain budget or something," she said sadly. "But that got cut last year. Everything is getting cut now, you know. So now we have to have dues. You know, just for a bus once a year for everyone to get together with other crops in the area and—"

"Other crops? What—do you *grow* your scrapbooks?"

Mrs. Ruddle laughed. Her brilliant teeth gleamed amidst the great parentheses of orange. "A 'crop' is a scrapbooking *club*. We all get together now and then and bring our best projects. Oh, and have a good lunch too."

"And talk about scrapbooks."

Paul handed back the cardboard, and Mrs. Ruddle snatched up her clipboard, jumped to her feet, and turned the key in the lock; the lights disappeared on the little traffic light. Then she was dashing down the hall, Paul trotting after her, closing his briefcase latches, raincoat over his arm.

"Scrapbooking's all the rage, see," Mrs. Ruddle said over her shoulder. "I printed this out for one of our members who doesn't have this particular template. Me, I don't print; I have a cutting machine. But Ruth, our fellow member? She still does scissors. It's more natural, that's true. But I prefer the cutter. You can go a lot faster."

"To cut out the leaves, I take it, and place in a, a scrapbook?"

"Right. It's extremely relaxing on the weekend. And totally creative. You can do anything you want, and if you don't like it—bingo—you just start all over." Suddenly she was no bureaucrat, but a common hobbyist. "You don't do scrapbooking, Paul? It's really therapeutic."

"I had an NBA basketball scrapbook when I was a kid," Paul said, still amazed.

Mrs. Ruddle swung around, so fast Paul would have run into her had he not dodged to the side and trotted two steps beyond. "You don't still have it by any chance, do you, Paul?" she blurted breathlessly. "I could use a thing or two from it if you've hung on to it."

"I'm afraid not. Lost the passion, I guess," Paul said with a pang of guilt.

Mrs. Ruddle was now stock-still with tension. "Oh. Oh, now you shouldn't have done that. Really, you shouldn't've. Are you sure you did?"

"I can't imagine that I've kept it."

Mrs. Ruddle looked down and scratched the back of her head; Paul realized this denoted irritation. "That's really too bad. Scrapbooking is the greatest pastime."

"But what do you make scrapbooks *about?*" Paul inquired, frankly curious. "It's a little late in life for worshipping NBA heroes—or Barbie dolls." He wondered if he'd gone too far. "Isn't it?" he added meekly.

Mrs. Ruddle was still looking down. "Family issues, mainly—vacations, about my girls, about my husband Perry. People make them about anything. I have a friend in Arlington—we're going to induct her into the crop next week? She just made one re: her divorce."

"Her divorce?" Paul blurted.

Mrs. Ruddle looked away, and Paul could see her eyes were misty. "Yes, it was wonderful therapy for her, and *so* touching—I just about cried. The last page is the divorce document itself—just sitting there behind a transparent." She dashed away again. "And she's really exploiting her non-man downtime these days. She can drive three hundred miles on a weekend, just trolling scrapbooking shops. She has a materials collection that I would *kill* for now. You mean you haven't heard of scrapbooking? I thought everyone had."

"As a hobby?" Paul called from behind. "Never."

Mrs. Ruddle stopped at an intersection of hallways near the elevators. "Well, I can see you've been posted abroad *far* too long, Paul. We really must see about apping you out for a *domestic* posting."

"So it seems," Paul said, though to be "apped out" sounded painful.

Now Mrs. Ruddle leaned in to him. "Paul, can I ask you to do me a favor? It's no big thing, but...."

"After this enlightening conversation, Mrs. Ruddle, you may count on it."

"Oh, please, call me Janet." She lowered her voice just a bit. "Look, could you possibly verify through your old things and see if you have that scrapbook? Just in case? I mean, I'm doing this scrapbook on my husband, and I'd like to use some old things, like basketball cards and the like. Really gives the final presentation some depth."

"Certainly," Paul lied. "I'll do my best."

"You could just pouch it to me."

Paul would have to rush all the way across Washington to the hotel for the crucial meeting, but he watched Mrs. Janet Ruddle, president of the State Department Scrapbooking Crop, stride all the way down the hall and disappear into an office—Ruth's, he supposed—before pushing the elevator button.

"So: such are the bricks in the wall of the American empire," he said in wonder. "Maybe I *have* been away too long."

15 El Ejido Park was now a plastic-tent city, and from across the street, Mary could smell kindling wood and damp wool; the usual afternoon rain had been particularly hard that day, scourging the streets so ferociously that traffic came to a standstill for about five minutes. It was only her second visit, and already the smell was like a welcome to her.

You've got a D cup to show him. If he isn't a complete fag, he'll talk to you where he won't talk to me.

"Well, you wanted me to get close to him, didn't you, Harry?" she murmured. "So I'm getting close."

Some nights he came to her home; on others, his men told him that the plainclothed policemen were watching the park closely. It was too dangerous.

She crossed Avenida de la Patria—Fatherland Avenue—beside which union workers were bathing in the public fountain, their wives pounding out sudsy laundry. Toddlers splashed about ecstatically, squealing like baby pigs. Quito city hall had raised hell about it all, but after the first week of the strike, lice had started to appear, and nobody wanted an epidemic. So traffic had been rerouted away from the fountain—much to the ire of the driving public. Now and then drivers lowered their windows and shouted insults at the workers.

El Ejido was so thick with trees that they formed a low ceiling over the entire area and cut out much of the public lighting. She had to feel her way along, and twice caught her neck on tent strings tied to tree branches and even monuments. So she walked crouched, and twice banged her feet on the rocks and busted cement chunks that held down the plastic.

The tents were everywhere now, even more numerous than before, crackling in chorus at the slightest breeze. Ponchos and blankets covered the few plastic floors; many beds were nothing but slabs of cardboard. Women swept them with pine boughs cut from the trees. Even here, cleanliness was a pride.

She navigated mainly by the small gas flames before which the thick, maternal women crouched at dented pots, cooking soups and muttering about the cold. These were people from the Pacific lowlands; to them cold began when a tee shirt or blouse no longer sufficed for warmth. Few had anything heavier than a shawl to put around their shoulders. The older children seemed to have stayed home with grandparents, and only the small children who still needed to nurse had come. They bounced everywhere, dodging through the laundry hung out on tent strings or slapping their hands in the mud puddles that formed everywhere. Inside the tents she saw heavy plastic jugs of water—filled patiently at the drinking fountain in the middle of the park. She saw two women crouched naked under shawls scrubbing themselves. To take a regular bath in the fountain, before the riot police sitting on their water cannon, was unthinkable.

"Miss, are you Mary?" blurted a voice. "From the television?"

Mary turned, trying to adjust her eyes to the dim light of the gas-flame on the ground between two women. Their tents were hung side by side. They sat together on some cinder bricks in front of their gas-bottle flame warming their hands. One seemed shaped like a potato, till her bulk moved under the poncho and Mary realized that she was nursing a child.

"Yes, I'm Mary from the television." She put a finger to her lips. "But don't tell anyone."

The women made the same gesture, shaking their heads vigorously.

"Oh, we liked your program very much!" whispered the nursing mother. "It was very funny."

Now the other jumped up. "Mary, can you tell us what the wage of work will be?"

The nursing woman: "We heard that the wage will be thirty dollars a day! *Thirty dollars!*"

"But we don't believe that," said the other with superiority. "People who say this are stupid. We think that the real price will be fourteen or fifteen dollars."

The nursing woman: "We hope for fifteen."

The standing woman: "Tell us, please, Mary! What have you

heard? Do you know anything?"

The nursing woman: "We are going to make good houses and have kitchens with real stoves."

The standing woman: "We also want to start businesses. I want to make a business that sells fruit and vegetables."

The nursing woman: "I want to have a shop that makes bread. I know how to make delicious bread—the most delicious bread in Ecuador!"

The standing woman: "And if our husbands make more money in the fields, we can make shops and have more money for our families."

The nursing woman: "Some day we will buy a computer—half and half. They say that you can run two businesses with one computer."

The standing woman: "They say it is necessary to maintain a proper business. Our businesses will be completely legal and important!"

"And our children will go to the university!"

The nursing woman: "We are going to be rich and fly to Miami in a plane!"

They giggled hilariously at the idea.

The standing woman: "Tell us, please, Mary. What salary is the most likely? It is sure that you have heard something!"

"Well, not much," Mary said vaguely; she didn't know what to say. "Are you sisters?"

"Yes, I am María Angelica, and she is María Inocencia." The standing woman gave her a kiss on each cheek. The nursing woman apologized for not standing up.

The standing woman: "Do you know, Mary? Have you heard anything?"

"Only a few rumors," Mary said, stalling. They were absurdly young—not yet twenty. She might have been talking to pioneer women in the 19th century. What did they know but a few geographical vagaries, basic math, the care of children, the orchard, and home? Five or six times in her few months in Ecuador she had had conversations with persons who had never heard of the United States. "Maybe fifteen," she said finally, not wanting to disappoint them.

The women thought this over, and Mary could almost see them mulling numbers and possibilities. "Yes, even still—fifteen," murmured the nursing one.

"Fifteen is okay," said the other stoutly. "In ten days that is 150 dollars and in twenty days 300."

"Three hundred dollars! We could buy a car! How fantastic, no?"

Mary said good-bye and plunged away towards the illuminated middle of the park, where a megaphoned voice was warbling. *I have dresses that cost 300 dollars.*

After a minute, she arrived at the drinking fountain, where people were standing in line to fill jugs from the single stream. Now and then, a particularly whiny child was lifted up to drink quickly. Here she waited. Alerted of her arrival by his invisible men, who watched the park constantly, Hondo would find her.

"And now they tell me I have to agree to an arbitrator," a sad voice buzzed through a megaphone. "I am *forced* to agree, my children! My arm was twisted! I argued and argued till I had lost my voice! How I resisted! Hour after hour, alone—totally alone, with everyone in the room against me. I kept saying, 'No, no, no, brothers, we can work this out, if we sweat together and reason with good faith! We are Ecuadorans—brothers! We can overcome the obstacles together if we just keep our heads and remember the great, the magnificent, the wonderful future that we will give to our people and the Ecuadoran nation, a future in which every family has a fine house and his own orchard with which to feed his children."

A pause for heavy panting that commemorated his struggles.

"But at the end, children, I had to give in. Here you are, day after day, heroic, calm, saintly, perfect, stoic as Inca gods, sitting in your tents under the rain. You are gods, you are gods of the Ecuadoran nation, and a hundred generations will venerate the Ecuadoran workers who sat here calmly, waiting for the word from their leaders, in whom they had deposited their ultimate and sacred trust."

It was Sixto Carrasco, the union lawyer. He stood on a platform— a wooden pallet—that sat on some oil drums, under the dim glow of a streetlamp, speaking into a megaphone mike. He had a massive beach-ball torso; wild gray hair and ragged beard made a bluish halo around his face. He flung out a fist, and his whole belly bounced and swung as if filled with water.

"Trust that has been betrayed at every moment!" he boomed. "Trust that I am doing my best to keep, my children, but the fascist forces of the American agents are twisting my arm, forcing my body to the

ground and my head into the water bucket!"

Carrasco wore only a light-blue shirt open far down his chest, the sleeves rolled up for that common-man touch. He was actually a very vain, sensual man, Mary could see. His huge belly indicated big appetites.

"Yes, my children, an arbitrator—God help us! I am beginning to wonder if this entire negotiation isn't a fraud. We are being cheated by the capitalists, lied to by the government, taken in by the growers, even by some of your own leaders! *Yes, your own leaders—the fingers of the gringos are everywhere!* I don't trust—I cannot trust—anyone in the negotiating room with me. No—maybe Napoleon, our brave *compañero* from the Machala region. He is at least an honest man."

"And what about the guy who risked his neck—for years—to organize all this?" Mary murmured. "Doesn't he get any credit?"

He didn't. Carrasco went on, swatting at his face with a handkerchief and then swinging it around as if batting away the demons.

"No, otherwise I am alone—*alone, my children!* And the only thing that keeps me standing upright, despite my fear and fatigue, discouraged and downhearted, is your presence out here, you who for the first time in the history of the Ecuadoran Republic are standing up to the forces of fascism and foul play. It is *you* who hold me upright!"

Another crackling thunder from the crowd, which thought and moved as one. Around her, Mary saw lost, dark Indian eyes wide with awe.

"But I will keep fighting and fighting and fighting for you, my children. Fighting and fighting and fighting so that one day we will emerge with victory and worth and respect and dignity and honor. We will rise up together and look God in the eye, my children. We will be better than God and our souls will shine to the ends of the universe! Yes, my children, your Sixto will keep fighting for you until his last breath, until the blood no longer runs in his veins, until his tongue can no longer form the words 'Long live Ecuador, our fatherland!'"

The crowd roared like an animal pricked with a pin. The crowd rushed forward and to the side, sweeping Mary along like a pebble on the beach.

"Sixto presidente! Sixto presidente! Sixto presidente!"

Then a solid, calm hand gripped her shoulder and steadied her.

"Isn't he pathetic?" Hondo said into her ear, his voice clear as a morning lark amidst the throbbing chant.

"Pathetic, but damn clever," Mary said, squeezing his hand a moment. "Makes himself out as the only one really interested in the workers."

Hondo chuckled. "When *he* was the one that it was necessary to drag into the strike. He opposed it till the last minute, till the workers at Costa actually started to stay home."

"An optimist, you mean."

"You ought to spend a morning in negotiations with him. He dominates everything. With any progress, he pulls its back. Only to agree to an arbitrator, we all argued with him for two solid days. He would not…Mary, stay here. Enrique will stay with you. It's my turn to speak." He slid away into the shadows.

Into his place stepped a boyish man who hardly reached Mary's shoulder, with gold outlining his teeth. He said good evening, hardly looking at her, his eyes on the men around her. On the previous night, a drunk man had tried to grope her, and Enrique had done something to his hand so that the man jerked away howling.

Carrasco was getting down—rigidly, awkwardly, as if he had bad knees. Mary figured that he probably did, having all that weight to support.

A man got on the little platform and raised the bullhorn. "Just two announcements from the strike committee. The first is that tomorrow night a band will come and we will have a dance." Whoops of joy, many from drunks near the platform. "However, it is important to remember at all times that there are many of us here and our living conditions are of the most primitive nature. We urge you to drink with responsibility and moderation, remembering the good of all."

A grudging rumble with scatterings of male laughter.

"The second announcement is the following: The local police, who are here to make our stay safe and beneficial"—hoots of derision—"have reported an increasing number of misdeeds and disgraces on the part of some *compañeros*. We have promised to take the appropriate measures. As a result, from this moment forward, if anyone creates a public problem, he will come before the Council of Elders for judgment. He will be sentenced to pay a fine and his house will be burnt."

The men hushed up. Apparently, the Council of Elders had real power.

"Thank you. Now Segundo Verdes, El Profesor, will inform us of the latest news of the negotiations, in which all of us have a very important interest."

A pleasant sizzle, like rain on the roof, wafted up from the crowd. As happened the other night, many people—now women as well—were calling "Hola, Profesor!" Suddenly the meeting was more a family gathering. Mary saw a few women pushing past to get closer to the front.

His shirt pockets still stuffed with papers, Hondo walked up the steps, took the microphone—a man at his feet held the megaphone—and nodded to the crowd. People began to shout to him—that had happened before too, and Mary hoped that Carrasco was hearing it.

"Profesor! I saw you in El Guabo!" shouted a man.

"You spoke to us in Balao!"

"Profesor! I am from El Aromo!"

"El Aromo?" said Hondo. "The beer in El Aromo was warm. Terrible!"

People laughed, and someone shouted, "They are all fools in El Aromo, Profesor. I invite you to Puerto San Jorge. The beer is fresh, and the girls also!"

Hondo laughed and motioned for people to quiet down. They did.

"Thank you, *compañeros,* thank you. *Compañeros,* it is a great pleasure to announce that our strike is spreading. I would like to thank our new friends from the Trujillo and Cuatro Vientos Plantations in the province of El Oro. They have also declared themselves on strike, awaiting the outcome of our negotiations."

A whoop went up. Hondo waited. Mary could see him opening and closing his hands, which he did when impatient. Finally:

"Today we have reached written agreement with the plantation owners to name an arbitrator who will hear the case of each side in the negotiations and suggest a price. The written agreement also stipulates that each side must abide by the new wage, whatever it is. We are looking at different names. We hope to find a man or woman who can look at both sides of the problem and set a fair wage."

The workers rumbled drily. But Hondo did not rise to their ire.

"Remember, *compañeros,* a fair wage does not mean that we deserve all the price of the fruit. Not at all. The plantation owners deserve their part too." A moan. "Yes, *compañeros,* yes, I insist: they deserve their part. Let's never forget that. We are not here to settle old scores but to build new futures. The owners are men and women just as we are."

He let that sink in.

"But they are men and women, *compañeros,* who have education. They read the books of the greatest men in history. They understand works of art. Look around you—each of you here, look around. What do you see? Men like yourself who can't read, men who live exactly as their grandfathers, and the grandfathers of their grandfathers. In the centuries since our liberation from Spanish rule, we haven't progressed one millimeter—not one millimeter! Why? Because we lack education. We lack culture."

Silence.

"You've all felt it these last few days, haven't you? You look at these well-dressed people here in the capital of our nation. For the first time you've seen the beautiful skyscrapers, the well-made parks with statues, like this one, El Ejido. Maybe you've seen the curtains hanging inside their pleasant houses. *They* have culture."

Silence. Ashamed, feet-shuffling silence. Mary would not have thought it possible.

"That is the true objective of our struggle—not money, not bread and roofing, but life as thinking, feeling men and women. To lift our children out of the mud that we inhabit today. To see our children go to school, go to university, go to work in a nice office, to have time and money to read a good book or listen to good music. That is why we are striking: not for more money, but for our dignity, for a higher form of culture—for ourselves and for our children. Remember that."

And that was all. Before anyone knew it, Verdes was stepping down from the pallet. The applause was not loud, but widespread.

"God bless you, *Profesor!*" called a woman's voice.

"You are a credit to the Ecuadoran nation, *Profesor!*"

"Thank you, *Profesor!* May you walk with God!"

That was amazing, she thought. *Who would have thought that you could talk to these people as adults?*

The crowd dispersed to the tents. Enrique led her to Hondo's.

"Well, how did it sound?" Hondo asked her as he walked in. "I hope people aren't going to get impatient. The plantation owners have made an excellent suggestion for an arbitrator: Doctor Antonio Melero, an important doctor."

"Yeah, his name was in the paper the other day. He's been mentioned for a Nobel Prize."

"It is the best option. Even Carrasco, who rejected all other names put to him, has said that he is a last resort. But he is still pushing for the ex-mayor of Havana. My god! As if the growers would agree to a flunky of Fidel Castro!"

A boy of about 12 was tugging at Hondo's sleeve, and he leaned down. After a while, Mary had the feeling that the boy wasn't delivering a simple message.

"Mary, I must to leave. Or…why don't you come? I think that you will see something, ah, unusual. Say hello to Leopoldo. He and his brother Alvaro are my *chasquis* here in Quito."

16

Hondo's assistants had the pick-up truck waiting for them on the street.

They entered colonial Quito, where the unbroken line of buildings along the sidewalks turned every street into a corridor. The sparse traffic crept along in single file on streets designed for horses and mules. Mary watched a sheep-wool vendor lumbering along under a netted burden as big as a small car. He walked past the wide door of an art gallery where a man in a good suit stood swirling a drink. The art dealer wrinkled his nose at the sheep smell and walked back into his shop.

Hondo also saw it. "We really are two peoples in one country, aren't we?" he said with a sigh. "Slowly airplanes and the Internet are bringing us together, but it will still take decades—if we don't kill one another first."

Sitting on Hondo's lap, the boy, Leopoldo, indicated a scarred doorway along the street between a paint-supplies store and a bakery. The driver stopped, and Hondo's two assistants hopped out of the back and slipped into its dim maw. Each cocked a gun—two phlegmatic rasps in the dark—for it had occurred to them that Leopoldo might have been sent by an enemy. The nightly fog was descending, and already the air had a cold bite.

But after a moment, a long whistle threaded out the doorway, and Hondo, the boy, and Mary followed.

They walked through a narrow canyon formed by three-story-high brick walls just five feet apart, turned left and continued on through four consecutive courtyards divided by blocks of apartments. Tiers of wet laundry strung between the second and third floors dripped on them, and girls were getting in their last games of hopscotch before bedtime. At the last courtyard, they walked up three dark flights of troublesome, uneven stairs—a sort of tunnel upward through the building—where cooking smells battled a carking fug of urine, and babies wept tiredly behind thin metal doors. Reaching the top of the stairs, they emerged onto a shaky, iron balcony that led around the corner of the building and up another half-dozen stairs. The fresh air was wonderful, and they all stopped a moment, panting because of the altitude; the men were from the Pacific lowlands and even less accustomed than Mary. Then Leopoldo pulled Hondo under a low doorway into the crawl space under the roof.

It was ancient, as the building must have been. The peak at its center was just high enough for Mary to stand up straight—and only then if she stood right beside one of the supporting columns of decrepit brick. From each of these columns, a ribbing of thick wooden branches and poles like rake handles, all dry and gray-white with age, slope-sagged down to the shin-high wall around the perimeter of the building. They were all that held up the ranks of baked-clay shingles of the roof. Gingerly, she pushed one with a finger; it rose easily.

This long room—perhaps four car-lengths—was home to many families, about seven on each side, each household a nest consisting of a castoff single mattress under a kerosene lantern hung from the branch-beams. Home was a circle of light; boundaries were defined by lines of milk cartons, plastic containers of every size, rusting frames of bedsprings turned on their sides, or piles of ancient newspapers. Each one's pantry lay along the walls where the lower ends of the beams rested: bananas, tomatoes, plastic cylinders of rice, pasteurized milk, a jar filled with salt, and for the richer ones camping-gas stoves and various plastic containers, like washtubs and buckets. The single toilet was in a corner walled off by shower curtains; two old men and a ten-year-old girl were lined up to use it; each held a child's beach pail with water for cleaning. It was amazingly quiet; even the children ran their toy cars over the mattresses humming a tiny *br-r-r-r* for the engines.

The bodyguards had stayed at the doorway. Walking slightly crouched, Hondo and Mary picked their way down the shoulder-wide center aisle after Leopoldo. Mary stepped carefully around a Michael Jackson tee shirt hung out to dry on the nubs of a tree branch. She smiled at a young woman sitting on her mattress, pulling her naked toddler away from the kerosene lantern hanging above them.

Imagine a fire in this place. Nobody would get out.

One thought struck her: the air was surprisingly cool and fresh. But now as she worked her way along, she discovered why: a constant flush of cool air slipped in under the tiles on the windy side, and here and there one was broken: a plastic bucket stood open beneath the hole to catch the rain. As she passed one, a woman dipped her little beach bucket in and went to join the line for the bathroom.

"Do you see those holes?" Hondo said over his shoulder. "That is how these people pay the rent. They keep water from leaking in below. Probably, many years ago, this started with one or two families living here."

Near the end of the room, they stopped at a narrow home-space, not four feet across, delimited by a pile of telephone books on one side and a wheel-less wheelbarrow tipped on its side, on the other. There was no mattress, no lantern, just a slab of cardboard and a pair of tee shirts and two shoeshine kits near the low wall. A small boy lay on a woolen poncho, which was folded over him, like a sandwich.

Leopoldo shoved it off. "Alvaro, wake up. The Professor is here," he called, gently pulling his brother around by the ankles into the light of the neighbor's lantern, exposing a small, round, Indian head, a nose so creamy and smooth it might have been poured from an ice-cream machine, the eyes closed in perfect half-circles. "Alvi," he snapped, almost as if angry. "Hey, Alvi, are you okay now? Wake up!"

Mary had to snap her hand over her mouth. *Oh no. Oh my god. That perfect little boy.*

"He's not crying anymore. Today he was really sick," said Leopoldo. "Today was the worst day."

Hondo knelt down to the boy. "When did he get hurt?"

"When he was bringing you a letter at night from the Estación Sur. A man tried to catch him. He was a fag, but Alvi was too fast. He grabbed Alvi, but Alvi slashed him with his knife and cut his neck or his ear. But the man kicked him in the back from behind."

Mary started. *His neck or his ear?* "Is he sure? Did he see the blood?"

"Yes, *señora*. The man took out his handkerchief and put it against the cut." Leopoldo demonstrated, bending his head over his shoulder as if holding a telephone. "Alvi saw it when he ran away. The fag was too slow for him," he added proudly. He reached over Alvaro, pulled up his shirt tail, and slid a switchblade out of his pocket. He touched a button, and the long blade leapt out like an alarmed snake—so fast Mary flinched.

Mary felt a shaft of numbness slide the length of her body. *Guy tried to take me down with a switchblade—a six-incher*, Harry Kruger had said.

"When was this?" Mary asked, but she already knew the answer: *It was Thursday night. Ruined a good shirt too.*

"Last Thursday," Hondo replied. He was bent low, pressing his ear to the boy's chest. "Strange—he didn't seem particularly hurt when I saw him. Just out of breath. I gave him a bottle of Coke and had him sit down for a minute before going back. He seemed okay when he left."

"Alvi was okay for the first few days, but then he got worse," Leopoldo added, touching the other button on the knife; the blade slid back in. "He looks better now. He's not crying."

"He's not crying because he's dead," Hondo said quietly in Spanish. "I'm sorry, Leo. Alvaro is dead."

Leopoldo frowned skeptically and kicked his brother's ankle. "Alvi! Get up! El Profesor wants to talk to you." He shrugged. "I think he's just sleeping."

Hondo turned the body to see the boy's back; on the right side, below the ribs, was a grayish-blue depressed area, like a coffee-cup saucer.

"See? It looks better today," said Leopoldo. "The mark used to be really big."

"The hit arrived directly to the kidney," he told Mary in English. "If he had taken it easy for a few days, he would have been fine probably.

But he never slowed down, and the wound must have reopened again and again." He wiped a tear away.

Leopoldo started tugging at Alvaro's arm, calling more gently now. Hondo put a hand on his shoulder. "Does anybody take care of you here?"

"Raimunda gives us dinner at night," he said, pointing towards the wheelbarrow, "only until our mother comes back."

Hondo looked over the edge of the wheelbarrow. "Can you continue to look after Leo?" he asked.

Mary moved a couple of steps to see her. Raimunda was a tiny Indian woman in her thirties with a round face and owlish cheeks. She was stirring some beans and rice around a tin pot.

"Yes, the little one, he was very sick." She crossed herself. She spoke in an Indian's sing-song Spanish. "I gave him some soup, but normally he is in the street all day with his brother. They give me some of their money from shining shoes. But I make them dinner," she added in defense. "And I wash their clothes. Her mother was my friend. She lived there when the little one was born and was nursing."

Hondo: "How long since you saw her?"

"Choo-sa!" Raimunda waved a hand as if throwing something over her shoulder.

Hondo nodded. "Well, thank you, Raimunda. You are very good. Leopoldo is my friend, and I'm going to find a school for him. I know one in Ibarra. It should take me a couple of weeks."

"Leopoldo is a good boy." A stern frown. "He should go to school."

Hondo began to gather Alvaro up in his arms. "Leo, listen to me. I'll come back for you in a few days. Okay?"

"Are you taking Alvi to a doctor?"

"He's not going to come back, Leo. He's dead."

For a long moment, Leopoldo looked at him, then frowned skeptically. Hondo turned to go. Mary was about to follow, but Leopoldo turned around, grabbed a shoeshine kit, and thrust it into Mary's hand. One of the flaps fell open, and she saw a young, smiling Jennifer Aniston in her *Friends* role as Rachel.

"I don't need a—"

"Wait." Leopoldo put down the flap on one side of the kit and dropped the knife in. "Just in case he wakes up. He shouldn't be without a knife."

Crouching, tears streaming down her face, Mary followed Hondo out. Women on either side of the aisle crossed themselves and muttered a little prayer. Everyone knew.

The man with the cut on his neck is going to pay for murdering that beautiful little boy, she swore.

17

"Just get 'er done, guys. Just get 'er done and report bay-ack when it is,'" Harry Kruger imitated in a Southern whine, deep into his second double whiskey and, Paul had found, his warm little streak of self-pity. His rubbery lips hung down at the corners, like a sad clown's. He had already opened his tie, but now he yanked the knot down to his chest, which was just as well, Paul thought. A suit sat on Harry poorly, but he had had to wear one to the high-level steering-committee meeting. "Like we're just supposed to snap our fingers or something. What the hell gets into them, Klippers?"

"That is the question, Harry," said Paul, sitting stool-by-stool with him at a bar at Washington National Airport.

"They want omelets but no busted eggshells," Harry went on. "'Y'all just get the workers back into their huts, and make sure they don't get any kind o' substantial raise. Just get 'er done.' Translation? 'Get it done, but without actually doing it.'"

"Not yes, not no—just the opposite," Paul responded—largely to give Harry the impression that he was listening. He was at that moment spinning a new plan, and spinning fast, since it had to be put into action before their plane left for Quito in ninety minutes.

The meeting with Doctor Antonio Melero had not gone well.

Paul had invited the doctor to the Committee on Agricultural Arrangements (CAGAR) meeting to ask him formally to arbitrate the banana negotiations—formally, because Paul had long before discussed the matter with him and gotten his approval. The doctor was something of a legend in Ecuador. Though he had lived in New York City for many years, he often wrote op-ed columns in El Comercio, wisely berating presidents, the military, and the ruling class in general, and would easily have had the eminence to arbitrate the talks.

To Paul's shock, however, the doctor came out of his hotel room dragging a red suitcase as large as a washing machine. When Paul told him they would come back to his room to pick up his suitcase before catching a cab to the airport, he only shrugged. Once in the CAGAR meeting room on the hotel's twelfth floor, the doctor shook hands warmly with everyone, announced that he had to fly to the Middle East to receive "a generous grant from the royal family of Dubai for experimental thyroid treatment," and added, "Your project sounds interesting and necessary, Mr. Klippen, and I do everything what is in my power to help my dear little Ecuador. But my flight leaves in less than two hours. I'm sorry." And out he had walked before the rippling astonishment of everyone there, unable to hear—as Paul very much did—the crashing and tinkling of his plan all around him.

The five-person committee, by turns, had then trashed Paul, Harry, their respective departments, and government in general— "You can't even *believe* in it anymore, not on any kind of *ongoing* basis, that is," Senator Strelling had bellowed—and stormed out of the room.

Paul now took another sip of his beer. "By the way, Harry, who was that revolting tub of lard, anyway? Mr. Just-get-it-done. Norman Broad-something? Not from your side of the sandbox too, was he?"

"Broadmaker: the guy who *invented* CAGAR," said Harry. "His lobby represents banana and pineapple interests in the U.S." He placed a peanut still in its shell on the bar, and Paul braced himself.

"Harry—*gently*, this time, huh?" he murmured, knowing that it was useless. What was good manners to Paul was censored power to Harry. Which was one of many reasons he had cut Harry out of his plan.

Harry's fist crashed down on the peanut, and the barman, an Ethiopian with almond-shaped face and a grizzled tuft of black hair, glanced over with alarm. "Y'know, I talked about this in CAGAR six months ago. I said, 'I'm telling you, this guy Verdes knows how to operate. This guy is trouble.' And did they give me funding? Did they give me a team to take him out? Did they my ass!"

The barman dropped a little bag of peanuts on the bar in front of Harry, who picked it up and tore it open.

"Well, it's not the end of the game, Harry," Paul said. "Still a few rays of light out there. I might have a Plan B that—"

Harry's hand rose and pointed out to the concourse. "Look. There's Strelling, that bastard. He was *supposed* to put some Senate muscle into CAGAR, but all he's done since day one is rant and bitch and... Wait a minute. Hell's he doing on the *international* concourse?"

Harry squinted. "Of course: Nassau. Some sun and fun after doing a little work, the asshole...Hey, take a gander!"

Paul sighed. Shuffling forward in the line, boarding pass in hand, the senator, a handsome man in his mid-forties, was talking on a cell phone.

"So? Harry, I have a new plan, and we're going to have to work together, and we'd best do it damn—"

"Know who he's talking to? Take a look at the redhead sweetcakes at the back of the line."

About thirty passengers behind him in line was a college-aged woman in jeans and a pink leotard, who had thick, red hair reaching below her shoulder blades. And now that Harry pointed it out, it was true: when one spoke, the other was listening.

"You're an observant man, Harry," Paul said admiringly. "I would never have picked out two—"

"Let's have some fun!"

Harry snatched out one of his own cell phones, found the senator's number, and on another phone tapped out a text message. He showed it to Paul:

WALK AWAY: SHE'S WORKING FOR MOSCOW.

"Harry—*please*. Let's not grudge a man his—"

"Fuck you, Mr. Clean-cut Christian Republican Bullshitter." Harry hit the Send button.

A moment later, as the senator closed his phone, it buzzed. He opened it and read the screen. His face went white. He closed the phone very slowly and stood immobile, rubbing a thumb over his cheek, so long that the passenger behind him had to give him a nudge. He turned and walked back along the line of passengers. Near the woman, he muttered something and kept walking, faster and faster straight out through security, waving his passport as if it were a wand that made all resistance disappear.

Harry chuckled and lifted his glass. "Have a nice day, asshole."

"Harry, I sometimes get the impression that you were one of those children who used to pull the legs off spiders."

"Frogs. And speaking of frogs…" Harry swung around on the stool and faced Paul squarely, lips a barbed sneer. "What the fuck were you doing at a CAGAR meeting, anyway? Barging your way in with this Melero guy like you're going to save the world? I didn't kick your ass in there—we had enough of that from CAGAR—but what the fuck were you doing? Why did Melero talk to *you*? You putting together an op without my okay?"

Paul took a sip of beer, slow enough to irritate Harry.

"The thing is, Harry, it's *my* op—has been from the beginning. Or at least it was till Doctor Melero blew it sky-high."

Harry stared hard at him. "*What* op? *I* haven't been informed."

"Of course not. I kept you out."

Harry's big lips parted, making a large race-track oval. Paul sipped more beer, put down his glass, and said, "Harry, do me a favor? Just drink your whiskey and listen till I finish, okay?"

And Harry did—even half-drunk he was a careful listener. In three minutes, Paul told him about the triangle of favors: the fixing of the workers' salary, followed by the plantations owners' contribution of twenty million dollars to an account in Panama, followed by President Tingo's permission to Americans to return to the airbase in Manta.

"American consumers happy, the Pentagon satisfied—all at no cost to our taxpayers," Paul finished. He raised his beer in a mock salute. "At State, they call it 'Operation Flexible Channel'—not *my* invention, I can assure you."

Harry Kruger's lips had slowly closed, and he had tilted away from Paul, as if looking at him through bifocals. Now he took a long gulp of whiskey—the first in some minutes. "Not bad," he said. "Not fucking bad at all. It *could* work. And the doctor was going to put the right price?"

"After a quiet word with me on the way to the airport, yes."

Harry's eyes narrowed. "What kind of quiet word with you?"

Paul tapped his briefcase, which sat on the bar beside him. "A nasty word about some past, ah, indiscretions in the university."

"Sex?" Harry asked, with obvious hope in his voice.

"Plagiarism—mainly. One word about it, and his Nobel Prize would be dead as road kill."

A smile muscled its way into Harry's broad face. "How come you don't work for us, Klippers?"

"Harry, you honor me."

"Of course, you kept me in the dark just to take all the credit for yourself."

Paul smiled. "Well, the State Department *is* a jungle, Harry, and a girl does need more than good legs to get ahead these days."

"Fuck you. I'm almost glad it didn't work out."

Paul looked at him a moment, blinked, and tapped an angry finger on the bar. "Well, *don't* be glad, Agent Kruger. No—gladness will not do at all right now. Because, you see, we—you, me, and nobody else—we have got to *get this thing done.* This is the most important thing we'll ever do in government service, Harry. We need a new plan and we need it *right now."*

"You'd have to clear it through CAGAR if it's—"

Paul continued with his crushing intensity. "Forget CAGAR; forget them. We have no time for them, and the stakes here are huge. If these workers pull off anything like success with this strike, *all Latin America* is going to see it and try the same thing. There'll be fruit-plantation strikes all the way up to the Mexican border. In a word, chaos. It's literally the end of the world as we know it."

"Calm the fuck down, Klippers. Don't get—"

"No, Harry, I repeat: *it is the end of the world as we know it.* Why do you think we've leaned so hard on socialist Cuba all these years? Because there's nothing worse than a successful example to follow. Just look at the Arab Spring movement: one guy burns himself alive in southern Tunisia, and now half the regimes in the Arab world are fighting for their lives. All we need is for one workers' fire to get started in Latin America, and the times of dirt-cheap fruit on our breakfast tables are over. *Over."*

"All right, all right. Jesus, Klippers. All right, you said you had a Plan B? I'm listening."

"Yes, but I'm going to need your help. I'm going to need cooperation—the kind that runs deep."

Harry shrugged his big shoulders. "Fine. Whatever. Let's hear it."

Paul drank his beer and adjusted his round glasses, though this did little to calm his intensity. His voice went low, but it fairly buzzed in Harry's ears. "First. Thumbs up or thumbs down now, Harry. No half-truths, no bullshit—we don't have time. Do you have any pull, any mole, any contact at all inside the banana workers negotiating committee?"

No answer.

"What I mean is this: the owners committee is no problem. Both of us have contacts and they'll do what we tell them. But if I pull another candidate for arbitrator out of my hat, can you get the workers to okay him?"

Harry looked sideways at Paul, then sideways at the Ethiopian barman, who was sulkily pulling a beer for a college kid who had sat down at the bar and popped open his laptop.

"Say I do."

"Harry, don't play coy with me! Do you have someone on the workers committee, or do you not? Someone who will okay a new candidate?"

"Klippers, do you have any idea what you're asking? You're asking about assets—deep assets—and your security clearance isn't all that—"

"Yes or no, Harry! I don't need a name. But it's this or we spin the bottle with an arbitrator that *they* choose. Do you want that?"

Quietly: "Okay, keep your pants on." A sigh. "There are three people on that negotiating committee, right? I have one."

Paul sighed—with relief. "I *knew* you were a resourceful man, Agent Kruger."

Harry grunted. "Only because *I* saw this thing coming and *I* got out in front of the curve six months ago." He drank. "So who's your arbitrator?"

Paul opened his briefcase and took out his smartphone. "There's a little story I've been watching unfold in Ecuador over the past thirty-six hours. About Jay Streets, the football player?"

"Oh yeah," said Harry hazily. "Flacks for DynoBank now. And he got into some trouble, right?"

Paul made a final tap on the screen to turn up the volume. "I'll give you the full run-down later. Right now I want you to watch the report of the press conference he had. He aced it, apparently, and the media in Ecuador is singing his praises today. *He's* our man."

18 Roger Asquotti stood at his office window, dabbing at the soft pouches under his eyes that a very expensive cream recommended by a specialist had failed to diminish after six months of use. The only change was that the pouches had a dirty-yellow tinge; even Katya, the beautiful office assistant, had looked at them curiously.

He stood cursing the street far below, cursed all the people on it and all of their relatives back to the Neanderthals, which was the last time in history that nobody made any excuses for snatching his neighbor's food and women. What a scam it all was, just like the pouch cream. A scam and a disappointment. *What a relief, what a step up for humanity when The Bomb finally goes off on Wall Street. Thank god computers and robots are slowly replacing humans. The sooner we end this travesty, the better.* Turning, he glanced with affection at the chessboard on his computer screen. *Look at that. It waits for you. Waits without impatience or judgment.*

"Hey, Rog', wussup?"

Asquotti turned and saw Jay Streets standing in his blond perfection, suit jacket hanging on one long finger over his shoulder, his coral-and-white pinstriped shirt fairly glowing, blue tie matching perfectly the blue pants, which themselves matched the blue eyes. *Is there a single defect between your hair and your toenails?* he thought with frank envy.

"Good morning, Jay. Don't sit down," he said, to his pleasure watching Streets snap to attention again. "It seems the Ecuador office wants you to make an appearance there—press conference and a few interviews."

"What—talking about giving away the money?"

"Talking about *your company,* more like it. Quito office thinks they can make some mileage out of you after the splash you made. People are calling the office asking about you."

"Yeah, I sure poured a bucket of water on *that* fire, huh?"

Should I put a star on your helmet? Asquotti asked silently.

Streets began swinging his torso from side to side, absently stretching it as he spoke. "Yup. Good press all over the place. One day I'm a capitalist monster, the next I'm upgraded to Robin Hood. Does that one-eighty you, or what?"

You expect anything different of fickle, stupid human beings? "Oh, you saved the day, no question," he said, and watched Streets fairly quiver with delight.

"Yeah, but is it really worth me going? I mean, the 10-hour down to Quito is no joy ride."

"Certainly. For the moment, you're a household name there," said Asquotti, glad to spoil Streets's day. "That's why the Quito office wants you—get in while the soup's hot."

"Yeah. Yeah, I get that," Streets said, pinching his lip thoughtfully. "Actually, that's a good idea. Get in their face a little, push the bank image. Do the pension bit for them. Hell, why didn't *I* think of that?" He shook his head with some irritation. "Rog', all I can say is, you're the best. I got a ton o' stuff to learn from you before you shuffle off to Retirement-land. I'm after your job when you leave, y'know. One of my mid-term goals."

"You don't say?" Asquotti chuckled. *You have them ordered, do you: short, medium and long? How wonderful to have goals. They relieve one of so much thought.*

Jay had pulled out a pocket agenda and was tapping at the screen. "So, like, when am I going? Hey, I got a promotional benefit tomorrow—a Newark literacy program. Reading's important, y'know."

"Really? When was the last time you read a book end to end?"

"I'm more of a magazine guy, actually, Rog'," Jay answered, studying the screen. "Guess I'll have to cancel a thing or two. How many days should I plan to be down there?"

"If you take off this evening, four should do it. I don't really know what Quito branch has in mind. But I told my secretary to make hotel reservations for four nights. You can always move up a day if necessary. Or take a day or two off and see the sights. Ecuador must be *fascinating.*"

"Yeah—great people," Jay said automatically, still mulling over his agenda. "Okay, well, if that's it, then, I'd better haul. Lots of shuffling to do. I'll let you know how things go down there."

"Send us a card," Asquotti proposed.

"You got it, homeboy. Later." And he smiled before leaving—probably, Asquotti figured, the same perfunctory smile he gave to adoring kids who handed him lukewarm Coke after practice.

Asquotti returned to his computer and moved a rook. *Whatever they're sticking you in the middle of, I hope it makes you sweat. I hope it makes you scream in panic and run for your life,* he thought. An old Harvard friend had called the night before to request the loan of Streets for a few days—said he was calling for a friend in Washington. No, he couldn't *possibly* go into it—all very hush-hush. Jay would just be missing a few days of work, that was all.

19 At six-fifteen, Paul left the U.S. Embassy and drove to the Hotel Martín. It was not a long drive, but in these few minutes, the equatorial evening vanished—from enough light for a basketball game, to full darkness. Paul took the elevator up to the ninth floor, checking it as he went: no security camera inside, but he would have to make sure in hotel security. When the doors opened, he stepped slowly out of the elevator and into the single long hallway before him: its security camera looked straight down the hallway into the elevator. Paul sighed with relief—it was set on a bracket near the ceiling. It would be the work of a moment, when he needed to, to have it turned it slightly toward the wall.

He walked to room 905 and knocked. Harry Kruger, wearing his gray windbreaker, opened the door and waved him in without a word because his mouth was full of hot dog, half of which lay in his hand oozing ketchup like a sacrificial victim.

The room stank of men, pizza, computer plastic and stale coffee cups; as he walked around, he quietly slid open the glass door to the terrace. The double bed had been stood on end and leaned against a wall, its bedclothes dumped in a corner. In another was a black packing case like a miniature coffin for the electronic console set up on the other side of the room. Beside it, a wicker wastebasket struggled to subdue the pizza boxes rammed into it.

"Paul Klippen—one of our local dips, intellectual author behind the op, with me, of course," Harry announced when he'd managed to swallow enough of his hot dog. Four men—all in tee shirts of various colors, three of them standing—were looking at the electronic console; one of them turned around and tossed out a "Hey, Paul."

"Head of e-tricks there is Ross Trbek," Harry went on.

The sitting man was lanky and too tall for the little folding chair, and sat with his knees pointing upwards and one arm hanging behind him. He had a headset-with-microphone wrapped around his bowling-ball of a bald head. He called out in three short Bostonian honks, not turning around: "Paul. Hey. How ya doin'?" He never moved his eyes from the eight nine-inch television monitors, set in two rows of four. "Now. Sound-check it," he said into the microphone. "Yeah, again. Try that fah cornah."

"Don't play poker with Trbek, is all you have to know about him. More luck than a damn elf," Harry went on. "How much you up as of last night, Terbs?"

"Four-seventy-five. But don't quote me. I have a system. Not luck. Algorithms. You know algorithms? Nothin' to fe-ah." He spoke in tracer-bullets of words.

"Algorithms, huh? Mine haven't bloomed this year yet," Paul said.

Trbek and the other laughed. "Hey! Not bad for a dip, Harry."

"Let's make him secretary of state," said one of the standing men. "One we got now's a wimp."

"Yeah. That'll do," said Trbek into his microphone. "Now try by the bathroom do-ah. Talk quiet….Yeah. Good enough. Christ alive: that HG5 is some nice ha'dwa'e. All right, now get the fuck out. *And don't get seen!*" He slapped some dials, swatted some switches and turned around; he had an ugly mustache scrawled across his upper lip. "Harry. We're up now. Prathuh—damn fool. Connected the cables bassassckwa'ds."

Paul took a look at the screens. Two agents had just finished wiring two hotel rooms for sound and image: Streets's and the one beside it. Of the top four screens, two were television channels: an NBA game between Seattle and Chicago—apparently still in its first quarter, the score 12–17—and a porno film showing a busy couple by the side of a swimming pool. The next two screens showed websites for prostitutes in Quito; the other agents were laboriously punching phone numbers into their cell phones.

"Anybody know what *francés sin* is?" said one of the agents, reading the blurb beside the photo of the girl. Paul felt his eyes open wide: the man's biceps were as thick as his own thighs. "I keep seeing that."

"A blowjob *without*—i.e., without the condom," said Harry Kruger. He looked over the man's shoulder. "That's Melania—I'd pass on her."

The agent turned. "Yeah?"

"Yeah—a dead squirrel in the road is sexier. At *that* house, let's see…" He leaned forward and touched the screen a few times. "That one. Check out Jade."

He turned to Paul and grinned. "Don't worry, it's all in their own rooms, own expenses. You get the final wage?"

Paul squared his feet patiently. "Just finished talking with Rafa Ramirez in Guayaquil. The banana barons don't like the switch of arbitrator, but they'll accept it as long as everything stays on plan."

"And how much?" he said.

"They say top price is eighteen dollars per day."

Harry grunted. "Tough—labor is looking for a minimum of twenty. All right: I'll inform the team."

"Do. Above that, the banana boys won't pay a nickel. Once the negotiations end and Streets names the wage, they'll transfer the twenty million."

"Oh, Klippers, by the way: it's going to be *three* people with Streets." A grin. "I talked to the psycho boys at Langley last night, and they suggested, ah, reinforcements."

"Two *big* reinforcements," chuckled the man with the huge biceps. "Trbek, pull up that jpeg. Take a look, Paul."

Paul felt a shock run through his stomach. "No. Thanks." He grabbed Harry's arm and jerked. "Harry, let's step out onto the terrace and get some much fresher air while you *explain* this change in our oh-so-carefully-laid plans." he said.

"Oh, I knew it. For God's sake, Klippen," Harry moaned.

The terrace overlooked El Ejido Park. Through the canopy of trees, bits of firelight peeped out where the strikers were making dinner. A bullhorn was squawking, and the reedy blather of children splashed here and there. Paul checked the adjoining terraces, waited for Harry to close the door, then faced him and jabbed his chest with a forefinger.

"Harry, we talked about—we *agreed on*—two men: one older for the wise-and-worldly touch, and a younger man that he could talk football with and keep his confidence. That was all, and that was enough."

"Well, I ran it past the psycho boys, and they said if you want short-term loyalty, you go with a girl. It's easy and reliable. Besides—hell—the guy deserves—"

"That's *not* quite my point here, Harry. I mean, can we think for a moment about if the op goes bad? Because if it does, this is how it's going to look: it's bad enough the government had to trick Streets into doing its dirty work for them; turns out they had to *prostitute* him too?"

"Oh, unclench, would you, Klippers? I don't see this thing derailing. Besides, look at it another way: the guy's going to do our dirty work—that's on target—so why don't we give him something for his services?"

"'Something for his services!'" Paul repeated, flapping his arms hopelessly.

Harry was still talking: "I mean, you should *see* this girl. She's got a body on her that just won't quit. I'm talking Playmate of the Year material, just a few years and some miles on her, that's all. Twenty-eight or so. Kind of babe that can handle anything."

"'Something for his services,'" Paul repeated one more time. "The idea being, I guess, that if Streets figures out the scam—God forbid—you've got a reply when he comes to punch you in the face."

"Exactly! Like, 'Try and tell me you didn't enjoy that.'"

"Funny, I feel no sense of consolation." He sighed. "And she's a Company asset? Somebody *inside* the tent? Please say yes, Harry."

"Contractor—like the other two. Charges eighteen grand a day *with* guarantee, but she's worth every penny. The other two are ten grand and five for the cameo."

"Guarantee…of what? Multiple orgasms?"

Harry rolled his eyes. "Nothing contagious between her legs—what else? What—you want to get hit with a lawsuit? Oh, and I got great references on her."

"Ah! Well, if Hugh Hefner gives her the seal of approval," said Paul facetiously, "that's good enough for me."

"No, as a matter of fact—a friend of mine in Nato, in Berlin. They used her on a couple of missions in East Europe, and they said she's great. Really focused."

Paul groaned. "'Focused.' My god. So easily do clichés come to our rescue."

"No, a real pro, Klippers," Harry insisted. "Listen. The guy told me she got a fifty-year-old Hungarian millionaire to show her where he was hiding his anti-aircraft missiles to sell to Iran. Twelve hours later he was in prison and she was in Paris. How's *that?*"

"Wonderful, Harry. *And* focused."

"Look, you don't have to take my word for it. Just a sec." He slid open the door a foot and called in. "Terbs, what's ETA on the team?"

"Late word is they're on the ground. Rillkey is sliding them through customs. Forty-five minutes tops."

"So stay and see for yourself, Klippers. This girl will blow you away—guaranteed."

Paul laughed out of sheer exasperation. "Harry, my problem is *not* with her beauty. Really it is not." He glanced out over the park, as if for help. "But I suppose there's no talking to you, is there? The die is cast."

"It'll go fine, Klippers," said Harry tiredly. "Besides, if Streets doesn't want to do anything, she's not going to—" He was trying to get past Paul and through the terrace door, but Paul blocked his way and shut the sliding door again, nearly catching Harry's fingers in it.

"All right, forget her. But from now on, Mr. Kruger, this is *your* op. Understand? Tomorrow morning I cable Washington and inform them the operation has been passed to surer hands than mine."

"Oh, for God's sake. Now don't go and—"

"Which means: *You* make the report, Harry. *You* take the credit—or the shit—and *you* deal with the lawsuit if it transpires that Streets resents being put out to stud for our tawdry little scam."

"Fine with me. I could use the promotion."

Paul patted his chest. "It's all yours, friend. You *have* checked to see if he's in a relationship, haven't you? Because that might—"

"Cell phone records indicate he's playing the field."

Paul smiled coldly. "Well, let's hope he's not seeing some gorgeous nature lover who hates cell phones."

"Oh, don't have a coronary, Klippers. This girl gets results. She gets a ten-percent bonus just for keeping Streets on the right price."

"*A bonus!* God, how you complicate things!" Paul huffed. He shoved the terrace door open with a bang and walked off.

"If it's worth doing, it's worth *over*doing," Harry called behind him, but Paul walked straight through the room, out the door, and down to the hall. For good measure, in case Harry was watching from behind, he swatted the elevator button.

But once the elevator doors closed behind him, Paul allowed himself a chuckle. "Well, that went better than I ever dreamed. A *girl,* good Lord! Could there *be* a better excuse for dumping the op on him?" He looked at his watch: seven-thirty. He would go right back to the embassy and send the cable to Washington now—make it sound bitter and disgusted, as if the op had just been snatched out of his hands.

He took out his cell phone and called his wife. "Sorry, my love, but I won't be home for another hour yet: nuclear emergencies, yellow hordes threatening to overrun us—the usual. Keep the Fendant cold for me, would you?"

20

The plane had banked more sharply than Jay liked and then descended to what looked like housetop level. Under his feet, Jay felt the wheels of the airplane humming into position and wondered if they were going to land on top of an apartment building.

"Jesus," he muttered. The last time he had landed it was night, and things hadn't been so clear. He saw moving cars, a donkey cart, two guys playing morning basketball in a park—which was so near that he could see one guy toss up a foul shot.

Somebody better put some runway down there, and fast.

Nobody did, however, and the plane continued its careful descent along the length of the city. A little Chevvy just like his first car in high school was turning onto a wide street, and a round bullfighting stadium slipped under the plane's right wing. If the plane's trajectory were any flatter, they would need to stop for traffic lights. But at the last second, a runway appeared to receive them, the plane clunked onto it, and the passengers applauded.

Jay realized that he was not all that glad to be back.

He went through customs. The policeman who stamped his passport extended a reverent hand and said, "Is a grea' honor that I give you the welco'e to the Ecuador Republic, Meester Stree's." Roger Asquotti was right: he was a household name. And while he was waiting for his bags, a couple of young women in tight jeans ran up to him and had their mother take their picture with him—then ran off before he could get a phone number. His current girlfriend, a marketing student at NYU, was ten thousand miles away, and the relationship was only a month old—nothing concrete yet. She had a nice personality.

Finally his big suitcase tumbled down the chute—he had brought clothes for every type of situation, plus four suits—and he rolled it out into the lobby, enjoying that spreading, fresh sense of liberation that topped off a long airplane journey. Around him Ecuadorans were falling into each other's arms as if they hadn't seen each other for a lifetime. Some were short, square Andean Indians; others, clearly the well-to-do, displayed every degree of mix between European and Indian. A bolt of loneliness shot through him—*Quito branch could have sent out a driver, at least,* he griped silently—and began patting his pockets for the address of his hotel.

"Hello there, Mr. Streets." The baritone voice was as solid as oak. The speaker was about 40 and had a trim jaw and good head of brown hair brushed back from his broad forehead. He wore a silk tie under a London Fog trenchcoat with a belt across his flat stomach—tied, not fastened, Jay noted approvingly. He wore glasses, but tasteful and of the kind that allowed his fine, brown eyes to show. He was the kind of man that Jay hoped to be in ten years—not one of the paunchy duffers slouching around DynoBank.

With his left hand, he flipped open a good wallet to reveal an i.d. card. "Michael Adams, U.S. Commerce Department—Special Operations," he said. "Can I call you Jay?"

"Jay's the name—don't see why not." He felt a solid hand in his own.

"Good. I'm Michael. Jay, is this all your stuff here?"

"That's it. You said you're from the Commerce Department?"

"Yeah. We've got a van over there." He signaled to a couple of Indian boys, who took the suitcase and began rolling it rumblingly behind Jay. The air sparkled with equatorial light, yet was chilly enough for Jay to zip up his jacket.

"Wait a minute," said Jay, looking around. "Maybe my company—DynoBank?—sent somebody, or—"

"We're the welcoming committee," Michael said with a note of apology. "Actually, the DynoBank thing is just an excuse."

Jay stopped. One of the boys bumped into him, but he hardly felt it.

Michael smiled. "You're in the Army now, Mr. Streets. Welcome."

Michael walked on, but Jay didn't move—and if Michael Special Ops didn't like it, too goddamn bad.

Michael looked back at him, then walked back a few steps. "Jay, the thing is this." A sheepish wiggle of the shoulders. "We've got a situation here and we need your help—simple as that. Nothing dangerous. We just need to use your face and your name."

"Oh! Okay. I can do that. Glad to help out."

Michael turned him down a row of parked cars. Ahead of them, a white van reversed alertly out of a space.

"This won't take long—extra day or two here in Quito. Don't worry about your company; we'll square it with them. Thing is, it's got to be you—you or nobody. Sorry, but on the run it's the best we could come up with. You're a patriotic American, am I right?"

"Yeah, sure. Patriotism's important."

"Good. 'Cause this is a five-star good cause that will earn you the thanks of your country and hundreds of thousands of Ecuadorans. It'll be fun too," he added, as if it hadn't occurred to him before.

"And you just need my face and name, right?" Jay asked carefully.

"That's right. If all you do is sit silent till your plane back to New York, that will be enough."

"Well, okay. Count me in."

Michael gave the boys a few bills each and grabbed the handle of Jay's suitcase. "Come on and meet the kids."

He rolled the case the last few yards up to the van and knocked twice—then a pause—and twice again on its side door. It was slid back by a muscular black man wearing a red-and-white-striped polo shirt that his chest and arms filled out. A thin gold chain lay around his thick neck, clinging to the hills and valleys of his clavicle. He lifted the suitcase in as if it weighed one pound rather than forty.

"There's the man! Hey, dog, hop in." The man extended his hand and pulled Jay up and into the cabin.

Jay sat down on a comfortable seat opposite the black man and a sparklingly beautiful woman of about twenty-six. She had elbow-length dark hair—brown with red highlights—and light-gray eyes. Her white shirt was tucked into her jeans, two buttons open, and stretched smooth over melon-like breasts supported by a lacy brassiere. Her triceps were full and high by the shoulders, a touch that Jay found sexy. No rings on her well-kept hands, feminine fingernails, glossy but not painted.

Michael had got into the front passenger seat. The van was moving before he had closed his door. "Jay, these are my assistants on the assignment: Dana Underwood and Skip Halday."

"Jay, hi. It's a pleasure." Dana's hand jangled with the many bracelets there, but was small and cool. Jay squeezed it with care. Her smile—full of white, strong teeth—had enough warmth to be friendly and enough steel to indicate that first things were first. Skip, however, smacked his hand into his.

"Hey, man, great to finally meet you, I gotta tell ya. Know I almost got to play against you? I started for OSU at tight end the year you checked into the pros."

"Really? How come you didn't turn pro later on?"

"Yo, what you think, dog—we *all* get drafted?" He grinned; there was a tiny gap between his two front teeth. "No, I finished my degree and turned into a damn bureaucrat." He flung his arms wide. "And here I am, turnin' fuckin' cartwheels for Commerce Special Ops—God bless it."

"Well, there's nothing wrong with a good career," Jay said generously.

"Yo! No complaints, dog. Seen the world with Special Ops. Man, just last month I was on another project in southern Italy. Spent about a month there—there and Greece."

"Sounds nice."

"Great food, babes know how to dress. Yo, Michael, whaddaya think?" he called up front. "Think we could get Jay an invite to try out for us when we're done here?"

Michael was consulting the screen of a smartphone. "Possible, sure."

"I'd need to be *invited?*" asked Jay.

"Yeah, well, you don't do a damn civil service exam for this kinda work, man. We ain't exactly your everyday bureaucrat."

"Not at *all*," Dana murmured, fingering the bangles on her wrist and making them tinkle. *No rings,* Jay noticed again.

"Why not?" said Jay, puzzled.

Michael put away the phone and climbed into the back with them. "Jay, I told you we're with Commerce Department Special Operations, and technically that's true. But Special Ops is just a kind of the umbrella organization. One section of Special Ops looks after American companies in countries where there's a civil war. Another covers international sporting events and concerts—just to make sure our athletes don't run into any trouble."

"Or make sure Bruce Springsteen doesn't," added Dana.

"And then we get 'em out when they *do* get in trouble. Lots of fun," Skip muttered darkly.

Michael: "*Our* unit does foreign union-management negotiations where American interests are involved. But since Uncle Sam doesn't *officially* stick his fingers into business affairs and especially not in another country, *officially* our unit is just a bunch of paper hangers."

"Yeah—yeah, I can see that," Jay answered, striving to sound intelligent. *Wow—it's just like TV.*

Dana: "Last year I think our budget was officially part of Commerce physical plant maintenance, wasn't it, Michael?"

He nodded. "This year they've knocked us over to transportation-slash-transportation procurement."

"Me, I'm on the payroll as a damn tax accountant," said Skip. "Know what my major was? Physical therapy! Gimme a bump, dog." He laughed and knocked his knuckles against Jay's. "My old lady thinks I'm a damn sales rep for a chemical company."

"Really? You can't tell her where you work?" Jay blurted, instantly ashamed. *I sound like a fan.*

"Hazards o' workin' Special Ops, dog. They lay it down for you on day one, and you take it or you leave it."

"Is that right?" Jay said in frank amazement. "So what about *your* resumé, Dana? I mean, if you don't mind my asking."

"Oh, nothing to brag about. I was a second-string running back at Yale," she deadpanned.

Jay laughed.

"Actually, I mainly work with Michael here. I graduated from Vassar four years ago—in English Lit, if you can believe that."

"Vassar—I'm impressed," said Jay, and he was. *These people are real pros!*

The van had nosed out of the parking lot and entered the heavy, stop-and-go traffic headed for downtown Quito. Michael had turned around in his seat and was conferring with the driver. Now he turned back. "Looks like we're clear," he said to Dana and Skip, who nodded. "Jay, we're going to get you set up at your hotel first."

"How did you know about my hotel?"

"R and D, homeboy—half our job," said Skip.

"Exactly. We've arranged for a room adjoining yours," said Michael. "You'll have about an hour to freshen up before DynoBank's Quito people contact you."

Dana leaned forward—her hair running over her shoulders a new way—and touched his knee. "Did you sleep at all on the plane, Jay? Are you tired?"

"Yeah, a bit. No big deal."

Michael clapped his hands together impatiently. "Fine. Okay, Jay, let me run it down for you. We don't have much time before you get to the hotel."

Jay arranged himself sideways in the seat to see him better. "Shoot."

"Okay. To put it in the simplest, briefest terms, what we're doing here is trying to head off a major disaster for the Ecuadoran economy and a minor one for ours, and we need your help. Now I know what you're thinking—that this is their country and they have to take care of their own affairs, and at Commerce everyone shares your sentiment, believe me."

"You can say *that* again, man," Skip muttered. "'Cause like we all got better things to do. I had a sweet vacation in Yosemite—nobody there, place to ourselves?—all lined up before this thing happened. My old lady's home screamin' bloody murder at me."

"Trouble is, if the Ecuadoran economy takes a bad hit, what are the consequences?" Michael went on patiently. He counted them on his shapely fingers. "Inflation, unemployment, more immigrants wanting to get into the United States, civil unrest, maybe war, and hardship for people who don't need another helping—and we *know* you're concerned about that."

"Yeah, sure am," said Jay, feeling Dana's eyes on him. The lapels and cuffs of her white blouse had a bit of lace on them, which Jay liked. And she had the confidence to show a triangle of cleavage right off the bat too. He liked a woman who knew how to be a woman.

"Now about three weeks ago at Commerce, a lot of the boys and girls who do analytical economics started getting uneasy about the fruit workers here. They're striking for higher wages—their good right, no problem in our book. Thing is, if they get the raise they're striking for, they might just drive the Ecuadoran economy over the brink."

Dana pulled a silver necklace out from deep in her bosom and fingered it. "And nobody really wanted to do anything because, as Michael said, everybody figures it's *their* problem, not ours."

Jay noted that correctness of the *as*. Roger Asquotti had corrected him on that mistake half a dozen times in his press statements before he got it right. *Classy babe.*

Michael: "But finally, things came to a boil here, and someone talked to someone who has face-time rights with the secretary—"

"Yo, dog, that's the Secretary o' *Commerce*," Skip added. "Not, like, y'know, Michael's secretary or somethin'." He put forth his fist, which Jay duly bumped with his own.

"Exactly," Michael said with a tight smile. "The Secretary of Commerce. And Mr. Secretary made a decision for action, which percolated down to Special Ops."

Dana: "As usual."

Jay: "To do what?"

"Well, Jay, again: it's not that Ecuadorans are stupid or can't run their own affairs; it's just that…" Michael's hands seemed to be trying to hold objects of different shapes as he searched for words. "Oh hell—*you've* been here before, Jay. You know what the people are like."

Skip: "Someone hadda step in and say, 'Yo, homies, just like fuckin' *chill*. Y'all chill before this gets outta hand and everybody's out of a fuckin' paycheck."

"I hear ya," Jay said sympathetically.

"To put it another way, Jay," said Michael, "do you let your mother dress you for a big night out?"

"No, I sure don't."

"Precisely. And you don't give a gun to a drunk, and you don't let people with third-grade educations set the wage for the country's biggest industry."

"I guess not," said Jay. "So who's going to set them?"

"You are!" said Dana with an unexpected giggle and spank of his knee.

"*Me?*"

"You duh man, dog!" cried Skip. "You duh big give-away-dem-twenties-like-they're-candy moth'fucker."

"How'm I going to do that?" Jay laughed, amazed.

But the driver whipped around and said, "Michael. Change—just to be sure. Now. Now as in *now*."

The van halted; looking through the windshield, Jay saw a traffic light four or five cars ahead. Without a word, Skip slid back the side door of the van. In the next lane, another identical van had pulled up, its door open too. Skip stepped across, turned and helped Dana because of her high heels, then Jay, then Michael. The driver lifted Jay's suitcase across to Skip and closed the door. Skip put the bag on the empty passenger seat beside the new driver. The four sat all together again.

"It's just a precaution, Jay," said Michael. "Where were we?"

The others acted as if they did this every day, so Jay did too.

"You were telling me how I was going to set the minimum wage."

"Precisely. Remember from your first trip that there were a lot of strikers protesting in the park in front of the Hotel Martín?"

"You know what hotel I was in on my first trip?" Jay asked, amazed.

"Yo, dog, we know that you last changed the oil in your car in the middle of January," said Skip. "Your sister is a third-year assistant prof in Sociology at Saint Olaf and your father runs the restaurant-and bar-licensing out at MSP airport. I mean, you see us three, but there's seventeen other people puttin' in time just a ten-minute drive away from the White House. Your shirt size is 19-37 and your shoe is a ten-and-a-half, and your office is on the thirtieth floor."

"That's 18–38, actually."

A gap-toothed grin. "I was just guessin', dog. Gimme a bump."

Jay did. "Still, that's pretty impressive."

"We're thorough," Dana added modestly.

"I guess," Jay said. *It really is just like TV!* "Well, to answer your question, Michael, um, I remember there was some kind of commotion out in the park. I asked the hotel receptionist about it and she told me it was something about banana workers and they were pretty pissed off about something and not to go over there."

"They're *striking* banana workers who have come up from the Ecuadoran Pacific side," said Michael. "Negotiations between their union leaders and plantation owners are going on right in your hotel." He turned more in his seat toward Jay. "They've been going at it for a week and a half now and our source says that they've recently decided to name an arbitrator to settle matters."

Dana touched his knee lightly again—or was it a stroke? "And that's where you come in."

Jay stared at them. He was shocked, and this embarrassed him. "They're gonna name...me?" he asked, strangling his voice to speak calmly.

"Like I say, dog: you duh man," Skip said.

Jay hoped to God he had control of his face. "But that's insane. I mean, that's just unbelievable. Why would anyone ask *me* to arbitrate their settlement? There have to be a hundred people in this country who'd be more qualified." His mouth wanted to run on, but he clamped it shut.

"Very simple: they want someone who's completely impartial," said Michael. "Someone who knows nothing about this specific situation. Each side will make a presentation, tell you what salary they want, and then you decide."

"Okay," Jay said slowly. "But even still: they have to agree on *me*, the two sides do, right?"

"And why not?" Michael counted on his fingers again. "One, you understand business, work in a major international bank and have quite a lot of money of your own to manage. Therefore the plantation owners will trust you. Two, you're a proven philanthropist. You literally gave away thousands of dollars to poor people on the street. And that will appeal to the unions."

Jay looked from one face to another. They were serious. He nearly told them the truth about the money, but reined himself in. A low pre-game panic was sputtering in his gut. "Michael, listen, I don't know about this. Are you sure there's not another—"

"Yo, homie, Special Ops to the rescue!" Skip said, swatting his shoulder. "Yeah, what we're here for, what you pay taxes for. We goin' set you up. We goin' walk you through it. We goin' tell you who to listen to and who's full o' shit. And then we goin' help you set a nice, sweet price so ev'body walks away with their own little cut o' the pie. And we goin' hang right with you till ev'body's shaken your hand and said muchas gracias and gone back to work. Ain't nobody goin' nowhere till this is all said and done and you're on the plane back to the good ol' U.S.A.—probably fly with us, come to think of it." He put out a fist, and Jay bopped it again.

"We'll be right next door," said Dana.

Michael: "And you'll be doing Ecuador *and* your own country a favor by setting a salary that people here can live on but *not* kill their economy."

Jay laughed: it was incredible. "Well. Well heck, I guess it sounds okay. That is, if they actually come up with *my* name to do this, which I still doubt."

Michael made a secret smile. "We can't tell you exactly how that's going to happen, Jay, but suffice it to say, we've got someone inside the negotiations. It *will* happen, that we can assure you."

"All set to fall, dog," Skip added. 'Cept that's kinda just between us, okay?"

"Yeah, sure."

From the front seat, the driver called back. "One block from Hotel Martín, Michael."

"Great. Pull over about twenty yards short."

"Okay? We're going to be right beside you, Jay," Michael said. "Or at least the kids will."

"Michael—I am a *woman*," said Dana with a melodramatic swish of her hair.

"When you're forty-six, you get to call twenty-somethings kids," Michael retorted.

"Where are *you* going to be, Michael?" Jay inquired.

"I'm going to make sure you're all up and running here in Quito," Michael said, "and then I've got to head for Kyoto, Japan. Kind of a shit job, but somebody has to do it."

"Sounds like you people really get around," said Jay.

"There's some months, man, when we just live in airports," said Skip.

"Me, I haven't been home in five weeks," said Dana. "I had to call my brother to tell him to go start my car and drive it a little so that the battery will stay charged."

Brother, Jay noted. *Not boyfriend, not husband.* "Sounds like pretty interesting work," said Jay.

"It's all about puttin' out fires, man," Skip said, shaking his head in wonder. "You never figured how many of 'em are out there burnin' away till you work for Special Ops."

The van stopped. Michael and Skip got out because the door was on their side. Before Jay could follow them, Dana laid a hand a cool hand on his own and winked. "You're in good hands—the best. I'll see you for dinner tonight, okay?"

"Lookin' forward to it," said Jay with what seductiveness he could marshal.

On the sidewalk, Michael shook Jay's hand. "Sorry not to leave you at the door of the hotel, Jay, but it's best that we're not seen together, okay?"

"Sure, Michael—not made of glass."

"I'll say he isn't," Dana called from the van, and Jay grinned at her.

"Great. So go get checked in, shower up, and go through with the day just as scheduled by your Quito branch. The kids'll call on you this evening—just your leave your terrace door unlocked. Oh, and before I forget, there's a small stipend—cash, of course, all off the books—for helping us out here. Can't promise a lot—I'll have to see what I can wring out of the budget gurus. The kids'll let you know."

"Oh, heck, I'm just happy to be of service."

"Good man." He hopped into the front of the fan again.

"Later, homes." Skip winked, got in the back, and closed the door—Dana, dark hair swinging, waved from inside—and the van moved on.

Just like on TV. I swear!

21 Hondo Verdes stood up to stretch his legs and recover his sanity. The talk between the workers union and Plantaciones Costa crabbed on and on, pale and unending and pointless like the taupe-colored walls of their Hotel Martín meeting room, which was nothing less than the entire sub-level of the hotel, as big as a hockey rink, though with supporting columns fat as elm trunks standing here and there. The Ecuadoran Department of Agriculture, panicking in the face of the surprise strike, had made the whole floor available to them, making a pharmaceutical convention find other accommodations.

He had nearly leapt for joy some days earlier when his two colleagues on the workers negotiating committee—if "colleagues" was the word for those shysters—had changed their minds and finally agreed to a suggestion the Costa committee had made: that they jointly name an arbitrator who would listen to both sides' point of view and set the per-diem wage. To his further amazement, both sides had signed a document agreeing to respect the arbitrator's decision. Surely, he had thought, an arbitrator could be chosen quickly and a wage decision would soon follow.

Which would be a godsend. The strikers in the park were tired and wet from the daily rains, and many were catching colds because they weren't used to the nightly fifty-degree cold at that altitude. If a pneumonia epidemic got started, the strikers would run for buses back down to the lowlands.

But naming an arbitrator was proving a nightmare as well. At first everyone had agreed on the suggestion of Doctor Antonio Melero, but the doctor had been called away on an emergency to the Middle East and would not be available. So the slow tug-of-war had begun.

One side would propose an eminent person to arbitrate, and the other side would make a show of considering, then bellow an objection. Some were clearly stupid, like Costa's suggestions of a former American senator or a member of the International Monetary Fund. Yet their other suggestions—a former leftist president of Peru, the head of the Organization of African States, the Ecuadoran vice-president of the International Red Cross—seemed to him fully reasonable.

Not for Sixto Carrasco. He would countenance nobody to the right of Fidel Castro and kept insisting on a former economic minister of Hugo Chavez's cabinet. The third member of the strikers' negotiating team, Napoleón García, was no better. Head of unions in the crucial area north of Guayaquil, he was Carrasco's poodle—or rather, his hound, since he had a long, doggy face and close-set eyes, and sat slouched in his chair like an elderly patient in a hospice. Hondo suspected that he was there merely to keep watch when Carrasco was absent, which was often. Otherwise he opened his mouth either to yawn or insult someone on the Costa committee.

Hondo walked around the vast room, glad to put a pillar between himself and Carrasco, who was bellowing at the three Costa negotiators that they would only be satisfied when workers had to pay *them* for the privilege of working on their plantations. How he loathed him. He loathed his massive head and belly and beard, his huge mane of graying hair always shoved back as if he were on a lion safari, his enormous mouth that opened inside the beard like the jaws of a thresher. He always went around in a shirt opened nearly to his belly button, the sleeves shoved up and wrinkled. You could hardly look at him without feeling that he had spent the morning digging ditches. But he had a closet full of suits tailored in Colón, Panama, Hondo knew, and a mansion in Ambato—inherited from his wealthy father, a former senator—where his domestic staff, all young women, tended to his—and his wife's—sexual demands.

Will we ever get on with this? Hondo thought as Carrasco screamed away at the Costa committee. Abelardo Marmalejo, an angry young man also on his way to obesity, screamed back that for the thirty-five dollars a day that Carrasco demanded he would go to work on the plantations himself and make a fortune.

"If you recommend total and complete card-carrying fascists as arbitrators, men who have signed ten contracts with Satan, how can we take any of your suggestions seriously?" Carrasco snapped.

"Only fascists recommend fascists!" added Napoleón, his little one-man cheerleading squad.

The owners committee across the table snarled back.

Hondo walked more, swinging his arms to loosen his shoulders. He wondered what Mary was doing. He had spent a few nights with her over the past ten days. He wondered if she would marry him. *Should I ask? Should I buy her a ring?* The thought of actually having a home and a wife was so wonderful that it made him sweat.

"Arnaldo Rodriguez? Mr. Simples, your suggestion is laughable! This suggestion is a travesty against our decency, common sense, and propriety. That man is nothing but the basest American puppet, a man whose crimes against humanity are legendary, and the most inveterate of liars!" Carrasco barked, and Hondo wondered if he was capable of saying a simple yes or no. Empty phrases gushed from his monstrous mouth like sewage from a pipe.

"That's nonsense. Rodriguez was a former U.N. official who had a reputation for siding with China and Russia."

Carrasco jumped to his feet, sending ripples through his belly. "Why do you insist on this scourge of the working man? Why? Isabel, was he your lover in America? Did he take what little—what speck—remains of your virtue, the only real possession that God ever gave you and the center of any decent, virtuous person's being?" He could not even insult a person, Hondo noted, without falling into rhetoric.

"When was the last time you *had* a lover, Carrasco?" Isabel said with a bored little giggle, her lime-green earrings shaking. "And just between us, how much did you pay for him?"

Marmalejo and Simples laughed. Carrasco roared back with gibberish about how some day the workers would tear her limb from limb.

Isabel Costa was of the Guayaquil landowning class that Hondo knew well: rich and young and irritable, her jeans so tight that might have been painted on and the waistband narrowed and doubled over itself by the pressure. Her breasts had been filled with silicon in Miami and were now framed gloriously in a stretchy yellow leotard that dipped to a deep V. Beside her at the table, little Miguel Simples, Costa's pale, boyish financial manager, could not stop peeping at her cleavage and gulping.

"But how can you reject the former secretary of labor of Costa Rica?" cried Abelardo Marmalejo, Costa's operating manager and largest minority investor. He was about thirty and had a childishly earnest air to him, with a tubby body and a great pumpkin head topped with soft, shaggy hair. The spectacles stretched across his fat face looked like swimmer's goggles. He owned the finest collection of model trains in Latin America, and Hondo knew that workers' wages were to him nothing but the train models they kept him from buying. "How? I still don't understand that. He's perfect."

Hondo returned to the table and, still standing, began to turn the pages of Napoleon's copy of the day's *El Comercio. He's perfect because you bribed him months ago,* he thought. *Spanish intelligence told me.*

"He's lived in mansions all his life," yawned Napoleón.

Marmalejo: "Like hell. He was a *union leader* before he went into the government! He was also a well-known defender of human rights, he's offered his good offices, and he's willing to come at a moment's notice. If you don't accept him, you won't accept anyone!"

Carrasco: "Our last offer is the honorable, wise, and superb ex-mayor of Havana, which is an offer acceptable to anyone with intelligence and a sense of culture, and with the interest, desire and the social obligation to move the talks forward. Even the most rightist of Nazis, like you, could accept him!"

"That's what you call a serious candidate?" shouted Marmalejo.

"You ought to—"

"Reject him and you might as well leave every banana in Ecuador to rot in the sun for the next five years! And your blood-soaked profits as well!" Carrasco said and slapped the table.

The Costa people visibly grayed. Bananas, which grow quickly, were spoiling by the ton every day.

Can it possibly be true that the lives of a hundred thousand Ecuadorans hang on this mud-slinging between children? thought Verdes, turning a page. *And that this corrupt madman holds the key to it all?*

But he was necessary; without him the strike had no weight. For the last three years Carrasco had been the big name on the Ecuadoran left. Only on his word had workers refrained last year from flooding Quito to overthrow President Tingo, another heartless bastard. It was a shrewd political move. By saving Tingo, he had positioned himself as the indispensable politician. He could well take the presidency in the upcoming elections.

"Please, everybody! We are here to reach *an agreement!*" wailed little Miguel Simples. He wore a basic blue suit and a basic pale face. He alone was willing to compromise and move things along. "This threat, Mr. Carrasco, has no place in our discussions. It is not only a dismissal of our efforts but of the Ecuadoran businessmen who have raised this country."

Oh no, why did you say that? thought Hondo with a sigh.

"'Raised this country?'" Carrasco roared. "Is that what you call the total enslavement, the inexorable impoverishment of three-quarters of all Ecuadoran workers? You, who eat the babies of the workers! You, who condemn them to a life of sickness and early death! You, who lay them in the mud and walk over them in order not to dirty your shoes!"

"Mr. Carrasco! Please!" he gasped.

Hondo turned another page. If it were up to himself and Simples alone, the whole matter would have been resolved in an hour.

Suddenly, Napoleon pointed a curled finger, since straightening it was too great an effort for him. Above the fold was a four-column story with photo. The headline read: *"Es cierto. Ha sido mi dinero, mi idea."* ("That's right. It was my money, my idea.")

"Hondo, what about *this* guy for arbitrator?" he murmured.

It was an interview with the American who had given away money in the streets of Quito.

Hondo had vaguely heard of the matter; with curiosity he glanced over the article. Having returned to Quito, Streets had given a short press conference the day before, had dinner with some local VIPs, and met with local DynoBank people, who were shamelessly exploiting the publicity. In the photo, he stood shaking the hand of the mayor.

Question: What do you hope the people will do with the money you've given out?

Answer: I don't know—get some decent food to eat, I guess. But each person knows his situation a lot better than I do. I guess my basic idea in giving out the money was that, you know, these people can put the money to much better use than I can."

That was elegant, thought Verdes. "Strange—he doesn't seem the type that worries about the problems of workers," he said to Napoleón.

"He gave away money—that proves that he has a heart."

"I'm not sure what it proves." Verdes was thinking back to the athletes he'd seen on TV interviews in America. They were self-centered and elitist. *Still, there's always one who breaks the mold, and America is full of mold-breakers.*

"Well?" said Napoleón.

Verdes nodded at Carrasco. "Go ahead—propose it to him. I don't care. I'd settle for Atilla the Hun if we could get on with things."

Napoleón looked at him. "Atilla the Hun?"

"Forget it."

Napoleón turned to Carrasco, who was sniping at Isabel Costa, then back to Verdes. "*You* propose it to him."

Verdes huffed. "What the hell is happening to you, Napoleón? Have you lost your balls?" He snatched away the newspaper.

"How much did you spend on those boobs, eh, Isa?" Carrasco was asking Isabel. "Have you ever thought of how many children could have had food in their bellies, could have had toys to play with, or could have received a complete education with that money? Or don't you know how to think?"

"Yes, but I might look like your wife. And that would be a tragedy."

"My wife is the flower of civilization, the cream of womanhood!

You dress in the blood of your people."

"You're a son of a bitch."

"You're nothing but a whore."

"*Sixto!*" Hondo snapped. "Shut up and take a look at this." He shoved the newspaper in front of him on the table. "He might be acceptable." To the Costa people: "Page 7 of today's *Comercio.*"

Carrasco glanced at the picture—and actually started reading the article.

Abelardo Marmalejo snatched his own copy of *El Comercio* out of his briefcase. So did Simples. For the first time that whole long morning, the hotel meeting room was quiet.

"M-m-m-m," giggled Isabel Montilla. "He gets *my* vote. Look at those shoulders."

Sixto Carrasco muttered, "Still…he works in a bank—*DynoBank.*"

"I saw him in the hotel yesterday afternoon," said Miguel Simples. "He must have a room here." He looked at Marmalejo, who nodded hastily and said, "I have no objection."

"He gave out money," murmured Carrasco. "For free? Why? What was the benefit to him?"

"Just to help people," said Napoleón. "I saw him on TV this morning."

"Hah—TV, the fascists' medium," Carrasco muttered—and kept reading. Then he sat back, pulling his gray beard. "He gave people money—cash—out of his pocket?" And then he grunted in amazement.

Which was as far as he had ever gotten. Hondo saw his chance and grabbed it. "We also accept the candidate," he said quickly.

Carrasco's great head snapped around as if he'd been bitten. "Who do you think you are? You're a double-talker from the slums of Guasmo, an ant on the shoulder of our movement who should have been brushed off years ago. *I'm* the one who—"

"Shut up!" Verdes snapped.

Carrasco laughed. His flying cackle was like a saw grinding against green wood. "*You* shut *me* up, little Hondo Verdes? *You* shut *me* up? If it weren't for me, you would still be in the muddy hills of Machala, shouting through a cardboard cone."

"If it weren't for you, we would have finished the negotiations by now. But what do you care? It's not you camped out in the park."

"I'm protecting the workers from the fascist lions waiting to tear them to pieces!"

"My goodness, you worry a lot about the fascists."

"Probably because you direct them."

"When they're not trying to kill me."

"Some day I'll expose you for the fraud, the pure and incorrigible liar, that you are!"

"Oh la la," giggled Isabel, and beside her, Simples stretched his arms and leaned over and looked deep into her yellow leotard.

Hondo: "Napoleón? What do you say?"

"Ah, I gotta think about it," he muttered.

"Fine then. We accept the candidate," Verdes repeated.

"We do not accept the candidate!" Carrasco shouted, swinging his fat arms around, hair flying. He might have been a child throwing a tantrum. "He is the tool of capitalist monsters like you. This is written on his fat white face. He is a millionaire American athlete. He works in a *bank*. He has blood money in his pockets. What difference does it make if he tosses a few bills to some poor people living in the street? He has—"

"Why don't you ask them, Carrasco?" snapped Hondo. "Ask that woman who got money—the one who lives in the ruins with her two babies. Ask *her* what a few hundred dollars mean."

"Bah!" Carrasco jumped out of his chair, bulk tossing about like a heaving sea. "You're a traitor! You're working for the fascist Americans, aren't you? Let there be no mistake about this. You are killing the first decent chance that the Ecuadoran worker has had in a thousand years to gain a decent, humane wage. You are the snake in our den—a viper! And the failure will be on *your* head, Segundo Verdes." He stopped, panting. He was so massive he could hardly move around without stopping for a breath. He glanced at the newspaper again, then swatted it off the table. "All right—I will accept your millionaire athlete, but I make one demand, and it is not negotiable."

"Yours never are."

"If he agrees to arbitrate, I want a twenty-four-hour guard of two of our workers in front of his hotel door. Got it? And no phone or Internet in his room, either. Our wages are at stake, and the fascists will do anything to bribe or threaten him."

"*Our* wages,'" Hondo chuckled, shaking his head. "My god—as if you were one of them. Your houses in Quito and Ambato could house five families each."

This stung. *"I will throw you to the dogs when we are done!"* Carrasco roared. *"To the dogs!* And we will see whether or not your millionaire athlete saves you!"

He stomped out, belly quivering and shaking like applause. At the door, he slapped it open and walked out, shouting to the waiting reporters, who jumped up from their chairs in the lobby and came running forward with cameras and microphones. "I have been betrayed! It is all a trick! This is the dirtiest play I have ever seen in all my years as a lawyer for the working man!"

Hondo sighed again. *What a liar. A liar and a traitor. That's the only way to fight him—keep handing him one fait accompli after another.*

Still—finally they were over the last hurdle. Only that was amazing. "Well, Mr. Simples, let's go talk to Streets and get on with this. You said that he is in this hotel?"

22 "How do you find the Quito?" the interviewer asked to kick off the interview. She had a high, squeaky voice and terrible English.

I take a plane—how else? he thought as he repeated the question and chuckled, which was what he always did in an interview to stall for time.

"Okay, you like the Quito?" she added.

"Oh, yeah, Quito's great." Jay felt he should say more: "Really beautiful, the way those green mountains rise over the city. What's the name of them again?"

"The Pichinchas."

"Yeah—Pichinchas. Great, fantastic. I like the way the city's strung out along the skirts of the mountains. It's really picturesque."

In fact, Jay was not sure at all that he liked the Quito anymore, but he was on the last interview of the day and he wasn't about to make fine distinctions if they weren't asked for. The questions were strictly softball, and it was easy to make hay for the bank. Yesterday and that morning had been taken up with shooting a commercial for the local DynoBank, a tedious process which involved a lot of moving around to shoot him against the mountains, against the Middle of the World Monument, looking over a spreadsheet with the local director and smiling at the supposedly excellent results. There was a lunch with a provincial governor—a greasy, grinning bastard—and a cocktail party with a lot of fancy people whose English, with one or two exceptions, sputtered like random bits of computer code. And in between there were the interviews, dreary but necessary.

His hotel room had only one easy chair, and out of politeness he had ceded it to the interviewer and sat hunched uncomfortably on a tiny folding chair that the camera crew had brought along. The questions went on—two pages of them, Jay could see. But from a long association with reporters, he was patient with people who needed his face and words to bring home the bacon.

Even this one. She was Angela Córdoba, who had introduced herself as "the presenter" of one of the local newscasts. She wore a sky-blue one-piece miniskirt with a cruelly pushed-up cleavage, and nylons which sank into sky-blue high heels. Her makeup and earrings were sky blue, as was the sponge cover of her microphone. Her sky-blue purse rested on the floor beside the chair like a faithful puppy.

Angela found the next question on her long list. "Have you watched the World Middle Monument?" she read. "How did you find it?" she asked with a groupie's dumb grin. She had spent a year living in New York and "spoke very well the English." She said she would translate his answers and put them in subtitles once back at her news studio. Remembering poor Rochelle's fate, Jay decided to keep his answers dead-center neutral.

Jay added enthusiasm to his face. "Yeah, I was there yesterday. It's really interesting. I mean, it's amazing how people can find the equator and put a big monument and museum right down the center of the line," he said. Yet he remembered Skip at dinner in their room the night before: *Tell you one thing, brother: the GPS on my cell isn't hair-trigger perfect, but it has that damn line a good hundred feet south o' the mark.*

Thank god for Dana and Skip, thought Jay. *After this stuff, you've just got to put on a T-shirt and say, 'Wussup, dog?'*

The sky-blue fingernails of Angela's left hand had risen to her cheek—a philosophic question was coming up. Out of the corner of his eye, Jay saw the cameraman checking his cell phone. He couldn't take it, either.

"Which was the more *surprising* thing that have saw you during your visit in the Quito?" she read.

The huge knots of cable on the utility poles. He said, "I guess the big crowd of people out in the park here. They're striking banana workers, I hear. At night, I can see their campfires from the balcony of my room here—dozens of them."

The cameraman's head jerked up. Standing against the doorframe of the bathroom reading a sports newspaper, the director harrumphed. Angela looked back at him, and he scowled and shook his head.

Uh-oh.

"Ah, can you think of another thing, Mr. Stree'? Something more funner? Is a complicated theme for me—for the public Ecuadoran."

"Ah, sure. Let's see." A glance at the cameraman, a two-beat hesitation so that it was easy to edit in the new answer. "I think the most surprising thing was, ah, how sudden the rain comes. The sky gets really, really dark, and then just a few drops fall, and then—*boom!*—somebody opens the tap, and the rain comes down like it was shot out of fire hoses. I've never seen rain like that before."

The director nodded and went back to his newspaper.

"Oooh!" squealed Angela, and a little puff of makeup burst from her gripped bosom. "Yes! Is truth! The rain, she can to be terrible!"

Jay chuckled. *Next question, Angela. Let's keep this thing moving.*

But Angela would not be hurried, and it was only when the director sawed at his throat 50 minutes later that Angela said something in Spanish into the camera, smiled, and wrapped it up. Jay gladly helped the techies wind up their cables and said good-bye to them all.

"And you can to call to me in any moment that you want," Angela gushed, propping her business card prominently against the lamp on the bedside table.

Two men appeared at the door before he closed it, and it was only with great self-restraint that Jay stifled a groan. The one on the left was a businessman, and Jay immediately understood him. He was thin and pale, with glum, empty eyes. Jay had met dozens at the bank—men who were always pestering him for photos or autographs for their nephews. The other man evaded categories; his smart, green eyes had the simple curiosity of a philosopher, and his body was spare and lean, with just the necessary muscularity, like a mountain climber. He wore a neat, khaki shirt with the pockets stuffed with papers. On his thick wrist rode a battered steel watch.

He spoke, in surprisingly clear English. "My name is Segundo Verdes; my associate is Miguel Simples. Mr. Streets, we have come for asking you a very important favor. Can we have a moment of your time?"

23

Jay Streets thanked the two guards outside his door for the orange juice that was his dinner; he had told them that his stomach was a bit upset. *"A sus ordenes, Señor Streets"*—at his orders, they replied.

He drank it down in one go and turned on the light beside his bed. Then he crossed the room, opened his terrace door, and with a now-practiced lunge, stepped over the barrier that separated his portion of the balcony from the next room's. There he tapped quietly on the glass. Skip opened the door.

"C'mon in, dog," he said. "Coast is clear."

"Hurry, Jay, it's gonna get cold!" called Dana.

"You sound like my mom," said Jay.

"Done with your interviews?" asked Dana. She was laying out silverware on the luggage bench, her long, dark hair tumbling gloriously over her shoulders. Her jeans were low-cut and tight, and her dark-red sweater had a deep V-neck that showed two heavenly scoops, full and close-set, especially now that she was bent over the plates. No shoes, only hotel slippers. She was so beautiful that he was grateful for Skip's presence to keep him on an even keel.

"Oh, babe, you don't know. I'm not done, I'm *well*-done. Cooked. Toasted. Burnt to a damn crisp. I've done enough interviews in the last couple of days to fill a book."

"Saw those two guys standin' guard at your room. Everything set for the negotiations?" Skip asked, handing him a fat, round glass of wine. He wore a light-blue denim shirt tucked into dark-blue chinos, with a cloth belt of different colors. Very sharp.

Jay chuckled and shook his head, amazed. "You were right—I'm the man." He took a sip of wine—lovely: smooth and with a tiny bite at the end. "You nailed it."

"Commerce Special Ops can't afford not to nail it, dog. Didn't I tell you we had a man inside the negotiating room?"

"And one guy was able to tip it? Wow!"

"Damn well better, man: we trained him."

"And paid him," Dana added. Having lit candles, she delicately blew out the match, her lips puckered up red and moist.

Jay took a long sip. "All right, how's this sound? Figuring in that the plantation owners have the same goals as you guys—low wages, that means—"

"Not low wages, just not sky-high wages," Skip corrected him.

"Right. But that means that your inside man who accepted me as mediator must be on the *workers'* committee." He looked at both slyly. "Am I right?"

Skip chuckled, displaying that oddly masculine gap in his strong teeth. "What'd I say, Danes? We gotta get Brother Jay a tryout for Special Ops." He bumped Jay's fist. "Man, could you dig that? You, me and Danes out in Stockholm or Jakarta or some sweet place workin' an op? Would that be like super-mega-cool or what? All expenses paid, homeboy—and doin' good for your country and not sittin' behind some dull desk all day? Fuck that shit, man!"

"You didn't answer my question. Which means I'm right, right?" said Jay.

Skip looked upwards comically. "Uh, um, I think it's time to eat, dog."

"Bastard."

"Come and get it," said Dana. She was tossing a salad. Three big steaks waiting on a long silver platter. "Jay, you sit on the bed beside me. They didn't deliver salad bowls. Guess we'll all have to eat out of the same one, camp-style."

"Oh, man, I'm so starved I'll eat off the floor," Jay said. "Where do you get this excellent grub? The lunch stuff I've had here was like insulation with spicy ketchup."

Skip was pulling the room's armchair up to the other side of the bench: "Probably was. No, man, tonight's feast comes from this Argentine restaurant a couple blocks away that specializes in steak. Got 'em to ship this up here to us. The wine, too. Hadda grease a palm to get it up the elevator, but no prob."

Jay adjusted the utensils around his plate as he waited for Skip to sit down. He was on his best manners; Dana and Skip were a class act. "Do we have another lesson tonight from Doc Jaworski?" he said, referring to the economist, a specialist in Latin America, who by Internet had given Jay a briefing on the Ecuadoran fruit situation the night before.

Skip: "Yeah, but just real short tonight. "He's got the final calculations for the wage. He's just checking the latest prices in the banana market and a few other things. We'll eat first and then get him on the screen."

Dana: "Okay, we ordered a rare, a medium, and a well. What's yours, Jay?"

"Medium—but hey, I'm easy. It's yours if you want it."

"Yours, man," said Skip. "I like 'em burnt."

"Dana? Last call."

"I like raw meat, in whatever form," she said with a flirty grin. "The important thing is that it's hot."

Wow—this is a girl after my own heart! thought Jay.

"Careful what you say, girl," said Skip. "You gonna eat those words."

Dana only smiled and served the steaks delicately onto large, heated plates. From another platter she added spoonfuls of sautéed mushrooms and onions. "Careful—the plates are pretty warm."

"How'd you keep 'em hot?"

Dana: "Old traveler's trick, dog: you run hot water in the bathtub, let the plates sit in it for twenty minutes or so, dry off, and ready to go."

Wow—these people are just ultra cool! thought Jay.

"Michael's gonna kill us when we hand him the bill for this," Dana giggled. "We had to pay extra to do takeout and everything."

Taking back a plate from Dana, Skip puffed out his cheeks: "Yeah, Michael, he's a good ol' guy, but he's a real s.o.b. when it comes to invoices. You get in with us, dog, don't forget. You don't wanna even think about crossing Michael with bad expenses."

"Way o' the world, you know: everybody has bosses," said Jay. "Few months ago, I bought a plane ticket to Memphis—company business—and lost the receipt? Forget it: Accounting Department wouldn't give me the time of day till my Visa bill arrived."

Dana: "We're keeping America supplied with cheap Ecuadoran fruit and keeping Ecuadorans safely employed into the bargain. Michael's getting his money's worth." She poured mushrooms over her steak. "Okay, I guess we're ready."

"Every man for himself!" cried Jay, taking his fork.

"Jussa sec', man," said Skip. "Mind if we say thanks for the Big Guy tonight?"

"No, no, hell. Go for it."

"Just haven't done it for a few days." He bowed his head, as did Dana. Jay quickly put down the fork.

"Lord, we thank you for this fine food and good company, even though we're all a long, long way from home. We thank you for our health and the enjoyment of a fine day. Bless my wife and baby. Amen."

"Amen," said Jay and Dana together.

Skip looked up, his gap-toothed grin as wide as a pumpkin's. "Nothin' like a prayer to open up the appetite, I always say. Now let's get it on!"

Jay ate a piece of steak and moaned. "Oh, man. Oh, baby!"

"Good stuff, huh?" said Skip with a grin.

"Makes me wish I had two stomachs."

Dana and Skip were solid, solid class. They held their wine glasses by the stems, as the fussy little woman Jay had hired for a day's lessons had taught him years earlier. Jay moved over a bit to give Dana more room, but she pulled him back.

"Don't go too far, sailor. I kind of like that big shoulder against mine."

Skip winked at him. "You heard the lady, dog. Hey, where's the smart money on the NBA playoffs? Me, I heard the Lakers are talkin' rings again."

"Forget the Lakers," Jay retorted. "It's the Bucks."

"*The Bucks?* Bucks couldn't beat a fuckin' girls gym class."

"And what's the matter with the fuckin' girls gym class?" Dana demanded.

Skip: "'Cause all you girls run around screamin', 'Ooooh, I'm gonna break my nails on the ball! Don't pass it to me! Oh my gawwwd!'"

"Up yours!" Dana laughed. She put a hand on Jay's shoulder. "Jay would never say a thing like that."

Jay: "Jay would say worse."

Dana: "I swear, just my luck to be all alone in a hotel room in a foreign country with a couple of hunky male chauvinists!" she cried with mock melodrama, swishing back her hair again. Jay loved it.

This is just like TV, I swear!

24 Down in the park, Hondo began pulling Mary gently through the crowd. On the pallet-stage, Sixto Carrasco was dancing around, pulling out the front of his shapeless shirt as if he had enormous breasts.

"Look at me, I am Isabel Montera, the owner of Costa Plantations. I can buy these big tits because the Americans pay me a lot of money for my bananas. And I don't give a nickel to my workers! I am a stoolie of the CIA and a traitor to my country, but I don't care because I have the biggest tits in Ecuador!"

The crowd laughed.

"My plantation slaves made me rich. I bought big, fat tits at the hospital and now I am going to be a top model! I am going to be a sex symbol!"

"Whore!"

"Death to the whore!" shouted someone.

"Death to the whore! Death to the whore!"

Carrasco: "Are we the cowards and fools they think we are?"

"No!"

"Are we better than them?"

"Yes!"

"Is our cause more just?"

"Yes!"

"Are we angels?"

"Yes!"

"Are we gods?"

"Yes!"

"Yes, my friends, we are angels, we are gods, we are better than God because we will triumph and lift the universe!"

"Six-to presidente, Six-to presidente, Six-to presidente."

"My god, who the hell does he think he is?" said Mary.

Hondo only tugged her down and to the right and into his tent. He sat Mary on a cot and turned on a penlight.

"Sixto is the Ecuadoran equal to one of your—what was the term? Your 'religious thumpers.'"

"Bible thumpers."

"That's it. He sounds crazy, although he knows exactly what he does." Hondo lit a match, twisted the knob of a bottle of camping gas, and a flame leapt up. He turned out the penlight.

"I wonder what would those people say if they knew the truth of poor Isabel Costa?" he said, pulling out cups and a water jug from unknown places. "She was the lead singer of a pop group in Argentina, and it just was starting to gain fans last year."

"Really?"

"Yes, the Marrupios, they were called—they made a fusion of salsa and Latin swing. She'd got that her father bankrolled the group, and after two years one of their albums started to sell well. That was her dream. She has a degree in Music from Ohio State University, by the way, and is an excellent pianist. But then Señor Costa was diagnosed with Alzheimer's, and that was the end of the Marrupios for Isabel. Someone had to run the business. Her mother knows nothing except how spend money on clothes. Her sister is equal—a useless figure of society; and her older brother is a cocaine addict who disappeared into Orlando, Florida, three years ago."

"Lovely family."

"A typical story of our rich class. They do not have the character to handle great money or great power. Take." He put out a package of sugar cookies. "So she had to take over Plantaciones Costa. She has put it on sale."

"What about the top managers? Can't they run the business?"

"In Ecuador, Mary, we trust only our families. Miguel Simples is honest, but basically only is a financial manager and doesn't understand the international fruit market. Marmalejo is in charge of operations and is tremendously corrupt. He takes a—what is the term?— a *ripoff*? No, a *rakeoff*. He takes a *rakeoff* from the Social Security payments he must to make for workers: just a tiny percentage each, but it sums to about fifty thousand dollars a year."

Mary felt the cot under her fingers: the cloth was damp just from the wet air. "You have good information."

"The Spaniards have been very good. We couldn't have done it without them." He sat down on a folding chair in front of her and pulled her forward, his hands sliding under her broad breasts. "I can't be with you two minutes without wanting to make love with you."

"Me neither."

"It's too bad all these people are around."

"But you'll come tonight, won't you?"

"Yes. God, yes, I will come tonight. And soon I will come every night."

They sat kissing till the water began to boil on the ring. With a sigh, Hondo stepped away. From a dark corner he pulled out a woolen poncho and started to put it on. "I'm sorry. Are you cold with only that jacket on? Would you like to wear this?"

"I'm fine, thanks."

"Good," he said with a shiver, putting it on. "I'm freezing. I never could stand the cold nights up in the mountains. I was very happy living in L.A."

"I'll have to include that in my report to Harry Kruger about you. He asked me to find you here and 'get close to you.' I can't put him off any longer."

Hondo uttered his tiny harrumph-laugh. "He must be worried. I can imagine that he is receiving a terrible pressure from the—what was that expression?—the 'big cheeses' in CIA headquarters."

Outside, Carrasco's harangue swelled and crashed steadily like a heavy surf on a beach. Hondo poured out the tea.

"Sixto will officially inform to Mr. Streets about the wage we are asking for—that is my agreement with him. He will do it in the manner most offensive possible, I would imagine, in order to get that Streets dismisses it completely." A look-out's glance out the tent. "He is my real enemy, you know—not the plantation owners. With them I can come to an agreement, one way or another. With Sixto, no. And at the end, either I will destroy him or he will destroy me."

Mary sipped her tea; it was hot, though strong and bitter, sugarless. Outside, the crowd chanted: *"Six-to presidente, Six-to presidente, Six-to presidente."*

"Do you think they'll elect him president?"

"I'm quite sure of it." A private laugh. "He has important backing. Did you know that his family disowned him? Years ago when he attacked to his mother and threw her down a stairway."

"My god! He did that?"

"His mother spent the rest of her life in a wheelchair, till she died, ah, four or five years ago it would be." A pause, another glance outside the tent, though two of his men were on guard there. "He frightens me. As I said, we are fighting to the death, he and I."

"Are you going to win the fight?" she asked quietly.

"I think so. First we need the wage agreement. Then I make my move—I plan to expose him as a traitor to the Council of Elders at the meeting when they confirm the new wage."

Mary sipped more tea—it slipped down like a warming hand in the clammy Andean night. "These Elders—are they good for anything?"

Hondo thought. "Well, in a sense. They are a band of old leftist, ah—yes!—old leftist *fuddy-duddies* which control the unions. Basically, they name the one who represents the workers on plantations—or change the representative if that person is corrupt, which is more common. They put the stamp of approval on whatever the negotiations produce. They're necessary. My men and I can't be in everywhere, so the workers on each individual plantation will have to insist in the new wages to the owner, and they won't do it without the Elders' approval. They think the Elders are the modern equivalent of Incan mystics or something. I wish we could—"

He stopped, listening. After a long moment, Mary heard it. A three-note whistle. Verdes put down his tea, snatched Mary's from her hand, and made the same whistle. "Come, Mary. Right now." He grabbed one or two objects and pulled her out of the tent by the elbow.

"What happened?"

"Sixto's heavy men, probably. They have entered the park to stir up trouble. Probably they will come for me. The government and your Mr. Kruger will not touch me during the negotiations, at least, but Sixto is not so discreet."

And in a blink they had slipped through the camp and stood on the street, where a car waited for them. They got in, and Hondo gave the driver an address a block from Mary's house.

"It will be safer in your house tonight," he said, laying a hand in hers. "Safer and better."

But he looked back through the rear window three times on the way, looked back for a good ten seconds each time, and Mary knew he was frightened.

25

Dinner was over and Skip was setting the dirty dishes in a metal container to take back to the restaurant. Dana had laid her arm over Jay's back and was smoothing his hair as Doctor Ted Jaworski came on the screen of her laptop. He was fortyish and baggy-eyed and ham-faced, and wore a wrinkled white business shirt. Grease could not tame his black hair, which had been combed back some time in the last month, and now stood up in spikes as if the result of a blast of wind. His collar and tie were open, for which his thick neck must have been grateful. He was harried and overworked and groaningly jolly.

"How was your daughter's game?" Jay asked. The previous night, Doctor Ted had said that he was missing his daughter's volleyball game.

"Great, thank you, Jay. Creamed 'em. I guess Becky served an ace, too. You shoulda been there." He was looking down at a quagmire of papers on his desk, shifting them and looking at them as if for a last statistic. Behind him, in profile, a middle-aged woman had a phone cocked under her chin as she tapped on an electronic agenda and looked at a computer screen. "Which is why we're gonna keep it short tonight, kids. I'm going home and catch the game on video. Becky got a copy."

"Oh—they recorded it, like for training purposes," said Jay.

"Right." A huff. "Okay, Mr. Streets, here we go: the buzz on the skinny on the low-down on the inside story—and you can quote me on that. Been here all night and all day tearin' apart spreadsheets, wonkin' figures and squeezin' a few tightasses for the latest price info."

Jay: "On behalf of the general public: thanks, Doc."

Dana massaged his neck with a hand.

"My pleasure. And hey, speakin' o' squeezes: Dana, let Jay alone long enough for him to concentrate on my words of wisdom, huh?"

"But he's so huggable!" Dana said, throwing her arms around his shoulders and kissing his cheek.

"Don't worry, Doc," said Jay, putting his arm around her back. "I've had to concentrate in worse conditions that this. Try catching a thirty-five-yard bullet on third-and-eight in the middle of a snowstorm." Dana wriggled a bit till his hand was resting against the base of her far-side breast.

Jaworski's eyes were wide. "Wow. Catch it?"

"Damn right. Against Washington in my next-to-last season. Broke the game open."

"Not bad," Jaworski said admiringly, and Jay felt Dana wriggle again. "Okay, Jay, I know you got a lot on your mind these days, so to simplify about two million stats, I'm just gonna plunk you down on ballpark numbers. After that, call it like you see it: ratchet up or down a buck or two dependin' on what they present to you tomorrow. You're a big boy, you know what EBITDA stands for. Anybody tries to pull the wool over your eyes, you're gonna to know it."

"I hope so, anyway," Jay said modestly.

"Now. Present minimum wage is 273 bucks a month, which if you figure 20 days of work a month—four weeks, five days—comes out to 13.65 bucks per day."

"That's less than two bucks an hour for an eight-hour day—ouch," Jay said.

"Well, don't forget nobody has to heat a house there in January—like I do. Now of course, the plantation owners will piss and moan over every nickel you raise it, but bottom line is they don't really start to feel the pinch and pass on added costs to American consumers till you're nearly at sixteen. At sixteen, they start to sweat." With a hopeless air, he stirred some papers on the desk. "I got a graph somewhere here, but people tell me the printouts don't show up too well on the screen."

"We're doing fine here, Doc," Jay replied helpfully.

"Now I don't want to be too exact about this, Jay. End o' the day, it's your call. You're the one on the ground, you're lookin' at faces and I'm lookin' at numbers. You could take a leap o' faith to seventeen, *maybe* eighteen bucks per diem—*maybe*—but that's pretty much the limit. Remember this is gonna raise the banana bill for the American family, and that's when the secretary o' commerce starts to hem and haw in front o' congressional committees, at which point I get fired, and Dana and Skip and Michael have to grow up and get real jobs."

"Ha-ha. As if we don't work 60-hour weeks for the taxpayer already," Dana said.

"Don't listen to her, Doc," said Jay. "You listen to these guys for a couple of days, and you'd think they were trying to raise the flag on Iwojima."

"You shit!" yelped Dana, slapping his shoulder.

"Give him one for me too, Danes," called Skip, who had put on his jacket.

Dana slapped Jay again.

Doctor Ted shrugged reasonably. "Now, thing is, you don't want to stick it too hard to either side here. The middlemen, those guys are gonna take their pound of flesh either way, so...."

"They always do," Jay replied ruefully. "So sixteen normal and eighteen tops." He shrugged. "Still doesn't sound like much. You're sure that much gives everybody a decent living, right? I'm talking feed the family, pay the mortgage, school books for the buckaroos? A few dollars to throw in a Dyno pension fund? I've spent the last couple of days plugging our pension funds, so I'd damn well better justify the extra time on this thing."

"Yeah, yeah, yeah—no problem to all that. Of course, the union people are gonna feed you all manner of ketchup crud, but yeah, long as people keep the family down to less than twenty-five kids— which I grant you is questionable—they should come out with a 27.5 percent discretional slice, which will do for a movie and a burger with the kids on Saturday night. Remember what I told you in my brilliant presentation yesterday: a family of five there can eat on six bucks a day, five if they stretch it. The union side is gonna load in the horse manure on that point, but don't buy. I got facts and figs that would support the Washington Monument." He picked up a load of paper and let it slump to the desk.From across the room, Skip put the box on a rolling cart and pushed it to the door. "I'm gonna get this stuff back to the restaurant," he called in a whisper. "See you tomorrow, dog. Good luck."

Jay and Dana waved good-bye.

"Now if there are any important fluctuations in wholesale banana prices over the next twenty-four hours or so, I'll let you know through Dana and Skip. And the Ecuadoran Finance Ministry is due to release quarterly inflation figs tomorrow, but I'm not expectin' any surprises." He looked down at his papers. "And that should do it."

"Great. Thanks, Doc."

"And Jay, do me a favor, huh? Remember that I'm not a politician, I'm your Uncle Ted. 'Cause if I've seen this kind of thing once, I've seen it a dozen times. The union guys put up a big multimedia bullshit presentation full of undernourished little girls and workers with dirty faces, and they're gonna tell you they can't get by on less than fifty a day. Ketchup crud, whole deal. You listen, you nod politely, make a sad face when you need to, and keep your counsel. And when it comes time to cut the pie…."

"I got it, Doc: sixteen to eighteen."

"Hell, those are the numbers everybody's figurin' on, anyway, and if they're not it's because nobody's told 'em God is a statistician, too."

"Zero tolerance on the ketchup crud, Doc—you got it," said Jay, and was pleased to feel Dana giggle silently beside him.

"All right, I got to get on with a Japanese tuna-shippin' question for Michael before I head for home, so I'm gonna…Hey, that reminds me: you don't know any Japanese translators with a specialty in finance, do you? Any there at DynoBank?"

"All the translation gets outsourced there. But call up, um…that would be Aaron Franken in Dyno's HR. He handles all the OS contracting—good egg. Tell him I gave you his name and he'll put you on the track."

Doc riffled some papers and grabbed a pen. "Aaron Franken in Dyno HR. Hey, thanks for the tip. I'll do that." He scribbled the name on a page. "Okay, well, good luck tomorrow. And Dana, tell that cad to behave like a gentleman. You're on a mission, for God's sake."

"Can't, Doc. Have you seen the body this guy has?" she sighed. "Bye."

She leaned forward and tapped a few keys; the screen went black. She lowered the top till it clicked home. "And that's that," she said quietly.

"Damn right that's that," Jay said, pulling her to him. She spread herself over him, hair falling forward and enveloping them in their own cavern of lust. Her hands swarmed under his shirt and up the hard curves of his abdomen. She was as hungry for it as he was.

"God, you're *perfect!*" she gasped.

"Skip isn't coming back here, is he?" Jay asked as she jerked his shirt off over his head.

"Skip's room is three doors down. I told him to eat his steak and get lost."

Hell, TV was never this good, thought Jay.

26 Just in case the guards checked, Jay spent the night in his own room. But in the morning, he climbed over the terrace barrier to have another round with Dana, who opened the terrace door to him naked, grinning and sleepily sexy.

He returned to his room just in time to hear the two guards at the door knock and ask him if his stomach felt better and what he wanted for breakfast. He told them, then showered and dressed and ate the toast and coffee and cereal in his room. New guards, El Zurdo and Estéban Miguel, followed him to the elevator and down to the lobby.

He still had a few minutes before the presentations started in the hotel's meeting room at nine o'clock—Skip winked at him from the entrance to the restaurant—so he wandered over to the gift shop and shuffled around among the ceramic tucans, posters of Cotopaxi Mountain, souvenir refrigerator magnets, bottles of aguardiente, Indian tapestries, and little bronze replicas of the Middle of the World Monument. Dana came in and stood looking over a table of coconut face-masks; Jay sidled up to her, though facing the other way, and examined postcards.

"All set to go, slugger?" she murmured, not turning her head.

"Are you kidding? I could take on five linebackers bare-handed right now."

Dana giggled. "I know what you mean. God, it's going to be a long day without you."

Jay shifted around so that the postcard rack blocked the view of the guards, who stood at the door. They were looking at something on the screen of a cell phone. "Yeah, you bet. I just hope the presentations don't drag on too long. I guess the owners present in the morning and the workers after lunch."

"Well, just remember what Doc said: No—"

"No ketchup crud," Jay interrupted. "None—promise. The number is sixteen, a little more if I'm in a good mood." Jay took out a couple of postcards.

"Twice last night and once this morning," said Dana, examining a set of dishware with the Middle of the World motif. "I swear, I have never wrapped myself around a body like that in my life! How did you ever get that way?"

"Lots of pumping iron and careful with the diet, babe—all it takes. And we're not through yet—remember that."

Dana smiled. "I sure hope not."

She was wearing a deep-cut white leotard that showed off those perfect breasts: wide as her torso and close-set. Jay felt his stomach tighten as he looked at them. He had rarely seen a pair that perfect even in Playboy. And she had been great in bed—almost too great. She gave and gave and gave; it was almost weird. In three go-rounds with her, he felt he hardly knew her as a lover. What did she like? How did she like it? He still didn't know. *But I'm gonna find out,* he told himself.

The other guard looked back again, saw him, and signaled: it was time to go. Jay nodded. The guard turned away.

"Okay, babe. Gotta run. How about a kiss for good luck?" He leaned towards her, but she jerked back.

"No, too risky."

"C'mon, Tweedledee and Tweedledum are looking the other way."

"Forget it—jobs have been blown for less. Someone might—"

"There's nobody else in the shop. C'mon." Jay turned squarely to her and leaned forward.

Dana jerked away. "No! Dammit, we're on a mission!" She scooted away towards a table of alpaca scarves.

Jay watched her, shocked. Who the hell was this?

He looked towards the guards, but they had seen nothing; neither had the employee behind the cash register, a teenage girl in a hotel uniform sitting on a small step-ladder, writing industriously in a book.

Turning on heel, Jay grabbed a refrigerator magnet—a Galapagos tortoise—and went to buy it. The girl was working on an English-as-a-second-language exercise book. "The Use of Still and Yet" was the title of the lesson.

As he paid for the magnet, Dana came up behind him and spoke very quietly into his ear: "Look, I'm sorry to be so business-like, but this is the key moment. Really, I'll see you tonight."

Jay took the little envelope, thanked the girl, and left. Walking off with his guards, he glanced through the shop window at her, and she winked, but it was a wink with a purpose—to keep him sweet—and Jay resented it, though he winked back.

First time since my sophomore year in college that a girl's refused me a kiss, he thought angrily.

27 "Moving on then. Next up on the agenda," George Kaufman went on, tilting his head back to look at his specs, "though nothing's written in stone in case he or she has anything he or she'd like to insert in on an ad-hoc basis."

"Or any other basis," Paul Klippen added, pouring himself another coffee.

Walt Boam giggled and started to work on his third powder donut of the meeting. Already white powder speckled his dark-brown face.

"Mary—what about Verdes?" Harry Kruger snapped. As usual, he sat slumped back wearing a rumpled polo shirt. Paul wondered if he had more than one suit. "You've got to do something around here to earn your keep instead of hosting TV shows. You get in bed with him yet?"

"Twice already."

"Wow!" giggled Walt Boam. "That was fast."

"Yeah?" said Harry, thick lips pulling back in an ugly grin. "What's his thing like?" He pointed at his groin.

Kaufman harrumphed. "Harry, we're all adults here and this is, of course, all in good fun. But Foreign Service professionals are not required to—"

"It's okay, George," Mary said. "Think donkeys, Harry. Elephants." Harry and Paul laughed; Walt managed a giggle.

Mary now fluffed her hair again and said, "Well, I really didn't have time to prepare anything this morning. I didn't even have time to get through drying my hair."

"So I've seen: a wet-hair day on top of it all," Paul said.

"Yeah, I got in late after the morning ride. I got a flat coming up from the Middle of the World." A breath. "Well, what can I tell you? He's a really incredible man."

Paul put a warning foot on Mary's: *Don't go over the top.*

"I heard he speaks English," said Harry.

"That's right—just about perfectly. He studied, if you can believe it, at Brigham Young University, on a student visa. He was sponsored—"

"Impossible," said Harry. "If he'd've taken a visa, he'd be in the records."

"He used his other second name, his mother's: Valenzuela. He was just a poor kid from the slums of Guasmo—outside of Guayaquil?"

"Ecuador's real third-largest city," Paul observed drily. "Now was that a career move, the Mormons, or a religious one?"

"Oh, a career move, to be sure. He couldn't stand them. But he let them redeem his soul, and pretty soon he was a standard fixture at one of their Mormon mission churches down in Guayaquil. Eventually he got to live in the church. They gave him room and board in exchange for being janitor. And he exchanged English and Spanish classes with the American boys down here doing their year of missionary work. You've seen them around here—college guys in white shirts and black ties."

"I've come across those guys down in remote Amazon villages," Walt said around his donut. "Gotta give 'em all the credit in the world, even if they're not your cup of tea: they're everywhere, just super-organized."

"Well, his English was so good, and he was always getting them to give him textbooks and everything—he devoured everything they had. And when he was twenty, some Mormons sponsored him to go to BYU. They made a huge fuss over him, sounded like. Got their senator involved, got BYU to overlook his lack of official accreditation—'cause he's self-taught? They let him in on the strength of a single SAT exam."

"He passed an SAT? Holy cow! That's real Abe Lincoln stuff!" cried George Kaufman.

Paul sipped his coffee and eyed Harry Kruger. With one hand he fingered the cut on his neck—the bandage was off but the tight stitches still gripped a pudgy line of pink flesh—and all the time he was weighing and remembering every word, listening even with his skin.

Mary was laughing. "But once he got Stateside, guess what? He spent about three days on BYU campus, said it wasn't for him after all, thanked everyone for their help, gave back the scholarship down to the last penny, and took off!"

"No!" Walt Boam gasped.

"My goodness, an honest man," Paul said. "Someone call Diogenes."

"Honest shmonest!" Kruger snapped. "He knew that the heat would be on if he kept the money. This way, no one put out an arrest warrant for him."

"No, he's just honest," Mary said.

Harry grunted. "It's easy to see who the junior dip is here, huh? All Immigration would ever have done was put out the standard bulletin on him; nobody would really have looked."

"Thank you, Agent Kruger for that timely commentary," said Paul. "Go on, Mary."

"Anyway," Mary went on, "he took a bus to Los Angeles and got a job cooking in a restaurant. And he lived in Watts and went to school right there in the neighborhood—at U.C.L.A. He stayed there for about ten years, just auditing classes. Then he came back here and started the union movement."

"So: very much the self-made man," Paul said. "Interesting."

"Self-made with the help of Spanish intelligence," Harry griped.

"Self-made or hand-made who cares?" Walt Boam groused around his donut. "Mary, it didn't occur to you to slip a little cyanide in his whatever-he-drinks, did it? Hell, I got growers down in Machala crying to me on the phone all day. This guy's gonna tear up structures and establishments that go back to time immemorial! The man has to be stopped, and I mean whatever way you—"

"What about Jay Streets?" Harry demanded. "How the hell does Verdes figure him? What does he expect of the guy?"

"Just impartiality, that's all. He says that anybody with an open mind will give them a decent price—maybe twenty-two."

Walt gripped his belly and moaned as if a donut had poisoned him. "Twenty-two! We're dead. Dead!"

"He has all planned out what he's going to say when it's his turn to give Streets the presentation. And he's really convincing—calm as a rock. I swear, he could sit down with a serial killer and turn him into a monk!"

Walt: "Lord help us!"

Paul said nothing, but watched Harry Kruger. He sat still, perfectly immobile, one hand on the table. Now, like a cobra sensing danger, a finger rose and arched back, and then settled again. When Kaufman moved on to the next point of the agenda, Harry jerked his phone out of his pocket, pretended he had a call, lumbered out, and did not return.

Paul knew that was a bad sign.

28

Jay Streets sat listening to the translation in his earjack. The first speaker was one of the men that had asked him to arbitrate, Miguel Simples, whose English apparently wasn't up to the task. He mainly showed a series of statistical graphs, stretching his meager body to point here and there on a computer screen big enough to be read across a baseball stadium.

The negotiating tables now formed a little rectangle: two long, false-maple tables, each with three black swivel chairs, were set up facing each other some ten feet apart. One chair was vacant on each side; Sixto Carrasco and Isabel Costa had passed up the morning presentations by the plantation owners.

Between the tables Jay sat at a smaller table, occasionally making a note on a pad of paper. The fourth side of the rectangle was formed by a speaker's lectern and the huge computer screen beside it. Bottles of water and pineapple juice and soft-drink huddled on each table as if in conference themselves, and Jay had already drunk an energy drink to keep himself alert: Simples was not exactly a stand-up comedian.

He squeaked along—voice as boyish as his body—with the nasal earnestness of a man who thought that all the world's ills could be righted if people would just be reasonable. If only people would put in an honest eight hours of work, if only they would spend their money carefully, have fewer children, settle for what they have, save their money for a better future…"Only is necessary *this*, Mr. Streets!" Simples kept insisting, which was all he said in English.

Only is necessary that this guy gives it up and takes a seat, Jay thought. He remembered Dana piling up her hair on her head as she undulated above him, her luscious breasts swinging from side to side.

"You don't mind if they're not a hundred percent natural?" she asked once, stopping for breath.

To which Jay buried his face in them again and said, "I can get used to it."

The interpreter cut into his thoughts. "Oh dear, we're gettin' into the speechy stuff now. Can't be helped in this country, you know." She was a shriveled Scotswoman who sat on a small metal chair some fifty feet away by the taupe-colored wall, a sleeveless green sweater on her lap, knitting needles churning like pistons as she spoke into a headset microphone.

Simples began pushing his palms downward, like a teacher trying to quiet her kids.

"It is only with the utmost effort in our labor, the most exacting and unstinting methods of cultivation, and the most meticulous, unrelenting twenty-four-hour care in calculation, that we are able to make any profit at all," he wailed. "We care for our workers as if they were our own sons, our own flesh and blood. Our shared passion in creating this product, the pride and symbol of the Ecuadoran nation, is the basis of a relationship that, with only a few tasteless incidents that one could cite as examples, unites us as men, as Ecuadorans, and as Americans of the New World, proud of the land we have mastered and bent to our needs, whims, and desires." Simples made a small bow and sat down.

"Muh goodness, the laddy does have a mouth on him when he fancies it, doesn't he?" added the interpreter. "Still, I've heard much worse. Worked a foreign policy meetin' last month, you know—Brits and Yanks. Ecuadorans spend half their time talkin' that bloody rot."

Segundo Verdes, the other guy that had come to ask Jay to arbitrate, caught his eye and raised an eyebrow in apology. Verdes, at least, was cool.

29 *He could sit down with a serial killer and turn him into a monk!*

Harry Kruger parked in the lot of an Italian restaurant, closed at that hour of the morning, and walked quickly to Mary's house. It was 9:45, and the woman who ran the hairdresser's downstairs from her apartment was a vain Argentine of 50 who did her hour of Pilates every morning at nine-thirty before opening her shop. He knew this from his brief affair with Mary.

Like all private houses among the upper class in Ecuador, it had a ten-foot-high wall topped with glass shards. Harry peeked between the black sheet-iron gate and its frame: the car was gone from the small front patio. His lock picks scratched and fluttered; he was in. He closed the door behind him; now he had some privacy.

"Wet hair," muttered Kruger, looking around the front patio and rubbing his hands. "Wet hair and flat tire. How come I hear my little bitch bell ringing?"

The small patio was just large enough to hold the car when it was parked there, the brick walls on either side lined with thick ivy that grew out of ceramic pots. Harry crossed in six strides and stooped to the front door with his picks—but stopped before inserting them. Beside the door was a little brick garden shed, and he remembered Mary saying that she kept her bike there. Its chintsy lock was the work of a moment. He stopped, though, because voices sounded on the other side of the patio's side wall. A mother and a whimpering child were coming out; the dentist was saying good-bye.

When they had gone, Kruger swung back the shed door. There stood Mary's bicycle, a red-framed Peugeot. He touched—caressed longingly—the seat, and found it cold. Then he took out the plastic water bottle and took a short drink of water. He spat it out: the water was brackish, plastic-tasting, easily days old.

Mary hadn't taken out her bicycle that morning, that was for sure.

The front door had a sophisticated lock that gave Harry a full minute of work, but he was soon upstairs and in Mary's studio apartment.

It wasn't at all as he'd remembered it from the one night he had spent there. The bedroom was actually bigger than the living room, though each was decorated in the earth colors he remembered. The down-feather bedspread, done in rust-orange and light green, was smooth, with a half-dozen pillows fluffed and in place. Above them hung a series of watercolors of Ecuadoran mountain ranges. A colorful Indian tapestry hung on the other wall. Looking around, he found between the bed and the wall a shin-high wastebasket, half-full of wadded-up tissues. Carefully, he began picking the top ones off.

They were wet. Soaked.

Harry stood up, amazed.

He went down further, and discovered that the ones below were drier, but not much. Harry's face darkened: it had been quite a night.

"So who the fuck is getting in where *I* can't?" he snapped, dropping the Kleenex back in.

He crossed the studio to the living-room area, touched the TV: cold. He glanced over the half-dozen bookshelves screwed into the wall, surveyed the little pinewood desk, touched the chair—cold— the laptop—cold—glanced over the bills and letters standing up between two polished-onyx bookends: bank statements, a letter from her brother in Oregon dated a month earlier, a postcard from Quevedo, Ecuador, with only a drawing of a winking stickman leaning on a cane, legs crossed, postmarked two weeks earlier.

He worked quickly around the room now, looking under cushions, checking through the dishes of the tiny kitchen—everything washed, dried and put away—picking through the clothes in her closet, and lovingly running his hands over her underwear.

Under which he found a stack of postcards.

There were eleven of them—some with stickman drawings, some with a single cryptic phrase: "Lights of Quito in the sky!" "It's you!" "Silent, lonely nights."

With a gasp, he whirled. He stared across the apartment at the little onyx-carved bookends and the letters between them—and the postcard.

Quevedo. Two weeks earlier. That had been the meeting point for the strikers to take buses up to Quito.

"What the fuck is going on here?" he snarled, running through the postcards again.

He noted the postmarks. Every four or five days, sometimes a week. And they coincided with Verdes's movements. Harry knew them by heart: his team had been trying to anticipate Verdes's next appearance for months, and never been able to.

Finally he reached the one dated furthest back in time. It coincided roughly with Mary giving him the cold shoulder after their night in bed.

He's a really incredible man, she'd said. And now that Harry thought about it, there was indeed a hint of gossamer in her eyes when she'd said it.

Harry Kruger stood frozen. A memory popped into his mind. After a high-school basketball game, he had been trying to make out with a cheerleader—"I just wanted to talk to you for a sec'"—under the bleachers of the gym, now completely empty, when suddenly a janitor appeared, turned off the lights, and left. The girl saw her chance and sprinted across the gym floor towards the red EXIT sign over the door. It opened and shut in a slow wink. Harry lumbered after her in the pitch dark. It was January, and the wind wailed, and something metallic was banging and banging back and forth on the roof like a failing heartbeat. It was a long walk across that dark gym, almost as if it were another country.

Harry shook himself. His professional instincts now came to the fore, and he slid the postcards back into place exactly, checked the room for traces of himself, checked the wastebasket again and noted the fact that among the Kleenex there were no condoms—though she'd made Harry wear one. A minute later he was re-locking the front gate.

He strode away, face stony. And once he'd turned the corner, to his amazement, he began to cry. It was embarrassing, but he couldn't stop. He had no handkerchief or Kleenex, so he had to keep wiping them away on the cuffs of his gray windbreaker.

It wasn't so much that she had not wanted to continue the relationship; he had been through that with women often enough, and besides, the initial conquest was what really gave him the buzz. No, it was that she had dumped him for another man—considered Harry inferior material.

"Well, guess what, bitch? When his fucking little strike fails and he dies, *you're* going to be there to watch," he sobbed. "Dump me for that motherfucker! Dump *me* for that, that motherfucker!" Harry wished he could find a harsher word, but none occurred to him. "And as for the bitch, that bitch I swear to Christ I'm going to nail her one more time—right up the ass. I'm gonna get that big butt up in the air, and I'm gonna do her straight up the ass! Even if I have to get two guys to hold her down for me."

He passed a couple of elderly women, who giggled at him.

"THE FUCK ARE YOU LOOKING AT?" he roared at them, and they shrieked and hurried off.

He fumbled out his cell phone and punched some buttons. "Al. How goes it? You guys in the air yet?"

"Choppers just starting to turn the blades, Harry," said Al Smick with his Carolinian accent. "Gonna be a piss of a long ride up there from the Colombian jungle, that's all I can say. Hey, they tell me they closed the base in Ecuador—years ago now. Hell's zat all about?"

"The last president—leftist piece of shit."

"I'll bring a bullet for him too. Ain't gonna be there, is he?"

"No, unfortunately. You just concentrate on taking out Verdes. You got your scope and everything, right?"

"Scope, piece, table and stool. All packed up and ready to go."

"How many bullets you bringing? More than one, right?"

"A dozen's standard practice for a long-range take-out. Hey, you gonna be on site?"

"If I can make it tomorrow morning, yeah. Depends."

"All right. Hey, you okay? Sounds like you got a cold."

"Sore throat." Harry snapped his phone shut and walked on.

30

The break was over. As Jay sat down in his chair, a chunky young man bounded to the lectern. "Okay, my turn now!" His fat—globular cheeks, chunky breasts, beer-barrel thighs—all jerked in unison. "Hey, Jay!" he cried, waving a hand widely. He might have been inviting Jay to come outside and play kick-the-can. "Hey, thanks for comin' in and helping us all out with this strike junk. We really appreciate it. And God—a former NFL player. This is really an honor!"

"Happy to help," said Jay expansively.

"Cool!" The man hooked a pair of tiny glasses behind his ears, or at least they looked tiny on the expanse of his pumpkin-like head. Loose bangs flapped over his forehead.

"Okay. Let's see. First: I'm Abelardo Marmalejo. But you can like call me Abe. That's what everybody called me when I like went to high school in Champagne, Illinois. I wasn't an exchange student, though. My family actually lived there. My dad was working as a chemical engineer there. I'm like totally Ecuadoran, though." He punched the air with a fist. "Go Bulls, like, huh?"

"Knicks fan myself, Abe—no offense."

"Hey, no problemo. Hey, you know what my nickname there was?" he giggled.

"What was that, Abes?"

"'Lardo'—you know, from Abelardo?"

"Because you're so skinny, right?"

"Right—that's right!" Marmalejo chuckled, his belly and shoulders bouncing around him as if he had brought his own private audience for his jokes. "Hey, but like don't call me that, okay?"

Jay noticed that Verdes's eyebrows tilted sharply.

"Wouldn't dream of it, Abes. Mine in high school was Straps—for jock strap?"

"No! You're fucking kidding me! *Straps?"* cried Abe.

"Right hand to God, buddy." A smile. "But don't call me that."

"Unbelievable, like. Wow." Abe took off his glasses, wiped his eyes, and put them back on. "All right, anyway, so-o-o-o, okay, what I'm going to do here today, Jay, is I'm gonna like give you an idea of the production side. That's my job at Costa. I mean, Miguel gave you an idea of the P and L stats. Me, I want you to see exactly what's involved for us growers when you raise the price we pay to our people. 'Cause bananas, man, only thing that's more labor-intense than the farming of—"

"Labor-intensive, you mean."

"Yeah—intensive. Thanks. Hey, if I make any big mistakes in English or anything, correct me, okay?"

"Will do."

"Like I was sayin', the only thing that's more labor-*intensive* is maybe like a Chinese rickshaw!" And again he and his blubber wobbled with laughter; out of politeness, Jay tossed up a chuckle.

"Okay! Now I'm going to tell you the story of how a banana gets to your plate."

"Sounds interesting."

Marmalejo connected a small computer to the screen and touched a button; the immense screen beside him blinked on. "Okay, I'm gonna try not to get too technical and all, but you got a college degree, right, Jay? I mean, that's what they told me."

"Damn right—worked like an s.o.b. for it too."

"Great. And you know something about economics and all that yucky stuff, right?"

"Well, I do work in a bank, Abe. It's macro and micro around the water-cooler all day, to be honest." Jay had the sense of Verdes's eyes on him.

"Okay, here we go!" He might have been on a roller coaster clacking up the first hill. "Now: what I'm gonna tell you, this, this, I swear, is the honest story, Jay." His chubby fingers lined up in a pharisaical little wall of warning. "Me, I'm in operations. Mainly, I study like stats and procedures and stuff like how to raise productivity. Then I make recommendations to the board of Costa. They decide. I'm not a politician. Heck, I hate politics!"

Jay remembered that Doctor Ted had said the exact same thing. *I don't know if I liked that guy very much,* he thought suddenly.

An image appeared on the screen: on the left a green banana sapling, on the right a grown banana tree with a blue plastic bag—like a trash liner—over a full vine of bananas. "Do you know, Jay, do you have any idea," he said with sudden solemnity, "I mean, do you have like *any fucking idea* how much labor is involved in putting a banana in your hand?"

"Gotta be honest with you, Abes: not much."

"Well, lemme tell you"—a pained expression as if someone had just stepped on his feet—"it's *unbelievable!* It takes years for trees to make any real money. And all that time you gotta treat 'em better 'n you treat your own mother, lemme tell ya. Lots of trees, they don't grow fruit good enough for the American consumer—in fact, most don't. Soon as the farmer sees he has a top-notch vine goin', he covers it with a special plastic bag to keep out the bugs and the parakeets. But the—"

"Parakeets?" blurted Jay.

Marmalejo looked at Verdes. *"Loros*—parakeets, right?"

Verdes: "You're right, Mr. Marmalejo—parakeets."

"Right—they'll come and eat up all your bananas if you aren't careful."

"So that's where parakeets come from—didn't know that," said Jay.

Marmalejo: "Yeah—okay, like I was saying, the crummy bananas, they're for domestic consumption." He threw his arms up, pulling up his suit jacket. "What do you think about that? Ecuador, the world's leader in bananas, and we don't even eat the best ones!"

"And we're grateful, Abes. I hope we're sendin' you guys a good load of bucks for it, too."

"Yeah, you better!" Marmalejo laughed. "Okay, so lemme explain exactly what I'm talkin' about."

With pictures flashing on the screen, as though it were an educational documentary for fifth-graders, Marmalejo explained that the banana vines had to be cared for with fungicides and pesticides. On big farms, the trees were also fumigated by air. Finally, the still-green banana vines were cut, loaded onto carts or hung on a moving cable, and taken to huge washing bins where the chemicals were washed off. Lastly, the vines were hung out to dry.

"It's only women that do that part," Abe added, as if it were all that women could be trusted to do. "And they're supposed to be like really super careful, 'cause the Cavendish banana variety bruises like if you just touch it. You wouldn't believe how many good bananas we lose that way."

The boxes were shipped to a central loading point before being shipped to the port and loaded into huge refrigerated containers. These were then stacked up on the deck of the ship and connected to the ship's electrical grid. The temperature had to be maintained perfectly constant. If the temperature rose, the bananas would arrive yellow and have to be dumped at sea. In fact, such is the hurry to get them to the supermarket before they ripen that the containers go directly off the ships and onto delivery trucks.

"See that?" Abelardo said a half-hour later, pointing at the last slide. "That's a real picture. The ship pulls into the dock, you got like thirty semis just sitting there waiting on the dock, their engines going, waiting to load the trailers."

Jay: "Needs good organization, huh?"

"Like a well-oiled machine, Jay," Abe said solemnly. "'Cause if it's not perfect, you don't sell bananas, man, lemme tell ya. Nobody's gonna buy soft bananas. You gotta like kiss the consumer's ass these days."

"Know the feeling, Abes. Banks are the same way." He had a vision of Dana's hands gripping the wooden headboard of the bed, her back arched, as he pounded her from behind. *God, could she take it!*

"Yeah, right—banks. So you'd know all about that. Okay, now you've seen all the labor-intensive steps necessary for to produce bananas. Why don't we talk about money now?"

"Money's what we're here for—don't see why not." *Maybe we're actually seeing some light at the end of this tunnel.*

"Now correct me if I'm wrong, Jay. After that slide presentation, you can really feel our pain, right? I mean, this is a labor-intensive set-up like from the ground up, right?"

"Absolutely, Abe. There's a lot more to it than I ever thought," Jay said sincerely.

"Okay, so I'm going to give you our proposal for a per-day wage." Abe stabbed the computer with his fat finger, and a group of figures appeared on the screen. "Okay, hundreds of thousands of people are involved in putting that banana on your plate, right? Wanna know how all this falls on the bottom line for us poor planters? Well, we feel that, at present supermarket prices, in order to get just a *little tiny profit* in the banana-cultivating business, uh—you don't have anything against making a profit, do you, Jay?"

"Not a thing. Makes the world go round."

"Right. We therefore cannot accept a per-diem price of more than fifteen dollars. And don't forget we provide lunch for two bucks, too, and even there we lose money. That amount, fifteen bucks, will make everybody happy—growers, workers, the industry as a whole—and the American consumer."

Napoleón, the hound-faced guy on the worker committee, laughed. Verdes merely nodded.

"Hey, and don't forget, Jay, on top of that, we have to pay Social Security like everyone else, and that's another chunk. That isn't really part of the negotiations, you know, but I just thought I'd mention that."

"All right, so your number is fifteen," *Doctor Ted was right—the growers are trying to pull down the number.*

"Now of course, *other* people"—this with a schoolboy sneer—"are going to get up here and bullshit you till you choke, but this is the truth. You put a higher wage and you can pretty much like kiss the Ecuadoran banana industry good-bye—which the workers committee wouldn't mind *at all*," he added with a barbed look their way, and Jay saw the spoiled child underneath.

Napoleon started to say something, but Verdes snapped at him in Spanish. Then he stood up. "Thank you, Mr. Marmalejo. Your presentation was coherent and concise and very helpful—as was the one of Mr. Simples."

Jay remembered how clear his English was, with just a small accent.

"I know that the rules of the debate allow that we give a critique of the owners' presentation, but that's really a formality. We're all very hungry. Let's break for the lunch, and then we'll make you our own presentation."

Napoleon's eyes went wide. *"Pero Hondo, qué haces?"* ("But Hondo, what are you doing?") he gasped.

"Hey, yeah, that's a good idea!" cried Abe excitedly. "Besides, there's not much to object to in my presentation, Jay. Like I said, it's good stuff—honest. I'm not a politician."

"Never doubted it, Abes."

"Mr. Streets, I would give you a lunch myself, but I'm afraid that our colleagues on the other committee would accuse me that I am trying to bribe you with a roast chicken. So I'm afraid you'll have to eat in your room under guard. One-thirty, Mr. Marmalejo?"

"Yeah, you bet. Let's eat!"

"I'll call the two guards, then." To Jay: "Another silly formality, but our colleague Mr. Carrasco insisted on it."

He walked out without a word to his colleague Napoleón, and to his amazement, Jay found himself eager for Verdes's presentation.

31 Paul Klippen was having a bad day. He sent three dull cables to Washington. He looked through applications for embassy internships. He tussled for nearly an hour with a Preliminary Parking Allocation Management form, which to his amazement asked for the dimensions of his car and a percentage estimation of the "car replacement possibility." But he couldn't concentrate on anything. He felt as if he were hacking at a flexible, green branch with a hatchet.

He looked around his little office—hardly four strides in any direction—at the exotic seashells from his posting in Cameroon that he'd had framed, at the photo of Cindy hanging from the cliff, at the curved Barbary knife from Morocco. He wondered if he would ever see them again after tomorrow; wondered if the next time he entered a government room it wouldn't be locked behind him with a menacing clang; wondered if they would waterboard him. And where.

In Guantanamo? Leavanworth? They would be boiling mad at him, that was for sure.

He wondered if he shouldn't steal a few embarrassing Top Secret documents: they might give him some bargaining power against a treason charge. But after hardly a moment, he rejected this. He had entered State an honest man and would leave with his head high—even if his wrists were in handcuffs.

He worried more about Cindy. Months earlier, when his plan shimmered on the horizon, he had quietly taken out an insurance policy for her if he were incapacitated for work—it gave him some solace.

They'll make an example of me. They'll make sure that all of us at State toe the line.

Maybe I should forget it. I haven't done anything wrong yet.

Rafa Ramirez called and had to be assured that everything was going fine. The money boys in Guayaquil had the twenty million ready to transfer to Panama, Paul told him, but nobody was moving a muscle till Jay Streets announced the wage in the morning.

"All right, Paulo. Sounds like everything is feelin' groovy," he said uneasily.

"Tell you what, Rafa, I'll stop by the operations room and be sure everything is running to plan," Paul said, more to get out of the office than anything else. Twenty minutes later, he walked into the Hotel Martín.

Paul found the ninth-floor operations room as he'd left it, except that the stink was worse and the trash had overwhelmed the little wastebasket and buried it like a colony of ants over a carcass. The cleaning lady had been shooed away, Paul learned, with fifty dollars to speed her steps. The same porn wailed on two of the video consoles, and the same rapt group stood with Harry Kruger behind Trbek, still sitting with one arm dangling behind him, still wearing the earphones, still watching his control panel and making needless adjustments here and there as a mother adjusts the blanket of her baby. Paul found Trbek's log of the operation—a single electronic tablet always at his side—and wandered out to the balcony where the air was fresh, reading:

847h. JS leaves for morning session.

1033h. Cleaning lady does room. No suspicious activity. (Video A259.3)

1210h. JS arrives (Video A269.6) from morning session.

1218h. JS watches CNN Sports (no news about Ecuador).

12:33h. Lunch arrives.

1252h. Dana signals from balcony. JS enters Dana-Skip room (Video A347.76) JS noncommental about morning sessions.

"*'Noncommental,'*" Paul sighed. "Good God."

Harry shuffled out onto the balcony, leaving the door open. "Terbs, you're recording this, right?" he called over his shoulder.

"Yeah."

Harry was eating a half sandwich out of a triangular plastic box. He showed it to Paul. "Wanna half? We got more. Chicken curry," he mushed, mouth full.

Paul shook his head. "My contact in Tingo's office is sweating bullets. I can tell him that all is well here?"

Harry swallowed hugely. "Far as we know, yeah."

"But he seems to be on track?"

"He seemed to take Doctor Ted the Economist pretty well last night. He just got back from the owners' presentations—hasn't said anything." A grin, and he jerked his thumb back towards the room. "Not that she's let him come up for air yet."

Paul froze solid. "That's…that on the screen is…." For some reason he couldn't think of Streets's name.

"That, Klippers, is the best part of the day."

"You mean that's him? And the girl?"

Harry burst out laughing. "Klippers, sometimes I wonder if—"

"Hey! Hey, what the hell is this?" Paul roared, charging into the room. "Turn that off right now!"

"For Chrissakes, Klippers—"

Paul shoved past the other men up to the console. It was true: the image was a bit shadowy, but he could make out Streets's blond hair mixed up with the woman and sheeting. "What the hell is this? You're *watching* them? Turn it off! Goddamn it, turn it off!" He was beside Trbek's big bald head, looking around wildly for a switch or a power button but could make no sense of it. He shoved him out of the way, too.

"Hey, get the fuck off my control board!" snapped Trbek, shoving back.

"I don't give a shit if—"

Which was as far as he got before practiced CIA arms spun him around and punched him in the gut—just under the breastbone, where it would hurt the most. The next thing Paul knew, Harry was frog-marching him out the door. He threw Paul, still doubled-over, against the wall of the corridor.

"Who the fuck do you think you are?" Harry snapped from the doorway. "You don't go messing around with a CIA op like that."

It took Paul forever to be able to straighten up. "For the love of God, Harry—that's an American national in there!" he gasped, still grasping his stomach. "We don't treat our people that way."

"Don't be a fucking Mother Teresa, Klippers. It all stays inside. Besides, the girl knows what's going on. She doesn't care. Hell, she's loving it."

"The girl knows the score. Streets doesn't."

"Who's looking at Streets?" Harry laughed.

"Turn that off, or I'm going right up there and bang on their door."

"Jesus." With a huff, Harry propped the door open with an empty pizza box lying on the floor and, grabbing Paul's tie, jerked him upright.

"No, you're not," he said. "And I'm gonna tell you *why* you're not. You're not because you want this op as bad as I do. This op is your one ticket to the better job titles, and you're not going to lose it." He shoved Paul back against the wall again.

Finally, Paul managed to catch his breath. "To hell with the op. Where the hell is your sense of decency? Not enough to set the guy up with a high-class hooker—you've got to *watch* him, too? *And* record it?"

"You see the same thing on the Net any day of the week, Klippers. Chrissakes, grow up. He'll never know the diff'. Not like they're whipping each other with chains."

"Harry, it's the *principle* of the thing," Paul pleaded. "The principle. Doesn't that *mean* anything to you?"

"Listen. All the vid—the whole op—gets chucked into Top Secret when it's all over. All he knows is he's having the best screw of his life. Costing my op eighteen long a day—I'll watch them as much as I damn well please."

Paul shook his head in pure, black exasperation. "We do nothing but talk past each other, Harry, don't we? Every time. Every single goddamn time. I swear, it's like talking to a pimply adolescent."

"You're not going to lift a finger over this, so cut the Virgin Mary crap." He went back into the room.

"Nobody's recording *me* in bed, are they?"

"Would if your wife could still move those hips," Kruger retorted. He kicked the pizza box into the hallway and shut the door.

32 Jay Streets saw Segundo Verdes walk to the lectern and, eyebrows crunched together in irritation, turn off the lit computer screen. He squeezed his hands together once, and Jay observed the good muscles in his forearms snap to attention. No paunch, no tie—just khaki, the full shirt pockets of a busy man, and scuffed brown shoes.

Good. Straight talk, man to man for once. All right, Doctor Ted knows his stuff and all, but if there's anything else worth listening to here, it comes from this guy.

"Good afternoon, Mr. Streets. Ah, my name is Segundo Verdes, in case you've forgotten. Before I begin, I would like to add two datas to Mr. Marmalejo's presentation. First, I believe that he gave you the impression that the banana trees require years of care before that they give profits. It is not true. A banana tree grows quickly in our excellent Ecuadoran soil, and begins to produce fruit within a year. After that, it continues growing and will give fruit for about ten years."

"I was talking about a plantation, Jay," Marmalejo put in, his big face turning red.

Isabel Montera, who had come for the afternoon session, sighed. Introduced to Jay, she had squeezed his big shoulders and squealed with delight. Now she sat back in her chair, one leg dangling, and with the other one swiveling her chair one way and another. Her lime-green hoop earrings and her massive breasts swung in time. Simple's eyes swung to her every time she swung the chair his way, as if the two were parts of the same machine.

"Yes, Mr. Marmalejo, why don't you jump in whenever you want? And Miss Costa also—you speak excellent English. There isn't need for making a formal answer a long time after Mr. Streets has forgotten the point. If I say something that you object, correct me."

"Um, all right," said Marmalejo, surprised. He had eaten too much and was sleepy.

"Just don't go off on a tangerine," said Isabel Costa, glancing at her watch.

"Yeah, anybody who has something to say, just spit it out," said Jay. *This guy is absolutely cool. This guy isn't afraid of anything.*

"Mr. Marmalejo also mentioned that Plantaciones Costa have to pay the Social Security on top of the wages, and this is true. But in reality, most Ecuadoran employers use loopholes to get away from paying it, including Costa, which pays Social Security only to the minority of its workers, the ones who work every day. Most of its workers come only a few days a week."

Simples, who had been following the translation on his earjack, stirred suddenly and spoke.

"He said, 'Nothing that we do is illegal,'" Marmalejo translated.

Verdes nodded. "Technically, no."

"You're getting pretty judgmental, man," grumbled Marmalejo.

Verdes: "Another relevant data is the following one: according to our National Institute of Statistics and Census, they say that a family of four need a income of 380 dollars a month. Now if a worker is earning only eleven dollars a day after lunch is taken out—"

Hound-faced Napoleón, who was also listening to the translation in the earjack, erupted, in Spanish, and Verdes snapped back.

Silence.

Jesus. What was that all about? thought Jay.

"I'm sorry, Mr. Streets. My colleague, Mr. Napoleón, was just pointing out that our partner, Mr. Carrasco, has the exclusive right to name the daily wage we are asking for. This is our coalition's agreement during these negotiations and I am obligated to respect. I answered to him that I simply am quoting an important statistic. You may consider it as you like. It's only a quite general, ah, benchmark."

"So how do people make up the shortfall?" Jay asked alertly. *And fuck if anybody tries to cut me off.* "I mean, let's do the math: Guy makes fifteen bucks a day under Mr. Simples's new per diem wage. Twenty days of work makes three hundred. So you need almost an extra hundred. Where's it gonna come from?"

Again Napoleon barked. Verdes hardly heard it.

"That is a question that every Ecuadoran family struggles with every month."

Jay nodded. "I'll bet it is."

"The trouble with statistics, though, is that they don't fill out the picture. The other problem is that our plantation workers make the living in dangerous circumstances."

Isabel Costa stirred, jerking upright. "Dangerous? What is dangerous?" she griped.

Verdes: "For example, the plastic bags that workers put over the bananas. These bags are, ah, impregnated—I hope that is the word—with pesticides and nematicides. These are—"

"Ah, nematicides?" Jay asked.

Marmalejo: "Those are the ones against fungus, Jay. Gotta have 'em. This is the tropics, you know."

"Thanks, Abes."

Verdes: "The trouble is that some nematicides used in Ecuador are prohibited in your country and Europe. And sometimes the workers have gloves to use the bags with, but other times they don't have. Or the gloves that they use are old and worthless."

"We give to the workers decent gloves," said Isabel Costa, turning to Marmalejo. "It is true, no?"

"Sure, always," said Marmalejo woodenly.

"Or the aerial fumigation," Verdes went on. "It is often made with workers in the fields because there's no time to abandon the fields. It is quite normal to work almost round-the-clock on a plantation, correct, Mr. Marmalejo?"

"So does a car factory—big deal. And besides, I told all our foremen to vacate the fields for fumigation." To Jay, with a hopeless shrug: "You wouldn't believe it, man. I got to be on top of those guys all the time."

Verdes smiled patiently and squeezed his hands together. "I'm sure that you do, Mr. Marmalejo. But as with everything in the banana business, one thing is the theory and another thing is the practice. The level of disease and birth deformation in the banana-producing area is horrendous—it is horrendous since decades. And the problem can be traced directly to the chemicals."

"Hey, Jay, I gotta interrupt here," said Marmalejo. "We deplore these human rights abuses just as much as the next guy. But hell, we're only responsible for what happens on our farms, not others. Hell, we can't be everywhere!" He threw his chubby arms wide in despair.

"Yes, that's the trick: no responsibility, to handle everything from the length of an arm," Verdes replied softly, looking at him. "The multinational fruit companies, that buy the fruit, rarely own any land, and the big plantation owners grow a relatively small number of crops and buy the rest from the thousands of small plantations in order to fulfill contracts with the multinationals. This is easy: the wholesale-banana markets in small towns run seven days a week. The labor needed on these small plantations is sometimes supplied by temp agencies which simply pull into a town in the morning and let the men they need get into the back of the pickup. Nobody is breaking the law, nobody has any legal responsibility—that is true. And if babies are born without eyes or legs, this is legal also."

"Hey, but a lot of that is also just from chemicals that get into the water supply," said Marmalejo, round face reddening again like a sinking moon. "I mean, heck, Jay, you gotta take this guy with a grain of salt."

"Don't worry, Abe. All under control." Jay remembered Doctor Ted: *Remember that I'm not a politician, I'm your Uncle Ted. 'Cause if I've seen this kind of thing once, I've seen it a dozen times. The union guys put up a big multimedia bullshit presentation full of undernourished little girls and workers with dirty faces, and they're gonna tell you they can't get by on less than fifty a day. Ketchup crud, whole deal.*

"Also Mr. Marmalejo mentioned the lunch. The standard charge for the plantation lunch is two dollars, as he said. But the standards for lunch vary widely. Some are terrible."

"Then why they spend half the day in the *cantina*?" snapped Isabel Costa. "If it is so bad—huh?"

"Perhaps because they are waiting that you enter and enjoy a meal with them, Miss Costa. A bit of the hard chicken and watered-down guayaba juice? Or haven't you had the pleasure?"

She huffed and started swinging again. "Hurry up," she muttered.

"Thank you—an excellent suggestion. You see, Mr. Streets, the economic aspect is actually the smaller part of our dispute with the plantation owners."

"'Jay,' will do there, Segundo."

A smile. "Jay, yes. Americans are first-name people, I've forgotten. Well, Jay, the economic aspect is very little in our plan. For one reason, because what we unions intend doing is to take two dollars from every worker's daily salary and provide the necessary social services for them to work with safety. I will explain you that more in a moment. For another, all of the extra wages we are asking for will simply be passed on to the supermarket chains and to the consumer. Bananas are one of the most profitable items in the store."

"Is that right? *Bananas?*" Jay said, amazed. He nearly called Segundo Verdes "Segs," but thought better of it: he wasn't that type.

"Bananas. Now, it will not cause a trauma if their profit on a banana falls. And besides, why is the duty of the supplier to bother about the trouble of the buyer? If Americans want our bananas, fine; if you don't, we send our products to China or Norway, and as they say in America, 'no hard feelings.'"

"Now hold on here a little, Segundo. That sounds a lot like those greedy bastards at OPEC, y'ask me. You know: take it or take it, and at our price?"

"Well, yes, but there *is* a difference," Hondo said. "Instead of the bananas, you can eat cheap apples from Iowa or the Canadian pears. You can introduce only gasoline in your car, but fruit? Well, there must be a dozen kinds in any supermarket."

Jay considered this. "All right. Point taken."

"Good. Now, with worker payrolls, we will take out a certain quantity to pay for social programs—more or less two dollars a day. We, the union, will take care of three aspects of plantation life: one, to make sure everyone is paid properly and to make sure they receive paid vacations."

"Paid vacations too?" sighed Isabel Costa and rubbed her forehead. "*Por el amor de dios!* They don't need paid vacations, Jay. Only it is necessary to go to the plantation and see for yourself. Every *day* is a paid vacation."

Napoleón growled something in Spanish.

That guy always seems to be asleep, Jay observed. *But he's got his eye on everything.*

Segundo Verdes: "Two, to check all the safety measures and the meals and to assure that a shower—even a primitive shower with plastic buckets—is available for the workers when they finish to work because they need to wash off the chemicals. And three, to give regular health checks to the workers, especially for chemical poisoning and parasites that they get in the fields. To the small plantations, we will organize mobile units on some pickup trucks that have the responsibility for maybe a dozen small plantations. Yes, our workers need more money in their pocket—there is no question. But as I constantly remind to workers, more money is little comfort if they are losing their vision or their children are born retarded."

No ketchup crud, Jay reminded himself sternly. "Wait. I don't know if I'm missing something here, but why do *you* need to do all that? What about the government here? How come *they* can't take care of that with—whatever—inspections and safety standards and all that?"

"Oh! The government!" sighed Isabel Costa.

"That's one place you don't want to go, man," said Abelardo.

Verdes smiled. "If there is one thing that we all agree in this room, Jay, it is that the workers and businessmen raise this country, not our terrible governments."

"Ah. Right," said Jay, embarrassed.

Verdes: "Our beautiful new airport with its 60-meters-high tower of control, finally being finished across the valley? For decades it was discussed—decades! Thirty years ago, Quito had already grown around the airport. Thirty years of airplanes screaming along the middle of our capital to land! Thirty years to build *one* airport with *one* runway!"

"Yeah, I hear those bastards coming in every morning," Jay said drily. He figured it was time to play Uncle Ted's trump card and pointed his pen at Verdes: "All right, Segundo, but here's the rub, as I see it: you give a big boost to wages, and Ecuadoran bananas won't be competitive on the world market. You said people could eat cheap apples, and that's exactly what they're gonna do if you start jacking up prices. Seems to me you're more likely to lose market than anything else, and that's not good for anybody."

"Not at all, Jay. That's a lot of oversimplified economics. Our market is virtually infinite."

"Bullshit," Jay griped. "Everything's supply and demand."

Verdes did not gesture much, but his mobile eyebrows leapt high. *"But children love bananas!* A child which hates everything put on his plate will fill himself on bananas. And with the rising middle classes of Asia, demand is the least of our worries. Ecuadoran bananas only will rise to the same price as the rest. Our salary raise here in Ecuador will be a, a small perturbation on the market."

"Ah, right. Yeah, I get it. Great. Can you just give me a minute here, Segundo?" Jay made a few notes. This wasn't at all what Uncle Ted had talked about. But it made sense—so did the safety program.

Still, there was Dana and Skip and Michael—and they were sharp people.

"All right, Segundo, I think I got the picture here. So let's talk bottom line. The present wage is about thirteen bucks a day, a little less if the worker gets lunch. Management is offering to go to fifteen. Where do you guys come out?"

The other guy, Napoleón, heard the translation through the earjack and coughed loudly.

A pained smile. "My colleague, Sixto Carrasco, will talk to you about that. I will only say that our plans call for each worker paying about two dollars a day for our program. So when you make the final salary, please remember that."

"Two is the number," Jay assured him.

"Thank you for your time and patience, Jay. I can understand that not all have been completely pleasant."

Napoleón went to the door and had scarcely touched it before Sixto Carrasco ripped it open and came thundering across the room. He wore a denim shirt open to the waist and baggy white pants and was roaring in Spanish.

Shit, who the hell is this? Jay thought, snatching his earjack:

"…that these liars and showmen have been telling you! The wage that I tell you is the price that God himself has handed me, and either you can put it or be damned for all time among the capitalists and hustlers of the world who wish to suck the blood and marrow from the sacred Ecuadoran worker. I give you your one chance in life to…"

A pause, and then the Scottish interpreter across the way, still going steadily with her knitting needles, sighed, "Oh my, it looks like we're in for a long blow. I'll let you know when he comes to the wage. If we're lucky, he might—whoops! Nod, dear. Nod very quickly. He just asked if you agree that Ecuadorans are the quintessence of sublimity. I suppose they might be up for it if they added some flowers to their gardens, don't you think?"

33 Al Smick, professional assassin, stood forlornly watching the last unmarked helicopter lift off, his tie flapping all over his pocked face like a pestering fly. He wore a business suit for the same reason that he did his work sitting down, his sniper rifle propped on a table: he was not a soldier, but a professional contract agent. Only his support team, the Forward Amphibious Interventions Cell—FAIC, as in FAIC you, went the slogan—was military.

Yes, he doted on the corporals and captains he came across in his work, heard their gripes with nostalgia, grinned with the best of them at the naked calendar girls in the Hummers, and loved to toss his own stories into the soup of scuttlebutt. But Al Smick was freelance; he was a contractor; he was not military. Not even the other men on the operation knew his real name.

True enough, he had started out in the Marines. He had worked the Panama and Grenada invasions, which he had enjoyed enormously, and went independent in the late 90s. He had racked up twenty-eight CKs—confirmed kills—for the CIA alone, his most memorable in Istanbul against an Al Qaeda section leader disguised as a peanut seller on the street. He had used a silencer—always dangerous for how it increased bullet drop—and shot him from the roof of a mechanic's garage at 400 yards. The target jerked back in his chair when the bullet hit, and remained looking at the sky as if to check the prospect of rain. The two women fifteen yards away down the sidewalk kept right on chatting, and when their children came out of guitar class, walked away without knowing that Death had just left its calling card.

But now Al stared blackly at the tubby chopper pulling up the last rope—the mountainside was too steep to land on—and lumbering away. Around him sturdy men in camouflaged uniforms ran through checklists and "secured the perimeter," but he didn't see them. The start of an op usually made him ecstatic with life, but now Al stood burning alive in the lava of bad luck: his table and chair had not arrived.

Hadn't he ordered, with days to spare, the field chair and table to set his little rifle tripod on? Yes, he had. Hadn't he described them— "just a little safari table, and a three-legged camp stool, so's I can spread my knees"—and added that any old thing would do? Yes, he had. Had he made a prima-donna's fuss, double-checked the order, bugged the equipment chief in charge of the op? No, he had not. Yet here he stood as if stranded at the airport, tie flapping from the chopper blast, banged-up rifle case in one hand, overnight bag in the other. Al had no table, Al had no chair.

"Well, hell, Mr. Crowley, what can I tell ya? I thought the guys were just pullin' muh dick on that one—Gawd as muh witness! Who ever heard of a sniper sittin' on a damn footstool?" the equipment officer had told him by cell phone a moment earlier. Al had hung up on him.

The grassy meadow where he stood lay on the rising ridge of a mountain, some fifty yards above the last vegetable orchards—carrots, they looked like, by the ragged green tassels growing out of the ground. But here no planting was possible, for rocky outcroppings had shouldered their way up into the steep slope. Hugging the ground to avoid radar detection, the chopper sailed off over the mountain behind them. Al walked dazedly around, kicking the long grass, disconsolate, talking feverishly to himself.

"Why should I go through with this?" he whined. "Fuck. Give me one good reason not to call back the chopper, fly to Larandia, and head for a cathouse. Never tried Colombian girls, anyway. Harry has an objective that needs taking out? Harry has an op that needs to be finished off? Then let *Harry* fucking take care of it."

"Mr. Crowley, sir? Would ya like me to help you set up?" asked Sergeant Trastow, saluting him. "I think I've re-conned a possible vantage just up the ridge here." He jerked his thumb upslope towards some boulders shrouded in green bushes.

"Fuck's it matter? Me, I can shoot anywhere, anyhow," Smick retorted sourly. "Just call me 'Clear-line-o'-sight Al.'"

The young sergeant reddened. "Uh, yessir," he said abashedly. "Uh, it's right over there beyond those rocks. Lemme give you a hand with your gear, sir." He reached for the rifle case but a sixth sense warned him, and he took the overnight bag instead and started away, though after ten steps he turned to see if Mr. Crowley was following. He was, sulkily. Trastow waited politely for him. He had been ordered to watch Mr. Crowley's back.

"Didn't anyone borrow you some fatigues, sir?" said Trastow, looking doubtfully at Smick's blue suit. "I can scrounge ya an extra pair, if ya like. Maybe have to roll up the cuffs a turn or two, but that's all in the ballgame. We're all pretty informal once we get into theater, ya know, 'specially when there's a BIV programmed," he added with an encouraging grin.

"Where's this vantage?" Al snapped.

34 "Thirty-seven dollars," Jay said. Dana lay against his chest. "Took him all fucking afternoon to get to it, and by that time we were all about in shellshock. It was like listening to some screechy TV preacher, only you couldn't change the channel. 'We want a just price, Señor Streets. We want dignity just like you and your rich friends, Señor Streets. The only difference is that we only want a decent life for our families. We don't want Ferraris and luxury hotels and high-priced whores. We are not materialistic, like you and your friends.'"

"Fuckwad. Leave it at fifteen and tell him to go fuck," Dana said.

"Yeah, something like that. Just to screw him, I'd like to lower the existing price and tell the workers, 'That's because you have a dumbshit for a spokesman. Get rid of him and call me back in a year when your contract runs out.'"

Giggling, Dana reached up and caressed his neck and face. "Well, after the press conference tomorrow it's all over. Hey, I'm forgiven for the thing this morning, right?"

"Yeah, sure," Jay said, tossing off the answer without thinking about it, which was a good thing, because it wasn't true.

"You don't sound too sincere."

"I am, I am." He kissed her quickly, running his hands over that perfect, smooth back to her behind in order to muster passion. "It's just that, I keep thinking this thing up and down. Jesus, thirty-seven dollars a day the guy wants! That's nothing to go on; he might as well have said a million."

"What difference does it make? Doctor Ted ran it all down to you. Call it sixteen or seventeen. Hell, I still don't know why they had to stick you in the middle of it all. It's not *your* problem."

"Yeah, maybe." He shrugged. "It's just that I'd like to give them *something*. I wish that Verdes guy had talked prices."

But he had. The meeting had ended when Carrasco, worked into a frenzy, shirt flapping, belly bouncing, leapt around the podium and ran up to Jay, screaming.

"Shit capitalista. You are fucking shit capitalista!" he shouted in English, leaning into him over the little table, belly shaking. "You make thirty-seven dollar wage, or you fucking shit! You understand!"

"Yeah, yeah, I get it," said Jay, waving away his bad breath. "Back off a little, would you?"

"I think you come fuck to my people, big capitalista. You fuck to us, huh? Huh?"

And with one heave he shoved the entire table over on top of Jay. Jay fell backwards off his chair.

"Get off me!" he snapped, sprawling. His right leg was caught under the edge of the table, and Carrasco was leaning on top of it. *"Ow! Shit! Get him off!"*

"Shit capitalista. You are fucking shit capitalista!" he screamed. "We want thirty-seven. Thirty-seven! Or we will remember you like one more fucking shit that—"

Verdes threw Napoleón out of the way and slammed into Carrasco with his shoulder, which was what it took to move that tub of lard.

"Bye, bye, shit capitalista," he called, laughing rustily. He strode away to the exit.

Verdes snatched away the table, grabbed Jay's hand and pulled him upright.

"Twenty-two, please," he whispered in his ear. "Twenty-two is enough." Then, stepping away, he started with apologies for Napoleón's sake.

Jay thought about telling Dana, but didn't; that was between Verdes and himself. "Yeah, well, I sort of wonder about Doctor Ted. I mean, it's not only money that's involved here, y'know," he said vaguely.

"I think he knows the situation better than all of those assholes combined," Dana said stoutly. "He knows both sides of the story, not just one." She raised up on one elbow and looked at him quite seriously. "And like I say, Jay, it isn't *your* problem. Leave it at seventeen and walk away."

Jay blew a puff of air towards the ceiling. "Yeah, normally I would, but you see, that one union guy, Verdes, said the salary really doesn't matter much on the world market. And there's the safety program too. It's not like they have a work-safety department that goes around checking working conditions or anything here."

"Fine and well, but that's not—"

"Wait, let me finish. I'm not going as far as that Carrasco guy. He can take a nice, long hike—like around Siberia, far as I'm concerned. But more than sixteen I am prepared to go, no question. Maybe more than eighteen."

"What—and stick it to Americans at the supermarket?" Dana said with alarm.

"Go fish, babe. Americans aren't going to starve if they can't buy cheap bananas. And hell, look at the overview. The better off the plantation workers are, the better off everyone is—for one because they'll have money to buy American products and stick their savings in DynoBank. I mean, that'd be publicity that even my boss Roger never thought of."

"Now just hold on a second here, Jay," Dana said, sitting up and pulling a sheet around herself, gray eyes sharp with anger. "Just hold on one goddamn minute. Skip, Michael and I didn't go through this whole thing on the spur of the moment and miss our vacations and stay another week in another damn hotel just so that you can go break out like a loose cannon. I mean, when they told me I had to fly fourteen hours and put out another fire, I could've killed someone. We set this whole thing up for you, and now you throw it back in our faces?"

"Well, these people did give me a responsibility, you know," Jay said weakly. "And that Verdes guy—you oughta listen to him. He is one class act. Really has his shit together. He has the whole thing figured out—wages, social programs, health stuff, the works," Jay said. "I mean, he's the kind of guy you don't want to disappoint, know what I mean?"

"Yes, but—"

He touched a bit of her thigh sticking out from under the sheet. "Besides, it's turned out okay for you, all this."

"Yes, of *course*," Dana said patiently. "Just by complete chance it's turned out great." She touched his cheek. "This was worth *forty* hours of flying, and once we get back to the U.S. I really want to see where this goes. So I'm not complaining, Jay—I'm not. But we got people to put in sixteen-hour days—miss their daughter's volleyball game among other things—to research the whole thing top-down for you, just to give you the whole story. And besides, it's not *our* salary that's going to rise or fall on what you say. Who's going to be more impartial than us?"

Jay nodded. "Yeah. Yeah, that's a good point."

"Of course it's a good point. It's the only point. Well, except that Skip and Michael and I might lose our jobs if you go too high."

"Really?"

"Special Ops pays well, buddy-boy, but they pay for results. People have been fired for less. And after all, I mean, are you going to trust: us or a bunch of guys wearing smelly llama wool?"

Special Ops to the rescue! Yeah, what we're here for, what you pay taxes for. We goin' set you up. We goin' walk you through it. We goin' tell you who to listen to and who's full o' shit. And then we goin' help you set a nice, sweet price so ev'body walks away with their own little cut o' the pie.

"Yeah, I guess," Jay admitted.

To Jay's surprise, she chuckled. "Besides, it's not exactly like *Segundo Verdes* is going to be disappointed if you say fifteen."

"What do you mean by that?"

An impish glance sideways. Then she pulled down the sheet and stretched out naked on him again, kissing him. Jay felt his groin inflate again as she fitted herself around him. "Verdes is our man," she whispered in his ear.

In a flash, Jay had her on her back, himself upright, looking down at her. "Segundo Verdes? *Your* guy? You've got to be kidding!"

"Life's full of surprises, huh?" Dana said with a grin, rubbing his chest slowly. "No, not kidding a bit; they filled us in during the briefing. I guess he's been on some Latin American fruit company's payroll for years. He keeps tabs on the union movements down here for them. I guess this is his last assignment. They're going to move him to Colombia after this."

Jay sat immobile for a long time, leaning back on one arm. He remembered Michael's words in the van: *We can't tell you exactly how that's going to happen, Jay, but suffice it to say, we've got someone inside the negotiations.* "Verdes. Geez. He seemed like a pretty straight guy."

"That's absolutely got to stay between us, though, right? I'm not allowed to tell you. But here you are, thinking he's some kind of saint."

"Yeah, sure," Jay said absently. "I guess you can't believe in anybody these days."

Dana was running a finger over his hand. "I only told you because I know I can trust you."

Jay moved a lock of her beautiful hair away from her face. "Yeah. Thanks, babe. 'Preciate it. Nothing is what it seems, huh?"

"*This* is what it seems." She swatted away the arm that supported him and pulled him down. "Now where were we?"

35

It was late afternoon, and Paul Klippen went for a jog; he wanted one last memory before starting a life in prison.

After changing clothes at home, he drove up Calle La Gasca to its steepest point, and from there reached the base of the TelefériQo, the cable-car ride up to the top of the Cruz Loma, at the top of the Pichinchas. The round-trip ticket was cheap—five bucks normally—but he paid the ten-dollar price for foreigners because he'd left behind his diplomatic i.d. This was doubly unjust because Paul didn't get on the cable car, but passed through the turnstile and walked off into the grassy brush to begin the grueling march up the mountain—his favorite exercise in Quito.

He stayed well to the right of the path and kept his eyes and ears open. A popular pastime of Quito youths is to load their mountain bikes on the cable cars' exterior racks and then enjoy kamikaze sublimity speeding nearly a mile down to the base of the cable cars—it took eight minutes, according to one kid he had asked. In his first hundred yards up the path, two blurred past—the last two of the day, it turned out, for it was getting dark.

The swift sun was slipping behind the Pichinchas, and the land quickly turned blue-gray. Paul climbed and climbed, panting and sweating, his tee shirt clapped wet to his back. His glasses steamed up so much that he took them off. Three-quarters of the way up, around 12,000 feet altitude, he stopped to take his fat plastic sports bottle out of his knapsack and drink some water. Leaning back against a boulder, he watched shadows fill the valleys like a rising tide till only the highest peaks were visible—the Cayambe fifty miles distant, the Antisana, and to the south the Cotopaxi—all with their broad coolie hats of snow, western sides blushing in the sunset's last kiss.

At his feet the improbable capital city clung to its mountain ledge. Beyond it, in a dungeon of darkness, lay the deep San Rafael Valley. Directly in front of him lay the long green square of La Carolina Park. Park lights now blinking on, he could just make out the line of basketball courts where the first steps of his plot had been taken. To his right, he made out the tight grid of the colonial section. It was hard to believe that those few-dozen blocks, the merest crossroads in the Andean wilderness, once comprised a national capital plotted for, warred over, and sung about in patriotic hymns. The red and green lights of a departing airliner caught his eye, and he followed its progress along the city till it gently banked east near the Cotopaxi and headed out over the Amazon jungle.

He nodded. This would do for a last vision of freedom.

He sidled around behind the boulder and drank off what was left of his water, unscrewed the lid of the bottle and vigorously shook the remaining drops out. Into it he dropped a few small rocks to weigh it down, then dropped in two credit cards, his detector of listening bugs, and a fat wad of hundred-dollar bills. Harry Kruger might be searching his home tomorrow at this hour, and there was no use leaving these for him to find. It was impossible to tell how events might twist and turn. If Paul needed to run—and if he had the chance—these things would come in handy.

For a moment, he thought of dropping in his wedding ring, but didn't: he might as well leave it for Cindy. He screwed the cap back on tight.

Then he took out a new gardening trowel, dug a slender hole, and buried the bottle.

That done, he stood up, panting in the thin air, and threw the trowel as hard as he could away down the mountain. It disappeared into the tall grass.

"Well, onward and upward," he muttered, turning up the slope.

He rode the cable car down with a couple of doctors from the altitude emergency-care clinic. They'd had four patients that day, they said, mostly from a gaggle of a chubby German ladies who indignantly griped that air was air and one ought to be able to breathe it wherever one went.

The lights of the city slowly rose and embraced him again. A lump formed in his throat as he thought about Cindy. Now that she was finally making progress with her therapy, he would love to be there to see it.

"Well, maybe someday I'll be able to see her walk into the prisoners' visiting room," he murmured to the window, "if they don't turn me into a zombie."

36 Pulling on a jacket, Hondo stood at the window of Mary's bedroom, looking up to the mountains. The equatorial stars shone in the clear sky, almost too bright to look at; they cast visible shadows on the floor. It was four in the morning.

"Streets believed me, I know that he did," said Hondo. "But something is holding to him. He wants to believe, he wants to help me—I can feel this. I don't know…perhaps your Mr. Kruger has managed grabbing him."

"But didn't you say he's escorted by two guys from the workers' committee? And they guard his door all night?" Mary asked, sitting on the edge of the bed in her nightgown.

"They are not professional guards, only assistants of Carrasco. I trust much more the decency of Streets. He is not a completely mature man, but he respects rules and he is trying to do an honest job." He slowly zipped up his jacket. "Yes, surely, surely: of course Kruger has contacted with him. And he has blackmailed to Streets. Still…"

"Still what?"

"I think Kruger has not been very successful. To blackmail is not so easy, you know—it requires technique. I did a seminar about it with the Spanish intelligence trainers. Maybe it was badly done."

Mary chuckled. "Well, if you want, I can ask him tomorrow. I'm supposed to escort him to the airport tomorrow after the announcement. He's taking the twelve-thirty flight to New York."

Hondo was checking his pockets for his things: money, papers, a pen, some type of map. "But you know…Streets listened to me carefully, I am sure. He would not have done that if already he had been blackmailed and told that he name a price of, for example, sixteen or seventeen dollars."

Mary shrugged. "So how good a wage is that?"

"Sixteen?" He pursed his lips. "With sixteen, the workers will starve a bit less—that's all. At nineteen they have a little space. But we could not ask them that they contribute serious money to the union for our programs. They would say no."

"When do you think they'd say yes?"

"At around twenty, if programs are available—and if we explain them to the women. *They* will move the mountain for us. That is why I quietly asked Mr. Streets for twenty-two: twenty for the worker, two for the union."

"That's nice and clear, at least."

Hondo shrugged, looking out the window again; Mary watched him outlined against the stars. "Yes, twenty-two is where we begin to fly, Mary. Give us that, and in five years you will see to healthy workers, fewer alcoholism, good mothers with less babies, and full classrooms of bright, noisy children in all the banana region. In ten years they will be in the universities. The hospitals will have healthy-birth babies and a finish to the nerve problems caused by the pesticides." He rammed a fist into his palm—so hard Mary jumped. "That is the dream, Mary. That is the dream. And it is possible, starting today."

"Sounds wonderful," Mary said quietly.

"It will be more than wonderful; it will be a new life in the entire region. But this reminds me." He turned and crouched and took her hands in his, his green eyes bright, the fine eyebrows high with hope.

"Mary, if anything happens to me, please would you take care about Leopoldo? You remember where to find to him? The door was on Buenos Aires Street, near the corner with Panama Street."

"I can find it."

"Good. There's a Lutheran orphanage in Ibarra directed by a Norwegian millionaire, Rolf Skoglund. They receive the kids and give them an education and teach them a trade. Would you be sure he enters in it?"

"Yeah, sure, but"—Mary swallowed—"what, uh, what could happen to you?"

It took Hondo a moment to answer. "After Streets makes his announcement, everybody will go to the meeting of the Council of Elders. It is in a special place in the country south of Quito. Do you know Machachi?"

"Yeah, down south about an hour's drive, I think."

"That's it. It is where people take the highway down to the lowlands. If the price is low, Carrasco will throw his men against me, and with them and an angry mob, it is possible that I don't survive. You have heard to him. With three sentences, he can make a crowd to boil."

"Well, if people are boiling in the park, your men will warn you."

"They won't be able to help to me. I will stand in the middle of a type of ancient Indian burial mound—very round. It forms a big C. I will confront Carrasco there in front of the Elders. If the price is good, I don't have anything to worry for—or at least I have less to worry for. Besides, I have evidence that completely discredits Carrasco. I intend to give this to the Council of Elders."

"Oh my god! Discredit him how?"

"Some photos." Hondo turned and crouched down in front of her. "I won't make you to keep secrets from your embassy—only about our relationship; that is fair. The photos I will not tell you yet. But I am also playing with my life by showing them. He will do anything to destroy me. The next hours will be crucial."

To lose him—my God! Mary thought, tears coming into her eyes. "Hey—maybe I could arrange political asylum for you!"

"Run away, and on top of it to the United States? No, I could never look any of my people at the eye again."

She looked down but he caught her chin and lifted it. "So—Leopoldo. Please?"

"Okay."

Then he kissed her and kissed her, kissed her till he had to tear himself away, and as she heard his footfalls echoing through the house—the dumb clunk of the front door—she put her head in her hands and wept.

37 Jaymond Arthur Streets handed his autograph to the American that had come down in the elevator with him and stepped out in the grip of a biting indignation he had never known before. He shook the hands of the two Indian guards—they peeled away—and strode stiffly across the lobby, oblivious to the roaring crowd of reporters, and into the huge meeting room and straight to the lectern, now set up before several rows of chairs. Shouted questions flew about him like a swarming flock of birds. Jay merely nodded, mouth set.

Segundo Verdes noticed his rigid stance and wondered what it portended. He stood behind the rows of chairs and far to the side, at the end of a long line of news cameras set on tripods, like storks in shallow water. He heard a murmured "testing, testing," and saw, over by the wall, the Scottish interpreter sat hunched over her knitting needles, microphone/earjack hung on her ear. What a job—repeating the sentences of others, however lame or false. He had done a few business-translation jobs to make extra money when he lived in Los Angeles, and had hated them even more than his janitorial work for the Mormons.

Across the room, Sixto Carrasco was bellowing into the microphone of a frightened reporter. A few steps away stood the rotund, snowman-like Abelardo Marmalejo, who was eating potato chips out of big bag as fast as he could shovel them in, worried little Miguel Simples fretting beside him. No sign of Isabel Costa, but this, it occurred to him, was the first common sense she had shown so far.

Streets blew into the microphone, then harrumphed loudly—proprietarily, which made Hondo shudder.

They've blackmailed him, thought Hondo. *With luck, we'll get seventeen.*

Jay Streets's talent as a receiver was his ability to concentrate on the ball even when he knew he was about to get smacked by the safety; it was a feature of his career that commentators had often highlighted. He needed all his concentration now to focus on his decision—he was still debating up or down a dollar or two—as people took their places, some putting in earjacks to hear the translation. He ran through his pre-conference checklist.

Check to be sure his suit jacket was buttoned: it was. Two deep breaths to loosen the shoulders. One foot slightly behind the other. Hands holding the sides of the lectern, but lightly, not clinging to it. Head and eyes level: speak to the TV cameras—they were the ones that sent his image, not the note-takers. He reached for the interpreter's earjack—then rejected it.

No Q and A today, friends. You wanted a number, that's what you get. I'm catching the noon flight out of here and it'll be a cold day in Bermuda when I ever come again.

"Okay, thanks for coming, everybody," he began, the sizzle of the crowd dying instantly. "Thanks for coming. I'm not going to keep you waiting. I've thought it all over."

Slow down. Delivery. Convince yourself first.

"I've thought it all over. I've tried to be as fair as possible and listen to both sides evenly. I've taken some notes, and I've reviewed them. I also spent some time looking over the statistics that the owners gave me, and I can tell you it's not an easy decision."

He stopped and took a breath—too long, too much dead air. But he just relaxed and started again.

"It's actually a *very* tough decision, and I can understand that not everybody is going to be happy with it. But just as in sports, if you lose, you accept it and shake the winner's hand. I'll tell you my decision, and that's all. After this, I'm not going to take any questions. Understand? No questions."

Two beats to wait for the translation to get through. Far over on his right, chubby Abe stood with both hands praying over his chest. Simple stood next to him, a cell phone to his mouth, waiting to inform someone.

Jay went on: "After a lot of thought, I've decided that the per diem rate for labor will be twenty-four dollars a day."

A loud buzz sizzled through the room.

He repeated the number in Spanish because he didn't want any mistakes: "*Veinticuatro.* Best I do. It's been a pleasure. Thanks to everyone. Good-bye. Adios."

And away he strode, reporters jumping to their feet, cameras swiveling, cables slithering, people tripping, the rows of chairs an instant mess. But near the door, he caught a glimpse of Verdes, eyebrows high, his green eyes wide with surprise.

And good luck to you, champ.

38

Al Smick wiped the morning dew off the footlockers where he would set up his rifle, and the drum of rocket flares that would serve as a chair. His tie was getting in his way, so he tucked it into his shirt. He was happy again. He had enjoyed camping out. Till past midnight he and the other five men had sat around a tiny fire—hardly bigger than a handkerchief—and traded battle stories about Iraq and Afghanistan and Panama. Al told them about operations in places where no operations had ever taken place—officially, at least.

The sentries had taken as prisoner a couple of Indians who twice a month climbed into the mountains with their donkey in order to bring back chunks of glacier ice from which to make ice cream. The Indians were given MREs to eat and told that all the Americans and equipment were part of joint maneuvers with the Ecuadoran Army. The men accepted this with an untroubled shrug and said, *"Mucho bueno, mucho bueno,"* which to Al's surprise was just about all of their Spanish, as they spoke only Quechua. They thanked the soldiers politely for the food and, in the spirit of contributing to the feast, took out a bottle of *chicha* and passed it around. Al poured himself a nice tot; it wasn't bad at all, and he told them so, repeating their *"mucho bueno."* The Indians were delighted and urged him to have more, and though it gave him something of a buzz, in the morning he felt right as rain. The Indians had breakfast and shook everyone's hand. The tactical commander having pronounced them "security-neutral," they ambled away up the mountain with their donkey.

The sun burst out of the mountains and rose quickly. Two FAIC agents dressed in green T-shirts planted microphones in the ground in front of the semi-circular Indian burial mound down below and climbed back from the valley, panting for breath in the high altitude. An hour later, a group of workers arrived and began setting up a long table and chairs on the open side of the mound. Behind them some ways, the first pickup arrived with nearly twenty people standing in its box. From his lookout behind the boulders and thick bushes nearly a half-mile away, he could hear them singing.

Al set up his little tripod and set the rifle on it, wiped the telescope lens with a chamois, loaded two bullets, the bolt sliding back and forth with a tiny, efficient click. He sighed and pulled the lapels of his suit jacket closed. He stood up to get out of the shadow of the bushes, and the sharp sun's warmth grew over him like a widening stain.

His satellite phone rang: Harry Kruger.

"Mornin', Harry. Hey, beautiful country ya got here. How's it goin'?"

"Half and half—there's been a wrinkle in the plan. Nothing that can't be smoothed out, though. You guys ready? Maybe I'm going to have to add targets to your list. I don't know—I'm still deciding. Are the mikes in place?"

"Harry, I'm a sniper," Al sniffed. "You want operational details, talk to the tac com. Hey—I haven't told you about my new piece."

"Stow it. How's security? Anybody see you?"

"Just some country boys the perimeter intercepted. Good guys, turned out. They had a bottle of moonshine on them too. Killer stuff. They called it *chicha*."

"You drank *chicha*? They ferment that shit with saliva, you know. Women chew the leaves and spit the juice into the bottle."

Al's face fell apart. "Fu-u-u-uck. Harry, you're shitting me."

"Forget it. You lived. All right, I'm going to call the tac com and--"

"Wait a minute, wait a minute, Harry. I didn't tell you about my new piece yet. Sweetest thing you ever—"

"Al, for God's sake."

"This'll just take a sec'. Listen, it's Tel Aviv-made. Bigass necked-down 30.06 cartridge holding a little .223 hollow-point."

"Great, Al. Now let me—"

But Smick wouldn't be shut up. "And you wouldn't believe what the Israelis charge you to make a bullet chamber for an XL cartridge and a .223 bore for the slug. Worth every shekel, though. It's like using a cannon to shoot a spitball. Does 5000 feet per second, trajectory flat as a ruler."

Harry sighed. "Well, it's gotta be a perfect shot. Okay, I gotta—"

"Hey—you said there's a wrinkle. What wrinkle?"

"Motherfucking Streets—he said twenty-four."

"Izzat right?" Al shook his head. "Thought you said that girl had him wrapped around her tits. What happened?"

"I don't know, I don't know. I talked to Trbek, and he can't figure it out either. The girl gave him one last check this morning, he told her eighteen. Solid as the Rock of Gibraltar. Then he goes downstairs, walks into the convention room and says twenty-four."

"Izzat right?" Al repeated. "You think he played her? What's the girl say?"

"She was out the door the second Streets went down the elevator. She and her team don't want to run into Streets at the airport. A private jet's waiting to take them to Bogo. But I'll tell you one thing—the second she looks at her bank account, she's gonna know she blew her bonus. All right, I got to get on to your tac com and tell him to patch everything through to Trbek at the hotel. I'm gonna grab

Klippen and head over there."

"Better hurry, Harry, they're already arriving here—half-dozen pickup-loads and a few buses just pulled up. Hey—they ride around standing up in pickup trucks. Can you believe that?"

"Keep me informed. And there's no trigger till I give the green light, get it?"

39

"A hard rain's a-gonna fall, Paulo. That's all what I can say," Rafa Ramirez said gloomily. "The presidente, he said that I hit the road, Jack, never comin' back no more, no more."

Paul heard a slow thumping and figured Rafa was bouncing the autographed ball around his office. Rafa had told him that he kept the ball on a stand on a corner of his desk.

"It's certainly a stick in the spokes, Rafa," said Paul. He sat in his office chair twirling a fountain pen—a birthday gift from Cindy—on the back of his thumb. "I talked to the banana barons just ten minutes ago. I tried to get them to tranfer at least part of the money, but that suggestion, to say the least, was met with no enthusiasm. I'm sorry."

"Yeah, I figured. Yesterday all my troubles seemed so far away, eh, man?"

"Well, for what it's worth, Rafa, the CIA took the whole operation out of my hands at the last minute. It's their fault, not mine."

"Ah—the CIA. Like bad, bad Leroy Brown."

"But tell your uncle that he's been a friend, and the U.S. State Department takes care of its friends. I've already made some calls this morning, and you can tell him he has a bright future. I've already looked into one possibility at the Organization of American States, another at the UN, and another at Florida State. You might be interested yourself, Rafa. He'll probably need an assistant, especially at the UN."

"Yeah? Really?"

"Sure. Decent salary, housing allowance, the works."

"Hey, Paulo, that makes great balls o' fire, man! Ah, well, maybe I wait for tomorrow for to tell him. Uncle Tata, he's full-tilt angry. Twist and shout—totally."

"He managed to put a smile on his face when he made a statement to the media congratulating the workers," Paul said drily.

"Hey, that was for the public, Paulo. Just a show. Like 'Me and Mrs. Jones got a thing goin' on.'"

"Sure."

Harry Kruger stuck his head through the doorway. His hair stuck up in tines everywhere, and his corduroy shirt—black again, today—was hanging out of his jeans. "Klippers, c'mon. Like right now. Crunch time."

Paul held up a hand: *Wait*. "So tell your uncle not to worry. Rafa, I'll call you back. The sky is falling here, you know."

Harry grabbed Paul's raincoat off the rack. "Let's go over to Trbek's room at the hotel. Since this is a joint op, you should be there while I'm…What the fuck are you doing?"

Paul had taken his raincoat and hung it up again. "Afraid not, Harry. I've got a rather busy day, in view of the, ah, rather bad news."

"Klippers, you're *coming*. This is no time for games."

"Games?" Paul walked back around his desk, sat, and held his glasses up to the ceiling to see if they were dirty. "Like the ones you played by changing our plans, right?"

"Klippen, for Chrissakes!" Harry swatted a chair out of the way and leaned over Paul's desk, his long, hard body rigid, fat lips set tightly. "Now get your ass up off that chair!"

Paul considered this request, polishing his glasses on the fat end of his tie. After a pleasant silence, he said, "And involve myself again in your stupid operation? I think not, Harry. What did I tell you? What did we *agree on*? An older man and a younger man, and what did you do instead? You gave him a porno queen. I'll bet Streets knew he was being scammed the moment he laid eyes on her. So what did he do? He made the best of a bad situation. He screwed her, enjoyed himself, strung everyone along, and named his price. Well, good for him: MVP of the whole stupid op."

Harry huffed. "It's not over yet. I've got cards to play that—"

Paul shook his head. "Oh no, Harry. Make no doubt: it's all over. All. Over. The price has been set: twenty-four dollars a day. The news has probably hit every city big and small in Latin America by now. By the end of the day, half of the continent is going to be on strike, seeing how well it's worked here."

"Well, it's on your head too, so get on the horn to those faggots at

State and tell them that we're going to—"

"It is not on my head and I don't need to call them. In fact, *they've* already called *me*. And guess what? They're unhappy. Specifically, the assistant secretary of state for Latin American affairs is unhappy. His assistant, the kindly Janet Ruddle, just called me ten minutes ago. She was enormously sympathetic in view of the months I had put into this op, and said that her boss intends to scrap his entire morning agenda in order to go to Langley and raise the matter with the— pardon the pun—*competent authorities.*"

"Goddammit, I'm telling you, there's *still a last card left to play.*" Harry pushed off the desk. "All right, *you* don't want to be in on the ground floor, that's *your* problem."

"What card?"

"The complete and utter discrediting of Segundo Verdes."

Paul shrugged. "And how would that help? The Council of Elders will approve the new wage, the workers will—"

"But what if they don't approve? What if they figure that where they can get twenty-four, they might well get thirty or thirty-five— and go on with the strike?"

"Go on with the strike?"

Harry was smiling—that ugly, supreme, fat-lipped clown smile, as when he had ruined the senator's fling at the airport. "Right. Say Verdes is disgraced and the strike goes on, hoping to hold out for more money, but somehow falls to pieces. The workers then crawl back into their huts with nothing."

Paul looked down at his desk blotter. "You can arrange that?" he said quietly.

"It's Plan B, but it'll work. What—you think I let everything ride on one guy saying one number?" Harry shook his head and grunted a laugh. "Fine, you don't have to be there. I still think of it as a joint op, but if you don't want to take part, go to hell. I *will* take the credit alone."

Paul considered this, then tilted sharply back in his chair. "Well, Harry, in my experience, Plan Bs rarely work. That's why they're Bs rather than As, you know."

"Very philosophic."

"No, this sounds to me like a very, very long shot, and you're about to take a big step down in your career—much bigger than if you'd left well enough alone. But it's *your* funeral. Send us a card from Timbuktu, okay?"

Which shook Harry. He started to say something, for once in his life refrained, then looked at his watch and trotted out and down the hall.

Paul sat looking at the open door, arms folded over his chest, thinking and thinking.

What on earth was Plan B?

40 Suitcase packed, handsome in his loose traveling clothes and sneakers, Jay Streets paid his bill at the reception desk and shook everyone's hand. He longed for the taxi and the airplane, but marshaled his good graces one last time and stood in the middle of the hotel staff and mugged while a security guy took their picture. Then he did the same for the security staff, some of whom abandoned their places in the parking garage and came running.

But at last he was in the taxi, where Mary Swanson from the State Department, who had called up from the lobby, awaited him to go to the airport. The idea hadn't pleased Jay, but when Mary Swanson told him that taxi drivers often took foreigners on the scenic route to fill out a fare, he was glad.

"God, what a morning," Jay panted, grinning and waving to the hotel staff through the back window. Finally the taxi nosed its way into the street. "All I want is an airplane seat under my butt."

"Yeah, I can imagine. By the way, I think you hit the price right on the head," Mary told him. "That's going to be great for the workers. Was it hard to make a decision?"

"Oh, not really," Jay said vaguely. "Sort of averaged it out. The workers wanted thirty-five, the owners seventeen. Just kind of split the diff, you know." He watched the traffic crawl up to a red light. "Hey, before I forget, is there a guy in the U.S. Embassy called, ah, Bill Klippen?"

"There's a Paul Klippen. Why?"

"That's it—Paul Klippen. And he's with you guys?"

"He's the embassy's top political officer. Why?"

"Oh, just wondering. I met him at a cocktail party a few days ago.

He asked me about pension plans. He sounded like, y'know, a pretty good guy. You know him?"

"Paul? He's one of the most decent, up-front guys I know there. And knowledgeable! He knows everything happening in this country, if not the world."

"Yeah, he sounded on the up-and-up. It's just that I forgot to get back to him, and, well, if you see him, tell him I'll do it first thing when I get back to the Apple. I've had kind of a busy week."

"Sure will. It's been a—"

Which was as far as Mary got when the front passenger door opened and a man with a round, piggish face got in; the taxi was stopped at a traffic light. To Mary's amazement, the driver had no objection. The door beside Jay Streets had opened, too, and he squawked in pain, made a ragged swinging motion with his arm, and tipped over into her lap, asleep. Beyond him a man—full-blooded Andean Indian, built square and close to the ground, with rutted cheeks—put the stun gun back into his pocket.

"What the hell are you doing?" Mary snapped in Spanish.

The man smiled politely but didn't answer. He closed the door and walked around the back, opened Mary's door and with no politeness at all shoved her over against Jay and sat down beside her.

"Why don't you *do* something?" Mary squealed in Spanish to the driver, banging him on the shoulder. But he was just waiting for the traffic light to turn green, tapping a finger on the wheel to the bouncing *cumbya* music from the radio.

41 A single ice cream vendor, sensing a business opportunity, had hitched a ride to the meeting on one of the pickup trucks crowded with strikers, who were now sitting on the semi-circular burial mound. The vendor quickly sold out his whole stock of Cokes and Orange Fantas—these stored at the top of the box—and ice cream sticks were moving nicely as well: people were hungry after the hour-long drive from Quito. His only competition was an old hag that had hitched a ride on one of the buses as it left Quito and was selling *chochos:* pieces of bread fried in oil.

But now even the vendor had stopped and was looking at the five-man Council of Elders, who were examining the four photos that

Segundo Verdes had taken from a half-sheet buff envelope and laid on their long table, which faced the semi-circle. As usual, Hondo had been short and to the point. Sixto Carrasco, who had bellowed for twenty minutes against their signing the agreement, stood smouldering at the side of the semi-circle, rubbing a hand down his long open shirt, occasionally emitting a cackle and saying that only a fool would believe mere photos.

Hondo turned away from the table and addressed the strikers around the mound, hands folded simply at his waist. "And that, *compañeros,* is my reply to Sixto's stupid notions, and his insistence that we not accept the new wage, but press on for thirty-five dollars a day. We cannot trust him when he says, 'This wage is a shame,' 'This wage will only ensure our poverty for another five hundred years.' He says this because that is precisely what the plantation owners want: no agreement. And he is their tool."

Sixto laughed—the sound was like a saw through metal—and shouted, "Once again in the long, sad history of our fatherland, the forces of fascism are speaking. Do not listen, my children. He is the voice of the devil offering temptation: 'Take this apple and bite deeply.'"

But silence answered him, Hondo noted with satisfaction. *Where are your screaming multitudes now, Sixto?* He had an urge to retort, but the experience of two years warming the fires of discontent in hundreds of villages had taught him many lessons. *No: every word counts now. Gloating will only bring out the people's dark side. If I play to the bright side, I will win.*

The two Elders on the ends of the table had stood up and were looking over the photos of their colleagues. They looked at the photos, at Sixto, and at the photos again.

"This is a travesty of such proportions that it has no name!" roared Sixto, the alarm palpitating in his voice. He hurtled across the clearing, belly bouncing over his belt that strained at the waist. *"Compañeros!* What have I"—he slapped his bare chest loudly three times—*"I, I, I* told you from the beginning? This man is not even a man! He is a viper sent by the devil—*by the president of the United States himself!*—to lead you back to slavery. Once again we are being tricked! Once again we are pouring our blood into the gringos' pockets!"

At the table, Father Pomasquí, Chief of the Elders, stood up. "Sixto, *enough!* You had your turn. We listened to you, and now we are listening to *Compañero* Verdes." He was a tall, thin man, and a priest, though officially defrocked in the Nineties for his defiance of Pope John Paul II. He had not given up his priestly clothes, however, and his longish, gray hair lay over his white collar. "All right, we have examined these photos. They seem to be proper. Explain your accusations, *Compañero* Verdes."

"You see, *compañeros,* our friend Sixto made his own agreement with the gringos months ago. As we all know, Carrasco is going to run for president. According to Spanish intelligence, the Americans will fund his election. And we all know what that means: once elected, he will take his orders from the American gringos. After President Rafael Correa threw the gringos out of their base in Manta—"

A small cheer went up.

"After that, and the continuation of these policies by President Atahualpa Tingo, the gringos want to control our country again, as they have for the last century. And Sixto Carrasco, as these photos clearly show, is the man they have chosen."

To the side Carrasco cackled. "Go ahead, *Compañero* Verdes. Tell your lies. I will soon show everyone who the gringo agent really is."

"What do you see in the photos?" someone shouted from the burial mound.

"Father Pomasquí, would you please tell everyone what you see in these photos?" said Hondo.

Pomasquí held up a photo. "This one is a photo of the American CIA director in the American Embassy in Quito. Horatio T. Kruger, it says at the bottom."

"That is a standard file photo," Verdes added.

"The other three photos are of this Señor Kruger in a car talking with Sixto Carrasco. Their faces are quite clear. It is them."

The crowd sizzled like water in a frying pan.

"Don't tell me you're going to believe photos!" Sixto roared. "Photos can be faked. Photos can be—"

"Sixto, *silence!*" shouted Father Pomasquí.

"The photos come with the stamp of Spain's Centro Nacional de Inteligencia," said Hondo. "I swear to you on my honor that neither they nor I have altered them. And as you can see, behind the car there is a tall building in construction. The Spanish agent was very clever in documenting these meetings. There are three of them, and in each one the building is a little more complete."

"Death to Sixto!"

"Sixto is a liar!"

Sixto only cackled again. "You fools! In one minute, I will show you how insane all of this is."

"Sixto Carrasco's your boy, Harry?" Al Smick said into his microphone, once the tactical commander beside him had told him what was going on.

Harry smiled. He was sitting beside Ross Trbek, watching the monitors, which showed long and close-up views of the burial mound. He touched the button on his microphone to talk to Al. "Grew him from a little seed. I'm gonna get him elected and then stick him in with the Venezuelans and a few other Commies. Two summit meetings and they'll all be at each other's throats."

"And that's really you in the pictures?"

Harry chuckled. "Don't worry. My hair's combed straight."

"You know about 'em?"

"Weeks ago. All under control."

This made Trbek rear back and stare at him. "Harry, for a man watching his key agent gettin' blown, you're calm as a pile of shit," he said in his Bostonian drawl.

"Calm as a pile of shit," Harry agreed. "It's all running to plan, Terbs."

Al's voice came over the earphones again: "Well, Jesus, Harry. Don't you think it might be a good idea for me to take out Verdes now—now as in 'right now'?"

Harry touched the button on his microphone. "Not the plan, Al. Take him out *now,* and all you do is make a martyr of him. *First* we discredit the bastard. This way, the crowd will tear him apart and go crawling back to Carrasco. See? It's love on the rebound. We make people ashamed of having doubted him. This way, people will follow him and continue the strike, and he'll lead them right back to where they started a month ago."

"How you gonna discredit Verdes?"

"You'll see. You just be ready."

"You're a sly, fucking bastard, Harry," Al giggled.

"Just stayed generally trained on Verdes. I'll give you the word."

Kruger released the button and turned to Trbek. "Chopper status?"

"Resting on the other side of the mountain, rotahs turning. Just give the word. ETA they say 75 seconds."

Hondo was slowly walking in front of the mound. In each hand he held two photos: one of Harry Kruger and the other three of Kruger in the car with Sixto. People crowded forward, jumping, bobbing and craning their heads to see.

"*Compañeros!* I ask you: are they wearing the same clothes?" Hondo asked loudly. "Are they the same clothes in all three photos? No. They are not. The shirts are different, and Mr. Kruger is wearing a tie in the third photo. You see the dates—none of them is even in the same month. Notice how the building behind them is taking shape. Does anyone know which one it is?"

"That is the new shopping center of Tenth of August Avenue," said a voice, and everyone turned. It was the ice-cream man, who had come down front. "*Galería de Compras,* it is called."

"That is correct. This shopping center is now finished and about to open."

"Yes! I saw the ads for the grand opening in Quito!" screamed a young woman who was breast-feeding her baby. "Sixto, you are a liar and a cheat!"

"Sixto, traitor!"

"Death to Sixto!"

Hondo waved them quiet, and the crowd quickly obeyed. "I believe that these two villains met there because the parking lot was full of trucks and construction equipment. But it also gave the Spanish intelligence agent good places to hide and take photos from."

"Death to Carrasco!"

"Carrasco, traitor!"

"Fakes! All fakes! When I show you the truth, you'll all cry with shame!" roared Sixto.

What does he have? Hondo wondered as he crossed the circle back to the table. He laid the photos there. "Father Pomasquí, as anyone can see, these photos clearly document a relationship between Sixto and the CIA."

The Elders sat in their seats, stony-faced. "All right, Sixto, you said you have something to say?" asked Father Pomasquí.

"Nothing, Father. Nothing at all." Sixto was walking past the table towards the parked trucks and buses and signaled. *"I will say nothing. I don't need to. I only wish to bring out a witness."*

Hondo Verdes jerked. *A witness?*

Carrasco saw a little group approaching and swaggered back in front of the table. "Faked photos?" Now he shouted: "YOU CAN WIPE YOUR ASSES WITH THEM! The truth will pour down like hail on this gathering"—he swung around, belly bobbing, and pointed a finger at Hondo—"and scourge the liars from our midst!"

Harry Kruger pushed the mike button and said, "Al, be ready. Keep a bead on Verdes. When I say go, you pull the trigger."

"Roger. Hey, you don't think that *chicha* shit is going to do anything to my liver, do you? Doctor told me to watch it."

Harry rolled his eyes. "Just be ready."

Jay Streets, having been awoken a few minutes before with an injection, stood in the center of the semi-circle, sullenly answering questions, Mary Swanson translating. The kidnappers had told him that if he wanted to make the six o'clock flight, he'd better answer the questions. He talked about his work in the bank, how he came to Ecuador, how he was asked to arbitrate.

Well, this is a bore. Those bastards in the cab had better make good on getting me to the evening flight, he thought.

The crowd buzzed every time he gave an answer, but seemed to be with him, and they'd damn well better be, since he had taken a chance on giving them a good wage—ten percent over what Verdes had recommended.

Sixto Carrasco, that fat bore, was asking the questions. One thing puzzled Jay: the crowd evidently knew Mary better than him. The moment they had walked out into the semi-circle, everyone had started shouting her name. Two women had run out and kissed her cheek.

Are these guys the ingrates of the century or what? Jay wondered, annoyed.

Segundo Verdes, off to the side, was watching, eyebrows crinkled in worry.

Sixto asked another question in Spanish, and Mary said in a loud voice, "Now, when you were in your hotel room, with guards outside the door, were you contacted by agents of the American government? Did they try to influence you?"

Shit. How the hell did he know that?

Jay thought fast. Mary had shown him a cell-phone message just a minute before they had been led out into the semi-circle. THE OPERATION HAS BEEN BLOWN. TELL EVERYTHING. DON'T LIE. YOU SHOULD BE OK IF YOU DON'T TRY TO COVER UP. SKIP. He took a breath.

"Yes, they contacted me. Two of their agents came in through the balcony."

He stopped to let Mary translate, and the crowd rumbled. Sixto roared an "Aahh!" and started a new question in Spanish.

Yeah, like I'm going to play your game, Fatman, Jay thought. *This is no goddamn courtroom. Nobody's cutting me off.*

"Mary, tell 'em this," he ordered loudly, interrupting Carrasco. He chose his words carefully. "I don't know who the two Americans worked for—that's the truth. I don't. They wanted me to set a wage of about sixteen-seventeen dollars. But when I made my decision on the actual wage, I only considered what people had told me from the two committees, the owners and the workers. The Americans' opinion didn't affect my decision."

Mary announced this in Spanish. The crowd seemed to believe him. Light applause started, then got heavier.

"*Gracias, Señor Streets,*" yelled someone.

"*Thankew, Meester Stree's,*" called another, and everyone laughed at the English.

"Um, *de nada, de nada.* You're welcome," called Jay in that direction.

Sixto began bellowing—about what Jay had no idea, but he had a lot to say. Then from the other side came a sharp stuccatto of protest: the priest at the table, some kind of retro-hippy with a collar, had cut him off.

A thought struck Jay: *Do they know about me and Dana?*

Sixto swung vindictively towards Mary and asked a question. And as he finished, Jay could see Segundo Verdes's eyes grow wide.

Oh, Jesus—more incoming. What—do they want to know if I got a blowjob?

Mary said, "Did the American agents say that they had a collaborator—a spy—on the workers' committee?"

Jay stiffened. "Yes," he blurted before he knew what he was saying. *Shit! Why'd I have to say that? They can't possibly know. Dana and I were in bed.*

But Mary had translated, and the crowd gasped. Jay glanced at Verdes. Now he was looking away and up to the mountains.

Sixto asked another question—again with triumph, Jay could see. "Identify the American collaborator," Mary translated.

Which was just what Jay had feared. Suddenly, the old mantra of many games came back to him. *Trust your instincts. Don't try to be a hero. When you move, move decisively. Indecision is worse than a mistake.*

He breathed out and made his shoulder relax; at most, he reset his feet minutely, widening his stance. He pointed briefly. "That guy. Sixto."

H arry Kruger's face fell open. "Mother...motherfuck," he sputtered. He turned to Trbek: "She told him Verdes, didn't she?"

"Yeah, sure. Yeah, I got that right heah in the log. Fuck!" he said, snatching up the electronic tablet and wiping a hand over it to pass the pages. "Yeah, right heah: yestahday, 4:48. 'Dana tells JS that Verdes is their agent, JS very surprised but accepts assertion.'"

On the monitors Harry was watching the crowd swarming off the burial mound like lava down a moutainside. Carrasco had disappeared under a rugby scrum of strikers.

Al Smick screamed in his earjack. "Harry! The crowd! I'm losing my scope on target!"

"Go! Go! Execute!" Harry shouted. "Terbs, tell the Three Bears to move!"

"Rogah that." He touched a button on the console. "Commence extraction, Three Bears."

The shot sounded through Harry's headphones, sharp like a marble falling on a wooden floor. On the monitor, the crowd jerked as one, like a school of fish. They began running towards the cars and buses.

"Target down," Al Smick reported. "Will re-tap when I get a clear shot."

"Yeah, yeah, roger, good take." Harry was gasping, his hands over the earphones, his mind flying: Had the girl double-crossed him? Or Skip? Did someone on Trbek's team have orders to spike the op? Was someone in Langley trying to discredit him?

He looked at the monitors. The area was emptying out. The tables and chairs where the Elders had sat were all awry. The ice cream vendor's box lay on its side atop the mound. In the middle of the semi-circle, Carrasco was on his hands on knees, dizzily trying to crawl. Fifty feet away, by the tables and chairs, Mary knelt down by Verdes, whose legs lay extended beside her. Harry could make out Mary's round head of curly hair.

"And take out…" He stopped.

Al: "Didn't copy that, Harry."

Trbek put a hand over his microphone. "You'd spend a month in Langley answering questions, Harry."

Harry nodded to him, then pointed a thick finger at the screen. "I'll pork you later on." He pressed the button on his mike. "Verdes— is that a good kill, Al?"

"Yeah, I think so."

Then Jay Streets dodged into the picture. He grabbed Mary, who didn't want to go. And finally he hoisted her in one movement over his shoulders and ran off.

"Want me to do the jock?" asked Al.

"Nah—he's famous. That'd be even worse."

"Worse 'n what?"

Trbek nudged him. "Choppahs fallin' on theatah, Harry. ETA twenty seconds. Game ovah."

Harry huffed hotly. "All right, Al. Re-tap Verdes."

"Got it."

Again the naked bang. Verdes head was now a bloody lump.

Harry was about to take off the headphones, when he jammed them back on. "And while you're at it, take out Sixto too—the guy down on all fours. Can't have *him* walking around with secrets."

"Guy on all fours—copy," said Al.

Another shot. Carrasco collapsed to the ground, arms under his body.

"You know, I told that dumbshit to watch his back," Harry told Trbek. "Finally I had a guy watch it for him, and good thing I did: turned out the Spanish CNI was on him like a cheap suit. I intercepted the photos a long time ago."

Two more shots: Sixto's head bounced twice.

Harry: "But someone fucked me, didn't they?"

Trbek nodded. "Somebody gave ya just enough rope, Harry."

Al: "I just double-tapped there, Harry. That's a lot of body he's got, you know."

"Roger."

"Closing time here, Harry. That'll be two confirmed kills."

"Roger, Al. Just put it on your bill, okay? Now get out of there before they put you on the evening news." Harry slouched back in his chair and jerked off the headphones. He watched the monitors a moment longer till they went black. "Gimme a screen shot of that bastard Sixto lying there with his head shot off, would you, Terbs?" he sighed. "Something to remember him by—while Langley is pulling my skin off."

42

Harry Kruger was recalled to Washington—not a good sign.

For weeks rumors percolated along the hemisphere of Washington committees quickly formed, boiling arguments enjoined, and reports hastily filed. A new CIA station chief arrived in Quito. He scowled at the lazy, non-American world around him and oozed Commitment, Loyalty and Patriotism from every pore. Paul found to his horror that he talked endlessly about his love of football and his hatred of Al Qaeda, and walked everywhere very fast, his long, thin legs scissoring the air.

El Comercio offered a watered-down account of the Elders meeting at the burial mound. Its headline was the death of Sixto Carrasco; the Elders' signing of the landmark agreement appeared in the second paragraph, the death of Segundo Verdes in the tenth, the roles of Mary Swanson and Jay Streets not at all.

Nor did the editor consider newsworthy the appearance of three unmarked helicopters pulling up equipment and several men—all in military fatigues except one in a business suit—and flying away over the mountain ridge. When Mary called to ask why, an editor told her that their reporter, who had arrived late, had heard about this, but could not find solid corroboration. Mary said she would be happy to provide it, but the editor answered that the news item was *"ya pasado"*: "past" or "overworked." Both translations had possibilities.

It hardly mattered. The media, both North American and South, were too busy covering the much bigger story: the strikes that blossomed on plantations throughout Latin America as far north as Mexico, some brutally repressed, others quite successful.

Over the next month, Paul Klippen was twice summoned to Washington for meetings of every tone from rabidly hostile to laudatory, and returned from the second trip to announce that with the usual State re-shuffling after upcoming mid-term elections, he would be named "assistant deputy director for hemispheric affairs." Still, as he pointed out to those who congratulated him, "the longer the job title, the smaller the influence." Alone with Mary, he added that the appointment was really State's spiteful shot at the CIA for taking away Paul's operation and then making a mess of it.

As to Mary, she took a vacation in America and returned ten pounds heavier.

Another month passed. Paul was considering going up the cable car path and digging up his water bottle when a new item circulated—not really a rumor, since it was confirmed by Consulate Guayaquil. Harry Kruger had stopped by there one day asking for some detailed roadmaps of the country and satellite photos of the region. He was a good deal thinner than the consul remembered, and dressed in fatigues and muddy hiking shoes. The consul gathered that he was looking for someone. But Harry took the documents and disappeared without really saying.

Until he confronted Paul Klippen in the embassy parking garage.

He stepped out from behind Walt Boam's huge SUV, and Paul knew that the jig was up. He could hear the door of his prison cell swinging slowly open.

"How about a drink to celebrate treason, Klippers?"

It was late afternoon and nearly dark outside; Paul was taking out his car keys. To his amazement, Harry was dressed not in fatigues but a good gray suit and silk tie, though the fluorescent lighting left both somewhat uniform and colorless.

"Harry! Hi. We've missed you in the country team meetings. The guy they sent to replace you?" Paul shook his head "No fun at all. Of course, Mary's turn on the rotating junior chair ended too—maybe that's part of it."

Harry just looked at him, nodding, his big lips pulled back in a wolf's smile. His pale face was reddish from too much sun.

Finally: "Couldn't find security video of you anywhere in the Hotel Martín. You were smart about it, having that cleaning lady move the security camera to the side—the one that would've looked down the hallway and into the elevator? She even had the sense to walk up to it fiddling with her little cleaner's cap. Never saw who she was, staff records were all a mess—no help at all."

"Security cameras and cleaning ladies." Paul shook his head. "Go fish, Harry." But even to himself this sounded bogus.

"Must've gone through those videos twenty times from end to end. Caught a back of a head there, bit of shoulder there—but not a thing worth taking to committee. Why'd you do it?"

"My goodness, you're all decked out. You're going to do a lady justice for once?"

"Big date tonight," Harry said patiently. "Bought this just an hour ago—had to be off the rack, though. Midriff isn't too loose, is it?" he added, turning slightly sideways.

"Not so anyone would notice. Does the girl know you're Company? Girls don't like being vetted, and you have that from the horse's mouth. Cindy took hell from the investigators, she being British."

A cold grin. "It's with Mary Swanson, so no problem. Called me up right out of the blue a few days ago. Said she'd heard I was in town again, thought we might get together, go over old times." A wink. "And that's just between us, huh? She didn't want me to advertise it."

"Smart lass."

Harry smiled indulgently. "Now don't fuck with me, Klippers. Or I'll hook you up to a lie-detector flutter so fast you'll think you were on a merry-go-round. As it is, I'm in a good mood and I'm willing to be generous."

"Generosity? In a CIA man? What's the country coming to?"

"I got on to you from the reporters' video," Harry went on. "From when Streets went into the conference room to give the number? There was Streets and the two Indian guards getting out of the elevator and him handing a notepad and pen back to a guy who was *still inside.* Like he'd given the guy an autograph and the guy was continuing down to the garage? But the shot's from the side, so you can't tell."

"What sleuthing, Harry! The taxpayer thanks you," said Paul, opening the trunk of his car and putting his briefcase inside. It was a foolish man who drove across Quito with important papers sitting on the passenger seat.

"Thing is, they were Carrasco's boys, and Carrasco is dead."

"I wonder why."

"Had to ask all over to find out who they were. Then I got a line on one of them—comes from an Amazon village down by El Puyo."

"Harry, we are moving this along, aren't we?" Paul sighed, closing the trunk. "Cindy has promised me a good old-fashioned English pudding tonight, and though she rarely makes one, it really is a—"

Harry wagged a finger. "No, no, Klippers. You're going to hear me out. After five weeks of 16-hour days to nab your ass, Langley screaming at me to come back and accept my dismissal, you're damn well going to hear the rest."

Paul crossed his arms and leaned back against the trunk. "All right. To the bitter end, Harry. Just stick to the high points, though, okay?" he said, which was the best imitation of blitheness he could do before impending disaster.

"Okay, I finally find the village, have to ask everyone in town about the guy, find his family's place, knock on the door, and guess what? He was dead."

"Well, don't look my way. Alibis left and right."

"He'd been bitten by a snake. He was trying to impress some girl with how quick he was, playing with a snake. Turns out the snake was quicker. He was dead before he hit the floor."

"Poor guy."

"Poor *me!*" Harry boomed. "Poor fucking me! Took me *fifteen more days* to find the other guy. Traced him to a town way down on the Peruvian border—guy called Sebas."

"Short for 'Sebastián'—very common nickname."

"There I got some answers. Sebas tells me that a guy was in the elevator when Streets and the guards came out of the room. American. He holds the doors for them, they get in, the guy asks Streets for an autograph, and down they all go in the elevator. All the time, the guy's talking to Streets—about football, he figures by the way they're throwing imaginary passes and catching 'em. But Sebas doesn't speak English and neither does the other guard, so they don't really know."

"Mary won't be happy if you're late," Paul warned, looking at his watch.

"Oh, it won't take me ten minutes to get over to her place," Harry said pleasantly, pulling back the sides of his suit jacket and putting his hands in his pockets. He was enjoying himself. "Anyhow, then I hit a roadblock. Sebas couldn't really describe the guy. Just a suit, lilly-white skin. Show him a half-dozen photos, but he shakes his head. So I leave him be, and I go back to the town hostal. This was yesterday, and time was running out on me because I had to drive up here to Quito for my date with Mary. It's too hot to sleep, and I'm lying there and *your* little mug wanders into my mind."

"Nothing erotic, I hope."

But Harry's momentum was unstoppable. "And at first I think, 'No, not ol' Klippers. Impossible. He's the one who started the whole thing. Operation Flexible Channel—all that.'"

Paul nodded. "That's how *my* reasoning would go too."

"But then I start remembering how understanding you were about me taking over your op."

"*Understanding?*" Paul exclaimed. "No. No, that's not the term I would use—not at all. I'd worked for six months putting together that op—sat in on nearly two hundred meetings for it—only to see it wrenched out of my hands at the moment of fruition by, um, *you,* if I remember."

An understanding smile that Paul resented. "But you didn't really put up a fight, did you? And that's just it, see? The longer I lay there thinking about it, the stranger it seemed that you took it so lying down. So I pull up a file photo of you on my phone, go back to Sebas the next morning—which was this morning. And his little brown face lights right up."

Paul clapped his hands slowly. "What wonderful detective work, Harry. America thanks you for keeping it safe."

But Harry was above sarcasm. "Thing is, though, Klippers, I can't figure out the why of it. At first I thought you just wanted to spite me, but I was driving up here all day, and I figure that can't be it. You're not the spiteful type." He shook his head. "I don't get it. Your future at State on the line, your one chance to get out of the Foreign Service rat race."

"Turns out I didn't need it. I had some meetings in Washington and—"

"I heard, I heard: you're going to be a big wheel at State. Still, I don't get it. I think: Did he sell out to the Chinese? Or the Spanish, looking to even out the banana market?"

"The Chinese—five million in a Swiss account, no questions asked."

Harry didn't even listen. "But no, I can't figure you for a sellout either. So what is it? Don't tell me you got some kind of attack of good old *moh*-rality. You're a diplomat, for Chrissakes."

Paul sighed. This was the end. *At least I had a few extra weeks with Cindy,* he thought. Just two days before, she had raised and straightened up her right leg; the growth-hormone shots were doing wonders. He looked out the end of the parking lot at the Pichinchas, black against a failing, blue sky. *Even at night, you just can't help looking at them,* he thought.

He sighed again. "I won't trouble you with moh-rality, Harry. To you morality is what works as opposed to what doesn't."

Harry laughed. "Why I'm Company, Klippers."

My god, what a simple little boy you are. You don't even know an insult when it's thrown in your face. "Call it…call it a sense of aesthetics, actually. Know what that is? A sense of how things should look. Focus. A sense of limits."

"Limits. I'm against limits. I'm a freedom guy."

"So I see. It just seemed, to be honest…"

Harry waited.

Paul shoved off the car, making Harry step back. "Where do we get people like you, Harry?" he snapped. "Not in Kansas City, that's for sure. Nobody there's asking the government for a handout."

"What handout?"

"Sending in our people to play dirty and make sure that plantation workers here have to live hand-to-mouth so that in the U.S. we can spend pennies on fruit: *that* handout."

"Bullshit, if it's in our interest—"

"Our interest! God! Always our sacred *interest!*" Paul shook his head. "People in Kansas City are willing to pay everyone fair prices for their products. They can get along just fine without your finely-measured calculations of *interest,* Harry."

Harry laughed. "Remember who you're talking about, Klippers. I mean *really* who: truck drivers, waitresses, marketing managers who spend their nights stretched out with a beer in front of the TV. Obese kids who spend their days eating potato chips and writing bullshit on social networks. Think they give a flying fuck what goes on in Ecuador, a country not even one in ten could find on a map? Somebody has to calculate the interests for them, and damn well we do. It's the difference between us and Mexico, us and Nigeria."

"Exactly what I've always suspected, Harry: end of the day, you and your spook colleagues have not the least respect for your own people. You're a government with a country attached to give it a little respectability."

Harry waved this idea away as too abstract. "What I don't get is why you went through with the whole thing. You spend six months putting together an op and then blow it all up? What the hell was *that* about?"

Paul's direct answer surprised him:

"Well, you get into a situation and you have to react. Or don't you know what that's about?"

"Only with girls," Harry joked.

Paul rolled his eyes, then went on: "Our ambassador, that reckless man, tasked me with heading off the labor unions and getting Americans back on the airbase in Manta. Bad ideas, both of them: the usual sticking our fingers into others' affairs. But of course, if *I* didn't carry out his orders, he would've gotten someone who would."

Harry's big lips fell open. "So, what—you planned to do it but not really do it, is that it? Christ!"

"Basically, yes. I linked it all together with the triangle plan and then messed it up. It's never hard to destroy a plan. If there was any kink at all, it was when Doctor Melero bowed out."

"*He* was in the original plan?" Harry asked, big mouth open in wonder. "Not Streets?"

"Of course he was. I'd spent months digging up dirt on his career in order to blackmail him into swinging the salary towards the workers. But then he slipped off to—what was it?—Dubai or wherever it was, so I filled in with Jay Streets. Truth is, he made things much easier. And your addition of the girl gave me the perfect excuse to hand over to you the soon-to-fail operation. On the morning of the announcement, I bribed a cleaning lady to move the camera a bit, waited for Streets with the elevator open, as if I'd just got in myself, and on the way down, I told him that he'd been scammed; Dana and Skip and the rest of them were just actors, contract free-lancers hired to sway him. He didn't—"

Harry nearly shouted: "For Chrissakes, Klippers, you couldn't compromise a bit? You couldn't be a diplomat and split some hairs? You couldn't tell him nineteen or twenty a day? *That* I could have sold to Langley. So we bleed the plantation owners a bit—big deal. And if we don't get Manta back, nobody's going to commit hara-kiri. But with *twenty-goddamn-four dollars a day,* it's—"

"*Harry!* Let me get a word in! I didn't tell Streets *any* number. I told him to choose whatever wage he thought was right. But he was pissed off big-time, I could tell. At the end, I wondered if he might hit *thirty*-four."

"And you had to bury my agent too—only for that you're going to hang, you know."

"Sixto Carrasco?" Paul said. "I didn't even know he was yours until I saw a confidential report in Washington. But I would imagine that if Streets knew the girl and the others were bogus, and if she had told him that Verdes was their man, it didn't require rocket science to conclude Carrasco was the real traitor."

Harry scowled. "And there went the best asset we've had here in the last fifty years. I was going to put him on the throne and tell him to wreck the new Latin leftists."

"Oh, Harry, *please,*" said Paul pityingly. "In a hundred years of relations with the hemisphere, our scheming has never done anyone a bit of good. You haven't noticed that our country is all but choking on Latinos fleeing poverty, have you?"

"And we've had cheap food for a hundred years too! That doesn't do it for you?"

Paul looked at him a moment, then shook his head at the floor.

"There's no arguing with you, Harry. There just isn't. We talk past each other every time."

"No, you just don't have an argument."

But Paul had walked away to the door of his car. "Well, it's all over for me now—but no complaints. I would never have forgiven myself if I hadn't done it. Go do your worst, Harry. Tell the whole world about me. I don't give a damn."

To his amazement, Harry followed after him. "Klippers, I said I was willing to be generous."

About to get into the car, Paul turned around, though more out of curiosity than hope. "My god, what could a CIA man possibly call 'generosity'?"

A calm smirk played on Harry's clown lips. "Now that I've got this thing by the balls"—he snapped his big square hand shut—"all I care about is setting the record straight in Langley: that it was *you* tipping off Streets at the last minute. After that, we can look at your career."

Paul looked into the dark eyes. "Why the generosity, Harry? And spare me the bullshit."

"Are you kidding? You're a rising star at State, Klippers!" He swatted Paul on the shoulder. "New assistant deputy whatever-it-is. Why should I turn you in for betrayal when you can be a big help to us?"

"A big help," Paul repeated blankly.

"Sure. Look, tomorrow I'm heading back to the States. First I'm going to take a team to New York and arrest Streets and take him—"

"*Arrest* him? For what?"

"For not telling me the truth the first time around when I went to see him six weeks ago. Wouldn't say a word. Just that he thought the workers made a better presentation and he split the difference on the per diem."

"What crime is that?" Paul said simply. "He wasn't under oath, and you're not a cop."

"It's a crime if I *make* it one," Harry snapped. "*This time*"—Harry's great lips crinkled into a professional sneer—"*this time* I pull the PATRIOT Act straightaway on him and don't fuck around looking for Indians in the fucking jungle. We put him in chains, and if I have anything to do with it, he'll end up in a nice quiet, out-of-the-way place we have out in Arizona where the cells are kept at around two degrees above freezing. And we put on the music nice and loud. And after forty-eight hours or so of that, I'm going to walk into his cell and put your picture in front of him and ask if he can explain his per-diem decision in a little more detail." A grin. "And speak up a little for the microphones, shithead."

Paul nodded, looking into the great, blank face. "And you'll do it, won't you?" he said softly.

"After getting my ass kicked up and down every hall in the Company? You're *damn fucking right* I will! *Then* I lay out the whole story at Langley and tell them that State has a traitor who from now on is going to suck our dicks if he doesn't want the same treatment as Streets. Get it?" He swatted Paul on the shoulder again. "You're going to be our boy at State, Klippers. The Company *loves* high-placed assets."

Paul nodded. "And through them bends the government to its will."

"Look at the bright side: we make sure our friends get ahead. Hell, having the Company behind you in Wash-town is better than the best resumé on earth."

"I've heard rumors that you guys have top officials on the leash. Members of Congress too."

A flat smile. "We don't like to brag. Now: all you have to do is tell me you'll agree to go along with your new life in Washington. Then you go home to your pudding, and I'll go pork Mary Swanson. We can talk details tomorrow."

Paul shrugged. "Well, I appreciate your concern, Agent Kruger, but my mother didn't raise me to betray my principles."

"You didn't have any trouble betraying your country."

"Actually, Harry, my country's principles of fair play and respect for others' sovereignty are ones that my mother and I hold very dear. Answer's no."

Harry laughed. He laughed so hard that he leaned against the car roof, his silk tie dangling. Walt Boam's secretary stared, waved uncertainly to Paul, got in her car, and drove off.

Harry stood up, wiping his eyes. "That's what they all say. I swear to God, every single one of 'em says that. We even have a seminar on it. And after a few months tangled in legal harassments and scandal, they all end up crawling back." He beat his chest, making a mess of his fine tie, and squawked, "'I didn't mean it! I'll be a good boy! He-e-e-e-elp!'"

Paul said nothing, hoping that he would be the exception and wondering if he would. He'd heard of government harassment going on for five, six, ten years—never reported in papers, never believed by local authorities. Just hell on earth for the victim.

Harry glanced at his watch, whirled around and walked away. "Gotta run. I'm staying at the Hotel Martín: Room 302, under the name of Michael Smith. Flight's not till noon tomorrow. You have my cell number. Take a good look at your wife tonight and ask yourself how long she can go on without you. 'Cause you'll spend a lot of the next twenty years in prison."

And Paul did think about this, all the way home. He also thought about how prison life might be, or the possibility of a decent minimum-security prison. And torture—that might be in the cards as well.

But this dark funk, which added a nostalgic poignancy to Cindy's fine pudding, didn't last long—less than ninety minutes. For Paul received an incoherent call from George Kaufman telling him to drop what he was doing and run for Quito police headquarters. Harry Kruger had been murdered.

43

What first caught the eye of the *Brigada de Homicidios* was the knife thrust through the right shoe and foot, which matched the gouge into the footrest of the shoeshine box. From the box and the size-6 and -7 blood prints of tennis shoes around the sprawled body, it was deduced that a gang of boys—three or four—had attacked and murdered Harry Kruger: first the thrust through the foot, making him bend down to pull out the knife, and then the hammer blow to the nape of the neck, which surely sent him into unconsciousness. It was so neatly done that, the police inspector felt, the boys may well have been under the direction of an adult. On the other hand, the body had twenty-one stabs and eight hammer blows, and this smacked of youthful fury. The police looked for a Fagan-like master of young hoodlums, but nothing ever turned up.

None of the actual weapons were ever found, nor were the contents of Harry's pockets—not so much as pocket change—another fact that indicated hoodlums. The sprinting bloody footprints ended abruptly at the end of the block—just around the corner from Mary Swanson's apartment, though she flatly denied any involvement with Harry, beyond a single call some days earlier to say that she hoped Langley hadn't been too hard on him.

It had been quite dark by then, and it was surmised that the boys were picked up by a waiting car: a classic tactic that kept the Fagan at arm's length from the act, just in case anything went wrong. Ecuadoran detectives pointed out that Harry was dressed in a new suit—he'd bought it that afternoon. "Is that how your agents go to empty a dead-letter box?" the lead detective asked. Paul translated, and the FBI agent on the scene only shrugged.

A day later, in an interview with *El Comercio*, the ambassador, with his usual deft coarseness, remarked that if Amerca had still had a base in Ecuador, the murder would never have happened. This caused quite a stir: protests in front of the embassy, editorials. The director of the *Brigada*, one of President Tingo's appointments, retorted that such arrogance was precisely why Ecuador had thrown the gringos out, and the investigation was quickly shelved. FBI requests for further action got knocked back to *mañana*.

A week after the murder, Mary Swanson knocked on Paul's office door. She handed him a plastic bag with a smartphone and a miniature cassette recorder with the tape inside. They had not talked much since Hondo's funeral; Mary got teary-eyed every time. "Better turn on your little gizmo," she told him.

Paul did; he had recovered it just the day before.

"I listened to the cassette," she said. "Interesting conversation you had with Harry. One question: did he shoot Hondo or order it done?"

Paul took out the hand-sized tape recorder—and looked at it dully.

"From what I gathered in Washington, there was a professional sniper under his orders." He put the bag in his desk drawer and locked it.

"That's what I figured." Mary wiped a tear away from her eye. Paul noticed that she was still gaining weight. Her face was round, and her lovely cheekbones diminished.

"How about a little coffee?"

"Perfect."

Paul made it, and they sat, silent, at his round meeting table.

"How close were you when Harry died?" Paul asked at last. "May I ask?"

"I stopped him at the corner before he got to my house and said I'd been talking to these nice shoeshine boys and it would really be nice if he would let them shine his shoes. Then I just walked away down the sidestreet, got into my car, and waited for the boys. I'd covered the whole interior of the car with plastic sheeting. I dropped them off at an orphanage in Ibarra—though we stopped to wash up and change clothes outside Quito."

Paul nodded. "The moment Harry told me you'd called I wondered what was in store for him."

"The one that stabbed Harry through the foot? He was the brother of a boy Harry killed." She wiped away another tear. "I heard him yelp—and it felt *fantastic*," she added with angry joy.

"Harry killed a child?" Paul blurted.

Mary explained about Alvaro's death and how she met up with Leopoldo in the attic some days later.

"Dear God," Paul gasped, taking off his glasses.

"Remember that famous video of Streets giving away the money? That was the kid in the video—the kid with the shoeshine kit who ran past: Alvaro. He was bringing a message to Hondo."

Paul thought back. "Yes, the boy running past—I remember. So that was how Harry got that cut on his neck. His story never really—"

"Too bad he didn't slash Harry's throat! Hondo might be alive today. He might be *alive!*" Mary buried her head in her handkerchief, sobbing.

Paul said nothing.

"I'm going to look like death warmed over for the rest of the day. And I'm up twenty-four pounds since Hondo died. I don't care. I don't care about anything anymore."

Paul shook his head. "My God, killing a boy. Even if he didn't mean to—just to kick a child that hard!"

"It was all the same to that bastard. If national security was involved, it was just one courier like another."

Paul nodded. Bitterness had infected her, and he wondered if it was a cause or a result of murdering Harry. Perhaps both.

They talked for a while longer till Paul had to leave for a meeting.

"Mary, can I give you my opinion? I wouldn't turn you in, but I think that once you've put your affairs in order, you ought to go to the FBI and tell them what you did."

"*Tell them?* For killing that piece of shit? Never! Paul, I'm amazed that *you* of all people—"

"Let me tell you something. You know why Cindy has done so well since her accident? Because she got over her anger. She put it behind her and looked forward. The doctors don't understand why she's done so well with her GH shots, but I do. It's because of her clean spirit. She's taken her knocks in life, but—"

"Confess, my ass!" Mary said, stalking to the door. "See you, Paul." And her thick heels sounded away down the corridor and seemed to echo a long time.

44 On a gray, ruminative afternoon some months later, when Paul Klippen could be sure that no connection between them had been established, he looked up Jay Streets in New York. Though they had only met that once, for thirty seconds, in the elevator, they greeted each other like old warriors back from the front. Then they took an aimless, timeless walk through Central Park, hands deep in their coat pockets. The lights in the buildings started to blink on all around the park.

Jay Streets had gone through a transformation in the months following his stint as wage arbitrator in Ecuador. He was only a few months older, but Paul found a certain cragginess about his jaw, a dry, appealing age around the eyes, an historic humility in his back as he ambled along, head down. Nearly the first thing that Jay told him was that he would soon be leaving DynoBank: "Once the marketing people have a new campaign dreamed up without me."

Paul asked what he would do, and Jay's answer was that he was forming an NGO: "Football Facilitators" would provide free football equipment to public-school systems, mainly at the high-school level, that were strapped for money. Only by floating the idea on his Facebook page, he had been flooded with pleas for assistance. Sports funding, like everything else, was failing. In many areas, high-school football leagues consisted of only two or three teams, or were forced to travel hundreds of miles to play a game. Jay intended to go around the NFL and the major colleges to get them to donate money, used equipment, and training material like blocking dummies and weight-lifting sets. Using his new knowledge of finance, he was researching insurance policies that would cover high school football for entire leagues, which was much cheaper than school-by-school insurance.

"It's about time I started giving back, I figured," Jay said. "God knows I sure benefited from well-funded programs." He jerked a thumb at his chin. "And it's about time I used my stupid mug for something other than a credit card."

As to the events in Quito, Jay was disgusted with himself. "You know something, Paul? I learned a lot from that experience. Mainly I learned that I can be a real chump. And it's time to stop being a real chump."

"How so?" Paul asked, stepping aside as a roller skater zipped past.

"Look: the sex with that Dana chick was one thing. But what really got me to swallow the story was all that good-times jive from that 'Skip' guy. *He's* the one who really made it all seem on the up-and-up. He knew just how to push my buttons and ease me into the con from the second I climbed into that van. Michael a little, but it was mainly Skip. All he had to do was talk the talk, and I fell for it."

"I see what you mean."

"And that really made me think, you know. I mean, it's like: 'What—I can be bought off by anybody who talks sports jive and does the bump?' Well, it's pretty sad, but I can. No question about it—they had me pegged from the beginning: the big dumb macho jock, just like ten thousand others. A little jive, a little sex, and I was ready to name a price I knew in my gut was all wrong. I'm sure glad you got to me in time."

"My pleasure."

Jay laughed suddenly. "And you know the funny thing, looking back on it, the one thing I'm glad about? I'm really glad that I gave out that cash to the poor people. I'd do it again if I went down there, only I'd take a wad of my own next time and give that out too. Hell, why not? They can use the cash a lot more than I can."

"Well, you certainly helped workers all throughout Latin America. They're grateful for that. There are strikes and rising salaries all over the place. And Verdes's programs are being replicated too. All it took was a spark."

"Yeah, I've been following that story. Hell, more power to 'em. I took some shit from a few of the power guys in the bank, know that?"

"Is that right?"

"Yeah, like, 'What the hell you think you're doing, making life miserable for the American consumer?' I was like, 'Yeah, right, like the American consumer doesn't have an extra five bucks to blow on fruit every week.' And this one time, in the men's club, this knuckle-dragger asshole started calling me a Communist and everything."

"I know the type," said Paul, remembering the ambassador.

"Oh. And this FBI guy—kind of a creep—came to talk with me a few weeks after I got back here."

"Wouldn't be…a big guy—thick lips, heavy torso?"

"Yeah, he a friend of yours?"

"'Friend' would be going it a bit."

"Oh—right," Jay said. "Well, at first the guy was nice enough—said he was just filling out a report on the Ecuador thing. Then he really started leaning on me to say why I named the price. Did I have any outside help? There was a rumor about some Americans contacting me in my room—what about that? I said it was all on my own—no mention of you. Shut him right down."

"Thanks."

"And I'll tell you something else." Jay stopped and lowered his voice. "The guy started getting really pissed off, right? And he pulled out this *video* of me and Dana having sex."

"No! Harry did that?" Paul blurted.

"I don't know how, but looks like that bitch was *taping* us too! Or probably Skip from the other room, seeing what he was missing. There were like two or three different angles on us too. It was all pretty dark and grainy, but if you looked close, you could tell it's us."

Paul ran a hand through his hair. "My God, there is no limit to that man."

Jay waved this away. "All right, so then the guy lets me watch a bit and he puts on this big grin—you know, with those big, rubbery lips of his? And he says to me, 'How'd you like to see this all over the Internet, you dumb-fuck jock? Nice, big scandal. What do you think they'll say in DynoBank? Huh? Might lose that nice, cushy six-figure job, huh? Girlfriend all upset, gossip websites having a ball with you.

No more Ten Best-Dressed Men nominations. So: remember some new details now? Quiet word to the wise when you were going down that elevator?' But I was like—"

Jay looked away, and to Paul's amazement, he squeezed the bridge of his nose. He was wiping away tears. "And you know, Paul—I haven't told anyone else this—but it's like right there, I did some kind of high jump. Just like I was doing a flop and arching my back and skimming over the bar—world record. And I looked at the guy, and I said, 'Like I give a shit about being a celeb anymore. Maybe six months ago that would've worked. But that was then and this is now. Go ahead. Put it on all over the Internet. Put it on the fucking Tonight Show if you want.' He couldn't believe it. He started threatening me and saying that he wasn't kidding, so I just told him to go stick the film sideways down his throat, and walked out on him. We were in a private meeting room in Dyno, see."

"Well done—Jay for president."

"And right then and there, two steps down the hall, I decided to leave DynoBank. That's it. I decided to do something different with myself. Time to stop being a damn manikin. Time to stop living high off the hog when I can get some stuff done. Time to stop a lot of things."

They went on walking. After some time, Paul asked, "Did the film ever come out?"

"No. That was the funny thing. Far as I know, it never came out anywhere."

"That *is* strange," Paul said, remembering the joke Harry had played on the senator in the airport. Then an idea hit him: "I would imagine, though, that the girl would have raised holy hell. Apparently, she does regular contract work for the strong-arm guys—CIA, Defense, others."

"Nice people," Jay grunted. "Who was the FBI guy, anyway? You said his name was Harry?"

"Oh, I've just kind of seen him around the embassy."

Then Paul started laughing. They had come out of the park now and stood on Central Park West, rheumatic rush-hour traffic inching past like people kicking their luggage forward at an airport check-in. Paul laughed and shook his head at the sidewalk.

"What's so funny?" asked Jay.

"You know, Jay, you asked me that question, and my first instinct was to remember that you don't have security clearance and to fob it off with a lie. Hell, you're an American citizen, you were central to an important operation. Why *shouldn't* you know? Why *shouldn't* I trust you?"

Jay shrugged. "Hey, I don't want to get you in trouble or anything."

"No—no trouble at all." He looked around. "You know a decent restaurant around here?"

Jay scanned the blocks in front of them. Across the street lay the West 60s. "Yeah, there's a terrific place for ribs just up there."

"Great. Tell you what: let me buy you dinner, and I'll tell you the whole story."

"You're on!"

They crossed the street. Paul said, "Okay, ever hear how huge cargo ships disappear at sea?"

THE END

ACKNOWLEDGEMENTS

BananaLink.org.uk kindly sent me a great lot of information about the tribulations of workers in Ecuador and other places. USLEAP also was very helpful. But the Internet won't really do for research, and although I lived in Quito for a year in the mid-80s, I returned to look at present conditions. There, my dear friend Geovanna Valencia gave up nearly the whole of her summer vacation to show me around and arrange excursions. And the Valencia family took me in as one of their own.

To learn the gentle arts of money-laundering, I relied on Robert Mazur's fascinating memoir of being an undercover agent amidst top money-launderers, *The Infiltrator* (Little, Brown, 2009). *Inside a U.S. Embassy* (Dorman, 2005), a very informative guide, filled me in on State Department minutiae such as the actual job titles and routines of embassy life.

Puzzled readers needn't wear out their eyes looking for Tumbacado; I made the name up. The scene that takes place there, however, was witnessed blow for blow in a certain Ecuadoran city by an English-teaching colleague. It just seemed to me polite not to mention exactly what city.

Lastly, to any reader whose interest in Ecuador is whetted by my story I strongly recommend a visit, and especially to its capital city at the feet of the Pichinchas. The tourist industry is well developed and can be enjoyed on the thinnest budget. Ecuador is also physically one of the most beautiful countries on earth, and home to some of the most welcoming, hospitable people anywhere—people who through the centuries have cheerfully endured every possible type of mismanagement and oppression at the hands of their leaders, in both the public and private sectors, and not a little brought to them by smiling foreigners.

And while in Quito, do stop one of the dirty-faced urchins who run around the streets with beaten shoeshine boxes, and give them some business, with a nice tip at the end. The money will go farther than you know.